Poor, Dear Margaret Kirby and Other Stories

Kathleen Norris

Contents

POOR, DEAR MARGARET KIRBY AND OTHER STORIES

BY

Kathleen Norris

POOR, DEAR MARGARET KIRBY

I

Y ou and I have been married nearly seven years," Margaret Kirby reflected bitterly, "and I suppose we are as near hating each other as two civilized people ever were!"

She did not say it aloud. The Kirbys had long ago given up any discussion of their attitude to each other. But as the thought came into her mind she eyed her husband--lounging moodily in her motor- car, as they swept home through the winter twilight--with hopeless, mutinous irritation.

What was the matter, she wondered, with John and Margaret Kirby-- young, handsome, rich, and popular? What had been wrong with their marriage, that brilliantly heralded and widely advertised event? Whose fault was it that they two could not seem to understand each other, could not seem to live out their lives together in honorable and dignified companionship, as generations of their forebears had done?

"Perhaps everyone's marriage is more or less like ours," Margaret mused miserably. "Perhaps there's no such thing as a happy marriage."

Almost all the women that she knew admitted unhappiness of one sort or another, and discussed their domestic troubles freely. Margaret had never sunk to that; it would not even have been a relief to a nature as self-sufficient and as cold as hers. But for years she had felt that her marriage tie was an irksome and distasteful bond, and only that afternoon she had been stung by the bitter fact that the state of affairs between her husband and herself was no secret from their world. A certain audacious newspaper had boldly hinted that there would soon be a sensational separation in the Kirby household, whose beautiful mistress would undoubtedly follow her first unhappy marital experience with another--and, it was to be hoped, a more fortunate--marriage.

Margaret had laughed when the article was shown her, with the easy flippancy that is the stock in trade of her type of society woman; but the arrow had reached her very soul, nevertheless.

So it had come to that, had it? She and John had failed! They were to be dragged through the publicity, the humiliations, that precede the sundering of what God has joined together. They had drifted, as so many hundreds and thousands of men and women drift, from the warm, glorious companionship of the honeymoon, to quarrels, to truces, to discussion, to a recognition of their utter difference in point of view, and to this final independent, cool adjustment, that left their lives as utterly separated as if they had never met.

Yet she had done only what all the women she knew had done, Margaret reminded herself in self-justification. She had done it a little more brilliantly, perhaps; she had spent more money, worn handsomer jewels and gowns; she had succeeded in idling away her life in that utter leisure that was the ideal of them all, whether they were quite able to achieve it or not. Some women had to order their dinners, had occasionally to go about in hired vehicles, had to consider the cost of hats and gowns; but Margaret, the envied, had her own carriage and motor-car, her capable housekeeper, her yearly trip to Paris for uncounted frocks and hats.

All the women she knew were useless, boasting rather of what they did not have to do than of what they did, and Margaret was more successfully useless than the others. But wasn't that the lot of a woman who is rich, and marries a richer man? Wasn't it what married life should be?

"I don't know what makes me nervous to-night," Margaret said to herself finally, settling back comfortably in her furs. "Perhaps I only imagine John is going to make one of his favorite scenes when we get home. Probably he hasn't seen the article at all. I don't care, anyway! If it SHOULD come to a divorce, why, we know plenty of people who are happier that way. Thank Heaven, there isn't a child to complicate things!"

Five feet away from her, as the motor-car waited before crossing the park entrance, a tall man and a laughing girl were standing, waiting to cross the street.

"But aren't we too late for gallery seats?" Margaret heard the girl say, evidently deep in an important choice.

"Oh, no!" the man assured her eagerly.

"Then I choose the fifty-cent dinner and 'Hoffman' by all means," she decided joyously.

Margaret looked after them, a sudden pain at her heart. She did not know what the pain was. She thought she was pitying that young husband and wife; but her thoughts went back to them as she entered her own warm, luxurious rooms a few moments later.

"Fifty-cent dinner!" she murmured. "It must be awful!"

To her surprise, her husband followed her into her room, without knocking, and paid no attention to the very cold stare with which she greeted him.

"Sit down a minute, Margaret, will you?" he said, "and let your woman go. I want to speak to you."

Angry to feel herself a little at loss, Margaret nodded to the maid, and said in a carefully controlled tone:

"I am dining at the Kelseys', John. Perhaps some other time--"

Her husband, a thin, tall man, prematurely gray, was pacing the floor nervously, his hands plunged deep in his coat pockets. He cleared his throat several times before he spoke. His voice was sharp, and his words were delivered quickly:

"It's come to this, Margaret--I'm very sorry to have to tell you, but things have finally reached the point where it's--it's got to come out! Bannister and I have been nursing it along; we've done all that we could. I went down to Washington and saw Peterson, but it's no use! We turn it all over--the whole thing--to the creditors to-morrow!" His voice rose suddenly; it was shocking to see the control suddenly fail. "I tell you it's all up, Margaret! It's the end of me! I won't face it!"

He dropped into a chair, but suddenly sprang up again, and began to walk about the room.

"Now, you can do just what you think wise," he resumed presently, in the advisory, quiet tones he usually used to her. "You can always have the income of your Park Avenue house; your Aunt Paul will be glad enough to go abroad with you, and there are personal things-- the house silver and the books--that you can claim. I've lain awake nights planning--" His voice shook again, but he gained his calm after a moment. "I want to ask you not to work yourself up over it," he added.

There was a silence. Margaret regarded him in stony fury. She was deadly white.

"Do you mean that Throckmorton, Kirby, & Son have--has failed?" she asked. "Do you mean that my money--the money that my father left me- -is GONE? Does Mr. Bannister say so? Why--why has it never occurred to you to warn me?"

"I did warn you. I did try to tell you, in July--why, all the world knew how things were going!"

If, on the last word, there crept into his voice the plea that even a strong man makes to his women for sympathy, for solace, Margaret's eyes killed it. John, turning to go, gave her what consolation he could.

"Margaret, I can only say I'm sorry. I tried--Bannister knows how I tried to hold my own. But I was pretty young when your father died, and there was no one to help me learn. I'm glad it doesn't mean actual suffering for you. Some day, perhaps, we'll get some of it back. God knows I hope so. I've not meant much to you. Your marriage has cost you pretty dear. But I'm going to do the only thing I can for you."

Silence followed. Margaret presently roused herself.

"I suppose this can be kept from the papers? We needn't be discussed and pointed at in the streets?" she asked heavily, her face a mask of distaste.

"That's impossible," said John, briefly.

"To some people nothing is impossible," Margaret said.

Her husband turned again without a word, and left her. Afterward she remembered the sick misery in his eyes, the whiteness of his face.

What did she do then? She didn't know. Did she go at once to the dressing-table? Did she ring for Louise, or was she alone as she slowly got herself into a loose wrapper and unpinned her hair?

How long was it before she heard that horrible cry in the hall? What was it--that, or the voices and the flying footsteps, that brought her, shaken and gasping, to her feet?

She never knew. She only knew that she was in John's dressing-room, and that the servants were clustered, a sobbing, terrified group, in the doorway. John's head, heavy, with shut eyes, was on her shoulder; John's limp body was in her arms. They were telling her that this was the bottle he had emptied, and that he was dead.

II

It was a miracle that they had got her husband to the hospital alive, the doctors told Margaret, late that night. His life could be only a question of moments. It was extraordinary that he should live through the night, they told her the next morning; but it could not last more than a few hours now. It was impossible for John Kirby to live, they said; but John Kirby lived.

He lived, to struggle through agonies undreamed of, back to days of new pain. There were days and weeks and months when he lay, merely breathing, now lightly, now just a shade more deeply.

There came a day when great doctors gathered about him to exult that he undoubtedly, indisputably winced when the hypodermic needle hurt him. There was a great day, in late summer, when he muttered something. Then came relapses, discouragements, the bitter retracing of steps.

On Christmas Day he opened his eyes, and said to the grave, thin woman who sat with her hand in his:

"Margaret!"

He slipped off again too quickly to know that she had broken into tears and fallen on her knees beside him.

After a while he sat up, and was read to, and finally wept because the nurses told him that some day he would want to get up and walk about again. His wife came every day, and he clung to her like a child. Sometimes, watching her, a troubled thought would darken his eyes; but on a day when they first spoke of the terrible past, she smiled at him the motherly smile that he was beginning so to love, and told him that all business affairs could wait. And he believed her.

One glorious spring afternoon, when the park looked deliriously fresh and green from the hospital windows, John received permission to extend his little daily walk beyond the narrow garden. With an invalid's impatience, he bemoaned the fact that his wife would not be there that day to accompany him on his first trip into the world.

His nurse laughed at him.

"Don't you think you're well enough to go and make a little call on Mrs. Kirby?" she suggested brightly. "She's only two blocks away, you know. She's right here on Madison Avenue. Keep in the sunlight and walk slowly, and be sure to come back before it's cold, or I'll send the police after you."

Thus warned, John started off, delighted at the independence that he was gaining day after day. He walked the two short blocks with the care that only convalescents know; a little confused by the gay, jarring street noises, the wide light and air about him.

He found the address, but somehow the big, gloomy double house didn't look like Margaret. There was a Mrs. Kirby there, the maid assured him, however, and John sat down in a hopelessly ugly drawing-room to wait for her. Instead, there came in a cheerful little woman who introduced herself as Mrs. Kippam. She was of the chattering, confidential type so often found in her position.

"Now, you wanted Mrs. Kirby, didn't you?" she said regretfully. "She's out. I'm the housekeeper here, and I thought if it was just a question of rooms, maybe I'd do as well?"

"There's some mistake," said John; and he was still weak enough to feel himself choke at the disappointment. "I want Mrs. John Kirby--a very beautiful Mrs. Kirby, who is quite prominent in--"

"Oh, yes, indeed!" said Mrs. Kippam, lowering her voice and growing confidential. "That's the same one. Her husband failed, and all but killed himself, you know--you've read about it in the papers? She sold everything she had, you know, to help out the firm, and then she came here--"

"Bought out an interest in this?" said John, very quietly, in his winning voice.

"Well, she just came here as a regular guest at first," said Mrs. Kippam, with a cautious glance at the door. "I was running it then; but I'd got into awful debt, and my little boy was sick, and I got to telling her my worries. Well, she was looking for something to do--a companion or private secretary position--but she didn't find it, and she had so many good ideas about this house, and helped me out so, just talking things over, that finally I asked her if she wouldn't be my partner. And she was glad to; she was just about worried to death by that time."

"I thought Mrs. Kirby had property--investments in her own name?" John said.

"Oh, she did, but she put everything right back into the firm," said Mrs. Kippam. "Lots of her old friends went back on her for doing it," the little woman went on, in a burst of loyal anger. "However," she added, very much enjoying her listener's close attention, "I declare my luck seemed to change the day she took hold! First thing was that her friends, and a lot that weren't her friends, came here out of curiosity, and that advertised the place. Then she slaves day and night, goes right into the kitchen herself and watches things; and she has such a way with the help-- she knows how to manage them. And the result is that we've got the house packed for next winter, and we'll have as many as thirty people here all summer long. I feel like another person, "the tears suddenly brimmed her weak, kind eyes, and she fumbled with her handkerchief. "You'll think I'm crazy running on this way!" said little Mrs. Kippam, "but everything has gone so good. My Lesty is much better, and as things are now I can get him into the country next year; and I feel like I owed it all to Margaret Kirby!"

John tried to speak, but the room was wheeling about him. As he raised his trembling hand to his eyes, a shadow fell across the doorway, and Margaret came in. Tired, shabby, laden with bundles, she stood blinking at him a moment; and then, with a sudden cry of tenderness and pity, she was on her knees by his side.

"Margaret! Margaret!" he whispered. "What have you done?"

She did not answer, but gathered him close in her strong arms, and they kissed each other with wet eyes.

III

A few weeks later John came to the boarding-house, nervous, discouraged, still weak. Despite Margaret's bravery, they both felt the position a strained and uncomfortable one. As day after day proved his utter unfitness for a fresh business start in the cruel, jarring competition of the big city, John's spirits nagged pitifully. He hated the boarding-house.

"It's only the bridge that takes us over the river," his wife reminded him.

But when a little factory in a little town, half a day's journey away, offered

John a manager's position, at a salary that made them both smile, she let him accept it without a murmur.

Her courage lasted until he was on the train, travelling toward the new town and the new position. But as she walked back to her own business, a sort of nausea seized her. The big, heroic fight was over; John's life was saved, and the debt reduced to a reasonable burden. But the deadly monotony was ahead, the drudgery of days and days of hateful labor, the struggle--for what? When could they ever take their place again in the world that they knew? Who could ever work up again from debts like these? Would John always be the weak, helpless convalescent, or would he go back to the old type, the bored, silent man of clubs and business?

Margaret turned a grimy corner, and was joined by one of her boarders, a cheerful little army wife.

"Well, we'll miss Mr. Kirby, I'm sure," said little Mrs. Camp, as they mounted the steps. "And by the way, Mrs. Kirby, you won't mind if I ask if we mayn't just now and then have some of the new towels on our floor--will you? We never get anything but the old, thin towels. Of course, it's Alma's fault; but I think every one ought to take a turn at the new towels as well as the old, don't you?"

"I'll speak to Alma," said Margaret, turning her key.

A lonely, busy autumn fellowed, and a winter of hard and thankless work.

"I feel like a plumber's wife," smiled Margaret to Mrs. Kippam, when in November John wrote her of a "raise."

But when he came down for two days at Christmastime, she noticed that he was brown, cheerful, and amazingly strong. They were as shy as lovers on this little holiday, Margaret finding that her old maternal, half-patronizing attitude toward her husband did not fit the case at all, and John almost as much at a loss.

In April she went up to Applebridge, and they spent a whole day roaming about in the fresh spring fields together.

"It's really a delicious little place," she confided to Mrs. Kippam when she returned. "The sort of place where kiddies carry their lunches to school, and their mothers put up preserves, and everybody has a surrey and an old horse. John's quite a big man up there."

After the April visit came a long break, for John went to Chicago in the July fortnight they had planned to spend together; and when he at last came to New

York for another Christmas, Margaret was in bed with a bad throat, and could only whisper her questions. So another winter struggled by, and another spring, and when summer came Margaret found that it was almost impossible to break away from her increasing responsibilities.

But on a fragrant, soft October day she found herself getting off the early train in the little station; and as a big man waved his hat to her, and they turned to walk down the road together, they smiled into each other's eyes like two children.

"Were you surprised at the letter?" said John.

"Not so much surprised as glad," said Margaret, coloring like a girl.

They presently turned off the main road, and entered a certain gate. Beyond the gate was an old, overgrown garden, and beyond that a house--a broad, shabby house; and beyond that again an orchard, and barns and outhouses.

John took a key from his pocket, and they opened the front door. Roses, looking in the back door, across a bare, wide stretch of hall, smiled at them. The sunlight fell everywhere in clear squares on the bare floors. It brightened the big kitchen, and glinted in the pantry, still faintly redolent of apples stored on shelves. It crept into the attic, and touched the scored casement where years ago a dozen children had recorded their heights and ages.

Margaret and John came out on the porch again, and she turned to him with brimming eyes. It suddenly swept over her, with a thankfulness too deep for realization, that this would be her world. She would sit on this wide porch, waiting for him in the summer afternoons; she would go about from room to room on the happy, commonplace journeys of house-keeping; would keep the fire blazing against John's return. And in the years to come perhaps there would be other voices about the old house; there would be little shining heads to keep the sunlight always there.

"Well, Margaret, do you like it?" said John, his arm about her, his face radiant with pride and happiness.

"Like it I" said Margaret. "Why, it's home!"

IV

So the Kirbys disappeared from the world. Sometimes a newcomer at Margaret's club would ask about the great portrait that hung over the library fireplace-- the portrait of a cold-eyed woman with beautiful pearls about her beautiful throat. Then the history of poor, dear Margaret Kirby would be reviewed--its triumphs, its glories, Margaret's brilliant marriage, her beauty, her wit. These only led to the final tragic scenes that had ended it all.

"And now she is grubbing away dear knows where!" her biographer would say carelessly. "Absolutely, they might as well be buried!"

But about seven years after the Kirbys' disappearance, it happened that four of Margaret's old intimates--the T. Illington Frarys and the Josiah Dunnings--were taking a little motor trip in the Dunnings' big car, through the northern part of the State. Just outside the little village of Applebridge, something mysterious and annoying happened to the car, which stopped short, and after some discussion it was decided that the ladies should wait therein, while the men walked back in search of help.

Mrs. Dunning and Mrs. Frary, settling themselves comfortably in the tonneau for a long wait, puzzled themselves a little over the name of Applebridge.

"I can just remember hearing of it," said Mrs. Dunning, sleepily, "but when or where or how I don't know."

They opened their books. A brilliant May afternoon throbbed, hummed, sparkled all about them. The big wheels of the motor were deep in grass and blossoms. On either side of the road, fields were gay with bees and butterflies. Larks looped the blackberry-vines with quick flights; mustard-tops showed their pale gold under the apple- blossoms.

Here and there a white cloud drifted in the deep, clear blue of the sky. There had been rains a day or two before, and in the fragrant air still hung a little chill, a haunting suggestion of wet earth and refreshed blossoms. Somewhere near, but out of sight, a flooded creek was tumbling noisily over its shallows.

Suddenly the Sunday stillness was broken by voices. The two women in the motor looked at each other, listening. They heard a woman's voice, singing; then a small boyish voice, then a man's voice. The speakers, whoever they were, apparently settled down in the meadow, not more than a dozen yards away, for a breathing space. A tangle of vines and bushes screened them from the motor-car.

"Mother, are me and Billy going to turn the freezer?" said a child's voice, and a man asked:

"Tired, old lady?"

"No, not at all. It's been a delicious walk," said the woman. The two sitting in the motor gasped. "Yes, yes, yes, lovey," the woman's voice went on, "you and Bill may turn, if Mary doesn't mind. Be careful of my fern, Jack!" And then, in German: "Aren't they lovely in all the grass and flowers, John?"

"Margaret!" breathed Mrs. Frary. "Poor, dear Margaret Kirby!"

"I hope they don't go by this way," whispered Mrs. Dunning, after an astounded second. "One's been so rude--don't you know--forgetting her!"

"She probably won't know us," Mrs. Frary whispered back, adjusting her veil in a stealthy way.

Mrs. Frary was right. The Kirbys presently passed with only a cursory glance at the swathed occupants of the motor-car. They were laughing like a lot of children as they scrambled through the hedge. John--a big, broad John, as strong and brisk as a boy--carried a tiny barefoot girl on his shoulder. Margaret, her beauty more startling than ever under the sweep of a gypsy hat; her splendid figure a little broader, but still magnificent under the cotton gown; her arms full of flowers and ferns, was escorted by two more children, sturdy little boys, who doubled and redoubled on their tracks like puppies. The tiny barefoot girl, in her father's arms, was only a tangle of blue gingham and drifting strands of silky hair; but the boys were splendidly alert little lads, and their high voices loitered in the air after the radiant, chattering little caravan had quite disappeared.

"Well!" said Mrs. Dunning, then.

"Poor, dear Margaret Kirby!" was on Mrs. Frary's lips; but she didn't say it.

She and Mrs. Dunning stared at each other a long minute, utterly at a loss. Then they reopened their books.

BRIDGING THE YEARS

The rain had stopped; and after long days of downpour, there seemed at last to be a definite change. Anne Warriner, standing at one of the dining-room windows, with the tiny Virginia in her arms, could find a decided brightening in the western sky. Roofs--the roofs that made a steep sky-line above the hills of old San Francisco--glinted in the light. The glimpse of the bay that had not yet been lost between the walls of fast-encroaching new buildings, was no longer dull, and beaten level by the rain, but showed cold, and ruffled, and steely-blue; there was even a whitecap or two dancing on the crests out toward Alcatraz. A rising wind made the ivy twinkle cheerfully against the old-fashioned brick wall that bounded the Warriners' backyard.

"I believe the storm is really over!" Anne said, thankfully, half aloud, "to-morrow will be fair!"

"Out to-morrow?" said Diego, hopefully. He was wedged in between his mother and the window-sill, and studying earth and sky as absorbedly as she.

"Out to-morrow, sweetheart," his mother promised. And she wondered if it was too late to take the babies out to-day.

But it was nearly four o'clock now; even the briefest airing was out of the question. By the time the baby was dressed, coated, and hooded, and little Diego buttoned into gaiters and reefer, and Anne herself had changed her house gown for street wear, and pinned on her hat and veil, and Helma, summoned from her ironing, had bumped Virginia's coach down the back porch steps, and around the wet garden path to the front door,--by the time all this was accomplished, the short winter daylight would be almost gone, she knew, and the crowded hour that began with the children's baths, and that ended their little day with bread-and-milky kisses to Daddy when he came in, and prayers, and cribs, would have arrived.

Anne sighed. She would have been glad to get out into the cool winter afternoon, herself, after a long, quiet day in the warm house. It was just the day and hour for a brisk walk, with one's hands plunged deep in the pockets of a heavy coat, and one's hat tied snugly against the wind. Twenty minutes of such walking, she thought longingly, would have shaken her out of the little indefinable mood of depression that had been hanging over her all day. She could have climbed the steep street on which the cottage faced, and caught the freshening ocean breeze full in her face at the corner; she could have looked down on the busy little thoroughfares of the Chinese quarter just below, and the swarming streets of the Italian colony beyond, and beyond that again to the bay, dotted now with the brown sails of returning fishing smacks, and crossed and recrossed by the white wakes of ferry-boats. For the Warriners' cottage clung to the hill just above the busy, picturesque foreign colonies, and the cheerful unceasing traffic of the piers. It was in a hopelessly unfashionable part of the city now; its old, dignified neighbors--French and Spanish houses of plaster and brick, with deep gardens where willow and pepper trees, and fuchsias, and great clumps of calla lilies had once flourished-- were all gone, replaced by modern apartment houses. But it had been one of the city's show places fifty years before, when its separate parts had been brought whole "around the Horn" from some much older city, and when homesick pioneer wives and mothers had climbed the board-walk that led to its gate, just to see, and perhaps to cry over, the painted china door-knobs, the colored glass fan-light in the hall, the iron-railed balconies, and slender, carved balustrade that took their hungry hearts back to the decorous, dear old world they had left so far behind them.

Jimmy and Anne Warriner had stumbled upon the Jackson Street cottage five years ago, just before their marriage, and after an ecstatic, swift inspection of it, had raced like children to the agent, to crowd into his willing hand a deposit on the first month's rent. Anne had never kept house before, she had no eyes for obsolete plumbing, uneven floors, for the dark cellar sacred to cats and rubbish. She and Jim chattered rapturously of French windows, of brick garden walks, of how plain little net curtains and Anne's big brass bowl full of nasturtiums would look on the landing of the absurd little stairway that led from the square hall to two useless little chambers above.

"Jimski--this floor oiled, and the rug laid cross-wise! And old tapestry papers from Fredericks! And the spindle-chair and Fanny's clock in the hall!"

"And the davenport in the dining-room, Anne,--there's no room in here, and your tea-table at the fireplace, with your copper blazer on it!"

"Oh, Jim, we'll have a place people will talk about!" Anne would sigh happily, after one of these outbursts. And when they made their last inspection before really coming to take possession of the cottage, she came very close to him,--Anne was several inches shorter than her big husband-to-be, and when she got as close as this to Jim she had to tip her serious little face up quite far, which Jim found attractive,--and said, in a little, breathless voice:

"It's going to be like a home from the very start, isn't it, Jim? And aren't you glad, Jim, that we aren't doing EXACTLY what every one else does, that you and I, who ARE a little different, Jim, are going to KEEP a little different? I mean that you really did do unusual work at college, and you really are of a fine family, and I am a Pendeering, and have travelled a lot, and been through Vassar,--don't you know, Jim? You don't think it's conceited for us to think we aren't quite the usual type, just between ourselves? Do you?"

Jim implied wordlessly that he did not. And whatever Jim thought himself, he was quite sincere in saying that he believed Anne to be peerless among her kind.

So they came to Jackson Street, and Anne made it quite as quaint and charming as her dreams. For a year they could not find a flaw in it.

Then little enchanting James Junior came, nick-named Diego for convenience, who fitted so perfectly into the picture, with his checked gingham, and his mop of yellow hair. Anne gallantly went on with her little informal luncheons and dinners, but she had to apologize for an untrained maid now, and interrupt these festivities with flying visits to the crib in the big bedroom that opened out of the dining-room. And then, very soon after Diego, Virginia was born--surely the most radiant, laughing baby that ever brought her joyous little presence into any home anywhere. But with Virginia's coming, life grew very practical for Anne, very different from what it had been in her vague hopes and plans of years ago.

The cottage was no longer quite comfortable, to begin with. The garden, shadowed heavily by buildings on both sides, was undeniably damp, and the fascinating railing of the little balconies was undeniably mouldy. The bath-room, despite its delightful size, and the ivy that rapped outside its window, was not a modern bath-room. The backyard, once sacred to geraniums and grass, and odd pots of shrubs, was sunny for the children's playing, to be sure, but no longer picturesque after their sturdy little boots had trampled it down, and with lines of their little clothes intersecting it. Anne began to think seriously of the big apartments all about, hitherto regarded as enemies, but perhaps the solution, after all. The modern flats were delightfully airy, high up in the sun, their floors were hard-wood, their bath-rooms tiled, their kitchens all tempting enamel, and nickel plate, and shining new wood. One had gas to cook with, furnace heat, hall service, and the joy of the lift.

"What if we do have to endure a dining-room with red paper and black wood-work, Jim," she would say, "and have near-Tiffany shades and a hall two feet square? It would be so COMFORTABLE!"

But if Jim agreed,--"we'll have a look at some of them on Sunday," Anne would hesitate.

"They're so horribly commonplace; they're just what every one else has!" she would mourn.

Commonplace,--Anne said the word over to herself sometimes, in the long hours that she spent alone with the children. That was what her life had become. The inescapable daily routine left her no time for unnecessary prettiness. She met each day bravely, only to find herself beaten and exhausted every night. It was puzzling, it was sometimes a little depressing. Anne reflected that she had always been busy, she was indeed a little dynamo of energy, her college years and the years of travel had been crowded with interests and enterprises. But she had never been tired before; she had never felt, as she felt now, that she could fall asleep at the dinner table for sheer weariness, and that no trial was more difficult to bear than Jim's cheerful announcement that the Deanes might be in later for a call, or the Weavers wanted them to come over for a game of bridge.

And what did she accomplish, after all? she thought sometimes. What mark did her busy days leave upon her life? She dressed and undressed the children, she bathed, rocked, amused them; indeed, she was so adoring a mother that sometimes whole precious fractions of hours slipped by while she was watching them, laughing at them, catching the little unresponsive soft cheeks to hers for the kisses that interfered so seriously with their important little goings and comings. She sewed on buttons and made puddings for Jim, she went for aimless walks, pushing Jinny before her in the go-cart, and guiding the chattering Diego with her free hand. She paused long in the market, uncomfortably undecided between the expensive steak Jim liked so much, and the sausages that meant financial balm to her own harassed soul. She commenced letters to her mother that drifted about half-written until Jinny captured and destroyed them. She sewed up rents in cloth lions and elephants, and turned page after page of the children's cloth books. Same and eventless, the months went by,--it was March, and the last of the rains,--it was July, and she and Jim were taking the children off for long Sundays in Sausalito, or on the Piedmont hills,--it was October, with the usual letter from Mother about Thanksgiving,--it was Christmas-time again! The seasons raced through their familiar surprises, and were gone. Anne had a desperate sense of wanting to halt them; just to think, just to realize what life meant, and what she could do to make it nearer her dreams.

So the first five years of their marriage slipped by, but toward the end with a perceptible brightening of the prospect in every direction. Not in one day, nor in one week, did the change come; it was just that things went well for Jim at the office, that the children were daily growing less helpless and more enchanting, that Anne was beginning to take an interest in the theatre again, and was charming in a new suit and a really extravagant hat. The Warriners began to spend their Sunday afternoons with real estate agents in Berkeley--not this year, perhaps, but certainly next, they told each other, they could CONSIDER that lovely one, with the two baths, and such a view, or the smaller one, nearer the station, don't you remember, Jim? where there was a sleeping-porch, and the garden all laid out? They would bring the children up in the open air and sunshine, and find neighbors, and strike roots, in the lovely college town.

Then suddenly, there were hard times again. Anne's health became poor, she was fitful and depressed, quite unlike her usual sunshiny self. Sometimes Jim found her in tears,--"It's nothing, dearest! Only I'm so MISERABLE all the time!" Sometimes she--Anne, the hopeful!--was filled with forebodings for herself and the child that was to come. No unnecessary expense could be incurred now, with this fresh, inevitable expense approaching. Especial concessions must be made to Helma, should Helma really stay; the whole little household was like a ship that shortens sail, and makes all snug against a storm. As a further complication, business matters began to go badly for Jim. Salaries were cut, new rules made, and an unpopular manager installed at the office. Anne struggled bravely to hide her mental and physical discomfort from Jim. Jim, cut to the heart to have to add anything to her care just now, touched her with a thousand little tendernesses; a joke over the burned pudding, a little name she had not heard since honeymoon days, a hundred barefoot expeditions about the bedroom in the dark, when Jinny awoke crying in the night, or Diego could not sleep because he was so "firsty." Tender and intimate days these, but the strain of them told on both husband and wife.

Things were at this point on the particular dark afternoon that found Anne with the two children at the window. All three were still staring out into the early dusk when Helma came in from the kitchen with an armful of damp little garments:

"Ef aye sprad dese hare, dey be dray en no tayme?" suggested Helma.

"Oh, yes! Spread them here by all means; then you can get a good start with your ironing to-morrow!" Anne agreed, rousing herself from her revery. "Put them all around the fire. And I MUST straighten this room!" she said, half to herself; "it's getting on to five!"

Followed by the stumbling children, she went briskly about the room, reducing it to order with a practised hand. Toys were piled in a large basket, scraps tossed into the fire, sewing materials gathered together and put out of sight, the rugs laid smoothly, the window- shades drawn. Anne "brushed up" the floor, pushed chairs against the wall, put a shovelful of coals on the fire, and finally took her rocker at the hearth, and sat with Virginia in her arms, and Diego beside her, while two silver bowls of bread and milk were finished to the last drop.

"There!" said she, pleasantly warmed by these exertions, "now for nighties! And Daddy can come as soon as he likes."

But Virginia was fretful and sleepy now, and did not want to be put down. So Diego manfully departed kitchenward with the empty bowls, and Anne, baby, rocker, and all, hitched her way across the room to the old chest of drawers by the hall door, and managed to secure the small sleeping garments with the little daughter still in her arms. She had hitched her way back to the fireplace again, and was very busy with buttons and strings, when Helma, appearing in the doorway, announced a visitor.

"Who?" said Anne, puzzled. "Did the bell ring? I didn't hear it. What is it?"

"Jantl'man," said Helma.

"A gentleman?" Anne, very much at a loss, got up, and carrying Jinny, and followed by the barefoot Diego, went to the door. She had a reassuring and instant impression that it was a very fine--even a magnificent--old man, who was standing in the twilight of the little hall. Anne had never seen him before, but there was no question in her heart as to his reception, even at this first glance.

"How do you do?" she said, a little fluttered, but cordial, too. "Will you come in here by the fire? The sitting-room is so cold."

"Thank you," said her caller, easily, with a little inclination of his head that seemed to acknowledge her hospitality. He put his hat, a shining, silk hat, upon the hall table, and followed her into the dining-room. Anne found, when she turned to give him the big chair, that he had pulled off his big gloves, too, and that Diego had put a confident, small hand into his.

He sat down comfortably, a big, square-built man, with rosy color, hair that was already silvered, and a fast-silvering mustache, and keen, kind eyes as blue as Virginia's. In the expression of these eyes, and in the lines about his fine mouth, was that suggestion of simple friendliness and sympathy that no man, woman, or child can long resist. Anne found herself already deciding that she LIKED this man. She went on with Jinny's small toilet, even while she wondered about her caller, and while she decided that Jim should have an overcoat of exactly this big, generous cut, and of exactly this delightful, warm-looking rough cloth, some day.

"Perhaps this is a bad hour to disturb these little people?" said the caller, smiling, but with something in his manner and in his rather deliberate and well-chosen speech, of the dignity and courtesy of an older generation.

"Oh, no, indeed!" Anne assured him. "I'm going right on with them, you see!"

Jinny, deliciously drowsy, gave the stranger a slow yet approving smile, from the safety of Anne's arms. Diego went to lay a small hand upon the gentleman's knee.

"This is my shoe," said Diego, frankly exhibiting a worn specimen, "and Baby has shoes, too, blue ones. And Baby cried in the night when the mirror fell down, didn't she, mother? And she broke her bowl, and bited on the pieces, and blood came down on her bib--"

"All our tragedies!" laughed Anne.

"Didn't that hurt her mouth?" said the caller, interestedly, lifting Diego into the curve of his arm.

Diego rested his golden mop comfortably against the big shoulder.

"It hurt her teef," he said dreamily, and subsided.

As if it were quite natural that the child should be there, the gentleman eyed Anne over the little head.

"I've not told you my name, madam," said he. "I am Charles Rideout. Not that that conveys anything to you, I suppose--?"

"But it does, as it happens!" Anne said, surprised and pleased. "Jim--my husband, is with the Rogers-Wiley Company, and I think they do a good deal of cement work for Rideout & Company."

"Surely," assented the man, "and your husband's name is--?"

"Warriner,--James Warriner," Anne supplied.

"Ah--? I don't place him," Mr. Rideout said thoughtfully. "There are so many. Well, Mrs. Warriner," he turned his smiling, bright eyes to her again, from the fire, "I am intruding on you this afternoon for a reason that I hope you will find easy to forgive in an old man. I must tell you first that my wife and I used to live in this house, a good many years ago. We moved away from it--let me see--we left this house something like twenty-six or --eight years ago. But we've talked a hundred times of coming back here some day, and having a little look about 'little Ten-Twelve,' as we always used to call it. I see your number's changed. But"--his gesture was almost apologetic--"we are busy people. Mrs. Rideout likes to live in the country a great part of the time; this neighborhood is inaccessible now--time goes by, and, in short, we haven't ever come back. But this was home to us for a good many years." He was speaking in a lower voice now, his eyes on the fire. "Yes, ma'am. Yes, ma'am," he said gently, "I brought Rose here a bride--thirty-three years ago."

"Well, but fancy!" said Anne, her face radiant, "just as we did! No wonder we said the house looked as if people had been happy in it!"

"There was a Frenchwoman here then," said Mr. Rideout, thoughtfully, "a queer woman! She played fast and loose until I didn't know whether we'd ever really get the place or not. This neighborhood was full of just such houses then, although I remember Rose used to make great capital out of the fact that ours was the only brick one among them. This house came around the Horn from Philadelphia, as a matter of fact, and"--his eyes, twinkling with indulgent amusement, met Anne's,--"and you know that before a lady has got a baby to boast of, she's going to do a little boasting about her new house!"

Anne laughed. "Perhaps she boasted about her husband, too," she said, "as I do, when Jimmy isn't anywhere around."

She liked the tender look, that had in it just a touch of pleased embarrassment with which he shook his head.

"Well, well, perhaps she did. Perhaps she did. She was very merry; pleased with everything; to this day my wife always sees the cheerful side of things first. A great gift, that. She danced about this house as if it were another toy, and she a little girl. We thought it a very, very lovely little home." His eyes travelled about the low walls. "I got to thinking of it to-day, wondered if it were still standing. I stood at your gate a little while,--the path is the same, and the steps, and some of the old trees,--a japonica, I remember, and the lemon verbenas. Finally, I found myself ringing your bell."

"I'm so glad you did!" Anne said. "There are lots of old trees and shrubs in the backyard, too, that you and your wife might remember. We think it is the dearest little house in the world, except that now we are rather anxious to get the children out of the city."

"Yes, yes," he agreed with interest, "much better for them somewhere across the bay. I remember that finally we moved into the country-- Alameda. The boy was a baby, then, and the two little girls very small. It was quite a move! Quite a move! We got one load started, and then had to wait and wait here--it was raining, too!--for the men to come for the other load. My wife's sister had gone ahead with the girls, but I remember Rose and I and the baby waiting and waiting,--with the baby's little coat and cap on top of a box, ready to be put on. Finally, I got Rose a carriage, to go to the ferry,-- quite a luxury in those days!" he interrupted himself, with a smile.

"And did the children love it,--the country?" said Anne, wistfully.

"Made them over!" said he, nodding reflectively. "Yes. I remember that the day after we moved was a Sunday, and we had quite a patch of lawn over there that I thought needed cutting. I shall never forget those little girls tumbling about in the cut grass, and Rose watching from the steps, with the baby in her lap. It made us all over." His voice fell again, and he stared smilingly into the fire.

"The children were born here, then?" said Anne.

"The little girls, yes. And the oldest boy. Afterward there was another boy, and a little girl--" he paused. "A little girl whom we lost," he finished gravely.

"Both these babies were born here," Anne said, after a moment. Her caller looked from one child to the other with an expression of interest and understanding that no childless man can ever wear.

"Our Rose was born here, our first girl," he said. "Sometimes a foggy morning even now will bring that morning back to me. My wife was very ill, and I remember creeping out of her room, when she had gone to sleep, and hearing the fog-horns outside,--it was early morning. We had an old woman taking care of her,--no trained nurses in those days!--and she was sitting here by this fireplace, with the tiny girl in her lap. Do you know--" his smile met Anne's--"do you know, I was so tired, and we had been so frightened for Rose, and it seemed to me that I had been up and moving about through unfamiliar things for so many, many hours, that I had almost forgotten the baby! I remember that it came to me with a shock that Rose was safe, and asleep, and that morning had come, and breakfast was ready, and here was the baby, the same baby we had been so placidly expecting and planning for, and that, in short, it was all right, and all over!"

"Oh, I KNOW!" Anne laid an impulsive hand for a second on his, and the eyes of the young wife, and of the man who had been a young father thirty years before, met in wonderful understanding. "That's- -that's the way it is," said Anne, a little lamely, with a swift thought for another foggy morning, when the familiar horn, the waking noises of the city, had fallen strangely on her own senses, after the terror and triumph of the night. Neither spoke for a moment. Diego's voice broke cheerily into the pause.

"I can undress myself," he announced, with modest complacence.

"Can you?" said Charles Rideout. "How about buttons?"

"I can't do buttons," Diego qualified firmly.

"Well, I think--I can--remember--how to unbutton--a boy!" said the man, with his pleasant deliberation, as he began on the button that was always catching itself on Diego's hair. Diego cheerfully extended little arms and legs in turn for the disrobing process. Presently a small heap of garments lay on the floor, and the children were quite delicious in baggy blue flannels. All the four were laughing and absorbed, when James Senior came in a few minutes later, and found them.

"Jim," said his wife, eagerly, rising to greet him, and to bring him, cold and ruddy, to the fireplace, "this is Mr. Rideout, dear!"

"How do you do, sir?" said Jim, stretching out his hand, and with a smile on his tired, keen, young face. "Don't get up. I see that my boy is making himself at home."

"Yes, sir; we've been having a great time getting undressed," said the visitor.

"Jim," Anne went on radiantly, "Mr. Rideout and HIS wife lived here years ago, when THEY were just married, and their children were born here too!"

"No--is that so!" Jim was as much pleased and surprised as Anne, as he settled himself with Virginia's web of silky hair against his shoulder. "Built it, perhaps, Mr. Rideout?"

"No. No, it was eight or ten years old, then. I used to pass it, walking to the office. We had a little office down on Meig's pier then. As a matter of fact, my wife never saw it until I brought her home to it. She was the only child of a widow, very formal Southern people, and we weren't engaged very long. So my brother and I furnished the house; used--" his eyes twinkled--"used to buy our pictures in a lump. We decided we needed about four to each room, and we'd go to a dealer's, and pick out a dozen of 'em, and ask him to make us a price!"

"Just like men!" said the woman.

"I suppose so. I know that some of those pictures disappeared after Rose had been here a while! And we had linen curtains--"

"Not linen!" protested Anne.

"Very--pretty--little--ruffled--curtains they were," he affirmed seriously. "Linen, with blue bands, in this bedroom, and red bands upstairs. And things--things--" he made a vague gesture--"things on the dressing-tables and bed to match 'em! I remember that on our wedding day, when I brought Rose home, we had a little maid here, and dinner was all ready, but no, Rose must run up and down stairs looking at everything in her little wedding dress--" Suddenly came another pause. The room was dark now, but for the firelight. Little Jinny was asleep in her father's arms, Diego blinking manfully. Neither husband nor wife, whose hands had found each other, cared to break the silence. But after a while Anne said:

"What WAS her wedding dress?"

Instantly roused, the guest raised bright, pleased eyes.

"The ladies' question, Warriner," said he. "It was silk, my dear, her first silk gown. Yellowish, or brownish, it was. And she had one of those little ruffled capes the ladies used to wear. And a little bonnet--"

"A BONNET!"

"A bonnet she had trimmed herself. I remember watching her, when we were engaged, making that trimming. You don't see it any more, but that year all the girls were making it. They made little bunches of grapes out of dried peas covered with chamois skin--"

"Oh, not really!" ejaculated Anne.

"Indeed, they did. Then they covered their bonnets with them, and with leaves cut out of the chamois skin. They were charming, too. My wife wore that bonnet a long time. She trimmed it over and over." He sighed, but there was a shade of longing as well as pity in his eyes. "We were young," he said thoughtfully; "I was but twenty-five; we had our hard times. The babies came pretty fast. Rose wasn't very strong. I worked too hard, got broken down a little, and expenses went right on, you know--"

"You bet I know!" Jim said, with his pleasant laugh, and a glance for Anne.

"Well," said Charles Rideout, looking keenly from one to the other, "thank God for it, you young people! It never comes back! The days when you shoulder your troubles cheerfully together,--they come to their end! And they are"--he shook his head--"they are very wonderful to look back to! I remember a certain day," he went on reminiscently, "when we had paid the last of the doctor's bills, and Rose met me down town for a little celebration. We had had five or six years of pretty hard sailing then. We bought her new gloves that day, I remember, and--shoes, I think it was, and I got a hat, and a book I'd been wanting. We went to a little French restaurant to dinner, with all our bundles. And that, that, my dear,--"he said, smiling at Anne,--"seemed to be the turning point. We got into the country next year, picked out a little house. And then, the rest of it all followed; we had two maids, a surrey, I was put into the superintendent's place--" a sweep of the fine hand dismissed the details. "No man and wife, who do what we did," said he, gravely, "who live modestly, and work hard, and love each other and their children, can FAIL. That's one of the blessed things of life."

Jim cleared his throat, but did not speak. Anne was frankly unable to speak.

"And now I mustn't keep these children out of bed any longer," said the older man. "This has been a--a lovely afternoon for me. I wish Mrs. Rideout had been with me." He stood up. "Shall I give you this little fellow, Mrs. Warriner?"

"We'll put the babies down," said Jim, rising, too, "and then, perhaps, you'd like to look about the house, Mr. Rideout?"

"But I know how a lady feels about having her house inspected--" hesitated the caller, with his bright, fatherly look for Anne.

"Oh, please do!" she urged them.

So the gas was lighted, and they all went into the bedroom, where Anne tucked the children into their cribs. She stayed there while the others went on their tour of inspection, patting her son's small, warm body in the darkness, and listening with a smile to the visitor's cheerful comments in kitchen and hallway, and Jim's answering laugh.

When she came blinking out into the lighted dining-room, the men were upstairs, and Helma, to Anne's astonishment, was showing in another caller,--and another Charles Rideout, as Anne's puzzled glance at the card in her hand, assured her. This was a tall young man, a little dishevelled, in a big storm coat, and with dark rings about his eyes.

"I beg your pardon, madam," said he, abruptly, "but was my father, Mr. Charles Rideout, here this afternoon?"

"Why, he's upstairs with my husband now!" Anne said, strangely disquieted by the young man's manner.

"Thank God!" said the newcomer, briefly. And he wiped his forehead with his handkerchief, and drew a deep short breath.

"He--I must apologize to you for breaking in upon you this way," said young Rideout, "but he came out in the car this afternoon, and we didn't know where he had gone. He made the chauffeur wait at the corner at the bottom of the hill, and the fool man waited an hour before it occurred to him to telephone me at the house. I came at once."

"He's been here all that time," Anne said. "He's all right. Your mother and father used to live here, you know, years ago. In this same house."

"Yes, I know we did. I think I was born here," said Charles Rideout, Junior. "I had a sort of feeling that he had come here, as soon as Bates telephoned. Dear old dad! He and mother have told us about this place a hundred times! They were talking about it for a couple of hours a few nights ago." He looked about the room as his father had done. "They were very happy here. There--" he smiled a little bashfully at Anne--"there never was a pair of lovers like mother and dad!" he said. Then he cleared his throat. "Did my father tell you--?" he began, and stopped.

"No," Anne said, troubled. He had told them a great deal, but not-- she felt sure--not this, whatever it was.

"That's why we worried about him," said his son, his honest, distressed eyes meeting hers. "You see--you see--we're in trouble at the house--my mother--my mother left us, last night--"

"Dead?" whispered Anne.

"She's been ill a good while," said the young man, "but we thought-- She's been so ill before! A day or two ago the rest of us knew it, and we wired for my married sister, but we couldn't get dad to realize it. He never left her, and he's not been eating, and he'd tell all the doctors what serious sicknesses she'd gotten over before--" And with a suddenly shaking lip and filling eyes, he turned his back on Anne, and went to the window.

"Ah!" said Anne, pitifully. And for a full moment there was silence.

Then Charles Rideout, the younger, came back to her, pushing his handkerchief into his coat pocket; and with a restored self-control.

"Too bad to bother you with our troubles," he said, with a little smile like his father's. "To us, of course, it seems like the end of the world, but I am sorry to distress YOU! Dad just doesn't seem to grasp it, he hasn't been excited, you know, but he doesn't seem to understand. I don't know that any of us do!" he finished simply.

"Here they are!" Anne said warningly, as the two other men came down the stairs.

"Hello, Dad!" said young Rideout, easily and cheerfully, "I came to bring you home!"

"This is MY boy, Mrs. Warriner," said his father; "you see he's turned the tables, and is looking after me! I'm glad you came, Charley. I've been telling your good husband, Mrs. Warriner," he said, in a lower tone, "that we--that I--"

"Yes, I know!" Anne said, with her ready tenderness, and a little gasp like a child's.

"So you will realize what impulse brought me here to-day," the older man went on; "I was talking to my wife of this house only a day or two ago." His voice had become almost inaudible, and the three young people knew he had forgotten them. "Only a day or two ago," he repeated musingly. And then, to his son, he added wistfully, "I don't seem to get it through my head, my boy. For a while to-day, I forgot--I forgot. The heart--" he said, with his little old-world touch of dignity--"the heart does not learn things as quickly as the mind, Mrs. Warriner."

Anne had found something wistful and appealing in his smile before, now it seemed to her heartbreaking. She nodded, without speaking.

"Dear old Dad," said Charles Rideout, affectionately. "You are tired out. You've been doing too much, sir, you want sleep and rest."

"Surely--surely," said his father, a little heavily. Father and son shook hands with Jim and Anne, and the older man said gravely, "God bless you both!" as he and his son went down the wet path, in the shaft of light from the hall door. At the gate the boy put his arm tenderly about his father's shoulders.

"Oh, Anne, Anne," said her husband as she clung to him when the door was shut, "I couldn't live one day without YOU, my dearest! But don't--don't cry. Don't let it make you blue,--he HAD his happiness, you know,--he has his children left!"

Anne tightened her arms about his neck.

"I am crying a little for sorrow, Jim, dearest!" she sobbed, burying her face in his shoulder. "But I believe it is mostly--mostly for joy and gratitude, Jim!"

THE TIDE-MARSH

What are you going to wear to-night in case you CAN go, Mary Bell?" said Ellen Brewster in her lowest tones.

"Come upstairs and I'll show you," said Mary Bell Barber, glancing, as they tiptoed out of the room, toward the kitchen's sunny big west window, where the invalid mother lay in uneasy slumber.

"My new white looks grand," said Ellen on the stairs. "I made it empire."

Mary Bell said nothing. She opened the door of her spacious bare bedroom, where tree shadows lay like a pattern on the faded carpet, and the sinking sun found worn places in the clean white curtains. On the bed lay a little ruffled pink gown, a petticoat foamy with lace, white stockings, and white slippers. Mary Bell caught up the gown and held the shoulders against her own, regarding the older girl meanwhile with innocent, exultant eyes. Ellen was impressed.

"Well, for pity's sake--if you haven't done wonders with that dress!" she ejaculated admiringly. "What on earth did you do to it?"

"Well--first I thought it was too far gone," confessed Mary Bell, laying it down tenderly, "and I wished I hadn't been in such a hurry to get my new hat. But I ripped it all up and washed it, and I took these little roses off my year-before-last hat, and got a new pattern,--and I tell you I WORKED! Wait until you see it on! I just finished pressing it this afternoon."

"Oh, say--I hope you can go now, after all this!" said Ellen, earnestly.

The other girl's face clouded.

"I'll never get over it if I don't!" she said. "It seems to me I never wanted to go anywhere so much in all my life! But some one's got to stay with mama."

"I'd go crazy,--not KNOWING!" said Ellen. "Who are you going to ask?"

"There it is!" said Mary Bell. "Until yesterday I thought, of course, Gran'ma

Scott would come. Then Mary died, and she went up to Dayne. So I went over and asked Bernie; her baby isn't but three weeks old, you know, and I thought she might bring it over here. Mama would love to have it! But late last night Tom came over, and he said Bernie was so crazy to go, they were going to take the baby along!"

"You poor thing!" said the sympathetic listener.

"I was nearly crazy!" said Mary Bell, crimping a pink ruffle with careful finger-tips. "I was working on this when he came, and after he'd gone I crumpled it all up and cried all over it! Well, I guess I didn't sleep much, and finally, I got up early, and wrote a letter to Aunt Matty, in Sacramento, and I ran over to Dinwoodie's with it this morning, and asked Lew if he was going up there to-day. He said he was, and he took the note for Aunt Mat. I told her about the dance, and that every one was going, and asked her to come back with Lew. He said he'd see her first thing!"

"Oh, she will!" said Ellen, confidently. "But, say, Mary Bell, why don't you walk over to the hotel with me now and ask Johnnie if she'll stay if your aunt doesn't come? I don't believe she and Walt are going."

"They mightn't want to leave the hotel on account of drummers on the night train," said Mary Bell, dubiously. "And that's the very time mama gets most scared. She's always afraid there are boes on the train."

"Boes!" said Ellen, scornfully, "what could a bo do!"

"Well, I WILL go over and talk to Johnnie," said Mary Bell, with sudden hope. "I'm going to get all ready except my dress, in case Aunt Mat comes," she confided eagerly, when she had kissed the drowsy mother, and they were on their way.

"Say, did you know that Jim Carr is going to-night with Carrie Parmalee?" said Ellen, significantly, as the girls crossed the clean, bare dooryard, under the blossoming locust trees.

Mary Bell's heart grew cold,--sank. She had hoped, if she DID go, that some chance might make her escort no other than Jim Carr.

"It'll make me sick if she gets him," said Ellen, frankly. Although engaged herself, she felt an unabated interest in the love-affairs about her.

"Is he going to drive her over?" asked Mary Bell, clearing her throat.

"No, thank the Lord for that!" said Ellen, piously. "No. It's all Mrs. Parmalee's doing, anyway! His horse is lame, and I guess she thought it was a good chance! He'll drive over there with Gus and mama and papa and Sadie and Mar'gret; and I guess he'll get enough of 'em, too!"

Mary Bell breathed again. He hadn't asked Carrie, anyway. And if she, Mary Bell, really went to the dance, and the pink frock looked well, and Jim Carr saw all the other boys crowding about her for dances--

The rosy dream brought them to the steps of the American Palace Hotel, for Deaneville was only a village, and a brisk walker might have circled it in twenty minutes. The hideous brown hotel, with its long porches, was the largest building in the place, except for hay barns, and fruit storehouses. Three or four saloons, a "social hall," the "general store," and the smithy, formed the main street, and diverging from it scattered the wide shady lanes that led to old homesteads and orchards.

"Johnnie," Walt Larabee's little black-eyed manager and wife, and the most beloved of Deaneville matrons, was in the bare, odorous hallway. She was clad in faded blue denim overalls, and a floating transparent kimono of some cheap stuff. Her coal-black hair was rigidly puffed and pinned, and ornamented with two coquettish red roses, and her thin cheeks were rouged.

"Well, say--don't you girls think you're the whole thing!" said the lady, blithely. "Not for a minute! Walt and me are going to this dance, too!"

She waved toward them one of the slippers she was cleaning.

"Walt said somethin' about it yes'day," continued Mrs. Larabee, with relish, "but I said no; no twelve-mile drive for me, with a young baby! But some folks we know came down on the morning train--you girls have heard me speak of Ed and Lizzie Purdy?"

"Oh, yes!" said Mary Bell, sick with one more disappointment.

"Well," pursued Johnnie, "they had dinner here, and come t' talk it over, Lizzie was wild to go, and Ed got Walt all worked up, and nothing would do but we must get out our old carryall, and take their Thelma and my Maxine along! Well, LAUGH--we were like a lot of kids! I'm crazy to dance just once in Pitcher's barn. We're going up early, and have our supper up there."

"We're going to do that, too," said Ellen, with pleasant anticipation. "Ma and I always help set tables, and so on! It's lots of fun!"

Mary Bell's face grew sober as she listened. It WOULD be fun to be one of the gay party in the big barn, in the twilight, and to have her share of the unpacking and arranging, and the excitement of arriving wagons and groups. The great supper of cold chicken and boiled eggs and fruit and pickles, the fifty varieties of cake, would be spread downstairs; and upstairs the musicians would be tuning their instruments as early as seven o'clock, and the eager boys and girls trying their steps, and changing cards. And then there would be feasting and laughing and talking, and, above all, dancing until dawn!

"Beg pardon, Johnnie?" she stammered.

"Well, looks like some one round here is in love, or something!" said Johnnie, freshly. "I never had it that bad, did you, Ellen? Ellen's been telling me how you're fixed, Mary Bell," she went on with deep concern, "and I was suggestin' that you run over to the general store, and ask Mis' Rowe--or I should say, Mis' Bates," she corrected herself with a grin, and the girls laughed--"if she won't sleep at your house tonight. Chess'll tend store. It'll be something fierce if you don't go, Mary Bell, so you run along and ask the bride!" laughed Johnnie.

"I believe I would," approved Ellen, and the girls accordingly crossed the grassy, uneven street to the store.

An immense gray-haired woman was in the doorway.

"Well, is it ribbon or stockings, or what?" said she, smiling. "The place has gone crazy! There ain't going to be a soul here but me to- night."

Mary Bell was silent. Ellen spoke.

"Chess ain't going, is he?" she asked.

The old woman shook with laughter.

"Chess ain't nothing but a regular kid," she said. "He was dying to go, but he knew I couldn't, and he never said a word. Finally, my boy Tom and his wife, and Len and Josie and the children, they all drove by on their way to Pitcher's; and Len--he's a good deal older'n Chess, you know--he says to me, 'You'd oughter leave Chess come along with the rest of us, ma; jest because he's married ain't no reason he's forgot how to dance!' Well, I burst right out laughing, and I says, 'Why didn't he say he wanted to go?' and Chess run upstairs for his other suit, and off they all went!"

There was nothing for it, then, but to wait for Lew Dinwoodie and the news from Aunt Mat.

Mary Bell walked slowly back through the fragrant lanes, passed now and then by a surrey loaded with joyous passengers already bound for Pitcher's barn. She was at her own gate, when a voice calling her whisked her about as if by magic.

"Hello, Mary Bell!" said Jim Carr, joining her. But she looked so pretty in her blue cotton dress, with the yellow level of a field of mustard-tops behind her, and beyond that the windbreak of gold- tipped eucalyptus trees, that he went on almost confusedly, "You-- you look terribly pretty in that dress! Is that what you're going to wear?"

"This!" laughed Mary Bell. And she raised her dancing eyes, to grow a little confused in her turn. Nature, obedient to whose law blossoms were whitening the fruit trees, wheat pricking through the damp earth, robins mating in the orchards, had laid the first thread of her great bond upon these two. They smiled silently at each other.

"I'm not even sure I'm going!" said Mary Bell, ruefully.

The sudden look of concern in his face went straight to her heart. Jim Carr really cared, then, that she couldn't go! Big, clever, kindly Jim Carr, who was superintendent at the power-house, and a comparative newcomer in Deaneville, was an important personage.

"Not going!" said Jim, blankly. "Oh, say--why not!"

Mary Bell explained. But Jim was encouraging.

"Why, of course your aunt will come!" he assured her sturdily. "She'll know what it means to you. You'll go up with the Dickeys, won't you? I'm going up early, with the Parmalees, but I'll look out for you! I've got to hunt up my kid brother now; he's got to sleep at Montgomery's to-night. I don't want him alone at the hotel, if Johnnie isn't there. If you happen to see him, will you tell him?"

"All right," said Mary Bell. And her spirits were sufficiently braced by his encouragement to enable her to call cheerfully after him, "See you later, Jim!"

"See you later!" he shouted back, and Mary Bell went back to the kitchen with a lightened heart. Aunt Mat wouldn't--COULDN'T--fail her!

She carried a carefully prepared tray in to her mother at five o'clock, and sat beside her while the invalid slowly finished her milk-toast and tea, and the cookies and jelly Mary Bell was famous for. The girl chatted cheerfully.

"You don't feel very badly about the dance, do you, deary?" said Mrs. Barber, as the gentle young hands settled her comfortably for the night.

"Not a speck!" answered Mary Bell, bravely, as she kissed her.

"Bernie and Johnnie going--married women!" said the old lady, sleepily. "I never heard such nonsense! Don't you go out of call, will you, dear?"

Mary Bell was eating her own supper, ten minutes later, when the train whistled, and she ran, breathless, to the road, to meet Lew Dinwoodie.

"What did Aunt Matty say, Lew?" called Mary Bell, peering behind him into the closed surrey, for a glimpse of the old lady.

The man stared at her with a falling jaw.

"Well, I guess I owe you one for this, Mary Bell!" he stammered. "I'll eat my shirt if I thought of your note again!"

It was too much. Mary Bell began to dislodge little particles of dried mud carefully from the wheel, her eyes swimming, her breast rising.

"Right in her part of town, too!" pursued the contrite messenger; "but, as I say--"

Mary Bell did not hear him. After a while he was gone, and she was sitting on the steps, hopeless, dispirited, tired. She sombrely watched the departing surreys and phaetons. "I could have gone with them--or with them!" she would think, when there was an empty seat.

The Parmalees went by; two carriage loads. Jim Carr was in the phaeton with Carrie at his side. All the others were in the surrey.

"I'm keeping 'em where I can have an eye on 'em!" Mrs. Parmalee called out, pointing to the phaeton.

Everybody waved, and Mary Bell waved back. But when they were gone, she dropped her head on her arms.

Dusk came; the village was very still. A train thundered by, and Potter's windmill creaked and splashed,--creaked and splashed. A cow-bell clanked in the lane, and Mary Bell looked up to see the Dickeys' cow dawdle by, her nose sniffing idly at the clover, her downy great bag leaving a trail of foam on the fresh grass. From up the road came the faint approaching rattle of wheels.

Wheels?

The girl looked toward the sound curiously. Who drove so recklessly? She noticed a bank of low clouds in the east, and felt a puff of cool air on her cheek.

"It feels like rain!" she said, watching the wagon as it came near. "That's Henderson's mare, and that's their wooden-legged hired man! Why, what is it?"

The last words were cried aloud, for the galloping old horse and driver were at the gate now, and eyes less sharp than Mary Bell's would have detected something wrong.

"What IS it?" she cried again, at the gate. The man pulled up sharply.

"Say, ain't there a man here, nowhere?" he demanded abruptly. "I've been banging at every house along the way; ain't there a soul in the place?"

"Dance!" explained Mary Bell. "The Ladies' Improvement Society in Pitcher's new barn. Why! what is it? Mrs. Henderson sick?"

"No, ma'am!" said the old fellow, "but things is pretty serious down there!" He jerked his hand over his shoulder. "There's some little fellers,--four or five of 'em!--seems they took a boat to-day, to go ducking, and they're lost in the tide-marsh! My God--an' I never thought of the dance!" He gave a despairing glance at the quiet street. "I come here to get twenty men--or thirty--for the search!" he said heavily. "I don't know what to do, now!"

Mary Bell had turned very white.

"There isn't a soul here, Stumpy!" she said, terrified eyes on his face. "There isn't a man in town! What CAN we do!--Say!" she cried suddenly, springing to the seat, "drive me over to Mrs. Rowe's; she's married to Chess Bates, you know, at the store. Go on, Stumpy! What boys are they?"

"I know the Turner boys and the Dickey boy is three of 'em," said the old man, "and Henderson's own boy, Davy--poor leetle feller!-- and Buddy Hopper, and the Adams boy. They had a couple of guns, and they was all in this boat of Hopper's, poking round the marsh, and it began to look like rain, and got dark. Well, she was shipping a little water, and Hopper and Adams wanted to tie her to the edge and walk up over the marsh, but the other fellers wanted to go on round the point. So Adams and Hopper left 'em, and come over the marsh, and walked to the point, but she wasn't there. Well, they waited and hallooed, but bimeby they got scared, and come flying up to Henderson's, and Henderson and me--there ain't another man there to- night!--we run down to the marsh, and yelled, but us two couldn't do nothing! Tide's due at eleven, and it's going to rain, so I left him, and come in for some men. Henderson's just about crazy! They lost a boy in that tide-marsh a while back."

"It's too awful,--it's just murder to let 'em go there!" said Mary Bell, heart-sick.

For no dragon of old ever claimed his prey more regularly than did the terrible pools and quicksands of the great marsh.

Mrs. Bates was practical. Her old face blanched, but she began to plan instantly.

"Don't cry, Mary Bell!" said she; "this thing is in God's hands. He can save the poor little fellers jest as easy with a one-legged man as he could with a hundred hands. You drive over to the depot, Stumpy, and tell the operator to plug away at Barville until he gets some one to take a message to Pitcher's barn. It'll be a good three hours before they even git this far," she continued doubtfully, as the old man eagerly rattled away, "and then they've got to get down to Henderson's; but it may be an all-night search! Now, lemme see who else we can git. Deefy, over to the saloon, wouldn't be no good. But there's Adams's Chinee boy, he's a good strong feller; you stop for him, and git Gran'pa Barry, too; he's home to-night!"

"Look here, Mrs. Bates," said Mary Bell, "shall I go?"

The old woman speculatively measured the girl's superb figure, her glowing strength, her eager, resolute face. Mary Bell was like a spirited horse, wild to be given her head.

"You're worth three men," said the storekeeper.

"Got light boots?"

"Yes," said the girl, thrilled and quivering.

"You run git 'em!" said Mrs. Bates, "and git your good lantern. I'll be gitting another lantern, and some whiskey. Poor little fellers! I hope to God they're all sneakin' home--afraid of a lickin'!--this very minute. And Mary Bell, you tell your mother I'll close up, and come and sit with her!"

It was a sorry search-party, after all, that presently rattled out of town in the old wagon. On the back seat sat the impassive and good-natured Chinese boy, and a Swedish cook discovered at the last moment in the railroad camp and pressed into service. On the front seat Mary Bell was wedged in between the driver and Grandpa Barry, a thin, sinewy old man, stupid from sleep. Mary Bell never forgot the silent drive. The evening was turning chilly, low clouds scudded across the sky, little gusts of wind, heavy with rain, blew about them. The fall of the horse's feet on the road and the rattle of harness and wheels were the only sounds to break the brooding stillness that preceded the storm. After a while the road ran level with the marshes, and they got the rank salt breeze full in their faces; and in the last light they could see the glitter of dark water creeping under the rushes. The first flying drops of rain fell.

"And right over the ridge," said Mary Bell to herself, "they are dancing!"

A fire had been built at the edge of the marsh, and three figures ran out from it as they came up: two boys and a heavy middle-aged man. It was for Mary Bell to tell Henderson that it would be hours before he could look for other help than this oddly assorted wagonful. The man's disappointment was pitiful.

"My God--my God!" he said heavily, as the situation dawned on him, "an' I counted on fifty! Well, 'tain't your fault, Mary Bell!"

They all climbed out, and faced the trackless darkening stretch of pools and hummocks, the treacherous, uncertain ground beneath a tangle of coarse grass. Even with fifty men it would have been an ugly search.

The marsh, like all the marshes thereabout, was intersected at irregular intervals by decrepit lines of fence-railing, running down from solid ground to the water's edge, half a mile away. These divisions were necessary for various reasons. In duck season the hunters who came up from San Francisco used them both as guides and as property lines, each club shooting over only a given number of sections. Between seasons the farmers kept them in repair, as a control for the cattle that strayed into the marsh in dry weather. The distance between these shaky barriers was some two or three hundred feet. At their far extremity, the posts were submerged in the restless black water of the bay.

Mary Bell caught Henderson's arm as he stood baffled and silent.

"Mr. Henderson!" she said eagerly, "don't you give in! While we're waiting for the others we can try for the boys along the fences! There's no danger, that way! We can go way down into the marsh, holding on,--and keep calling!"

"That's what I say!" shrilled old Barry, fired by her tone.

The Chinese boy had already taken hold of a rail, and was warily following it across the uneven ground.

"They've BEEN there three hours, now!" groaned Henderson; but even as he spoke he beckoned to the two little boys. Mary Bell recognized the two survivors.

"You keep those flames so high, rain or no rain," Henderson charged them, "that we can see 'em from anywheres!"

A moment later the searchers plunged into the marsh, facing bravely away from lights and voices and solid earth.

Stumbling and slipping, Mary Bell followed the fence. The rain slapped her face, and her rubber boots dragged in the shallow water. But she thought only of five little boys losing hope and courage somewhere in this confusing waste, and her constant shouting was full of reassurance.

"Nobody would be scared with this fence to hang on to!" she assured herself, "no matter how fast the tide came in!" She rested a moment on the rail, glancing back at the distant fire, now only a dull glow, low against the sky.

Frequently the rail was broken, and dipped treacherously for a few feet; once it was lacking entirely, and for an awful ten feet she must bridge the darkness without its help. She stood still, turning her guttering lantern on waving grasses and sinister pools. "They are all dancing now!" she said aloud, wonderingly, when she had reached the opposite rail, with a fast-beating heart. After an endless period of plunging and shouting, she was at the water's very edge.

There was light enough to see the ruffled, cruel surface of the river, where its sluggish forces swept into the bay. Idly bumping the grasses was something that brought Mary Bell's heart into her throat. Then she cried out in relief, for it was not the thing she feared, but the little deserted boat, right side up.

"That means they left her!" said Mary Bell, trembling with nervous terror. She shouted again in the darkness, before turning for the homeward trip. It seemed very long. Once she thought she must be going aimlessly back and forth on the same bit of rail, but a moment more brought her to the missing rail again, and she knew she had been right. Blown by the wind, struck by the now flying rain, deafened by the gurgling water and the rising storm, she fought her way back to the fire again. The others were all there, and with them three cramped and chilled little boys, crying fright and relief, and clinging to the nearest adult shoulder. The Chinese boy and Grandpa Barry had found them, standing on a hummock that was still clear of the rising tide, and shouting with all their weary strength.

"Oh, thank God!" said Mary Bell, her heart rising with sudden hope.

"We'll get the others, now, please God!" said Henderson, quietly. "We were working too far over. You said they were all right when you left them, Lesty?" he said to one of the shivering little lads.

"Ye-es, sir!" chattered Lesty, eagerly, shaking with nervousness. "They was both all right! Davy wanted to git Billy over to the fence, so if the tide come up!"--terror swept him again. "Oh, Mr. Henderson, git 'em--git 'em! Don't leave 'em drowned out there!" he sobbed frantically, clutching the big man with bony, wet little hands.

"I'm going to try, Lesty!"

Henderson turned back to the marsh, and Mary Bell went too.

"Billy who?" said Mary Bell; but her heart told her, before Henderson said it, that the answer would be, "Jim Carr's kid brother!"

"Are you good for this?" said Henderson, when the four fittest had reached that part of the marsh where the boys had been found.

She met his look courageously, his lantern showing her wet, brave young face, crossed by dripping strands of hair.

"Sure!" she said.

"Well, God bless you!" he said; "God--bless--you! You take this fence, I'll go over to that 'n."

The rushing, noisy darkness again. The horrible wind, the slipping, the plunging again. Again the slow, slow progress; driven and whipped now by the thought that at this very instant--or this one-- the boys might be giving out, relaxing hold, abandoning hope, and slipping numb and unconscious into the rising, chuckling water.

Mary Bell did not think of the dance now. But she thought of rest; of rest in the warm safety of her own home. She thought of the sunny dooryard, the delicious security of the big kitchen; of her mother, so placid and so infinitely dear, on her couch; of the serene comings and goings of neighbors and friends. How wonderful it all seemed! Lights, laughter, peace,--just to be back among them again, and to rest!

And she was going away from it all, into the blackness. Her lantern glimmered,--went out. Mary Bell's cramped fingers let it fall. Her heart pounded with fear of the inky dark.

She clung to the fence with both arms, panting, resting. And while she hung there, through rain and wind, across darkness and space, she heard a voice, a gallant, sturdy little voice, desperately calling,--

"Jim! Ji-i-m!"

Like an electric current, strength surged through Mary Bell.

"O God! You've saved 'em, you've got 'em safe!" she sobbed, plunging frantically forward. And she shouted, "All right--all right, darling! Hang on, boys! Just HANG ON! Hal-lo, there! Billy! Davy! Here I am!"

Down in pools, up again, laughing, crying, shouting, Mary Bell reached them at last, felt the heavenly grasp of hard little hands reaching for hers in the dark, brushed her face against Billy Carr's wet little cheek, and flung her arm about Davy Henderson's square shoulders. They had been shouting and calling for two long hours, not ten feet from the fence.

Incoherent, laughing and crying, they clung together. Davy was alert and brave, but the smaller boy was heavy with sleep.

"Gee, it's good you came!" said Davy, simply, over and over.

"You've got your boots on!" she shouted, close to his ear; "they're too heavy! We've got a long pull back, Davy,--I think we ought to go stocking feet!"

"Shall we take off our coats, too?" he said sensibly.

They did so, little Billy stumbling as Mary Bell loosened his hands from the fence. They braced the little fellow as well as they could, and by shouted encouragement roused him to something like wakefulness.

"Is Jim coming?" he shouted.

Mary Bell assented wildly. "Start, Davy!" she urged. "We'll keep him between us. Right along the fence! What is it?" For he had stopped.

"The other fellers?" he said pitifully.

She told him that they were safe, safe at the fire, and she could hear him break down and begin to cry with the first real hope that the worst was over.

"We're going to get out of this, ain't we?" he said over and over. And over and over Mary Bell encouraged him.

"Just one more good spurt, Davy! We'll see the fire any minute now!"

In wind and darkness and roaring water, they struggled along. The tide was coming in fast. It was up to Mary Bell's knees; she was almost carrying Billy.

"What is it, Davy?" she shouted, as he stopped again.

"Miss Mary Bell, aren't we going toward the river!" he shouted back.

The sickness of utter despair weakened the girl's knees. But for a moment only.

Then she drew the elder boy back, and made him pass her. Neither one spoke.

"Remember, they may come to meet us!" she would say, when Davy rested spent and breathless on the rail. The water was pushing about her waist, and was about his armpits now; to step carelessly into a pool would be fatal. Billy she was managing to keep above water by letting him step along the middle rail, when there was a middle rail. They made long rests, clinging close together.

"They ain't ever coming!" sobbed Davy, hopelessly. "I can't go no farther!"

Mary Bell managed, by leaning forward, to give him a wet slap, full in the face. The blow roused the little fellow, and he bravely stumbled ahead again.

"That's a darling, Davy!" she shouted. A second later something floating struck her elbow; a boy's rubber boot. It was perhaps the most dreadful moment of the long fight, when she realized that they were only where they had started from.

Later she heard herself urging Davy to take just ten steps more,-- just another ten. "Just think, five minutes more and we're safe, Davy!" some one said. Later, she heard her own voice saying, "Well, if you can't, then hang on the fence! DON'T let go the fence!" Then there was silence. Long after, Mary Bell began to cry, and said softly, "God, God, you know I could do this if I weren't carrying Billy." After that it was all a troubled dream.

She dreamed that Davy suddenly said, "I can see the fire!" and that, as she did not stir, he cried it again, this time not so near. She dreamed that the sound of splashing boots and shouting came down across the dark water, and that lights smote her eyelids with sharp pain. An overwhelming dread of effort swept over her. She did not want to move her aching body, to raise her heavy head. Somebody's arm braced her shoulders; she toppled against it.

She dreamed that Jim Carr's voice said, "Take the kid, Sing! He's all right!" and that Jim Carr lifted her up, and shouted out, "She's almost gone!"

Then some one was carrying her across rough ground, across smooth ground, to where there was a fire, and blankets, and voices--voices- -voices.

"It makes me choke!" That was Mary Bell Barber, whispering to Jim Carr. But she could not open her eyes.

"But drink it, dearest! Swallow it!" he pleaded.

"You were too late, Jim, we couldn't hold on!" she whispered pitifully. And then, as the warmth and the stimulant had their effect, she did open her eyes; and the fire, the ring of faces, the black sky, and the moon breaking through, all slipped into place.

"Did you come for us, Jim?" she murmured, too tired to wonder why the big fellow should cry as he put his face against hers.

"I came for you, dear! I came back to sit with you on the steps. I didn't want to dance without my girl, and that's why I'm here. My brave little girl!"

Mary Bell leaned against his shoulder contentedly.

"That's right; you rest!" said Jim. "We're all going home now, and we'll have you tucked away in bed in no time. Mrs. Bates is all ready for you!"

"Jim," whispered Mary Bell.

"Darling?"--he put his mouth close to the white lips.

"Jim, will you remind Aunty Bates to hang up my party dress real carefully? In all the fuss some one's sure to muss it!" said Mary Bell.

WHAT HAPPENED TO ALANNA

A capped and aproned maid, with a martyred expression, had twice sounded the dinner-bell in the stately halls of Costello, before any member of the family saw fit to respond to it.

Then they all came at once, with a sudden pounding of young feet on the stairs, an uproar of young voices, and much banging of doors. Jim and Danny, twins of fourteen, to whom their mother was wont proudly to allude as "the top o' the line," violently left their own sanctum on the fourth floor, and coasted down such banisters as lay between that and the dining-room. Teresa, an angel-faced twelve-year-old in a blue frock, shut 'The Wide, Wide World' with a sigh, and climbed down from the window-seat in the hall.

Teresa's pious mother, in moments of exultation, loved to compare and commend her offspring to such of the saints and martyrs as their youthful virtues suggested. And Teresa at twelve had, as it were, graduated from the little saints, Agnes and Rose and Cecilia, and was now compared, in her mother's secret heart, to the gracious Queen of all the Saints. "As she was when a little girl," Mrs. Costello would add, to herself, to excuse any undue boldness in the thought.

And indeed, Teresa, as she was to-night, her blue eyes still clouded with Ellen Montgomery's sorrows, her curls tumbled about her hot cheeks, would have made a pretty foil in a picture of old Saint Anne.

But this story is about Alanna of the black eyes, the eight years, the large irregular mouth, the large irregular freckles.

Alanna was outrunning lazy little Leo--her senior, but not her match at anything--on their way to the dining-room. She was rendering desperate the two smaller boys, Frank X., Jr., and John Henry Newman Costello, who staggered hopelessly in her wake. They were all hungry, clean, and good-natured, and Alanna's voice led the other voices, even as her feet, in twinkling patent leather, led their feet.

Following the children came their mother, fastening the rich silk and lace at her wrists as she came. Her handsome kindly face and her big shapely hands were still moist and glowing from soap and warm water, and the shining rings of black hair at her temples were moist, too.

"This is all my doin', Dad," said she, comfortably, as she and her flock entered the dining-room. "Put the soup on, Alma. I'm the one that was goin' to be prompt at dinner, too!" she added, with a superintending glance for all the children, as she tied on little John's napkin.

F.X. Costello, Senior, undertaker by profession, and mayor by an immense majority, was already at the head of the table.

"Late, eh, Mommie?" said he, good-naturedly. He threw his newspaper on the floor, cast a householder's critical glance at the lights and the fire, and pushed his neatly placed knives and forks to right and left carelessly with both his fat hands.

The room was brilliantly lighted and warm. A great fire roared in the old-fashioned black marble grate, and electric lights blazed everywhere. Everything in the room, and in the house, was costly, comfortable, incongruous, and hideous. The Costellos were very rich, and had been very poor; and certain people were fond of telling of the queer, ridiculous things they did, in trying to spend their money. But they were very happy, and thought their immense, ugly house was the finest in the city, or in the world.

"Well, an' what's the news on the Rialter?" said the head of the house now, busy with his soup.

"You'll have the laugh on me, Dad," his wife assured him, placidly. "After all my sayin' that nothing'd take me to Father Crowley's meetin'!"

"Oh, that was it?" said the mayor. "What's he goin' to have,--a concert?"

"--AND a fair too!" supplemented Mrs. Costello. There was an interval devoted on her part to various bibs and trays, and a low aside to the waitress. Then she went on: "As you know, I went, meanin' to beg off. On account of baby bein' so little, and Leo's cough, and the paperers bein' upstairs,--and all! I thought I'd just make a donation, and let it go at that. But the ladies all kind of hung back--there was very few there--and I got talkin'--"

"Well, 'tis but our dooty, after all," said the mayor, nodding approval.

"That's all, Frank. Well! So finally Mrs. Kiljohn took the coffee, and the Lemmon girls took the grab-bag. The Guild will look out for the concert, and I took one fancy-work booth, and of course the Children of Mary'll have the other, just like they always do."

"Oh, was Grace there?" Teresa was eager to know.

"Grace was, darlin'."

"And we're to have the fancy-work! You'll help us, won't you, mother? Goody--I'm in that!" exulted Teresa.

"I'm in that, too!" echoed Alanna, quickly.

"A lot you are, you baby!" said Leo, unkindly.

"You're not a Child of Mary, Alanna," Teresa said promptly and uneasily.

"Well--WELL--I can help!" protested Alanna, putting up her lip. Can't I, mother? "CAN'T I, mother?"

"You can help ME, dovey," said her mother, absently. "I'm not goin' to work as I did for Saint Patrick's Bazaar, Dad, and I said so! Mrs. O'Connell and Mrs. King said they'd do all the work, if I'd just be the nominal head. Mary Murray will do us some pillers-- leather--with Gibsons and Indians on them. And I'll have Lizzie Bayne up here for a month, makin' me aprons and little Jappy wrappers, and so on."

She paused over the cutlets and the chicken pie, which she had been helping with an amazing attention to personal preference. The young Costellos chafed at the delay, but their mother's fine eyes saw them not.

"Kelley & Moffat ought to let me have materials at half price," she reflected aloud. "My bill's two or three hundred a month!"

"You always say that you're not going to do a thing, and then get in and make more than any other booth!" said Dan, proudly.

"Oh, not this year, I won't," his mother assured him. But in her heart she knew she would.

"Aren't you glad it's fancy-work?" said Teresa. "It doesn't get all sloppy and mussy like ice-cream, does it, mother?"

"Gee, don't you love fairs!" burst out Leo, rapturously.

"Sliding up and down the floor before the dance begins, Dan, to work in the wax?" suggested Jimmy, in pleasant anticipation. "We go every day and every night, don't we, mother?"

"Ask your father," said Mrs. Costello, discreetly.

But the Mayor's attention just then was taken by Alanna, who had left her chair to go and whisper in his ear.

"Why, here's Alanna's heart broken!" said he, cheerfully, encircling her little figure with a big arm.

Alanna shrank back suddenly against him, and put her wet cheek on his shoulder.

"Now, whatever is it, darlin'?" wondered her mother, sympathetically, but without concern. "You've not got a pain, have you, dear?"

"She wants to help the Children of Mary!" said her father, tenderly. "She wants to do as much as Tessie does!"

"Oh, but, Dad, she CAN'T!" fretted Teresa. "She's not a Child of Mary! She oughtn't to want to tag that way. Now all the other girls' sisters will tag!"

"They haven't got sisters!" said Alanna, red-cheeked of a sudden.

"Why, Mary Alanna Costello, they have too! Jean has, and Stella has, and Grace has her little cousins!" protested Teresa, triumphantly.

"Never mind, baby," said Mrs. Costello, hurriedly. "Mother'll find you something to do. There now! How'd you like to have a raffle book on something,--a chair or a piller? And you could get all the names yourself, and keep the money in a little bag--"

"Oh, my! I wish I could!" said Jim, artfully. "Think of the last night, when the drawing comes! You'll have the fun of looking up the winning number in your book, and calling it out, in the hall."

"Would I, Dad?" said Alanna, softly, but with dawning interest.

"And then, from the pulpit, when the returns are all in," contributed Dan, warmly, "Father Crowley will read out your name,-- With Mrs. Frank Costello's booth--raffle of sofa cushion, by Miss Alanna Costello, twenty-six dollars and thirty-five cents!"

"Oo--would he, Dad?" said Alanna, won to smiles and dimples by this charming prospect.

"Of course he would!" said her father. "Now go back to your seat, Machree, and eat your dinner. When Mommer takes you and Tess to the matinee to-morrow, ask her to bring you in to me first, and you and I'll step over to Paul's, and pick out a table or a couch, or something. Eh, Mommie?"

"And what do you say?" said that lady to Alanna, as the radiant little girl went back to her chair.

Whereupon Alanna breathed a bashful "Thank you, Dad," into the ruffled yoke of her frock, and the matter was settled.

The next day she trotted beside her father to Paul's big furniture store, and after long hesitation selected a little desk of shining brass and dull oak.

"Now," said her father, when they were back in his office, and Teresa and Mrs. Costello were eager for the matinee, "here's your book of numbers, Alanna. And here, I'll tie a pencil and a string to it. Don't lose it. I've given you two hundred numbers at a quarter each, and mind the minute any one pays for one, you put their name down on the same line!"

"Oo,--oo!" said Alanna in pride. "Two hundred! That's lots of money, isn't it, Dad? That's eleven or fourteen dollars, isn't it, Dad?"

"That's fifty dollars, goose!" said her father making a dot with the pencil on the tip of her upturned little nose.

"Oo!" said Teresa, awed. Hatted, furred, and muffed, she leaned on her father's shoulder.

"Oo--Dad!" whispered Alanna, with scarlet cheeks.

"So NOW!" said her mother, with a little nod of encouragement and warning. "Put it right in your muff, lovey. Don't lose it. Dan or Jim will help you count your money, and keep things straight."

"And to begin with, we'll all take a chance!" said the mayor, bringing his fat palm, full of silver, up from his pocket. "How old are you, Mommie?"

"I'm thirty-seven,--all but, as well you know, Frank!" said his wife, promptly.

"Thirty-six AND thirty-seven for you, then!" He wrote her name opposite both numbers. "And here's the mayor on the same page,-- forty-four! And twelve for Tessie, and eight for this highbinder on my knee, here! And now we'll have one for little Gertie!"

Gertrude Costello was not yet three months old, her mother said.

"Well, she can have number one, anyway!" said the mayor. "You make a re-jooced rate for one family, I understand, Miss Costello?"

"I DON'T!" chuckled Alanna, locking her thin little arms about his neck, and digging her chin into his eye. So he gave her full price, and she went off with her mother in a state of great content, between rows and rows of coffins, and cases of plumes, and handles and rosettes, and designs for monuments.

"Mrs. Church will want some chances, won't she, mother?" she said suddenly.

"Let Mrs. Church alone, darlin'," advised Mrs. Costello. "She's not a Catholic, and there's plenty to take chances without her!"

Alanna reluctantly assented; but she need not have worried. Mrs. Church voluntarily took many chances, and became very enthusiastic about the desk.

She was a pretty, clever young woman, of whom all the Costellos were very fond. She lived with a very young husband, and a very new baby, in a tiny cottage near the big Irish family, and pleased Mrs. Costello by asking her advice on all domestic matters and taking it. She made the Costello children welcome at all hours in her tiny, shining kitchen, or sunny little dining-room. She made them candy and told them stories. She was a minister's daughter, and wise in many delightful, girlish, friendly ways.

And in return Mrs. Costello did her many a kindly act, and sent her almost daily presents in the most natural manner imaginable.

But Mrs. Church made Alanna very unhappy about the raffled desk. It so chanced that it matched exactly the other furniture in Mrs. Church's rather bare little drawing-room, and this made her eager to win it. Alanna, at eight, long familiar with raffles and their ways, realized what a very small chance Mrs. Church stood of getting the desk. It distressed her very much to notice that lady's growing certainty of success.

She took chance after chance. And with every chance she warned Alanna of the dreadful results of her not winning, and Alanna, with a worried line between her eyes, protested her helplessness afresh.

"She WILL do it, Dad!" the little girl confided to him one evening, when she and her book and her pencil were on his knee. "And it WORRIES me so."

"Oh, I hope she wins it," said Teresa, ardently. "She's not a Catholic, but we're praying for her. And you know people who aren't Catholics, Dad, are apt to think that our fairs are pretty--pretty MONEY-MAKING, you know!"

"And if only she could point to that desk," said Alanna, "and say that she won it at a Catholic fair."

"But she won't," said Teresa, suddenly cold.

"I'm PRAYING she will," said Alanna, suddenly.

"Oh, I don't think you ought, do you, Dad?" said Teresa, gravely. "Do you think she ought, Mommie? That's just like her pouring her holy water over the kitten. You oughtn't to do those things."

"I ought to," said Alanna, in a whisper that reached only her father's ear.

"You suit me, whatever you do," said Mayor Costello; "and Mrs. Church can take her chances with the rest of us."

Mrs. Church seemed to be quite willing to do so. When at last the great day of the fair came, she was one of the first to reach the hall, in the morning, to ask Mrs. Costello how she might be of use.

"Now wait a minute, then!" said Mrs. Costello, cordially. She straightened up, as she spoke, from an inspection of a box of fancy- work. "We could only get into the hall this hour gone, my dear, and 'twas a sight, after the Native Sons' Banquet last night. It'll be a miracle if we get things in order for to-night. Father Crowley said he'd have three carpenters here this morning at nine, without fail; but not one's come yet. That's the way!"

"Oh, we'll fix things," said Mrs. Church, shaking out a dainty little apron.

Alanna came briskly up, and beamed at her. The little girl was driving about on all sorts of errands for her mother, and had come in to report.

"Mother, I went home," she said, in a breathless rush, "and told Alma four extra were coming to lunch, and here are your big scissors, and I told the boys you wanted them to go out to Uncle Dan's for greens, they took the buckboard, and I went to Keyser's for the cheese-cloth, and he had only eighteen yards of pink, but he thinks Kelley's have more, and there are the tacks, and they don't keep spool-wire, and the electrician will be here in ten minutes."

"Alanna, you're the pride of me life," said her mother, kissing her. "That's all now, dearie. Sit down and rest."

"Oh, but I'd rather go round and see things," said Alanna, and off she went.

The immense hall was filled with the noise of voices, hammers, and laughter. Groups of distracted women were forming and dissolving everywhere around chaotic masses of boards and bunting. Whenever a carpenter started for the door, or entered it, he was waylaid, bribed, and bullied by the frantic superintendents of the various booths. Messengers came and went, staggering under masses of evergreen, carrying screens, rope, suit-cases, baskets, boxes, Japanese lanterns, freezers, rugs, ladders, and tables.

Alanna found the stage fascinating. Lunch and dinner were to be served there, for the five days of the fair, and it had been set with many chairs and tables, fenced with ferns and bamboo. Alanna was charmed to arrange knives and forks, to unpack oily hams and sticky cakes, and great bowls of salad, and to store them neatly away in a green room.

The grand piano had been moved down to the floor. Now and then an audacious boy or two banged on it for the few moments that it took his mother's voice or hands to reach him. Little girls gently played The Carnival of Venice or Echoes of the Ball, with their scared eyes alert for reproof. And once two of the "big" Sodality girls came up, assured and laughing and dusty, and boldly performed one of their convent duets. Some of the tired women in the booths straightened up and clapped, and called "encore!"

Teresa was not one of these girls. Her instrument was the violin; moreover, she was busy and absorbed at the Children of Mary's booth, which by four o'clock began to blossom all over its white-draped pillars and tables with ribbons and embroidery and tissue paper, and cushions and aprons and collars, and all sorts of perfumed prettiness.

The two priests were constantly in evidence, their cassocks and hands showing unaccustomed dust.

And over all the confusion, Mrs. Costello shone supreme. Her brisk, big figure, with skirts turned back, and a blue apron still further protecting them, was everywhere at once; laughter and encouragement marked her path. She wore a paper of pins on the breast of her silk dress, she had a tack hammer thrust in her belt. In her apron pockets were string, and wire, and tacks. A big pair of scissors hung at her side, and a pencil was thrust through her smooth black hair. She advised and consulted and directed; even with the priests it was to be observed that her mild, "Well, Father, it seems to me," always won the day. She led the electricians a life of it; she became the terror of the carpenters' lives.

Where was the young lady that played the violin going to stay? Send her up to Mrs. Costello's.--Heavens! We were short a tablecloth! Oh, but Mrs. Costello had just sent Dan home for one.--How on earth could the Male Quartette from Tower Town find its way to the hall? Mrs. Costello had promised to tell Mr. C. to send a carriage for them.

She came up to the Children of Mary's booth about five o'clock.

"Well, if you girls ain't the wonders!" she said to the tired little Sodalists, in a tone of unbounded admiration and surprise. "You make me ashamed of me own booth. This is beautiful."

"Oh, do you think so, mother?" said Teresa, wistfully, clinging to her mother's arm.

"I think it's grand!" said Mrs. Costello, with conviction. There was a delighted laugh. "I'm going to bring all the ladies up to see it."

"Oh, I'm so glad!" said all the girls together, reviving visibly.

"An' the pretty things you got!" went on the cheering matron. "You'll clear eight hundred if you'll clear a cent. And now put me down for a chance or two; don't be scared, Mary Riordan; four or five! I'm goin' to bring Mr. Costeller over here to-night, and don't you let him off too easy."

Every one laughed joyously.

"Did you hear of Alanna's luck?" said Mrs. Costello. "When the Bishop got here he took her all around the hall with him, and between this one and that, every last one of her chances is gone. She couldn't keep her feet on the floor for joy. The lucky girl! They're waitin' for you, Tess, darlin', with the buckboard. Go home and lay down awhile before dinner."

"Aren't you lucky!" said Teresa, as she climbed a few minutes later into the back seat with Jim, and Dan pulled out the whip.

Alanna, swinging her legs, gave a joyful assent. She was too happy to talk, but the other three had much to say.

"Mother thinks we'll make eight hundred dollars," said Teresa.

"GEE!" said the twins together, and Dan added, "If only Mrs. Church wins that desk now."

"Who's going to do the drawing of numbers?" Jimmy wondered.

"Bishop," said Dan, "and he'll call down from the platform, 'Number twenty-six wins the desk.' And then Alanna'll look in her book, and pipe up and say, 'Daniel Ignatius Costello, the handsomest fellow in the parish, wins the desk.'"

"Twenty-six is Harry Plummer," said Alanna, seriously, looking up from her chance book, at which they all laughed.

"But take care of that book," warned Teresa, as she climbed down. "Oh, I will!" responded Alanna, fervently.

And through the next four happy days she did, and took the precaution of tying it by a stout cord to her arm.

Then on Saturday, the last afternoon, quite late, when her mother had suggested that she go home with Leo and Jack and Frank and Gertrude and the nurses, Alanna felt the cord hanging loose against her hand, and looking down, saw that the book was gone.

She was holding out her arms for her coat when this took place, and she went cold all over. But she did not move, and Minnie buttoned her in snugly, and tied the ribbons of her hat with cold, hard knuckles, without suspecting anything.

Then Alanna disappeared and Mrs. Costello sent the maids and babies on without her. It was getting dark and cold for the small Costellos.

But the hour was darker and colder for Alanna. She searched and she hoped and she prayed in vain. She stood up, after a long hands-and- knees expedition under the tables where she had been earlier, and pressed her right hand over her eyes, and said aloud in her misery, "Oh, I CAN'T have lost it! I CAN'T have. Oh, don't let me have lost it!"

She went here and there as if propelled by some mechanical force, a wretched, restless little figure. And when the dreadful moment came when she must give up searching, she crept in beside her mother in the carriage, and longed only for some honorable death.

When they all went back at eight o'clock, she recommenced her search feverishly, with that cruel alternation of hope and despair and weariness that every one knows. The crowds, the lights, the music, the laughter, and the noise, and the pervading odor of pop-corn were not real, when a shabby, brown little book was her whole world, and she could not find it.

"The drawing will begin," said Alanna, "and the Bishop will call out the number! And what'll I say? Every one will look at me; and HOW can I say I've lost it! Oh, what a baby they'll call me!"

"Father'll pay the money back," she said, in sudden relief. But the impossibility of that swiftly occurred to her, and she began hunting again with fresh terror.

"But he can't! How can he? Two hundred names; and I don't know them, or half of them."

Then she felt the tears coming, and she crept in under some benches, and cried.

She lay there a long time, listening to the curious hum and buzz above her. And at last it occurred to her to go to the Bishop, and tell this old, kind friend the truth.

But she was too late. As she got to her feet, she heard her own name called from the platform, in the Bishop's voice.

"Where's Alanna Costello? Ask her who has number eighty-three on the desk. Eighty-three wins the desk! Find little Alanna Costello!"

Alanna had no time for thought. Only one course of action occurred to her. She cleared her throat.

"Mrs. Will Church has that number, Bishop," she said.

The crowd about her gave way, and the Bishop saw her, rosy, embarrassed, and breathless.

"Ah, there you are!" said the Bishop. "Who has it?"

"Mrs. Church, your Grace," said Alanna, calmly this time.

"Well, did you EVER," said Mrs. Costello to the Bishop. She had gone up to claim a mirror she had won, a mirror with a gold frame, and lilacs and roses painted lavishly on its surface.

"Gee, I bet Alanna was pleased about the desk!" said Dan in the carriage.

"Mrs. Church nearly cried," Teresa said. "But where'd Alanna go to? I couldn't find her until just a few minutes ago, and then she was so queer!"

"It's my opinion she was dead tired," said her mother. "Look how sound she's asleep! Carry her up, Frank. I'll keep her in bed in the morning."

They kept Alanna in bed for many mornings, for her secret weighed on her soul, and she failed suddenly in color, strength, and appetite. She grew weak and nervous, and one afternoon, when the Bishop came to see her, worked herself into such a frenzy that Mrs. Costello wonderingly consented to her entreaty that he should not come up.

She would not see Mrs. Church, nor go to see the desk in its new house, nor speak of the fair in any way. But she did ask her mother who swept out the hall after the fair.

"I did a good deal meself," said Mrs. Costello, dashing one hope to the ground. Alanna leaned back in her chair, sick with disappointment.

One afternoon, about a week after the fair, she was brooding over the fire. The other children were at the matinee, Mrs. Costello was out, and a violent storm was whirling about the nursery windows.

Presently, Annie, the laundress, put her frowsy head in at the door. She was a queer, warm-hearted Irish girl; her big arms were still streaming from the tub, and her apron was wet.

"Ahl alone?" said Annie, with a broad smile.

"Yes; come in, won't you, Annie?" said little Alanna.

"I cahn't. I'm at the toobs," said Annie, coming in, nevertheless. "I was doin' all the tableclot's and napkins, an' out drops your little buke!"

"My--what did you say?" said Alanna, very white.

"Your little buke," said Annie. She laid the chance book on the table, and proceeded to mend the fire.

Alanna sank back in her chair. She twisted her fingers together, and tried to think of an appropriate prayer.

"Thank you, Annie," she said weakly, when the laundress went out. Then she sprang for the book. It slipped twice from her cold little fingers before she could open it.

"Eighty-three!" she said hoarsely. "Sixty--seventy--eighty-three!"

She looked and looked and looked. She shut the book and opened it again, and looked. She laid it on the table, and walked away from it, and then came back suddenly, and looked. She laughed over it, and cried over it, and thought how natural it was, and how wonderful it was, all in the space of ten blissful minutes.

And then, with returning appetite and color and peace of mind, her eyes filled with pity for the wretched little girl who had watched this same sparkling, delightful fire so drearily a few minutes ago.

Her small soul was steeped in gratitude. She crooked her arm and put her face down on it, and sank to her knees.

"NEW white dress, is it?" said Mrs. Costello in bland surprise. "Well, my, my, my! You'll have Dad and me in the poorhouse!"

She had been knitting a pink and white jacket for somebody's baby, but now she put it into the silk bag on her knee, dropped it on the floor, and with one generous sweep of her big arms gathered Alanna into her lap instead. Alanna was delighted to have at last attracted her mother's whole attention, after some ten minutes of unregarded whispering in her ear. She settled her thin little person with the conscious pleasure of a petted cat.

"What do you know about that, Dad?" said Mrs. Costello, absently, as she stiffened the big bow over Alanna's temple into a more erect position. "You and Tess could wear your Christmas procession dresses," she suggested to the little girl.

Teresa, apparently absorbed until this instant in what the young Costellos never called anything but the "library book," although that volume changed character and title week after week, now shut it abruptly, came around the reading-table to her mother's side, and said in a voice full of pained reminder:

"Mother! EVERY ONE will have new white dresses and blue sashes for Superior's feast!"

"I bet you Superior won't!" said Jim, frivolously, from the picture- puzzle he and Dan were reconstructing. Alanna laughed joyously, but Teresa looked shocked.

"Mother, ought he say that about Superior?" she asked.

"Jimmy, don't you be pert about the Sisters," said his mother, mildly. And suddenly the Mayor's paper was lowered, and he was looking keenly at his son over his glasses.

"What did you say, Jim?" said he. Jim was instantly smitten scarlet and dumb, but Mrs. Costello hastily explained that it was but a bit of boy's nonsense, and dismissed it by introducing the subject of the new white dresses.

"Well, well, well! There's nothing like having two girls in society!" said the Mayor, genially, winding one of Teresa's curls about his fat finger. "What's this for, now? Somebody graduating?"

"It's Mother Superior's Golden Jubilee," explained Teresa, "and there will be a reunion of 'lumnae, and plays by the girls, you know, and duets by the big girls, and needlework by the Spanish girls. And our room and Sister Claudia's is giving a new chapel window, a dollar a girl, and Sister Ligouri's room is giving the organ bench."

"And our room is giving a spear," said Alanna, uncertainly.

"A spear, darlin'?" wondered her mother. "What would you give that to Superior for?" Jim and Dan looked up expectantly, the Mayor's mouth twitched. Alanna buried her face in her mother's neck, where she whispered an explanation.

"Well, of course!" said Mrs. Costello, presently, to the company at large. Her eye held a warning that her oldest sons did not miss. "As she says, 'tis a ball all covered with islands and maps, Dad. A globe, that's the other name for it!"

"Ah, yes, a spear, to be sure!" assented the Mayor, mildly, and Alanna returned to view.

"But the best of the whole programme is the grandchildren's part," volunteered Teresa. "You know, Mother, the girls whose mothers went to Notre Dame are called the 'grandchildren.' Alanna and I are, there are twenty-two of us in all. And we are going to have a special march and a special song, and present Superior with a bouquet!"

"And maybe Teresa's going to present it and say the salutation!" exulted Alanna.

"No, Marg'ret Hammond will," Teresa corrected her quickly. "Marg'ret's three months older than me. First they were going to have me, but Marg'ret's the oldest. And she does it awfully nicely, doesn't she, Alanna? Sister Celia says it's really the most important thing of the day. And we all stand round Marg'ret while she does it. And the best of it all is, it's a surprise for Superior!"

"Not a surprise like Christmas surprises," amended Alanna, conscientiously. "Superior sort of knows we are doing something, because she hears the girls practising, and she sees us going upstairs to rehearse. But she will p'tend to be surprised."

"And it's new dresses all 'round, eh?" said her father.

"Oh, yes, we must!" said Teresa, anxiously.

"Well, I'll see about it," promised Mrs. Costello.

"Don't you want to afford the expense, mother?" Alanna whispered in her ear. Mrs. Costello was much touched.

"Don't you worry about that, lovey!" said she. The Mayor had presumably returned to his paper, but his absent eyes were fixed far beyond the printed sheet he still held tilted carefully to the light.

"Marg'ret Hammond--whose girl is that, then?" he asked presently.

"She's a girl whose mother died," supplied Alanna, cheerfully. "She's awfully smart. Sister Helen teaches her piano for nothing,-- she's a great friend of mine. She likes me, doesn't she, Tess?"

"She's three years older'n you are, Alanna," said Teresa, briskly, "and she's in our room! I don't see how you can say she's a friend of YOURS! Do you, mother?"

"Well," said Alanna, getting red, "she is. She gave me a rag when I cut me knee, and one day she lifted the cup down for me when Mary Deane stuck it up on a high nail, so that none of us could get drinks, and when Sister Rose said, 'Who is talking?' she said Alanna Costello wasn't 'cause she's sitting here as quiet as a mouse!'"

"All that sounds very kind and friendly to me," said Mrs. Costello, soothingly.

"I expect that's Doctor Hammond's girl?" said the Mayor.

"No, sir," said Dan. "These are the Hammonds who live over by the bridge. There's just two kids, Marg'ret and Joe, and their father. Joe served the eight o'clock Mass with me one week,--you know, Jim, the week you were sick."

"Sure," said Jim. "Hammond's a nice feller."

Their father scraped his chin with a fat hand.

"I know them," he said ruminatively. Mrs. Costello looked up.

"That's not the Hammond you had trouble with at the shop, Frank?" she said.

"Well, I'm thinking maybe it is," her husband admitted. "He's had a good deal of bad luck one way or another, since he lost his wife." He turned to Teresa. "You be as nice as you can to little Marg'ret Hammond, Tess," said he.

"I wonder who the wife was?" said Mrs. Costello. "If this little girl is a 'grandchild,' I ought to know the mother. Ask her, Tess."

Teresa hesitated.

"I don't play with her much, mother. And she's sort of shy," she began.

"I'll ask her," said Alanna, boldly. "I don't care if she IS going on twelve. She goes up to the chapel every day, and I'll stop her to-morrow, and ask her! She's always friendly to me."

Mayor Costello had returned to his paper. But a few hours later, when all the children except Gertrude were settled for the night, and Gertrude, in a state of milky beatitude, was looking straight into her mother's face above her with blue eyes heavy with sleep, he enlightened his wife further concerning the Hammonds.

"He was with me at the shop," said the Mayor, "and I never was sorrier to let any man go. But it seemed like his wife's death drove him quite wild. First it was fighting with the other boys, and then drink, and then complaints here and there and everywhere, and Kelly wouldn't stand for it. I wish I'd kept him on a bit longer, myself, what with his having the two children and all. He's got a fine head on him, and a very good way with people in trouble. Kelly himself was always sending him to arrange about flowers and carriages and all. Poor lad! And then came the night he was tipsy, and got locked in the warehouse--"

"I know," said Mrs. Costello, with a pitying shake of the head, as she gently adjusted the sleeping Gertrude. "Has he had a job since, Frank?"

"He was with a piano house," said her husband, uneasily, as he went slowly on with his preparations for the night. "Two children, has he? And a boy on the altar. 'Tis hard that the children have to pay for it."

"Alanna'll find out who the wife was. She never fails me," said Mrs. Costello, turning from Gertrude's crib with sudden decision in her voice. "And I'll do something, never fear!"

Alanna did not fail. She came home the next day brimming with the importance of her fulfilled mission.

"Her mother's name was Harmonica Moore!" announced Alanna, who could be depended upon for unfailing inaccuracy in the matter of names. Teresa and the boys burst into joyous laughter, but the information was close enough for Mrs. Costello.

"Monica Moore!" she exclaimed. "Well, for pity's sake! Of course I knew her, and a sweet, dear girl she was, too. Stop laughing at Alanna, all of you, or I'll send you upstairs until Dad gets after you. Very quiet and shy she was, but the lovely singing voice! There wasn't a tune in the world she wouldn't lilt to you if you asked her. Well, the poor child, I wish I'd never lost sight of her." She pondered a moment." Is the boy still serving Mass at St. Mary's, Dan?" she said then.

"Sure," said Jim. For Dan was absorbed in the task of restoring Alanna's ruffled feelings by inserting a lighted match into his mouth.

"Well, that's good," pursued their mother. "You bring him home to breakfast after Mass any day this week, Jim. And, Tess, you must bring the little girl in after school. Tell her I knew her dear mother." Mrs. Costello's eyes, as she returned placidly to the task of labelling jars upon shining jars of marmalade, shone with their most radiant expression.

Marg'ret and Joe Hammond were constant visitors in the big Costello house after that. Their father was away, looking for work, Mrs. Costello imagined and feared, and they were living with some vague "lady across the hall." So the Mayor's wife had free rein, and she used it. When Marg'ret got one of her shapeless, leaky shoes cut in the Costello barn, she was promptly presented with shining new ones, "the way I couldn't let you get a cold and die on your father, Marg'ret, dear!" said Mrs. Costello. The twins' outgrown suits were found to fit Joe Hammond to perfection, "and a lucky thing I thought of it, Joe, before I sent them off to my sister's children in Chicago!" observed the Mayor's wife. The Mayor himself heaped his little guests' plates with the choicest of everything on the table, when the Hammonds stayed to dinner. Marg'ret frequently came home between Teresa and Alanna to lunch, and when Joe breakfasted after Mass with Danny and Jim, Mrs. Costello packed his lunch with theirs, exulting in the chance. The children became fast friends, and indeed it would have been hard to find better playfellows for the young Costellos, their mother often thought, than the clever, appreciative little Hammonds.

Meantime, the rehearsals for Mother Superior's Golden Jubilee proceeded steadily, and Marg'ret, Teresa, and Alanna could talk of nothing else. The delightful irregularity of lessons, the enchanting confusion of rehearsals, the costumes, programme, and decorations were food for endless chatter. Alanna, because Marg'ret was so genuinely fond of her, lived in the seventh heaven of bliss, trotting about with the bigger girls, joining in their plans, and running their errands. The "grandchildren" were to have a play, entitled "By Nero's Command," in which both Teresa and Marg'ret sustained prominent parts, and even Alanna was allotted one line to speak. It became an ordinary thing, in the Costello house, to hear the little girl earnestly repeating this line to herself at quiet moments, "The lions,--oh, the lions!" Teresa and Marg'ret, in their turn, frequently rehearsed a heroic dialogue which began with the stately line, uttered by Marg'ret in the person of a Roman princess: "My slave, why art thou always so happy at thy menial work?"

One day Mrs. Costello called the three girls to her sewing-room, where a brisk young woman was smoothing lengths of snowy lawn on the long table.

"These are your dresses, girls," said the matron. "Let Miss Curry get the len'ths and neck measures. And look, here's the embroidery I got. Won't that make up pretty? The waists will be all insertion, pretty near."

"Me, too?" said Marg'ret Hammond, catching a rapturous breath.

"You, too," answered Mrs. Costello in her most matter-of-fact tone. "You see, you three will be the very centre of the group, and it'll look very nice, your all being dressed the same--why, Marg'ret, dear!" she broke off suddenly. For Marg'ret, standing beside her chair, had dropped her head on Mrs. Costello's shoulder and was crying.

"I worried so about my dress," said she, shakily, wiping her eyes on the soft sleeve of Mrs. Costello's shirt-waist; when a great deal of patting, and much smothering from the arms of Teresa and Alanna had almost restored her equilibrium, "and Joe worried too! I couldn't write and bother my father. And only this morning I was thinking that I might have to write and tell Sister Rose that I couldn't be in the exhibition, after all!"

"Well, there, now, you silly girl! You see how much good worrying does," said Mrs. Costello, but her own eyes were wet.

"The worst of it was," said Marg'ret, red-cheeked, but brave, "that I didn't want any one to think my father wouldn't give it to me. For you know"--the generous little explanation tugged at Mrs. Costello's heart--"you know he would if he COULD!"

"Well, of course he would!" assented that lady, giving the loyal little daughter a kiss before the delightful business of fitting and measuring began. The new dresses promised to be the prettiest of their kind, and harmony and happiness reigned in the sewing-room.

But it was only a day later that Teresa and Alanna returned from school with faces filled with expressions of utter woe. Indignant, protesting, tearful, they burst forth the instant they reached their mother's sympathetic presence with the bitter tale of the day's happenings. Marg'ret Hammond's father had come home again, it appeared, and he was awfully, awfully cross with Marg'ret and Joe. They weren't to come to the Costellos' any more, or he'd whip them. And Marg'ret had been crying, and THEY had been crying, and Sister didn't know what was the matter, and they couldn't tell her, and the rehearsal was no FUN!

While their feeling was still at its height, Dan and Jimmy came in, equally roused by their enforced estrangement from Joe Hammond. Mrs. Costello was almost as much distressed as the children, and excited and mutinous argument held the Costello dinner-table that night. The Mayor, his wife noticed, paid very close attention to the conversation, but he did not allude to it until they were alone.

"So Hammond'll take no favors from me, Mollie?"

"I suppose that's it, Frank. Perhaps he's been nursing a grudge all these weeks. But it's cruel hard on the children. From his comin' back this way, I don't doubt he's out of work, and where Marg'ret'll get her white dress from now, I don't know!"

"Well, if he don't provide it, Tess'll recite the salutation," said the Mayor, with a great air of philosophy. But a second later he added, "You couldn't have it finished up, now, and send it to the child on the chance?"

His wife shook her head despondently, and for several days went about with a little worried look in her bright eyes, and a constant dread of the news that Marg'ret Hammond had dropped out of the exhibition. Marg'ret was sad, the little girls said, and evidently missing them as they missed her, but up to the very night of the dress rehearsal she gave no sign of worry on the subject of a white dress.

Mrs. Costello had offered her immense parlors for the last rehearsal of the chief performers in the plays and tableaux, realizing that even the most obligingly blind of Mother Superiors could not appear to ignore the gathering of some fifty girls in their gala dresses in the convent hall, for this purpose. Alanna and Teresa were gloriously excited over the prospect, and flitted about the empty rooms on the evening appointed, buzzing like eager bees.

Presently a few of the nuns arrived, escorting a score of little girls, and briskly ready for an evening of serious work. Then some of the older girls, carrying their musical instruments, came in laughing. Laughter and talk began to make the big house hum, the nuns ruling the confusion, gathering girls into groups, suppressing the hilarity that would break out over and over again, and anxious to clear a corner and begin the actual work. A tall girl, leaning on the piano, scribbled a crude programme, murmuring to the alert-faced nun beside her as she wrote:

"Yes, Sister, and then the mandolins and guitars; yes, Sister, and then Mary Cudahy's recitation; yes, Sister. Is that too near Loretta's song? All right, Sister, the French play can go in between, and then Loretta. Yes, Sister."

"Of course Marg'ret'll come, Tess,--or has she come?" said Mrs. Costello, who was hastily clearing a table in the family sitting-room upstairs, because it was needed for the stage setting. Teresa, who had just joined her mother, was breathless.

"Mother! Something awful has happened!"

Mrs. Costello carefully transferred to the book-case the lamp she had just lifted, dusted her hands together, and turned eyes full of sympathetic interest upon her oldest daughter,--Teresa's tragedies were very apt to be of the spirit, and had not the sensational urgency that alarms from the boys or Alanna commanded.

"What is it then, darlin'?" said she.

"Oh, it's Marg'ret, mother!" Teresa clasped her hands in an ecstasy of apprehension. "Oh, mother, can't you MAKE her take that white dress?"

Mrs. Costello sat down heavily, her kind eyes full of regret.

"What more can I do, Tess?" Then, with a grave headshake, "She's told Sister Rose she has to drop out?"

"Oh, no, mother!" Teresa said distressfully. "It's worse than that! She's here, and she's rehearsing, and what DO you think she's wearing for an exhibition dress?"

"Well, how would I know, Tess, with you doing nothing but bemoaning and bewildering me?" asked her mother, with a sort of resigned despair. "Don't go round and round it, dovey; what is it at all?"

"It's a white dress," said Teresa, desperately, "and of course it's pretty, and at first I couldn't think where I'd seen it before, and I don't believe any of the other girls did. But they will! And I don't know what Sister will say! She's wearing Joe Hammond's surplice, yes, but she IS, mother!--it's as long as a dress, you know, and with a blue sash, and all! It's one of the lace ones, that Mrs. Deane gave all the altar-boys a year ago, don't you remember? Don't you remember she made almost all of them too small?"

Mrs. Costello sat in stunned silence.

"I never heard the like!" said she, presently. Teresa's fears awakened anew.

"Oh, will Sister let her wear it, do you think, mother?"

"Well, I don't know, Tess." Mrs. Costello was plainly at a loss. "Whatever could have made her think of it,--the poor child! I'm afraid it'll make talk," she added after a moment's troubled silence, "and I don't know what to do! I wish," finished she, half to herself, "that I could get hold of her father for about one minute. I'd--"

"What would you do?" demanded Teresa, eagerly, in utter faith.

"Well, I couldn't do anything!" said her mother, with her wholesome laugh. "Come, Tess," she added briskly, "we'll go down. Don't worry, dear; we'll find some way out of it for Marg'ret."

She entered the parlors with her usual genial smile a few minutes later, and the flow of conversation that never failed her.

"Mary, you'd ought always to wear that Greek-lookin' dress," said Mrs. Costello, en passant. "Sister, if you don't want me in any of the dances, I'll take meself out of your way! No, indeed, the Mayor won't be annoyed by anything, girls, so go ahead with your duets, for he's taken the boys off to the Orpheum an hour ago, the way they couldn't be at their tricks upsettin' everything!" And presently she laid her hand on Marg'ret Hammond's shoulder. "Are they workin' you too hard, Marg'ret?"

Marg'ret's answer was smiling and ready, but Mrs. Costello read more truthfully the color on the little face, and the distress in the bright eyes raised to hers, and sighed as she found a big chair and settled herself contentedly to watch and listen.

Marg'ret was wearing Joe's surplice, there was no doubt of that. But, Mrs. Costello wondered, how many of the nuns and girls had noticed it? She looked shrewdly from one group to another, studying the different faces, and worried herself with the fancy that certain undertones and quick glances WERE commenting upon the dress. It was a relief when Marg'ret slipped out of it, and, with the other girls, assumed the Greek costume she was to wear in the play. The Mayor's wife, automatically replacing the drawing string in a cream-colored toga lavishly trimmed with gold paper-braid, welcomed the little respite from her close watching.

"By Nero's Command" was presently in full swing, and the room echoed to stately phrases and glorious sentiments, in the high-pitched clear voices of the small performers. Several minutes of these made all the more startling a normal tone, Marg'ret Hammond's everyday voice, saying sharply in a silence:

"Well, then, why don't you SAY it?"

There was an instant hush. And then another voice, that of a girl named Beatrice Garvey, answered sullenly and loudly:

"I WILL say it, if you want me to!"

The words were followed by a shocked silence. Every one turned to see the two small girls in the centre of the improvised stage, the other performers drawing back instinctively. Mrs. Costello caught her breath, and half rose from her chair. She had heard, as all the girls knew, that Beatrice did not like Marg'ret, and resented the prominence that Marg'ret had been given in the play. She guessed, with a quickening pulse, what Beatrice had said.

"What is the trouble, girls?" said Sister Rose's clear voice severely.

Marg'ret, crimson-cheeked, breathing hard, faced the room defiantly. She was a gallant and pathetic little figure in her blue draperies. The other child was plainly frightened at the result of the quarrel.

"Beatrice--?" said the nun, unyieldingly.

"She said I was a thief!" said Marg'ret, chokingly, as Beatrice did not answer.

There was a general horrified gasp, the nun's own voice when she spoke again was angry and quick.

"Beatrice, did you say that to Marg'ret?"

"I said--I said--" Beatrice was frightened, but aggrieved too. "I said I thought it was wrong to wear a surplice, that was made to wear on the altar, as an exhibition dress, and Marg'ret said, 'Why?' and I said because I thought it was--something I wouldn't say, and Marg'ret said, did I mean stealing, and I said, well, yes, I did, and then Marg'ret said right out, 'Well, if you think I'm a thief, why don't you say so?'"

Nobody stirred. The case had reached the open court, and no little girl present could have given a verdict to save her little soul.

"But--but--" the nun was bewildered, "but whoever did wear a surplice for an exhibition dress? I never heard of such a thing!" Something in the silence was suddenly significant. She turned her gaze from the room, where it had been seeking intelligence from the other nuns and the older girls, and looked back at the stage.

Marg'ret Hammond had dropped her proud little head, and her eyes were hidden by the tangle of soft dark hair. Had Sister Rose needed further evidence, the shocked faces all about would have supplied it.

"Marg'ret," she said, "were you going to wear Joe's surplice?"

Marg'ret did not answer.

"I'm sure, Sister, I didn't mean--" stammered Beatrice. Her voice died out uncomfortably.

"Why were you going to do that, Marg'ret?" pursued the nun, quite at a loss.

Again Marg'ret did not answer.

But Alanna Costello, who had worked her way from a scandalized crowd of little girls to Marg'ret's side, and who stood now with her small face one blaze of indignation, and her small person fairly vibrating with the violence of her breathing, spoke out suddenly. Her brave little voice rang through the room.

"Well--well--" stammered Alanna, eagerly, "that's not a bad thing to do! Me and Marg'ret were both going to do it, weren't we, Marg'ret? We didn't think it would be bad to wear our own brothers' surplices, did we, Marg'ret? I was going to ask my mother if we couldn't. Joe's is too little for him, and Leo's would be just right for me, and they're white and pretty--" She hesitated a second, her loyal little hand clasping Marg'ret's tight, her eyes ranging the room bravely. She met her mother's look, and gained fresh impetus from what she saw there. "And MOTHER wouldn't have minded, would you, mother?" she finished triumphantly.

Every one wheeled to face Mrs. Costello, whose look, as she rose, was all indulgent.

"Well, Sister, I don't see why they shouldn't," began her comfortable voice. The tension over the room snapped at the sound of it like a cut string. "After all," she pursued, now joining the heart of the group, "a surplice is a thing you make in the house like any other dress, and you know how girls feel about the things their brothers wear, especially if they love them! Why," said Mrs. Costello, with a delightful smile that embraced the room, "there never were sisters more devoted than Marg'ret and my Alanna! However"--and now a business-like tone crept in--"however, Sister, dear, if you or Mother Superior has the slightest objection in the world, why, that's enough for us all, isn't it, girls? We'll leave it to you, Sister. You're the one to judge." In the look the two women exchanged, they reached a perfect understanding.

"I think it's very lovely," said Sister Rose, calmly, "to think of a little girl so devoted to her brother as Margaret is. I could ask Superior, of course, Mary," she added to Mrs. Costello, "but I know she would feel that whatever you decide is quite right. So that's settled, isn't it, girls?"

"Yes, Sister," said a dozen relieved voices, the speakers glad to chorus assent whether the situation in the least concerned them or not. Teresa and some of the other girls had gathered about Marg'ret, and a soothing pur of conversation surrounded them. Mrs. Costello lingered for a few satisfied moments, and then returned to her chair.

"Come now, girls, hurry!" said Sister Rose. "Take your places, and let this be a lesson to us not to judge too hastily and uncharitably. Where were we? Oh, yes, we'll go back to where Grace comes in and says to Teresa, 'Here, even in the Emperor's very palace, dost dare....' Come, Grace!"

"I knew, if we all prayed about it, your father'd let you!" exulted Teresa, the following afternoon, when Marg'ret Hammond was about to run down the wide steps of the Costello house, in the gathering dusk. The Mayor came into the entrance hall, his coat pocket bulging with papers, and his silk hat on the back of his head, to find his wife and daughters bidding the guest good-by. He was enthusiastically imformed of the happy change of event.

"Father," said Teresa, before fairly freed from his arms and his kiss, "Marg'ret's father said she could have her white dress, and Marg'ret came home with us after rehearsal, and we've been having such fun!"

"And Marg'ret's father sent you a nice message, Frank," said his wife, significantly.

"Well, that's fine. Your father and I had a good talk to-day, Marg'ret," said the Mayor, cordially. "I had to be down by the bridge, and I hunted him up. He'll tell you about it. He's going to lend me a hand at the shop, the way I won't be so busy. 'Tis an awful thing when a man loses his wife," he added soberly a moment later, as they watched the little figure run down the darkening street.

"But now we're all good friends again, aren't we, mother?" said Alanna's buoyant little voice. Her mother tipped her face up and kissed her.

"You're a good friend,--that I know, Alanna!" said she.

"S IS FOR SHIFTLESS SUSANNA"

You look glorious. What's the special programme you've laid out for this morning, Sue?" said Susanna's husband, coming upon her in her rose garden early on a certain perfect October morning.

"I FEEL glorious too" young Mrs. Fairfax said, returning his kiss and dropping basket and scissors to bestow all her attention upon his buttonhole rose. "There is no special occasion for all this extravagance," she added, giving a complacent downward glance at the filmy embroideries of her gown, and her small whiteshod feet. "In fact, to-day breaks before me a long and delicious blank. I don't know when I have had such a Saturday. I shall write letters this morning--or perhaps wash my hair--I don't know. And then I'll take Mrs. Elliot for a drive this afternoon, or take some fruit to the Burkes, maybe, and stop for tea at the club. And if you decide to dine in town, I'll have Emma set my dinner out on the porch and commence my new Locke. And if you can beat that programme for sheer idle bliss," said Susanna, "let me hear you do it!"

She finished fastening his rose, stepped back to survey it, and raised to his eyes her own joyous, honest blue eyes, which still were as candid as a nice child's. Jim Fairfax, keenly alive to the delight of it, even after six months of marriage, kissed her again.

"You know, Jim," said Susanna, when they were presently sauntering with their load of roses toward the house and breakfast, "apropos of this new dress, I believe I put it on just BECAUSE there was no real reason for it. It is so delightful sometimes to get into dainty petties, and silk stockings, and a darling new gown, just as a matter of course! All my life, you know, I've had just one good outfit at a time, and sometimes less than that, and all the things I wore every day were so awfully plain--!"

"I know, my darling," Jim said, a little gravely. For he was always sorry to remember that there had been long years of poverty and struggle in Susanna's life before the day when he had found her, an underpaid librarian in a dark old law library, in a dark old street. Susanna, buoyant, ambitious, and overworked, had never stopped in her hard daily round long enough to consider herself pitiful, but she could look back from her rose garden now to the days before she knew Jim, and join him in a little shudder of reminiscence.

"I don't believe a long, idle day will ever seem anything but a joyous holiday to me," she said now. "It seems so curious still, not to be expected anywhere every morning!"

"Well, you may as well get used to it," Jim told her smilingly. But a few minutes later, when Susanna was busy with the coffee-pot, he looked up from a letter to say: "Here's a job for you, after all, to-day, Sue! This--" and he flattened the crackling sheets beside his plate, "this is from old Thayer."

"Thayer himself?" Susanna echoed appreciatively. For old Whitman Thayer, in whose hands lay the giving of contracts far larger than any that had as yet been handled by Jim or his senior partners in the young firm of Reid, Polk & Fairfax, Architects, was naturally an enormously important figure in his and Susanna's world. They spoke of Thayer nearly every night, Jim reporting to his interested wife that Thayer had "come in," or "hadn't come in," that Thayer had "seemed pleased," that Thayer had "jumped" on this, or had "been tickled to death" with that; and the Fairfax domestic barometer varied accordingly.

"Go ON, Jim," said Susanna, in suspense.

"Why, it seems that his wife--she's awfully sweet and nice," Jim proceeded, "is coming into town this afternoon, and she wonders if it would be too much trouble for Mrs. Fairfax to come in and lunch with her and help her with some shopping."

"Jim, it doesn't say that!" But Susanna's eyes were kindling with joy at the thought. "Oh, Jim, what a chance! Doesn't that look as if he really liked you!"

"Liked YOU, you mean," Jim said, giving her the letter. "Now I call that a very friendly, decent thing for them to do," young Mr. Fairfax went on musingly. "If you and she like each other, Sue--"

"Oh, don't worry, we will!" Mrs. Fairfax was always sure of her touch upon a feminine heart.

"Wonder why he didn't think of Mrs. Reid or Mrs. Polk?" said Jim.

"Oh, Jim, they are sort of--stiff, don't you know?" Susanna returned to her coffee, seasoning Jim's cup carefully before she added, with a look of naive pleasure that Jim thought very charming: "You know I rather THOUGHT that Mr. Thayer liked me just that one day I saw him!"

"Well, you'll like her," Jim prophesied. "She's very sweet and gentle, not very strong. They live right up the line there somewhere. She rarely comes into town. Old Thayer is devoted to her, and he always seems--" Jim hesitated. "I don't know," he went on, "I may be all wrong about this, Sue, but Thayer always seems to be protecting her, don't you know? I don't imagine he'd want to run her up against society women like Jane Reid and Mrs. Polk. You're younger and less affected; you're approachable. I don't know, but it seems to me that way. Anyway," he finished with supreme satisfaction, "I wouldn't take anything in the world for this chance! It shows the old man is really in earnest."

"He says she'll be at the office at eleven," said Susanna. "That means I must get the ten twenty-two."

"Sure. And take a taxi when you get to town. Got money? Got the right clothes?"

"Hydrangea hat," Susanna decided aloud. "New pongee, and pongee coat hung in careless elegance over my arm. As the last chime of eleven rings I will step into your office--"

"I hope to goodness you will!" said Jim, with an anxious look. "You'll really get there, won't you, Sue? No slips?"

This might have seemed overemphatic to an unprejudiced outsider. But no one who really knew Susanna would have blamed her young husband for an utter disbelief in the likelihood of her getting anywhere at any given time. Susanna's one glaring fault was a cheerful indifference to the fixed plans of others. Engagements she forgot, ignored, or cancelled at the last minute; dinner guests, arriving at her lovely home, never dreamed how often the consternation of utter surprise was hidden under the hilarious greetings of hostess and host. Dressmakers and dentists charged Susanna mercilessly for forgotten appointments; but an adoring circle of friends had formed a sort of silent conspiracy to save her from herself, and socially she suffered much less than she deserved.

"But some day you'll get an awful jolt; you'll get the lesson of your life, Sue," Jim used to say, and Susanna always answered meekly:

"Oh, Jim, I know it!"

"My mother used to have a nursery rhyme about me," she told Jim on one occasion. "It was one of those 'A is for Amiable Annie' things, you know; 'K is for Kind little Katie, whose weight is one hundred and eighty'--you've heard them, of course? Well, 'S was for Shiftless Susanna.' I know the next line was, 'But such was the charm of her manner'--but I've forgotten the rest. Whether mother made that up for my especial benefit or not, I don't know."

"Well, you have the charm all right," Jim was obliged to confess, for Susanna had an undeniable genius for adjustment and placation. Nobody was angry long at Susanna, perhaps because so many other people were always ready to step in gladly and fill any gaps in her programme. She was too popular to be snubbed. And her excuses were always so reasonable!

"You know I simply lose my mind at the telephone," she would plead. "I accept anything then--it never occurs to me that we may have engagements!" Or, "Well, the Jacksons said Thursday," she would brilliantly elucidate, "and Mrs. Oliver said the twentieth, and it never OCCURRED to me that it was the same day!"

And she was always willing--this was the maddening part of Susanna!- -to own herself entirely in the wrong, and always ended any conversation on the subject with a cheerful: "But anyway, I'm improving, you admit that, don't you, Jim? I'm not nearly as bad as I used to be!"

She said now very seriously: "Jim, darling, you may depend upon me. I realize what this means, and I am perfectly delighted to have the chance. At eleven to-day, 'one if by land, and two if by sea,' I'll be at your office. Trust me!"

"I do, dearest," Jim said. And he went down the drive a little later, under the blazing glory of the maples with great content in his heart. Susanna, going about her pretty house briskly, felt so sure of herself that the day's good work seemed half accomplished already.

She had adjusted the skirt of the pongee suit, and pinned the hydrangea hat at a fascinating angle when the telephone rang.

Susanna slipped her bare arms into the stiff sleeves of a Mandarin coat and crossed the hall to the instrument.

"Hello, Susanna!" said the cheerful voice of young Mrs. Harrington, a neighbor and friend, at the other end of the telephone. "I just rang up to know if I could come over early and help you out with anything and whether--"

"Help me out with anything?" Mrs. Fairfax's voice ranged through delicate shades of surprise to dawning consternation. "Help me out with what?"

"Why, you told me yourself that this was the day of the bridge-club lunch at your house!" Mrs. Harrington said, almost indignantly. But immediately she became mirthful. "Oh, Susanna, Susanna! You haven't forgotten--oh, you HAVE! Oh, you poor girl, what will you do! Listen, I could bring a--"

"Oh, my goodness, Ethel--and I've got to go to town!" Susanna's tone was hushed with a sort of horror. "And those seven women will be here at half-past twelve! And not ONE thing in the house--"

"Oh, you could get Ludovici as far as the lunch goes, Sue. But the girls will think it's odd, perhaps. Couldn't you wait and take the one o'clock?"

"Yes, I'll get Ludovici," Susanna decided hastily. "No, I couldn't do that. But I'll tell you what I COULD do. If you'll be an angel, Ethel, and do the honors until I get here, I could lunch early, get through my business in town, and get the one-fifty train for home--"

"Well, that'll be all right. I'll explain," said the amiable Mrs. Harrington.

A few minutes later Mrs. Fairfax left the telephone and went down to the kitchen to explain to Emma and Veronica, the maids, that there would be a luncheon for eight ladies served by a caterer, in her home, that day, and that they must simply assist him. She herself must be in town unfortunately, but Mrs. Harrington had very kindly offered to come over and be hostess and play the eighth hand of bridge afterward. Emma and Veronica, perhaps more hardened to these emergencies than are ordinary maids, rose to the occasion, and Susanna hurried off to her train satisfied that as far as the actual luncheon was concerned, all would go well. But what the seven women would think was another story!

"I don't suppose Mrs. Thayer wants to do so very much shopping," said Susanna to herself, hurrying along. "If I meet her at eleven and we lunch at one, say, I don't see why I shouldn't get the one- fifty train home. I'd get here before the girls had fairly started playing bridge, and explain--somehow one can always explain things so much better in person--"

"Or suppose we lunched at half-past twelve," her uneasy thoughts ran on. "That gives us an hour and a half to shop--that ought to be plenty. But we mustn't lose a minute getting started! Mrs. Thayer will come up in her motor--that will save us time. We can start right off the instant I get to Jim's office."

She stopped at the caterer's for a brief but satisfactory interview. The caterer was an artist, but his enthusiasms this morning were wasted upon Susanna.

"Yes, yes--cucumber sandwiches by all means," she assented hastily, "and the ices--just as you like! Plain, I think--or did you say in cases? I don't care. Only don't fail me, Mr. Ludovici."

Fail her? Mr. Ludovici's lexicon did not know the word. Susanna breathed more freely as she crossed the sunny village street to the train.

The station platform was deserted and bare. Susanna, accustomed to a breathless late arrival, could saunter with delightful leisure to the ticket-seller's window.

"You've not forgotten the new time-table?" said the agent, pleasantly, when they had exchanged greetings.

"Oh, does the change begin to-day?" Susanna looked blank.

"October sixteenth, winter schedule," he reminded her buoyantly. "Going to be lots of engagements missed to-day!"

"But mine is very important and I cannot miss it," said Susanna, displeased at his levity. "I MUST be in Mr. Fairfax's office at eleven."

"You won't be more than ten or twelve minutes late," said young Mr. Green, consolingly. "You tell Mr. Fairfax it's up to the N.Y. and E.W."

Susanna smiled perfunctorily, but took her place in the train with a sinking heart. She would be late, of course, and Jim would be angry, of course. Late to-day, when every minute counted and the programme allowed for not an instant's delay! Her eyes on the flying countryside, she rehearsed her part, found herself eloquently explaining to a pacified Jim, capturing a gracious Mrs. Thayer, successfully reaching home again, and explaining to an entirely amiable bridge club.

It could be done, of course, but it meant a pretty full day! Susanna's mind reverted uneasily to the consideration that she had already bungled matters. Oh, well, if she was late, she was late, that was all; and if Jim was furious, why, Jim would simply have to be furious! And she began her explanations again--

After all, it was but fifteen minutes past eleven when she walked into her husband's office. But neither Jim nor Mrs. Thayer was there.

"Mr. Fairfax went out not three minutes ago," said the pretty stenographer in the outer office. Susanna, brought to a full stop, stared at her blankly.

"Went out!"

"Yes, with Mrs. Thayer to the dentist. He said to say he was afraid you had missed your train. There's a note."

The note was forthwith produced. Susanna read it frowningly. It was rather conspicuously headed "Eleven-twelve!"

DEAREST GIRL: Can't wait any longer. Mrs. T. must see her dentist (Archibald). I'm taking her up. Thayers and we lunch at the Palace at one-thirty. Wait for me in my office. J. F.

"Oh, what is the matter with everything to-day!" Susanna burst out in exasperation. "He's wild, of course. When does he ever sign himself 'J. F.' to me! When did they go?" she asked Miss Perry, briefly, with an unreasonable wish that she might somehow hold that irreproachable young woman responsible.

"Just about three minutes ago," said Miss Perry. "He said that if you had missed your train, you wouldn't be here for more than an hour, and it was no use waiting."

"You see, it was a changed time-table, and he forgot it just as I did," explained Susanna, pleased to find him fallible, even to that extent.

"But HE was on time," fenced Miss Perry, innocently.

"They don't change the business trains," Susanna said coldly. And she decided that she disliked this girl. She opened a magazine and sat down by the open window.

The minutes ticked slowly by. The telephone rang, doors opened and shut, and men came and went through the office. Susanna, opposed in every fibre of her being to passive waiting, suddenly rose.

"Dr. Archibald is in the First National Bank Building, isn't he?" she inquired. "I think I'll join Mrs. Thayer up there. There's no use in my waiting here."

Miss Perry silently verified Dr. Archibald's address in the telephone book, and to the First National Bank Building Susanna immediately made her way. It was growing warmer now and the streets seemed noisy and crowded, but no matter--"If I can only get to them and SEE Jim!" thought Susanna.

In the pleasant shadiness of Dr. Archibald's office, rising from a delightful mahogany arm-chair, Susanna presently asked if Mrs. Thayer could be told that Mrs. Fairfax was there.

"I think Mrs. Thayer is gone," said the attendant pleasantly. "I'm not sure, but I'll see."

In a few minutes she returned to inform Mrs. Fairfax that Mrs. Thayer had just come in to have a bridge replaced, and was gone.

"You don't know where?" Susanna's voice was a trifle husky with repressed emotion. She realized that she was getting a headache.

No, the attendant didn't know where.

So there was nothing for it but to go back to Jim's office, and back Susanna accordingly went. She walked as fast as she could, conscious of every separate hot step, and was nervous and headachy when she entered Miss Perry's presence again.

Mr. Fairfax and Mrs. Thayer had not come in; no, but Miss Perry reported that Mr. Fairfax had telephoned not ten minutes ago, and seemed very anxious to get hold of his wife.

"Oh, dear, dear!" lamented Susanna. "And where is he now?"

Miss Perry couldn't say. "I wrote his message down," she said, with sympathetic amusement at Susanna's crushed dismay. And, referring to her notes, she repeated it:

"Mr. Fairfax said that Mrs. Thayer had had an appointment to see a sick friend in a hospital this afternoon. But she has gone right out there now instead, so that you and she can go shopping after lunch. You are, please, to meet Mr. Fairfax and the Thayers at the Palace for luncheon at half-past one; there'll be a table reserved. Mr. Fairfax has a little business to attend to just now, but if you don't mind waiting in the office, he thinks it's the coolest place you could be. He wanted to know if you had the whole afternoon free- -"

"Oh, absolutely!" Susanna assented eagerly. This was not the time to speak or think of the bridge club.

"And that was all," finished Miss Perry, "except he said perhaps you would like to look at the plans of the orphanage. Mr. Fairfax got them out to show to Mr. Thayer this afternoon. I can get them for you."

"Oh, thank you! I do want to see them!" said Susanna, gratefully. And she established herself comfortably by the open window, the orphanage plans, a stiff roll of blue paper, in her lap, her idle eyes following the noonday traffic in the street below.

What a shame to have to sit here doing nothing, to-day of all days, for nearly two hours! Susanna thought. Why, she could have met her luncheon guests, seen that the meal was at least under way, apologized in person, and then started for town. As it was, they might be angry, and no wonder! And these were her neighbors and very good friends, after all, the women upon whose good feeling half the joy of her country home and garden depended. It was too bad!

She glanced at the blue-prints, but one of her sudden inspirations turned the page blank. What time was it? Ten minutes of twelve. She referred to her new time-table. Ten minutes of--why, she could just catch the noon train, rush home, meet her guests, explain, and come back easily on the one o'clock. But would it be wise? Why not?

Her thoughts in a jumble, Susanna hastily gathered her small possessions together, moved to a decision by the always imperative argument that in a few minutes it would be too late to decide.

"Heavens! I'm glad I thought of that!" she ejaculated, seating herself in the train as the noon whistles shrilled all over the city. A moment later she was a trifle disconcerted to find the orphanage plans still in her hand.

"Well, this is surely one of my crazy days!" Susanna strapped the stiff sheets firmly to her handbag. "I must not forget to take those back," she told herself. "Jim will ask for them the very first thing."

Her house; when she reached it, seemed quiet, seemed empty. Susanna crossed the porch, wondering, and encountered the maid.

"Emma! Nobody come?"

"Sure you had the wrong day of it," said Emma, beaming. "Mrs. Harrington fomed about an hour ago, and she says 'tis NEXT Saturday thin!"

"What do you mean?" said Susanna, sharply.

"'Tis not to-day they're comin', Mrs. Fairfax--"

"Nonsense!" Susanna said under her breath. She flew to her desk and snatched up the scribbled card of engagements. "Why, it's no such thing!" she said indignantly. "Of course it's to-day! October sixteenth, as plain as print." And with her eyes still on the card she reached for her desk telephone.

"Ethel," said Susanna, a moment later. "Listen, Ethel, this is Susanna. Ethel, what made you say the club luncheon wasn't to-day? This is my day to have the girls.... Certainly.... Why, I don't care what she said, I have it written down!... Why, I think that's very funny.... I have it written.... No, you can laugh all you want to, but I know I'm right.... No, that's nothing. Jim will eat it all up to-morrow; he says he never gets enough to eat on Sundays.... But I can't understand, and I don't believe YET that I... Yes, it's written right here; I've got my eyes on it now! It's the most extraordinary...."

A little vexed at Mrs. Harrington's unbounded amusement, Susanna terminated the conversation as soon as was decently possible, and went kitchenward. In her anxiety not to miss her train back to the city, she refused Teresa's offer of dainty sandwiches, pastries, and tea, and merely stopped long enough to brush up her hair and to ascertain by carefully enumerating them out loud that she had her purse, her gloves, the orphanage plans, and the new time-table.

"This will seem very funny," said poor Susanna, gallantly to herself, as she took her seat in the train and tried to ignore a really sharp headache, "when once I see them! If I can only get hold of Jim, and if the afternoon goes smoothly, I shan't mind anything!"

Only ten minutes late for her luncheon engagement, Susanna entered the cool depths of the restaurant and, piloted by an impressed head waiter, looked confidently for her own party. It was very pleasant here, and the trays of salads and iced things that were borne continually past her were very inviting.

But still there was no Mrs. Thayer and no Jim. Susanna waited a few nervous minutes, sat down, got up again, and finally, at two o'clock, went out into the blazing, unfriendly streets, and walked the five short squares that lay between the restaurant and her husband's office. A hot, dusty wind blew steadily against her; the streets were full of happy girls and men with suit-cases, bound for the country and a day or two of fresh air and idleness. Miss Perry was putting the cover on her typewriter as Susanna entered the office, her own suit-case waiting in a corner. She looked astonished as Susanna came in.

"My goodness, Mrs. Fairfax!" she ejaculated. "We've been trying and trying to get you by telephone! Mr. Fairfax was so anxious to get hold of those orphanage plans. Mr. Thayer wanted--"

"I've been following him about all day," said Susanna, with an undignified, but uncontrollable gulp. She sat down limply. "WHAT happened to the luncheon plan?" she asked forlornly. "Where is Mr. Fairfax?"

Miss Perry, perhaps softened by the sight of Susanna's filling eyes and tired face, became very sympathetic. "Isn't it TOO bad--I know you have! But you see Mrs. Thayer couldn't see her friend in the hospital this morning, so she came right down here and got here not ten minutes after you left. She said she couldn't wait for you, as she had to be back at the hospital at two, so she would do a little shopping herself and let the rest wait."

"Well," said Susanna, after a pause in which her very soul rebelled, "it can't be helped, I suppose! Did Mr. Fairfax go out with her?"

"He was to take her somewhere for a cup of tea and then he was going home."

"Going home! But I've just come from there!"

"He thought he'd probably catch you there, I think. He was anxious to get hold of those plans."

"Oh, I could CRY--" Susanna began despairingly. But indeed Miss Perry needed no assurance of that. "I could cry!" said Susanna again. "To-day," she expanded, "has been simply one miserable accident after another! I hope it'll be a lesson to me! Well--" She broke off short, for Miss Perry, while kind, was human, and was visibly conscious that she had promised her brother and sister-in- law to be at their house in East Auburndale, a populous suburb, long before it was time to put the baby to bed. "I suppose there's nothing for me to do but go home," finished Susanna, discontentedly.

"Accidents will happen!" trilled Miss Perry, blithely, hurrying for her car.

Susanna went thoughtfully home, reflecting soberly upon the events of the day. If she could but live this episode down, she told herself; but meet and win Mrs. Thayer somehow in the near future; but bring Jim to the point of entirely forgetting and forgiving the whole disgraceful day, she would really reform. She would "keep lists," she would "make notes," and she would "think twice." In short, she would do all the things that those who had her good at heart had been advising for the past ten years.

Of course, if the Thayers were resentful--refused to be placated-- Susanna made a little wry mouth. But they wouldn't be!

Still deep in stimulating thoughts of a complete reformation, Susanna reached home again, crossed the deep-tiled porch with its potted olives and gay awnings, entered the big hall now dim with afternoon shadows. Now for Jim--!

But where was Jim?

"Mr. Fairfax is home, Emma?"

"Oh, there you are, Mrs. Fairfax! And us trying and trying to telefome you! No ma'am, he's not home. He left on the three-twenty. He'd only come out in a rush for some papers, and he had to get back to town to see some one at once. There's a note--"

Susanna sat down. Her head was splitting, she was hungry and exhausted, and, at the effort she made to keep the tears out of her eyes, a wave of acute pain swept across her forehead. She opened the note.

If you can find a reliable messenger [said the note, without preamble], I wish you would get those orphanage plans to me at Thornton's office before six. I have to meet him there at four. The matter is really important, or I would not trouble you. I'll dine with Thayer at the club. J.F. The pretty hallway and the glaring strip of light beyond the open garden door swam suddenly before Susanna's eyes. The hand that held the note trembled.

"I could not be so mean to him!" said Susanna to herself. "But perhaps he was tired and hot--poor Jim!" And aloud she said with dignity: "I shall have to take this paper--these plans--in to Mr. Fairfax, Emma. I'll catch the four-twenty."

"You'll be dead!" said Emma, sympathetically.

"My head aches," Mrs. Fairfax admitted briefly. But when she was upstairs and alone she found herself suddenly giving way to the long deferred burst of tears.

After a while she bathed her eyes, brushed her hair, and substituted a more substantial gown for the pongee. Then she started out once more, refreshed and more cheerful in spite of herself, and soothed unconsciously by the quiet close of the lovely autumn afternoon.

Her own gateway was separated by a flight of shallow stone steps from the road, and Susanna paused there on her way to the train to gather her skirts safely for the dusty walk. And while she was standing there she found her gaze suddenly riveted upon a motor-car that, still a quarter of a mile away, was rapidly descend the slope of the hill, its two occupants fairly shaken by its violent and rapid approach. The road here was not wide, and curved on a sharp grade, and Susanna always found the descent of a large car, like this one, a matter of half-terrified fascination. But surely with this car there was more than the ordinary danger, she thought, with a sudden sick thumping at her heart. Surely here was something all wrong! Surely no sane driver--

"That man is drunk," she said, quite aloud. "He cannot make it! He can't possibly--ah-h-h!"

Her voice broke on a gasp, and she pressed one hand tight over her eyes. For with swift and terrible precision the accident had indeed come to pass. The car skidded, turned, hung for a sickening second on one wheel, struck the stone of the roadside fence with a horrible grinding jar and toppled heavily over against the bank.

When Susanna uncovered her eyes again, and before she could move or cry out in the dumb horror that had taken possession of her, she saw a man in golfing wear run from the Porters' gate opposite; and another motor, in which Susanna recognized the figure of a friend and neighbor, Dr. Whitney, swept up beside the overturned one. When she ran, as she presently found herself running, to the spot, other men and women had gathered there, drawn from lawns and porches by this sudden projection of tragedy into the gayety of their Saturday afternoon.

"Hurt?" gasped Susanna, joining the group.

"The man is--dead, Billy says," said young Mrs. Porter, in lowered tones, with an agitated clutch of Susanna's arm. "And, poor thing! she doesn't realize it, and she keeps asking where her chauffeur is and why he doesn't come to her!"

"Wouldn't you think people would have better sense than to keep a man like that!" added another neighbor, Dexter Ellis, with a bitterness born entirely of nervousness. "He was drunk as a lord! Young and I were just coming out of my side gate--"

Every one talked at once--there was a confusion of excited comment. Somebody had flung a carriage robe over the silent form of the man as it lay tumbled in the dust and weeds; Susanna glanced toward it with a shudder. Somehow she found herself supporting the car's other occupant, the woman, who was half sitting and half lying on the bank where she had fallen. The woman had opened her eyes and was looking slowly about the group; she had pushed away the whiskey the doctor held to her lips, but she looked sick and seemed in pain.

"I had just put the baby down when I heard Dex shout--" Susanna could hear Mrs. Ellis saying behind her in low tones. "Oh, it is, it's an outrage--they should have regarded it years ago," said another voice. "Merest chance in the world that we took the side gate," Dexter Ellis was saying, and some man's voice Susanna did not know reiterated over and over: "Well, I guess he's run his last car, poor fellow; I guess he's run his last car--"

"You feel better, don't you?" the doctor asked his patient, encouragingly. "Just open your mouth and swallow this." And Susanna said gently: "Just try it; you'll feel so much stronger!"

The woman turned upon her a pair of eyes as heavy as a sick animal's, and moistened her lips. "Arm," she said with difficulty.

"Her arm's broken," said the doctor, in a low tone, "and I think her leg, too. Kane has gone to wire for the ambulance. We'll get her right into town."

"You can't take her to town!" Susanna ejaculated, turning so that she might not be heard by the sufferer. "Take her in to my house."

"The hospital is really the most comfortable place for her, Mrs. Fairfax," the doctor said guardedly. "I am afraid there is internal injury. Her mind seems some-what confused. You can't undertake the responsibility--"

"Ah, but you can't jolt the poor thing all the way into town--" Susanna began again. Mrs. Porter, at her shoulder, interrupted her in an earnest whisper:

"Sue, dear, it's always done. It won't take very long, and nobody expects you--"

"I know just how Susanna feels," interrupted Mrs. Ellis, "but after all, you never can tell--we don't know one thing about her--"

"She'll be taken good care of," finished the doctor, soothingly.

"Please--don't let them frighten--my husband--" said the woman herself, slow-ly, her distressed eyes moving from one face to another. "If I could--be moved somewhere before he hears--"

"We won't frighten him," Susanna assured her tenderly. "But will you tell us your name so we may let him know?"

The injured woman frowned. "I did tell you--didn't I?" she asked painfully.

"No"--Susanna would use this tone in her nursery some day--"No, dear, not yet."

"Tell us again," said the doctor, with too obvious an intention to soothe.

The woman gave him a look full of dignified reproach.

"If I could rest on your porch a little while," she said to Susanna, ignoring the others rather purposely, "I should be quite myself again. That will be best. Then I can think--I can't think now. These people--and my head--"

And she tried to rise, supporting herself with a hand on Susanna's arm. But with the effort the last vestige of color left her face, and she slipped, unconscious, back to the grass.

"Dead?" asked Susanna, very white.

"No--no! Only fainted," Dr. Whitney said. "But I don't like it," he added, his finger at the limp wrist.

"Bring her in, won't you?" Susanna urged with sudden decision. "I simply can't let her be taken 'way up to town! This way--"

And, relieved to have it settled, she led them swiftly across the garden and into the house, flung down the snowy covers of the guest- room bed, and with Emma's sympathetic help established the stranger therein.

"Trouble," whispered the injured woman apologetically, when she opened her eyes upon walls and curtains rioting with pink roses, and felt the delicious softness and freshness of the linen and pillows about her.

"Oh, don't think of that--I love to do it!" Susanna said honestly, patting her head. "A nurse is coming up from the village to look out for you, and she and the doctor are going to make you more comfortable."

The woman, fixing her with a dazed yet curiously intent look, formed with her lips the words, "God bless you," and wearily shut her eyes. Susanna, slipping out of the room a few minutes later, said over and over again to herself, "I don't care--I'm glad I did it!"

Still, it was not very reassuring to hear the big hall clock strike six, and suddenly to notice the orphanage plans lying where they had been flung on the hall table.

"I wish it was the middle of next year," said Susanna, thoughtfully, going out to sink wearily into a porch chair, "or even next week! I'd pretend to be asleep when Jim came home to-night," she went on gloomily, "if it wasn't my duty to sit up and explain that there are a perfect stranger and a trained nurse in the house. Of course, being there as I was, any humane person would have to do what I did, but it does seem strange, this day of all days, that I had to be there! And I wish I had thought to send those plans in by messenger- -that would have been one thing the less to worry about, at least!-- What is it, Emma?"

For Emma, mildly repeating some question, had come out to the porch. "Would you like tea, Mrs. Fairfax? I could bring it out here like you had it last week with your book."

Susanna brightened. After all, she had not eaten for a long while; tea would be very welcome. And the porch was delightful, and there was the new Locke.

"Well, that was my original idea, Emma," said she, "and although the day has not gone quite as I had planned, still there's no reason why the idea should be changed. Bring a supper-tea, Emma, lots of sandwiches--I'm combining three meals in one, Miss Smith," she broke off to explain smilingly, as the nurse, trimly clad in white, came to the doorway. "I've not eaten since breakfast. You must have some tea with me. And how is she? Is her mind clearer?"

"Oh, dear me, yes! She's quite comfortable," Miss Smith said cheerfully. "Doctor thinks there's no question of internal trouble. Her arm is broken and her ankle badly wrenched, but that's all. And she's so grateful to you, Mrs. Fairfax. It seems she has a perfect horror of hospitals, and she feels that you've done such a remarkably kind thing--taking her in. She asked to see you, and then we're going to try to make her sleep. Oh, and may I telephone her husband?"

"Oh, she could give you his name then!" cried Susanna, in relief. "Oh, I am glad! Indeed, you may telephone. Who is she?"

Miss Smith repeated the name and address.

Susanna, stared at her blankly. Then the most radiant of all her ready smiles lighted her face.

"Well, this is really the most extraordinary day!" she said softly, after a pause. "I'll come right up, Miss Smith, but perhaps you might let me telephone for you first. I can get her husband easily. I know just where he is. He and my own husband are dining together this evening, as it happens--"

THE LAST CAROLAN

A blazing afternoon of mid-July lay warmly over the old Carolan house, and over the dusty, neglected gardens that enclosed it. The heavy wooden railing of the porch, half smothered in dry vines, was hot to the touch, as were the brick walks that wound between parched lawns and the ruins of old flowerbeds. The house, despite the charm of its simple, unpretentious lines, looked shabby and desolate. Only the great surrounding trees kept, after long years of neglect, their beauty and dignity.

At the end of one of the winding paths was an old fountain. Its wide stone basin was chipped, and the marble figure above it was discolored by storm and sun. Weeds--such weeds as could catch a foothold in the shallow layer of earth--had grown rank and high where once water had brimmed clear and cool, and great lazy bees boomed among them. Cut in the granite brim, had any one cared to push back the dry leaves and sifted earth that obscured them, might have been found the words:

>Over land and water blown,   Come back to find your own.

A stone bench, sunk unevenly in the loose soil, stood near the fountain in the shade of the great elms, and here two women were sitting. One of them was Mary Moore, the doctor's wife, from the village, a charming little figure in her gingham gown and wide hat. The other was Jean Carolan, wife of the estate's owner, and mother of Peter, the last Carolan.

Jean was a beautiful woman, glowing with the bloom of her early thirties. Her eyes were moving contentedly over house and garden. She gave Mrs. Moore's hand a sudden impulsive pressure. "Well, here we are, Mary!" she said, smiling, "just as we always used to plan at St. Mary's--keeping house in the country near each other, and bringing up our children together!"

"I never forgot those plans of ours," said the doctor's wife, her eyes full of pleasant reminiscence. "But here I've been, nearly eleven years, duly keeping house and raising four small babies in a row. And what about YOU? You've been gadding all over Europe--never a word about coming home to Carolan Hall until this year!"

"I know," said Mrs. Carolan, with a charming air of apology. "Oh, I know! But Sid had to hunt up his references abroad, you know, and then there was that hideous legal delay. I really have been frantic to settle down somewhere, for years. And as for poor Peter! The unfortunate baby has been farmed out in Italy, and boarded in Rome, and flung into English sanitariums, just as need arose! The marvel is he's not utterly ruined. But Peter's unique--you'll love him!"

"Who's he like, Jean?"

"Oh, Sidney! He's Carolan all through." With the careless words a thin veil of shadow fell across her bright face, and there came a long silence.

Carolan Hall! Jean had never seen it before to-day. Looking at the garden, and the trees, and the roof that showed beyond, she felt as if she had not truly seen it until this minute. All its gloomy history, half forgotten, lightly brushed aside, came back to her slowly now. This was the home of her husband's shadowed childhood; it was here that those terrible events had taken place of which he had so seriously told her before their wedding day.

Here old Peter Carolan, her little Peter's great-grandfather, had come with his two dark boys and his silent wife, eighty years before. A cruel, passionate man he must have been, for stories presently crept about the county of the whippings that kept his boys obedient to him. Rumor presently had an explanation of the wife's shadowed life. There had been a third boy, the first-born, whom no whippings could make obedient. That boy was dead.

The day came when old Peter's blooded mare refused him obedience, too, and stood trembling and mutinous before the bars he would have had her take. He presently had his way, and the lovely, frightened creature went bravely over. But after that he rode her at that fence day after day, and sometimes the wood rang for an hour with his shouting and urging before she would essay the leap. While he forced her, Madam Carolan sat at the one library window that gave on the road, and knotted her hands together and waited. She waited, one gusty March evening, until the shouting stopped, and the bewildered mare came trotting riderless into view. Then she and the maids ran to the wood. But even after that she still sat at that window at the end of every day, a familiar figure to all who came and went upon the road.

The sons, Sidney and Laurence, grew up together, passionate, devoted, and widely loved. Sidney married and went away for a few years; but presently he came back to his mother and brother, bringing with him the motherless little Sidney who was Jean's sunny big husband now. This younger Sidney well remembered the day--and had once told his wife of it--when his father and his uncle fell to sudden quarrelling in their boat, during a morning's fishing on the placid river. He remembered, a small watcher on the bank, that the boat upset, and that, when his uncle reached the shore, it was to work unavailingly for hours over his father's silent form, which never moved again. The boy was sent away for a while, but came back to find his uncle a silent, morose shadow, pacing the lonely garden in unassailable solitude, or riding his horse for hours in the great woods. Sometimes the little fellow would sit with his grandmother in the library window, where she watched and waited. Always, as he went about the garden and yards, he would look for her there, and wave his cap to her. He missed her, in his unexpressed little-boy fashion, when she sat there no longer, although she had always been silent and reserved with him. Then came his years of school and travel, and in one of them he learned that the Hall was quite empty now. Sidney meant to go back, just to turn over the old books, and open the old doors, and walk the garden paths again; but, somehow, he had never come until to-day. And now that he had come, he, and Jean, and Peter, too, wanted to stay.

Jean sighed.

"You knew Madam Carolan, didn't you, Mary?"

"No--no, I didn't," said Mrs. Moore, coloring uneasily. "I've seen her, though, as a small girl, at the window. I used to visit Billy's--my husband's--people when we were both small, you know, and we often came to these woods."

"I've been thinking of the house and its cheerful history," said Jean, with a little shudder. "Sweet heritage for Peterkin!"

"Heritage--nonsense!" said the other woman, hardily. "Every one tells me that your husband is the gentlest and finest of them all-- and his father was before him. I don't believe such things come down, anyway."

"Well," smiled Sidney's wife, a little proudly, "I've never seen the Carolan temper in the nine years we've been married!"

"Exactly. Besides, it's not a temper--just strong will."

"Sidney has WILL enough," mused Jean.

"Oh, all men have," said the doctor's wife contentedly. "Billy, now! He won't STAND a locked door. One night--I never shall forget!--the children locked themselves in the nursery, and Will simply burst the door in. Nobody makes a fuss or worries over THAT!"

If the illustration was beside the point, neither woman perceived it.

"There, you see!" said Jean, glad to be quite sure of conviction. "It never really worries me," she added, after a moment, "for Peter adores his father, and is only too eager to obey him. If Peter--and it's impossible!--ever DID really work himself up to disobedience, why, I suppose he'd get a thrashing,"--she made a wry face,--"and they'd love each other all the more for it."

"Of course they would," agreed the other cheerfully.

"There must have been some way in which Madam Carolan could have managed them," pursued Jean, thoughtfully. "The women of that generation were a poor-spirited lot, I imagine. One isn't quite a child!" There was another little pause in the hot murmuring silence of the garden, and then, with a sudden change of manner, she rose to her feet. "Mary! come and meet Sidney and the kiddy!" she commanded.

"Well, I rather hoped you were going to present them," said Mrs. Moore, rising too, and gathering up sunshade and gloves.

They threaded the silent garden paths again, passed the house, and crossed a neglected stable yard, where a great red motor-car had crushed a path for itself across dry grass and weeds. In the stable itself they found Sidney Carolan, the little Peter, and a couple of servants--the chauffeur with oily hands, and the wrinkled old Italian maid, very gay in scarlet gown and headdress.

Jean's husband had all the Carolan beauty and charm, and was his most gracious and radiant self to-day. His sunny cordiality gave Mary no chance to remember that she had a little feared the writer and critic. But, after the first moment, her eye was irresistibly drawn to the child.

Tawny-haired, erect, and astonishing in the perfection of his childish beauty, Peter Carolan advanced her a bronzed, firm little hand, and gave her with it a smile that seemed all brilliant color-- white teeth, ocean-blue eyes, and poppied cheeks. His square little figure was very boyish in the thin silk shirt and baggy knickerbockers, and a wide hat, slipping from his yellow mane, added a last debonair touch to his picturesque little person. He was flushed, but gracious and at ease.

"You're one of the reasons we came!" he said in a rich little voice- -when his mother's "You've heard me speak of Mrs. Moore, Peter?" had introduced them. "You have boys, too, haven't you?"

"I have three," said Mrs. Moore, in the rational, unhurried tone that only very clever people use to children. "Billy is nine, George seven, Jack is three; and then there's a girl--my Mary."

"I come next to Billy," calculated little Peter, his eyes very eager.

"You and he will like each other, I hope," said Billy's mother.

"I hope we will--I hope so!" he assented vivaciously. "I've been thinking so!"

Mrs. Carolan presently suggested that he go off with Betta to pack the luncheon things in the car, and the three watched his sturdy, erect little figure out of sight. Mrs. Moore heard his gay voice break into ready Italian as they went.

A horde of workmen took possession of Carolan Hall a few days later, and for happy weeks Jean and Mary followed and directed them. The Moore children and Peter Carolan explored every fascinating inch of house and garden. Linen and china were unpacked, old furniture polished, and old paintings restored.

Mrs. Moore, with her two oldest sons frolicking about her like excited puppies, came up to Carolan Hall one exquisite morning a month later. Brush fires were burning in the thinning woods, and the blue, fragrant smoke drifted in thin veils across the sunlight.

A visit to the circus was afoot, and Peter Carolan, seated on the porch steps in the full glory of starched blue linen and tan sandals, leaped up to join his friends in a war-dance of wild anticipation.

Jean came out, also starched and radiant, kissed her guests, piled some wraps into the waiting motor, and engineered the group into the shaded dining-room, where the excited children were somehow to be coaxed into eating their luncheon. Sidney came in late, to smile at them all from the top of the table.

It was rapidly dawning on the adult consciousness that, above every other sound, the voices of the children were really reaching inexcusable heights, when a burst of laughter and a brief struggle between Peter and Billy Moore resulted in an overturned mug, the usual rapidly spreading pool of milk, and the usual reckless mopping. Peter's silver mug fell to the floor, and rolled to the sideboard, where it lay against the carved mahogany base, winking in the sun.

"Peter!" said Jean, severely. "No, don't ring, Sidney! He did that by his own carelessness, and mother can't ask poor, busy Julia to pick up things for boys who are noisy and rude at the table. Go pick up your mug, dear!"

"Yes. Quite right!" approved Sidney, under his breath.

Peter, who had been laughing violently a moment before seemed rather inclined to regard the incident as a tribute to his own brilliancy. He caught his heels in a rung of his chair, raised himself to a standing position, and turned a bright little face to his mother.

"But--but--but what if I don't WANT to pick it up, mother?" he said gayly.

The little Moore boys, still bubbling, giggled outright, and Peter's cheeks grew pink. He was innocently elated with this new role of clown.

"What do you mean?" said Sidney's big voice, very quietly. There was a pause. Peter slowly turned his eyes toward his father.

"Oh, please, Sidney!" said Jean, a shade impatiently. "He thinks he has some reason." She turned to Peter. "What do you mean, dear?" she asked pleasantly.

Peter looked about the group. He was confused and excited at finding himself so suddenly the centre of attention.

"Well--well--why are you all looking at me?" he asked in his confident little treble, with his baffling smile.

"Dearie, did you hear mother tell you to get quietly down and pick up your mug?" demanded Jean, authoritatively.

"Well--well, you know, I don't want to, mother, because Billy and I were both reaching for that mug," drawled Peter, "and maybe it was Billy who--"

"Now, look here, son!" said his father, controlling his impatience with difficulty, "we've had enough of this! You do it because your mother told you to, and you do it right NOW!"

"And don't let anything spoil this happy day," pleaded Jean's tender voice.

"Can't I let it stay there, mother?" suggested Peter, brilliantly, "and have my milk in a glass? I don't want my mug! It can just lie there--"

His mother unsmilingly interrupted this pleasantly offered solution.

"Peter! Father and mother are waiting."

"Gee--I'll pick it up!" said Billy Moore, good-naturedly, slipping to the floor.

Sidney reached for the little boy, and brought him to anchor in the curve of his big arm, without once glancing at him.

"Thank you, Billy," he said, "but Peter will pick it up himself. Now, Peter! We don't care who knocked it down, or whose fault it was. Your mother told you to pick up your mug, and we are waiting to have you do it. Don't talk about it any more. Nobody thinks it is at all smart or funny for boys to disobey their mothers!"

"It will take you JUST one second, dear," interpolated Jean softly, "and then we will all go upstairs and get ready, and forget all about it."

"Just a little too much c-i-r-c-u-s!" spelled Mrs. Moore, in the pause.

"Pick it up, son!" said Sidney, very calm.

Peter stopped smiling. He breathed hard and took a firm hold of his chair.

"Go on. Go ahead!" said his father, briskly, encouragingly.

The child moved his eyes from the mug to his father's face, but did not stir.

"Peter?" said Sidney. A white line had come about his mouth.

For a long moment there was not a sound in the rooms. Julia stood transfixed at the door. Mrs. Moore's eyes were on her plate. Jean's lips were shut tight; she was breathing as if she had been running.

"I won't!" said Peter, simply, with a quick breath.

"Sid!" said Jean, hurriedly. "Sidney!"

"Just a moment, Jean," said her husband, without glancing at her. "You will do it now, or have father punish you to make you do it," he said to the boy. "Father can't have boys here who don't obey, you know. Every one obeys. Soldiers have to, engineers have to, even animals have to. Are you going to do what mother told you to?"

"No," said little Peter. "I said I wouldn't, and now I won't!"

"He is hot and excited now," said Jean, quickly, in French, "but I'll take him upstairs and quiet him down. He'll come to his senses. Leave him to me, dear!"

"Much the wisest thing to do, Sidney," supplemented Mrs. Moore, in the same tongue.

"Certainly!" said his father, coldly. "Give him time. Let him understand that if he doesn't obey, it means no circus. That's reasonable, I think, Jean?"

"Oh, perfectly! Perfectly!" Mrs. Carolan assented nervously. Nothing more was said as she took the boy's hand and led him away. The others heard Peter chatting cheerfully as he mounted the stairway a moment later.

"The boys and I will go down and look at Nellie's puppies," said Mrs. Moore, acutely uncomfortable.

Her host muttered something about closing his mail.

"But are we going to the circus?" fretted little George Moore. His mother hardly heard him.

A moment later, Julia, the maid, appealed to her submissively.

"Shall you pick up the cup?" repeated the doctor's wife. "No. No, indeed, I wouldn't, Julia. Yes, you can clear the table, I think; we've all finished."

She led her sons down to the fascinating realm of dogs and horses, vaguely uneasy, yet unwilling to admit her fears. An endless warm half hour crept by. Then, glancing toward the house, she saw Sidney and Jean deep in conversation on the porch, and a moment later Sidney came to find her.

The boy was obstinate, he told her briefly--adding, with a look in his kind eyes that was quite new to her, that Peter had met his match, and would realize it sooner or later. Mary protested against there being any further talk of the circus that day, but Sidney would not refuse the disappointed eyes of the small Moores. In the end, the doctor's family went off alone in the motor-car.

"Don't worry, Mary," said Sidney, kindly, as he tucked her in comfortably. "Peter's had nothing but women and servants so far. Now he's got to learn to obey!"

"But such a baby, Sidney!" she reminded him.

"He's older than I was, Mary, when my poor father and Uncle Larry--"

"Yes--yes, I know!" she assented hurriedly. "Good-by!"

"Good-by!" repeated a hardy little voice from an upper window. Mary looked up to see Peter, composed and smiling, looking down from the nursery sill.

All the next day, and the next, Mary Moore's thoughts were at the Hall. She told her husband all about it on the afternoon of the second day, for no word or sign had come from Jean, and real anxiety began to haunt her. She and the doctor were roaming about their pretty, shabby garden, Mrs. Moore's little hand, where she loved to have it, in the crook of his big arm. The doctor, stopping occasionally to shake a rose post with his free hand, or to break a dead blossom from its stalk, scowled through the recital, even while contentedly enjoying his wife, his garden, and his pipe.

Before he could make a definite comment, they were interrupted by Sidney himself, who brought his big riding horse up close to the fence and waved his whip with a shout of greeting. The doctor went to meet him, Mary, a little pale, following.

"Good day to you!" said Sidney Carolan, baring his head without a smile. "I'm bound to Barville; my editor is there for a few days, and I may have to dine with him. I stopped to ask if Mary would run in and see Jean this afternoon. She's feeling a little down."

"Of course I will!" said Mary, heartily.

There was a pause.

"Mary's told you that we're having an ugly time with the boy?" said Sidney, then, combing his horse's mane with big gloved fingers.

"Too bad!" said the doctor, shaking his head and pursing his lips.

"No change, Sidney?" Mary asked gravely.

"No. No, I think the little fellow is rather gratified by the stir he's making. He--oh, Lord knows what he thinks!"

"Give him a good licking," suggested the doctor.

"Oh, I'd lick him fast enough, Bill, if that would bring him round!" his father said, scowling. "But suppose I do, and it leaves things just where they are now? That's all I CAN do, and he knows it. His mother has talked to him; I've talked to him." He looked frowningly at the seam of his glove. "Well, I mustn't bother you. He's a Carolan, I suppose--that's all!"

"And you're a Carolan," said the doctor.

"And I'm a Carolan," assented the other, briefly.

Mary found Jean, serious and composed over her sewing, on the cool north veranda. When they had talked awhile, they went up to see Peter, who was sprawled on the floor, busy with hundreds of leaden soldiers. He was no longer gay; there was rather a strained look about his beautiful babyish eyes. But at Jean's one allusion to the unhappy affair, he flushed and said with nervous decision:

"Please don't, mother! You know I am sorry; you know I just CAN'T!"

"He has all his books and toys?" said Mary when they went downstairs again.

"Oh, yes! Sidney doesn't want him to be sick. He's just to be shut up on bread and milk until he gives in. I must say, I think Sid is very gentle," said Jean, leaning back wearily in her chair, with closed eyes. Her voice dropped perceptibly as she added, "But he says he is going to thrash him to-morrow."

"I think he ought to," said Mary Moore, sturdily. "This isn't excitement or show-ing off any more; it's sheer naughty obstinacy over a perfectly simple demand!"

"Oh, but I couldn't bear it!" whispered Jean, with a shudder. A moment later she added sensibly, "But he's right, of course; Sidney always is."

Peter was duly whipped the next day. It was no light punishment that Sidney gave his son. Jean's gold-mounted riding-crop had never seen severer service. The maids, with paling cheeks, gathered together in the kitchen when Sidney went slowly upstairs with the whip in his hand; and Betta and her mistress, their hands over their ears, endured a very agony while the little boy's cries rang through the house. Sidney went for a long and lonely walk afterward, and later Jean went to her son.

Mrs. Moore heard of this event from her husband, who stopped at the Hall late that evening, and found Peter asleep, and Jean restless and headachy. He spent a long and almost silent hour pacing the rose terrace with Sidney in the cool dark. Late into the night the doctor and his wife lay wakeful, discussing affairs at the Hall.

After some hesitation, Mrs. Moore went the next day to find Jean. There was no sound as she approached the house, and she stepped timidly into the big hall, listening for voices. Presently she went softly to the dining-room, and stood in the doorway. The room was empty. But Mary's heart rose with a throb of thanksgiving. Peter's silver mug was in its place on the sideboard. She went swiftly to the pantry where Julia was cleaning the silver.

"Julia!" she said eagerly, softly, "I notice that the baby's cup is back. Did he give in?"

The maid, who had started at the interruption, shook her head gravely.

"No'm. Mrs. Carolan picked it up."

"MRS. Carolan?"

"Yes'm. She seemed quite wildlike this morning," went on the maid, with the simple freemasonry of troubled times, "and after Peter went off with Mrs. Butler, she--"

"Oh, he went off? Did his father let him go?" Mary's voice was full of relief. Mrs. Butler was Jean's cousin, a cheery matron who had taken a summer cottage at Broadsands, twenty miles away.

Julia's color rose; she looked uneasy.

"Mr. Carolan had to go to Barville quite early," she evaded uncomfortably, "and when Mrs. Butler asked could she take Peter, his mother said yes, she could."

"Thank you," Mary said pleasantly, but her heart was heavy. She went slowly upstairs to find Jean.

Peter's mother was lying in a darkened bedroom, and the face she turned to the door at Mary's entrance was shockingly white. They exchanged a long pressure of fingers.

"Headache, Jean, dear?"

"Oh, and heartache!" said Jean, with a pitiful smile. "Sid thrashed him yesterday!" she added, with suddenly trembling lips.

"I know." Mary sat down on the edge of the bed and patted Jean's hand.

"I've let him go with Alice," said Jean, defensively. "I had to!" She turned on her elbow, her voice rising. "Mary, I didn't say one word about the whipping, but now--now he threatens to hold him under the stable pump!" she finished, dropping back wearily against her pillows. Mrs. Moore caught her breath.

"Ah!" They eyed each other sombrely.

"Mary, would YOU permit it?" demanded Mrs. Carolan, miserably.

"Jeanie, dearest, I don't know what I'd do!"

After a long silence, Mary slipped from the bedside and went noiselessly to the door and down the stairs, vague ideas of hot tea in mind. In the dining-room she was surprised to find Sidney, looking white and exhausted, and mixing himself something at the sideboard.

"I'm glad you're with Jean," he said directly. "I'm off to get the boy! The car is to be brought round in a few minutes."

Mrs. Moore went to him, and laid her fingers on his arm.

"Sidney!" she protested sharply, "you must stop this--not for Peter; he's as naughty as he can be, like all other boys his age sometimes; but you don't want to kill Jean!" And, to her self-contempt, she began to cry.

"My dear girl," he said concernedly, "you mustn't take this matter too hard. Jean knows enough of our family history to realize--"

"All that is such nonsense!" she protested angrily. But she saw that he was not listening. He compared his watch with the big dining-room clock, and then, quite as mechanically picked Peter's mug from the group of bowls and flagons on the sideboard, studied the chasing absently for a moment, and, stooping, placed the mug just as it had fallen four days before. Mary watched as if fascinated.

A moment later she ran upstairs, her heart thundering with a sense of her own daring. She entered the dark bedroom hurriedly, and leaned over Jean.

"Jean! Jean, I hate to tell you! But Sidney's going to leave in a few minutes to bring Peter home. He's going after him."

She had to repeat the message before the meaning of it flashed into the heavy eyes so near her own. Then Jean gathered her filmy gown together, and ran to the door.

"He shall not!" she said, panting, and Mary heard her imperative call, "Sidney! Sidney!" as she ran downstairs. Then she heard both their voices.

With an intolerable consciousness of eavesdropping, Mrs. Moore slipped out of the house by the servants' quarters, and crossed the drying lawn at the back of the house, to gain the old grape arbor beyond. She sat there with burning cheeks and a fast-beating heart, and gazed with unseeing eyes down the valley.

Presently she heard the horn and the scraping start of the motor- car, and a moment later it swept into view on the road below. Sidney was its only occupant.

Mrs. Moore sat there thinking a long while. Dull clouds banked themselves in the west, and the rising breeze brought dead leaves about her feet.

She sat there half an hour--an hour. The afternoon was darkening toward dusk when she saw the motorcar again still a mile away. Even at this distance, Mary could see that Peter was sitting beside his father in the tonneau, and that the little figure was as erect and unyielding as the big one.

She rose to her feet and stood watching the car as it curved and turned on the winding road that led to the gates of Carolan Hall. Even when the gates were entered, both figures still faced straight ahead.

Suddenly Sidney leaned toward the chauffeur, and a moment later the car came to a full stop. Mary watched, mystified. Then Sidney got out, and stretched a hand to the boy to help him from his place. The simple little motion, all fatherly, brought the tears to her eyes. A moment later the driver wheeled the car about, to take it to the garage by the rear roadway, and Sidney and his son began to walk slowly toward the house, the child's hand still in his father's. Once or twice they stopped short, and once Mary saw Sidney point toward the house, and saw, from the turn of Peter's head, that his eyes were following his father's. Her heart rose with a wild, unreasoning hope.

When a dip in the road hid them, Mary turned toward the house, not knowing whether to go to Jean or to slip away through the wood. But the instant her eye fell on Madam Carolan's window she knew what had halted Sidney, and a wave of heartsickness made her breath come short.

Jean had taken her place there, to watch and wait. She was keeping the first vigil of her life. Mary could see how the slight figure drooped in the carved chair; she remembered, with a pang, the other patient, drooping figure that had stamped itself upon her childish memory so many years ago. The suffocating tears rose in her throat. A sudden sense of helplessness overwhelmed her.

Obviously, the watcher had not seen Sidney and Peter. Her head was resting on her hand, and her heavy eyes were fixed upon some sombre inner vision that was hers alone.

Mary crossed behind the house, and, as they came up through the shrubbery, met Sidney and his son at the side door. Sidney's face was tired, but radiant with a mysterious content. Peter looked white--awed. He was clinging with both small brown hands to one of his father's firm, big ones.

"I know what you're going to say, Mary," said Sidney, in a tone curiously gentle, and with his oddly bright smile. "I know she's there. But we're going to her now, and it's all right. Peter and I have been talking it over. I saw her there, Mary, and it was like a blow! SHE'S not the one who must suffer for all this. Peter and I are going to start all over again, and settle our troubles without hurting a woman; aren't we, Peter?"

The little boy nodded, with his eyes fixed on his father's.

"So the episode is closed, Mary," said Sidney, simply. "And the next time-- if there is a next time!--Peter shall make his own decision, and abide by what it brings. The mug goes back to its place to- night, and--and we're going to tell mother that she never need watch and wait and worry about us again!"

They turned to the steps; but, as the boy ran ahead, Sidney came back to say in a lower tone:

"I--it may be weakness, Mary, but I can't have Jean doing what--what SHE did, you know! I tried to give the boy some idea, just now, of the responsibility of it. Nobody spared my grandmother, but Jean SHALL be spared, if I never try to control him or save him from himself again!"

"Ah, Sidney," Mary said, "you have done more, in taking him into your confidence, than any amount of punishing could do!"

"Well, we'll see!" he said, with a weary little shrug. "I must go to Jeanie now."

As he mounted the steps, Peter reappeared in the darkened doorway. The child looked like a little knight, with his tawny loose mop of hair and short tunic, and the uplifted look in his lovely eyes.

"Shall we go to her now, Dad?" said the little treble gallantly. And, as the boy came close to Sidney's side, Mary saw the silver mug glitter in his hand.

MAKING ALLOWANCES FOR MAMMA

At the head of her own breakfast table,--a breakfast table charmingly littered with dark-blue china and shining glass, and made springlike by a great bowl of daisies,--Mary Venable sat alone, trying to read her letters through a bitter blur of tears. She was not interested in her letters, but something must be done, she thought desperately, to check this irresistible impulse to put her head down on the table and cry like a child, and uninteresting letters, if she could only force her eyes to follow the lines of them, and her brain to follow the meaning, would be as steadying to the nerves as anything else.

Cry she would NOT; for every reason. Lizzie, coming in to carry away the plates, would see her, for one thing. It would give her a blazing headache, for another. It would not help her in the least to solve the problem ahead of her, for a third and best. She must think it out clearly and reasonably, and--and--Mary's lip began to quiver again, she would have to do it all alone. Mamma was the last person in the world who could help her, and George wouldn't.

For of course the trouble was Mamma again, and George--

Mary wiped her eyes resolutely, finished a glass of water, drew a deep great breath. Then she rang for Lizzie, and carried her letters to the shaded, cool little study back of the large drawing-room. Fortified by the effort this required, she sank comfortably into a deep chair, and began to plan sensibly and collectedly. Firstly, she reread Mamma's letter.

Mary had seen this letter among others at her plate, only an hour ago. A deep sigh, reminiscent of the recently suppressed storm, caught her unawares as she remembered how happy she and George had been over their breakfast until Mamma's letter was opened. Mary had not wanted to open it, suggesting carelessly that it might wait until later; she could tell George if there was anything in it. But George had wanted to hear it read immediately, and of course there had been something in it. There usually was something unexpected in Mamma's letters. In this one she broke the news to her daughter and son-in-law that she hated Milwaukee, she didn't like Cousin Will's house, children, or self, she had borrowed her ticket money from Cousin Will, and she was coming home on Tuesday.

Mary had gotten only this far when George, prefacing his remarks with a forcible and heartfelt "damn," had said some very sharp and very inconsiderate things of Mamma. He had said--But no, Mary wouldn't go over that. She would NOT cry again.

The question was, what to do with Mamma now. They had thought her so nicely settled with Cousin Will and his motherless boys, had packed her off to Milwaukee only a fortnight ago with such a generous check to cover incidental expenses, had felt that now, for a year or two at least, she was anchored. And in so many ways it seemed a special blessing, this particular summer, to have Mamma out of the way,-- comfortable and happy, but out of the way. For Mary had packed her three babies and their nurse down to the cottage at Beach Meadow for the summer, and she and George had determined--with only brief weekend intervals to break it--to try staying in the New York house all summer.

Ordinarily Mary, too, would have been at Beach Meadow with the children, seeing George only in the rare intervals when he could run up from town, two or three times a season perhaps, and really rather more glad than otherwise to have Mamma with her. But this promised to be a trying and overworked summer for him, and Mary herself was tired from a winter of close attention to her nursery, and to them both the plan seemed a most tempting chance for jolly little dinners together, Sunday and evening trips in the motor, roof-garden shows and suppers. They had had too little of each other's undivided society in the three crowded years that had witnessed the arrival of the twins and baby Mary, there had been infantile illnesses, Mary's own health had been poor, Mamma had been with them, nurses had been with them, doctors had been constantly coming and going, nothing had been normal. Both Mary and George had thought and spoken a hundred times of that one first, happy year of their marriage, and they wanted to bring back some of its old free charm now. So the children, with Miss Fox, who was a "treasure" of a trained nurse, and Myra, whose Irish devotion was maternal in its intensity, were sent away to the seaside, and they were living on the beach all day, and sleeping in the warm sea air all night, and hardier and browner and happier every time they rushed screaming out to welcome mother and daddy and the motor-car for a brief visit. And Mamma was with Cousin Will. Or at least she HAD been--

Well, there was only one thing certain, Mary decided,--Mamma could not come to them. That would spoil all the summer they had been planning so happily. To picnic in the hot city with one beloved companion is one thing, to keep house there for one's family is quite another. Mamma was not adaptable, she had her own very definite ideas. She hated a dimly lighted drawing-room, and interrupted Mary's music--to which George listened in such utter content--with cheery random remarks, and the slapping of cards at Patience. Mamma hated silences, she hated town in summer, she made jolly and informal little expeditions the most discussed and tedious of events. If George, settling himself happily in some restaurant, suggested enthusiastically a planked steak, Mamma quite positively wanted some chicken or just a chop for herself, please. If George suggested red wine, Mamma was longing for just a sip of Pommerey: "You order it, Georgie, and let it be my treat!"

It never was her treat, but that was the least of it.

No, Mamma simply couldn't come to them now. She would have to go to Miss Fox and the children. Myra wouldn't like it, and Mamma always interfered with Miss Fox, and would have to take the second best bedroom, and George would probably make a fuss, but there was nothing else to do. It couldn't be helped.

Sometimes in moments of less strain, Mary was amused to remember that it was through Mamma that she had met George. She, Mary, had gone down from, her settlement work in hot New York for a little breathing spell at Atlantic City, where Mamma, who had a very small room at the top of a very large hotel, was enjoying a financially pinched but entirely carefree existence. Mary would have preferred sober and unpretentious boarding in some private family herself, but Mamma loved the big dining-room, the piazzas, the music, and the crowds of the hotel, and Mary amiably engaged the room next to hers. They had to climb a flight of stairs above the last elevator stop to reach their rooms, and rarely saw any one in their corridors except maids and chauffeurs, but Mamma didn't mind that. She knew a score of Southern people downstairs who always included her in their good times; her life never lacked the spice of a mild flirtation. Mamma rarely had to pay for any of her own meals, except breakfast, and the economy with which she could order a breakfast was a real surprise to Mary. Mamma swam, motored, danced, walked, gossiped, played bridge, and golfed like any debutante. Mary, watching her, wondered sometimes if the father she had lost when a tiny baby, and the stepfather whose marriage to her mother, and death had followed only a few years later, were any more real to her mother than the dreams they both were to her.

On the day of Mary's arrival, mother and daughter came down to the wide hotel porch, in the cool idle hour before dinner, and took possession of big rocking-chairs, facing the sea. They were barely seated, when a tall man in white flannels came smilingly toward them.

"Mrs. Honeywell!" he said, delightedly, and Mary saw her mother give him a cordial greeting before she said:

"And now, George, I want you to know my little girl, Ma'y,--Miss Bannister. Ma'y, this is my Southe'n boy I was telling you about!"

Mary, turning unsmiling eyes, was quite sure the man would be nearer forty than thirty, as indeed he was, grizzled and rather solid into the bargain. Mamma's "boys" were rarely less; had he really been at all youthful, Mamma would have introduced him as "that extr'ornarily intrusting man I've been telling you about, Ma'y, dear!"

But he was a nice-looking man, and a nice seeming man, except for his evidently having flirted with Mamma, which proceeding Mary always held slightly in contempt. Not that he seemed flirtatiously inclined at this particular moment, but Mary could tell from her mother's manner that their friendship had been one of those frothy surface affairs into which Mamma seemed able to draw the soberest of men.

Mr. Venable sat down next to Mary, and they talked of the sea, in which a few belated bathers were splashing, and of the hot and distant city, and finally of Mary's work. These topics did not interest Mamma, who carried on a few gay, restless conversations with various acquaintances on the porch meanwhile, and retied her parasol bow several times.

Mamma, with her prettily arranged and only slightly retouched hair, her dashing big hat and smart little gown, her red lips and black eyes, was an extremely handsome woman, but Mr. Venable even now could not seem to move his eyes from Mary's nondescript gray eyes, and rather colorless fair skin, and indefinite, pleasant mouth. Mamma's lines were all compact and trim. Mary was rather long of limb, even a little GAUCHE in an attractive, unself-conscious sort of way. But something fine and high, something fresh and young and earnest about her, made its instant appeal to the man beside her.

"Isn't she just the biggest thing!" Mamma said finally, with a little affectionate slap for Mary's hand. "Makes me feel so old, having a great, big girl of twenty-three!"

This was three years short of the fact, but Mary never betrayed her mother in these little weaknesses. Mr. Venable said, not very spontaneously, that they could pass for sisters.

"Just hear him, will you!" said Mamma, in gay scorn. "Why there's seventeen whole years between us! Ma'y was born on the day I was seventeen. My first husband--dearest fellow ever WAS--used to say he had two babies and no wife. I never shall forget," Mamma went on youthfully, "one day when Ma'y was about two months old, and I had her out in the garden. I always had a nurse,--smartest looking thing you ever saw, in caps and ribbons!--but she was out, I forget where. Anyway our old Doctor Wallis came in, and he saw me, with my hair all hanging in curls, and a little blue dress on, and he called out, 'Look here, Ma'y Lou Duval, ain't you too old to be playin' with dolls?'"

Mary had often heard this, but she laughed, and Mr. Venable laughed, too, although he cut short an indication of further reminiscence on Mamma's part by entering briskly upon the subject of dinner. Would Mrs. Honeywell and Miss Bannister dine with him, in the piazza, dining-room, that wasn't too near the music, and was always cool, and then afterward he'd have the car brought about--? Mary's first smiling shake of the head subsided before these tempting details. It did sound so cool and restful and attractive! And after all, why shouldn't one dine with the big, responsible person who was one of New York's biggest construction engineers, with whom one's mother was on such friendly terms?

That was the first of many delightful times. George Venable fell in love with Mary and grew serious for the first time in his life. And Mary fell in love with George, and grew frivolous for the first time in hers. And in the breathless joy that attended their discovery of each other, they rather forgot Mamma.

"Stealing my beau!" said the little lady, accusatively, one night, when mother and daughter were dressing. Mary turned an uncomfortable scarlet.

"Oh, don't be such a little goosie!" Mrs. Honeywell said, with a great hug. And she artlessly added, "My goodness, Mary, I've got all the beaux I want! I'm only too tickled to have you have one at last!"

By the time the engagement, with proper formality, was announced, George's attitude toward his prospective mother-in-law had shifted completely. He was no longer Mamma's gallant squire, but had assumed something of Mary's tolerant, protective manner toward her. Later, when they were married, this change went still further, and George became rather scornful of the giddy little butterfly, casually critical of her in conversations with Mary.

Mrs. Honeywell enjoyed the wedding as if she had been the bride's younger sister now allowed a first peep at real romance.

"But I'm going to give you one piece of advice, dearie," said she, the night before the ceremony. Mary, wrapped in all the mysterious thoughts of that unreal time, winced inwardly. This was all so new, so sacred, so inexpressible to her that she felt Mamma couldn't understand it. Of course she had been married twice herself, but then she was so different.

"It's this," said Mrs. Honeywell, cheerfully, after a pause. "There'll come a time when you'll simply hate him--"

"Oh, Mamma!" Mary said, with distaste.

"Yes, there will," her mother went on placidly, "and then you just say to yourself that the best of 'em's only a big boy, and treat him as you'd treat a boy!"

"All right, darling!" Mary laughed, kissing her. But she thought to herself that the men Mamma had married were of very different caliber from George.

Parenthood developed new gravities in George, all life became purer, sweeter, more simple, with Mary beside him. Through the stress of their first married years they became more and more closely devoted, marvelled more and more at the miracle that had brought them together. But Mamma suffered to this. The atmosphere of gay irresponsibility and gossip that she brought with her on her frequent visitations became very trying to George. He resented her shallowness, her youthful gowns, her extravagances. Mary found herself eternally defending Mamma, in an unobtrusive sort of way, inventing and assuming congenialities between her and George. It had been an unmitigated blessing to have the little lady start gayly off for Cousin Will's, only a month ago--And now here she was again!

Mary sighed, pushed her letters aside, and stared thoughtfully out of the window. The first of New York's blazing summer days hung heavily over the gay Drive and the sluggish river. The Jersey hills were blurred with heat. Dull, brief whistles of river-craft came to her; under the full leafage of trees on the Drive green omnibuses lumbered; baby carriages, each with its attendant, were motionless in the shade. Mary drew her desk telephone toward her, pushed it away again, hesitated over a note. Then she sent for her cook and discussed the day's meals.

Alone again, she reached a second time for the telephone, waited for a number, and asked for Mr. Venable.

"George, this is Mary," said Mary, a moment later. Silence. "George, darling," said Mary, in a rush, "I am so sorry about Mamma, and I realize how trying it is for you, and I'm so sorry I took what you said at breakfast that way. Don't worry, dear, we'll settle her somehow. And I'll spare you all I can! George, would you like me to come down to the office at six, and have dinner somewhere? She won't be here until tomorrow. And my new hat has come, and I want to wear it--?" She paused; there was a moment's silence before George's warm, big voice answered:

"You are absolutely the most adorable angel that ever breathed, Mary. You make me ashamed of myself. I've been sitting here as BLUE as indigo. Everything going wrong! Those confounded Carter people got the order for the Whitely building--you remember I told you about it? It was a three-million dollar contract."

"Oh, George!" Mary lamented.

"Oh, well, it's not serious, dear. Only I thought we 'had it nailed.' I'd give a good deal to know how Carter does it. Sometimes I have the profoundest contempt for that fellow's methods--then he lands something like this. I don't believe he can handle it, either."

"I hate that man!" said Mary, calmly. George laughed boyishly.

"Well, you were an angel to telephone," he said. "Come early, sweetheart, and we'll go up to Macbeth's,--they say it's quite an extraordinary collection. And don't worry--I'll be nice to Mamma. And wear your blessed little pink hat--"

Mary went upstairs ten minutes later with a singing heart. Let Mamma and her attendant problems arrive tomorrow if she must. Today would be all their own! She began to dress at three o'clock, as pleasantly excited as a girl. She laid her prettiest white linen gown beside the pink hat on the bed, selected an especially frilled petticoat, was fastidious over white shoes and silken stockings.

The big house was very still. Lizzie, hitherto un-compromisingly a cook, had so far unbent this summer as to offer to fill the place of waitress as well as her own. Today she had joyously accepted Mary's offer of a whole unexpected free afternoon and evening. Mary was alone, and rather enjoying it. She walked, trailing her ruffled wrapper, to one of the windows, and looked down on the Drive. It was almost deserted.

While she stood there idle and smiling, a taxicab veered to the curb, hesitated, came to a full stop. Out of it came a small gloved hand with a parasol clasped in it, a small struggling foot in a gray suede shoe, a small doubled-up form clad in gray-blue silk, a hat covered with corn-flowers.

Mamma had arrived, as Mamma always did, unexpectedly.

Mary stared at the apparition with a sudden rebellious surge at her heart. She knew what this meant, but for a moment the full significance of it seemed too exasperating to be true. Oh, how could she!--spoil their last day together, upset their plans, madden George afresh, when he was only this moment pacified! Mary uttered an impatient little sigh as she went down to open the door; but it was the anticipation of George's vexation--not her own--that stirred her, and the sight of Mamma was really unwelcome to Mary only because of George's lack of welcome.

"No Lizzie?" asked Mamma, blithely, when her first greetings were over, and the case of Cousin Will had been dismissed with a few emphatic sentences.

"I let her go this afternoon instead of to-morrow, Muddie, dear. We're going down town to dinner."

"Oh; that's nice,--but I look a perfect fright!" said Mrs. Honeywell, following Mary upstairs. "Nasty trip! I don't want a thing but a cup of tea for supper anyway--bit of toast. I'll be glad to get my things off for a while."

"If you LIKE, Mamma, why don't you just turn in?" Mary suggested. "It's nearly four now. I'll bring you up some cold meat and tea and so on."

"Sounds awfully nice," her mother said, getting a thin little silk wrapper out of her suit-case. "But we'll see,--there's no hurry. What time are you meeting Georgie?"

"Well, we were going to Macbeth's,--but that's not important,--we needn't meet him until nearly seven, I suppose," Mary said patiently, "only I ought to telephone him what we are going to do."

"Oh, telephone that I'll come too, I'll feel fine in half an hour," Mrs. Honeywell said decidedly.

Mary, unsatisfied with this message, temporized by sitting down in a deep chair. The room, which had all been made ready for Mamma, was cool and pleasant. Awnings shaded the open windows; the rugs, the wall-paper, the chintzes were all in gay and roseate tints. Mrs. Honeywell stretched herself luxuriously on the bed, both pillows under her head.

"I'm sure she'd be much more comfortable here than tearing about town this stuffy night!" the daughter reflected, while listening to an account of Cousin Will's dreadful house, and dreadful children.

It was so easy when Mamma was away to think generously, affectionately of her, to laugh kindly at the memory of her trying moods. But it was very different to have Mamma actually about, to humor her whims, listen to her ceaseless chatter, silently sacrifice to her comfort a thousand comforts of one's own.

After a half hour of playing listener she went down to telephone George.

"Oh, damn!" said George, heartily. "And here I've been hustling through things thinking any minute that you'd come in. Well, this spoils it all. I'll come home."

"Oh, dearest,--it'll be just a 'pick-up' dinner, then. I don't know what's in the house. Lizzie's gone," Mary submitted hesitatingly.

"Oh, damn!" George said forcibly, again.

"What does your mother propose to do?" he asked Mary some hours later, when the rather unsuccessful dinner was over, Mamma had retired, and he and his wife were in their own rooms. Mary felt impending unpleasantness in his tone, and battled with a rising sense of antagonism. She tucked her pink hat into its flowered box, folded the silky tissue paper about it, tied the strings.

"Why, I don't know, dear!" she said pleasantly, carrying the box to her wardrobe.

"Does she plan to stay here?" George asked, with a reasonable air, carefully transferring letters, pocket-book, and watch-case from one vest to another.

"George, when does Mamma ever plan ANYTHING!" Mary reminded him, with elaborate gentleness.

There was a short silence. The night was very sultry, and no air stirred the thin window-curtains. The room, with its rich litter of glass and silver, its dark wood and bright hangings, seemed somehow hot and crowded. Mary flung her dark cloud of hair impatiently back, as she sat at her dressing table. Brushing was too hot a business tonight.

"I confess I think I have a right to ask what your mother proposes to do," George said presently, with marked politeness.

"Oh, Georgie! DON'T be so ridiculous!" Mary protested impatiently. "You know what Mamma is!"

"I may be ridiculous," George conceded, magnificently, "but I fail to see--"

"I don't mean that," Mary said hastily. "But need we decide tonight?" she added with laudable calm. "It's so HOT, dearest, and I am so sleepy. Mamma could go to Beach Meadow, I suppose?" she finished unthinkingly.

This was a wrong move. George was disappearing into his dressing- room at the moment, and did not turn back. Mary put out all the lights but one, turned down the beds, settled on her pillows with a great sigh of relief. But George, returning in a trailing wrapper, was mighty with resolution.

"I mean to make just one final remark on this subject, Mary," said George, flashing on three lights with one turn of the wrist, "but you may as well understand me. I mean it! I don't propose to have your mother at Beach Meadow, not for a single night--not for a day! She demoralizes the boys, she has a very bad effect on the nurse. I sympathize with Miss Fox, and I refuse to allow my children to be given candy, and things injurious to their constitutions, and to be kept up until late hours, and to have their first perceptions of honor and truth misled--"

"George!"

"Well,' said George, after a brief pause, more mildly, "I won't have it."

"Then--but she can't stay here, George. It will spoil our whole summer."

"Exactly," George assented. There was another pause.

"I'll talk to Mamma--she may have some plan," Mary said at last, with a long sigh.

Mamma had no plan to unfold on the following day, and a week and then ten days went by without any suggestion of change on her part. The weather was very hot, and Lizzie complained more than once that Mrs. Honeywell must have her iced coffee and sandwiches at four and that breakfast, luncheon, and dinner regularly for three was not at all like getting two meals for two every day, and besides, there was another bedroom to care for, and the kitchen was never in order! Mary applied an unfailing remedy to Lizzie's case, and sent for a charwoman besides. Less easily solved were other difficulties.

George, for example, liked to take long motoring trips out of the city, on warm summer evenings. He ran his own car, and was never so happy as when Mary was on the driver's seat beside him, where he could amuse her with the little news of the day, or repeat to her long and, to Mary, unintelligible business conversations in which he had borne a part.

But Mamma's return spoiled all this. Obviously, the little lady couldn't be left to bounce about alone in the tonneau. If Mary joined her there, George would sit silently, immovably, in the front seat, chewing his cigar, his eyes on the road. Only when they had a friend or two with them did Mary enjoy these drives.

Mamma had an unlucky habit of scattering George's valuable books carelessly about the house, and George was fussy about his books. And she would sometimes amuse herself by trying roll after roll on the piano-player, until George, perhaps trying to read in the adjoining library, was almost frantic. And she mislaid his telephone directory, and took telephone messages for him that she forgot to deliver, and insisted upon knowing why he was late for dinner, in spite of Mary's warning, "Let him change and get his breath Mamma, dear,--he's exhausted. What does it matter, anyway?"

Sometimes Mary's heart would ache for the little, resourceless lady, drifting aimlessly through her same and stupid days. Mamma had always been spoiled, loved, amused,--it was too much to expect strength and unselfishness of her now. And at other times, when she saw the tired droop to George's big shoulders, and the gallant effort he made to be sweet to Mamma, George who was so good, and so generous, and who only asked to have his wife and home quietly to himself after the long day, Mary's heart would burn with longing to put her arms about him, and go off alone with him somewhere, and smooth the wrinkles from. his forehead, and let him rest.

One warm Sunday in mid-July they all went down to Long Island to see the rosy, noisy babies. It was a happy day for Mary. George was very gracious, Mamma charming and complaisant. The weather was perfection, and the children angelic. They shared the noonday dinner with little George and Richard and Mary, and motored home through the level light of late afternoon. Slowly passing through a certain charming colony of summer homes, they were suddenly hailed.

Out from a shingled bungalow, and across a velvet lawn streamed three old friends of Mamma's, Mrs. Law'nce Arch'bald, and her daughter, 'Lizabeth Sarah, who was almost Mamma's age, and 'Lizabeth Sarah's husband, Harry Fairfax. These three were rapturously presented to the Venables by Mrs. Honeywell, and presently they all went up to the porch for tea.

Mary thought, and she could see George thought, that it was very pleasant to discuss the delicious Oolong and Maryland biscuit, and Southern white fruit-cake, while listening to Mamma's happy chatter with her old friends. The old negress who served tea called Mamma "chile," and Mrs. Archibald, an aristocratic, elderly woman, treated her as if she were no more than a girl. Mary thought she had never seen her mother so charming.

"I wonder if the's any reason, Mary Lou'siana, why you can't just come down here and stay with me this summah?" said Mrs. Archibald, suddenly. "'Lizabeth Sarah and Harry Fairfax, they're always coming and going, and Lord knows it would be like havin' one of my own girls back, to me. We've room, and there's a lot of nice people down hereabouts--"

A chorus arose, Mrs. Honey well protesting joyously that that was too much imp'sition for any use, 'Lizabeth Sarah and Harry Fairfax violently favorable to the idea, Mrs. Archibald magnificently overriding objections, Mary and George trying with laughter to separate jest from earnest. Mrs. Honeywell, overborne, was dragged upstairs to inspect "her room," old Aunt Curry, the colored maid and cook, adding her deep-noted welcome to "Miss Mar' Lou." It was arranged that Mamma should at least spend the night, and George and Mary left her there, and came happily home together, laughing, over their little downtown dinner, with an almost parental indulgence, at Mamma.

In the end, Mamma did go down to the Archibald's for an indefinite stay. Mary quite overwhelmed her with generous contributions to her wardrobe, and George presented her with a long-coveted chain. The parting took place with great affection and regret expressed on both sides. But this timely relief was clouded for Mary when Mamma flitted in to see her a day or two later. Mamma wondered if Ma'y dearest could possibly let her have two hundred dollars.

"Muddie, you've overdrawn again!" Mary accused her. For Mamma had an income of a thousand a year.

"No, dear, it's not that. I am a little overdrawn, but it's not that. But you see Richie Carter lives right next do' to the Arch'balds,"--Mamma's natural Southern accent was gaining strength every day now,--"and it might be awkward, meetin' him, don't you know?"

"Awkward?" Mary echoed, frowning.

"Well, you see, Ma'y, love, some years ago I was intimate with his wife," her mother proceeded with some little embarrassment, "and so when I met him at the Springs last year, I confided in him about-- laws! I forget what it was exactly, some bills I didn't want to bother Georgie about, anyway. And he was perfectly charmin' about it I"

"Oh, Mamma!" Mary said in distress, "not Richard Carter of the Carter Construction Company? Oh, Mamma, you know how George hates that whole crowd! You didn't borrow money of him!"

"Not that he'd ever speak of it--he'd die first!" Mrs. Honeywell said hastily.

"I'll have to ask George for it," Mary said after a long pause, "and he'll be furious." To which Mamma, who was on the point of departure, agreed, adding thoughtfully, "I'm always glad not to be here if Georgie's going to fly into a rage."

George did fly into a rage at this piece of news, and said some scathing things of Mamma, even while he wrote out a check for two hundred dollars.

"Here, you send it to her," he said bitterly to Mary, folding the paper with a frown. "I don't feel as if I ever wanted to see her again. I tell you, Mary, I warn you, my dear, that things can't go on this way much longer. I never refused her money that I know of, and yet she turns to this fellow Carter!" He interrupted himself with an exasperated shrug, and began to walk about the room. "She turns to Carter," he burst out again angrily, "a man who could hurt me irreparably by letting it get about that my mother-in-law had to ask him for a petty loan!"

Mary, with a troubled face, was slowly, silently setting up a game of chess. She took the check, feeling like Becky Sharp, and tucked it into her blouse.

"Come on, George, dear," she said, after an uneasy silence. She pushed a white pawn forward. George somewhat unwillingly took his seat opposite her, but could not easily capture the spirit of the game. He made a hasty move or two, scowled up at the lights, scowled at the windows that were already wide open to the sultry night, loosened his collar with two impatient fingers.

"I'd give a good deal to understand your mother, Mary," he burst out suddenly. "I'd give a GREAT deal! Her love of pleasure I can understand--her utter lack of any possible vestige of business sense I can understand, although my own mother was a woman who conducted an immense business with absolute scrupulousness and integrity--"

"Georgie, dear! What has your mother's business ability to do with poor Mamma!" Mary said patiently, screwing the separated halves of a knight firmly together.

"It has this to do with it," George said with sudden heat, "that my mother's principles gave me a pretty clear idea of what a lady does and does not do! And my mother would have starved before she turned to a comparative stranger for a personal loan."

"But neither one of her sons could bear to live with her, she was so cold-blooded," Mary thought, but with heroic self-control she kept silent. She answered only by the masterly advance of a bishop.

"Queen," she said calmly.

"Queen nothing!" George said, suddenly attentive.

"Give me a piece then," Mary chanted. George gave a fully aroused attention to the game, and saving it, saved the evening for Mary.

"But please keep Mamma quiet now for a while!" she prayed fervently in her evening devotions a few hours later. "I can't keep this up-- we'll have serious trouble here. Please make her stay where she is for a year at least."

Two weeks, three weeks, went peaceably by. The Venables spent a happy week-end or two with their children. Between these visits they were as light-hearted as children themselves, in the quiet roominess of the New York home. Mamma's letters were regular and cheerful, she showed no inclination to return, and Mary, relieved for the first time since her childhood of pressing responsibility, bloomed like a rose.

Sometimes she reflected uneasily that Mamma's affairs were only temporarily settled, after all, and sometimes George made her heart sink with uncompromising statements regarding the future, but for the most part Mary's natural sunniness kept her cheerful and unapprehensive.

Almost unexpectedly, therefore, the crash came. It came on a very hot day, which, following a week of delightfully cool weather, was like a last flaming hand-clasp from the departing summer. It was a Monday, and had started wrong with a burned omelette at breakfast, and unripe melons. And the one suit George had particularly asked to have cleaned and pressed had somehow escaped Mary's vigilance, and still hung creased and limp in the closet. So George went off, feeling a little abused, and Mary, feeling cross, too, went slowly about her morning tasks. Another annoyance was when the telephones had been cut off; a man with a small black bag mysteriously appearing to disconnect them, and as mysteriously vanishing when once their separated parts lay useless on the floor. Mary, idly reading, and comfortably stretched on a couch in her own room at eleven o'clock, was disturbed by the frantic and incessant ringing of the front doorbell.

"Lizzie went in to Broadway, I suppose," she reflected uneasily. "But I oughtn't to go down this way! Let him try again."

"He"--whoever he was--did try again so forcibly and so many times that Mary, after going to the head of the kitchen stairs to call Lizzie, with no result, finally ran down the main stairway herself, and gathering the loose frills of her morning wrapper about her, warily unbolted the door.

She admitted George, whose face was dark with heat, and whose voice rasped.

"Where's Lizzie?" he asked, eying Mary's negligee.

"Oh, dearie--and I've been keeping you waiting!" Mary lamented. "Come into the dining-room, it's cooler. She's marketing."

George dropped into a chair and mopped his forehead.

"No one to answer the telephone?" he pursued, frowning.

"It's disconnected, dear. Georgie, what is it?--you look sick."

"Well, I am, just about!" George said sternly. Then, irrelevantly, he demanded: "Mary, did you know your mother had disposed of her Sunbright shares?"

"Sold her copper stock!" Mary ejaculated, aghast For Mamma's entire income was drawn from this eminently safe and sane investment, and Mary and George had never ceased to congratulate themselves upon her good fortune in getting it at all.

"Two months ago," said George, with a shrewdly observant eye.

Mary interpreted his expression.

"Certainly I didn't know it!" she said with spirit.

"Didn't, eh? She SAYS you did," George said.

"Mamma does?" Mary was astounded.

"Read that!" Her husband flung a letter on the table.

Mary caught it up, ran through it hastily. It was from Mamma: She was ending her visit at Rock Bar, the Archibalds were going South rather early, they had begged her to go, but she didn't want to, and Mary could look for her any day now. And she was writing to Georgie because she was afraid she'd have to tell him that she had done an awfully silly thing: she had sold her Sunbright shares to an awfully attractive young fellow whom Mr. Pierce had sent to her--and so on and so on. Mary's eye leaped several lines to her own name. "Mary agreed with me that the Potter electric light stock was just as safe and they offered seven per cent," wrote Mamma.

"I DO remember now her saying something about the Potter," Mary said, raising honest, distressed eyes from the letter, "but with no possible idea that she meditated anything like this!"

George had been walking up and down the room.

"She's lost every cent!" he said savagely. And he flung both hands out with an air of frenzy before beginning his angry march again.

Mary sat in stony despair.

"Have you heard from her today?" he flung out.

His wife shook her head.

"Well, she's in town," George presently resumed, "because Bates told me she telephoned the office while I was out this morning. Now, listen, Mary. I've done all I'm going to do for your mother! And she's not to enter this house again--do you understand?"

"George!" said Mary.

"She is not going to ENTER MY HOUSE," reiterated George. "I have often wondered what led to estrangements in families, but by the Lord, I think there's some excuse in this case! She lies to me, she sets my judgment at naught, she does the things with my children that I've expressly asked her not to do, she cultivates the people I loathe, she works you into a state of nervous collapse--it's too much! Now she's thrown her income away,--thrown it away! Now I tell you, Mary, I'll support her, if that's what she expects--"

"Really, George, you are--you are--Be careful!" Mary exclaimed, roused in her turn. "You forget to whom you are speaking. I admit that Mamma is annoying, I admit that you have some cause for complaint,--but you forget to whom you are speaking! I love my mother," said Mary, her feeling rising with every word. "I won't have her so spoken of! Not have her enter the house again? Why, do you suppose I am going to meet her in the street, and send her clothes after her as if she were a discharged servant?"

"She may come here for her clothes," George conceded, "but she shall not spend another night under my roof. Let her try taking care of herself for a change!"

There was a silence.

"George, DON'T you see how unreasonable you are?" Mary said, after a bitter struggle for calm.

"That's final," George said briefly.

"I don't know what you mean by final," his wife answered with warmth. "If you really think--"

"I won't argue it, my dear. And I won't have my life ruined by your mother, as thousands of men's lives have been ruined, by just such unscrupulous irresponsible women!"

"George," said Mary, very white, "I won't turn against my mother!"

"Then you turn against me," George said in a deadly calm.

"Do you expect her to board, George, in the same city that I have my home?" Mary demanded, after a pause.

"Plenty of women do it," George said inflexibly.

"But, George, you know Mamma! She'd simply be here all the time; it would come to exactly the same thing. She'd come after breakfast, and you'd have to take her home after dinner. She'd have her clothes made here, and laundered here, and she'd do all her telephoning..."

"That is exactly what has got to stop," said George. "I will pay her board at some good place. But I'll pay it... she won't touch the money. Besides that, she can have an allowance. But she must understand that she is NOT to come here except when she is especially invited, at certain intervals."

"George, DEAR, that is absolutely absurd!"

"Very well," George said, flushing, "but if she is here to-night, I will not come home. I'll dine at the club. When she has gone, I'll come home again."

Mary's head was awhirl. She scarcely knew where the conversation was leading then, or what the reckless things they said involved. She was merely feeling blindly now for the arguments that should give her the advantage.

"You needn't stay at the club, George," she said, "for Mamma and I will go down to Beach Meadow. When you have come to your senses, I'll come back. I'll let Miss Fox go, and Mamma and I will look out for the children--"

"I warn you," George interrupted her coldly, "that if you take any such step, you will have a long time to think it over before you hear from me! I warn you that it has taken much less than this to ruin the happiness of many a man and woman!"

Mary faced him, breathing hard. This was their first real quarrel. Brief times of impatience, unsympathy, differences of opinion there had been, but this--this Mary felt even now--was gravely different. With a feeling curiously alien and cold, almost hostile, she eyed the face opposite her own; the strange face that had been so familiar and dear only at breakfast time.

"I WILL go," she said quietly. "I think it will do us both good."

"Nonsense!" George said. "I won't permit it."

"What will you do, make a public affair of it?"

"No, you know I won't do that. But don't talk like a child, Mary. Remember, I mean what I say about your mother, and tell her so when she arrives."

After that, he went away. A long time passed, while Mary sat very still in the big leather chair at the head of the table. The sunlight shifted, fell lower,--shone ruby red through a decanter of claret on the sideboard. The house was very still.

After a while she went slowly upstairs. She dragged a little trunk from a hall closet, and began quietly, methodically, to pack it with her own clothes. Now and then her breast rose with a great sob, but she controlled herself instantly.

"This can't go on," she said aloud to herself. "It's not today--it's not to-morrow--but it's for all time. I can't keep this up. I can't worry and apologize, and neglect George, and hurt Mamma's feelings for the rest of my life. Mamma has always done her best for me, and I never saw George until five years ago--

"It's not," she went on presently, "as if I were a woman who takes marriage lightly. I have tried. But I won't desert Mamma. And I won't--I will NOT!--endure having George talk to me as he did today!"

She would go down to the children, she would rest, she would read again during the quiet evenings. Days would go by, weeks. But finally George would write her--would come to her. He must. What else could he do?

Something like terror shook her. Was this the way serious, endless separations began between men and their wives? Her mind flitted sickly to other people's troubles: the Waynes, who had separated because Rose liked gayety and Fred liked domestic peace; the Gardiners, who--well, there never did seem to be any reason there. Frances and the baby just went to her mother's home, and stayed home, and after a while people said she and Sid had separated, though Frances said she would always like Sid as a friend--not very serious reasons, these! Yet they had proved enough.

Mary paused. Was she playing with fire? Ah, no, she told herself, it was very different in her case. This was no imaginary case of "neglect" or "incompatibility." There was the living trouble,-- Mamma. And even if tonight she conceded this point to George, and Mamma was banished, sooner or later resentment, bitter and uncontrollable, would rise again, she knew, in her heart. No. She would go. George might do the yielding.

Once or twice tears threatened her calm. But it was only necessary to remind herself of what George had said to dry her eyes into angry brilliance again. Too late now for tears.

At five o'clock the trunk was packed, but Mamma had not yet arrived. There remained merely to wait for her, and to start with her for Beach Meadow. Mary's heart was beating fast now, but it was less with regret than with a nervous fear that something would delay her now. She turned the key in the trunk lock and straightened up with the sudden realization that her back was aching.

For a moment she stood, undecided, in the centre of her room. Should she leave a little note for George, "on his pincushion," or simply ask Lizzie to say that she had gone to Beach Meadow? He would not follow her there, she knew; George understood her. He knew of how little use bullying or coaxing would be. There would be no scenes. She would be allowed to settle down to an existence that would be happy for Mamma, good for the children, restful--free from distressing strain--for Mary herself.

With a curious freedom from emotion of any sort, she selected a hat, and laid her gloves beside it on the bed. Just then the front door, below her, opened to admit the noise of hurried feet and of joyous laughter. Several voices were talking at once. Mary, to whom the group was still invisible, recognized one of these as belonging to Mamma. As she went downstairs, she had only time for one apprehensive thrill, before Mamma herself ran about the curve of the stairway, and flung herself into Mary's arms.

Mamma was dressed in corn-colored silk, over which an exquisite wrap of the same shade fell in rich folds. Her hat was a creation of pale yellow plumes and hydrangeas, her silk stockings and little boots corn-colored. She dragged the bewildered Mary down the stairway, and Mary, pausing at the landing, looked dazedly at her husband, who stood in the hall below with a dark, middle-aged man whom she had never seen before.

"Here she is!" Mamma cried joyously. "Richie, come kiss her right this minute! Ma'y, darling, this is your new papa!"

"WHAT!" said Mary, faintly. But before she knew it the strange man did indeed kiss her, and then George kissed her, and Mamma kissed her again, and all three shouted with laughter as they went over and over the story. Mary, in all the surprise and confusion, still found time to marvel at the sight of George's radiant face.

"Carter--of all people!" said George, with a slap on the groom's shoulder. "I loved his dea' wife like a sister!" Mamma threw in parenthetically, displaying to Mary's eyes her little curled-up fist with a diamond on it quite the width of the finger it adorned. "Strangely enough," said Mr. Carter, in a deep, dignified boom, "your husband and I had never met until to-day, Mrs.--ah, Mary-- when-" his proud eye travelled to the corn-colored figure, "when this young lady of mine introduced us!"

"Though we've exchanged letters, eh?" George grinned, cutting the wires of a champagne bottle. For they were about the dining-room table now, and the bride's health was to be drunk.

Mary, managing with some effort to appear calm, outwardly congratulatory, interested, and sympathetic; and already feeling somewhere far down in her consciousness an exhilarated sense of amusement and relief at this latest performance of Mamma's,--was nevertheless chiefly conscious of a deep and swelling indignation against George.

George! Oh, he could laugh now; he could kiss, compliment, rejoice with Mamma now, he could welcome and flatter Richard Carter now, although he had repudiated and insulted the one but a few hours ago, and had for years found nothing good to say of the other! He could delightedly involve Mary in his congratulations and happy prophecies now, when but today he had half broken her heart!

"Lovely!" she said, smiling automatically and rising with the others when the bridegroom laughingly proposed a toast to the firm that might some day be "Venable and Carter," and George insisted upon drinking it standing, and, "Oh, of course, I understand how sudden it all was, darling!" "Oh, Mamma, won't that be heavenly!" she responded with apparent rapture to the excited outpourings of the bride. But at her heart was a cold, dull weight, and her sober eyes went again and again to her husband's face.

"Oh, no!" she would say to herself, watching him, "you can't do that, George! You can't change about like a weathercock, and expect me to change, too, and forget everything that went before! You've chosen to dig the gulf between us--I'm not like Mamma, I'm not a child--my dignity and my rights can't be ignored in this fashion!"

No, the matter involved more than Mamma now. George should be punished; he should have his scare. Things must be all cleared up, explained, made right between them. A few weeks of absence, a little realization of what he had done would start their marriage off again on a new footing.

She kissed her mother affectionately at the door, gave the new relative a cordial clasp with both hands.

"We'll let you know in a week or two where we are," said Mamma, all girlish confusion and happiness. "You have my suit-case, Rich'? That's right, dea'. Good-by, you nice things!"

"Good-by, darling!" Mary said. She walked back into the empty library, seated herself in a great chair, and waited for George.

The front door slammed. George reappeared, chuckling, and rubbing his hands together. He walked over to a window, held back the heavy curtain, and watched the departing carriage out of sight.

"There they go!" he said. "Carter and your mother--married, by Jove! Well, Mary, this is about the best day's work for me that's come along for some time. Carter was speaking in the carriage only an hour ago about the possibility of our handling the New Nassau Bridge contract together. I don't know why not." George mused a moment, smilingly.

"I thought you had an utter contempt for him as a business man," Mary said stingingly--involuntarily, too, for she had not meant to be diverted from her original plan of a mere dignified farewell.

"Never for him," George said promptly. "I don't like some of his people. Burns, his chief construction engineer, for instance. But I've the greatest respect for him! And your mother!" said George, laughing again. "And how pretty she looked, too! Well, sir, they walked in on me this afternoon. I never was so surprised in my life! You know, Mary," said George, taking his own big leather chair, stretching his legs out luxuriously, and eying the tip of a cigar critically, "you know that your mother is an extremely fascinating woman! You'll see now how she'll blossom out, with a home of her own again--he's got a big house over on the Avenue somewhere, beside the Bar Kock place--and he runs three or four cars. Just what your mother loves!"

Mary continued to regard her husband steadily, silently. One look at the fixed expression of contempt on her face would have enlightened him, but George was lighting his cigar now, and did not glance at her.

"I'll tell you another thing, Mary," said George, after a match- scratching-and-puffing interlude, "I'll tell you another thing, my dear. You're an angel, and you don't notice these things as I do, but, by Jove, your mother was reaching the point where she pretty nearly made trouble between us! Fact!" he pursued, with a serious nod. "I get tired, you know, and nervous, and unreasonable--you must have had it pretty hard sometimes this month between your mother and me! I get hot--you know I don't mean anything! If you hadn't the disposition of a saint, things would have come to a head long ago. Now this very morning I talked to you like a regular kid. Mary, the minute I got back to the office I was ashamed of myself. Why, ninety-nine women out of a hundred would have raised the very deuce with me for that! But, by Jove--" his voice dropped to a pause.

"By Jove," George went on, "you are an angel! Now tell me the honest truth, old girl, didn't you resent what I said to-day, just for a minute?"

"I certainly did," Mary responded promptly and quietly, but with an uncomfortable sense of lessened wrath. "What you said was absolutely unwarrantable and insulting!"

"I'll BET you did!" said George, giving her a glance that was a little troubled, and a little wistful, too. "It was insulting, it was unwarrantable. But, my Lord, Mary, you know how I love your mother!" he continued eagerly. "She and I are the best of friends. We rasp each other now and then, but we both love you too much ever to come to real trouble. I'm no angel, Mary," said George, looking down his cigar thoughtfully, "but as men go, I'm a pretty decent man. You know how much time I've spent at the club since we were married. You know the fellows can't rope me into poker games or booze parties. I love my wife and my kids and my home. But when I think of you, and realize how unworthy I am of you, by Heaven--!" He choked, shook his head, finding further speech for a moment difficult. "There's no man alive who's worthy of you!" he finished. "The Lord's been very good to me."

Mary's eyes had filled, too. She sat for a minute, trying to steady her suddenly quivering lips. She looked at George sitting there in the twilight, and said to herself it was all true. He WAS good, he WAS steady, he was indeed devoted to her and to the children. But-- but he had insulted her, he had broken her heart, she couldn't let him off without some rebuke.

"You should have thought of these things before you--" she began, with a very fair imitation of scorn in her voice. But George interrupted her. His hands were clasped loosely between his knees, his head hanging dejectedly.

"I know," he said despondently, "I know!"

Mary paused. What she had still to say seemed suddenly flat. And in the pause her mother's one piece of advice came to her mind. After all it only mattered that he was unhappy, and he was hers, and she could make him happy again.

She left her chair, went with a few quick steps to her husband's side, and knelt, and put her cheek against his shoulder. He gave a great boyish laugh of relief and pleasure and put his arms about her.

"How old are you, George?" she said.

"How old am I? What on earth--why, I'm forty," he said.

"I was just thinking that the best of you men is only a little boy, and should be treated as such!" said Mary, kissing him.

"You can treat me as you like," he assured her, joyously. "And I'm starving. And unless you think there is any likelihood of Mamma dropping in and spoiling our plan, I would like to take you out to dinner."

"Well, she might," Mary agreed with a happy laugh, "so I'll simply run for my hat. You never can be sure, with Mamma!"

THE MEASURE OF MARGARET COPPERED

Duncan Coppered felt that his father's second marriage was a great mistake. He never said so; that would not have been Duncan's way. But he had a little manner of discreetly compressing his lips, when, the second Mrs. Coppered was mentioned, eying his irreproachable boots, and raising his handsome brows, that was felt to be significant. People who knew and admired Duncan--and to know him was to admire him--realized that he would never give more definite indications of filial disapproval than these. His exquisite sense of what was due his father's wife from him would not permit it. But all the more did the silent sympathy of his friends go out to him.

To Harriet Culver he said the one thing that these friends, comparing notes, considered indicative of his real feeling. Harriet, who met him on the Common one cold afternoon, reproached him, during the course of a slow ride, for his non-appearance at various dinners and teas.

"Well, I've been rather bowled over, don't you know? I've been getting my bearings," said Duncan, simply.

"Of course you have!" said Harriet, with an expectant thrill.

"I'd gotten to count on monopolizing the governor," pursued Duncan, presently, with a rueful smile. "I shall feel no end in the way for a while, I'm afraid, Of course, I didn't think Dad would always keep"-his serious eyes met Harriet's--"always keep my mother's place empty; but this came rather suddenly, just the same."

"Had your father written you?" said Harriet, confused between fear of saying the wrong thing and dread of a long silence.

"Oh, yes!" Duncan attempted an indifferent tone. "He had written me in August about meeting Miss Charteris and her little brother in Rome, you know, and how much he liked her. Her brother was an invalid, and died shortly after; and then Dad met her again in Paris, quite alone, and they were married immediately."

He fell silent. Presently Harriet said daringly: "She's--clever; she's gifted, isn't she?"

"I think you were very bold to say that, dear!" said Mrs. Van Winkle, when Harriet repeated this conversation, some hours later, in the family circle.

"Oh, Aunt Minnie, I had to--to see what he'd say."

"And what did he say?" asked Harriet's mother,

"He looked at me gravely, you know, until I was ashamed of myself," the girl confessed, "and then he said: 'Why, Hat, you must know that Mrs. Coppered was a professional actress?'"

"And a very obscure little actress, at that," finished Mrs. Culver, nodding.

"Pacific Coast stock companies or something like that," said Harriet. "Well, and then, after a minute, he said, so sadly, 'That's what hurts, although I hate myself for letting it make a difference.'"

"Duncan said that?" Mrs. Van Winkle was incredulous.

"Poor boy! With one aunt Mrs. Vincent-Hunter and the other an English duchess! The Coppereds have always been among Boston's best families. It's terrible," said Mrs. Culver.

"Well, I think it is," the girl agreed warmly. "Judge Clyde Potter's grandson, and brought up with the very nicest people, and sensitive as he is--I think it's just too bad it should be Duncan!"

"There's no doubt she was an actress, I suppose, Emily?"

"Well," said Harriet's mother, "it's not denied." She shrugged eloquently.

"Shall you call, mother?"

"Oh, I shall have to once, I suppose. The Coppereds, you know. Every one will call on her for Carey's sake," said Mrs. Culver, sighing.

Every one duly called on Mrs. Carey Coppered, when she returned to Boston; and although she made her mourning an excuse for declining all formal engagements, she sent out cards for an "at home" on a Friday in January. She was a thin, graceful woman, with the blue- black Irish eyes that are set in with a sooty finger, and an unexpectedly rich, deep voice. Her quiet, almost diffident manner was obviously accentuated just now by her recent sorrow; but this did not conceal from her husband's friends the fact that the second Mrs. Coppered was not of their world. Everything charming she might be, but to the manner born she was not. They would not meet her on her own ground, she could not meet them on theirs. In her own home she listened like a puzzled, silenced child to the gay chatter that went on about her.

Duncan stood with his father, at his stepmother's side, on her afternoon at home, prompting her when names or faces confused her, treating her with a little air of gracious intimacy eminently becoming and charming under the circumstances. His tact stood between her and more than one blunder, and it was to be noticed that she relied upon him even more than upon his father. Carey Coppered, indeed, hitherto staid and serious, was quite transformed by his joy and pride in her, and would not have seen a thousand blunders on her part. The consensus of opinion, among his friends, was that Carey was "really a little absurd, don't you know?" and that Mrs. Carey was "quite deliciously odd," and that Duncan was "too wonderful-- poor, dear boy!"

Mrs. Coppered would have agreed that her stepson was wonderful, but with quite a literal meaning. She found him a real cause for wonder- -this poised, handsome, crippled boy of nineteen, with his tailor, and his tutor, and his groom, and the heavy social responsibilities that bored him so heartily. With the honesty of a naturally brilliant mind cultivated by hard experience, and much solitary reading, she was quite ready to admit that her marriage had placed her in a new and confusing environment; she wanted only to adapt herself, to learn the strange laws by which it was controlled. And she would naturally have turned quite simply to Duncan for help.

But Duncan very gently, very coldly, repelled her. He was representative of his generation. Things were not LEARNED by the best people; they were instinctively KNOWN. The girls that Duncan knew--the very children in their nurseries--never hesitated over the wording of a note of thanks, never innocently omitted the tipping of a servant, never asked their maid's advice as to suitable frocks and gloves for certain occasions. All these things, and a thousand more, his stepmother did, to his cold embarrassment and annoyance.

The result was unfortunate in two ways. Mrs. Coppered shrank under the unexpressed disapproval into more than her native timidity, rightly thinking his attitude represented that of all her new world; and Carey, who worshipped his young wife, perceived at last that Duncan was not championing his stepmother, and for the first time in his life showed a genuine displeasure with his son.

This was exquisitely painful to Margaret Coppered. She knew what father and son had been to each other before her coming; she knew, far better than Carey, that the boy's adoration of his father was the one vital passion of his life. Mrs. Ayers, the housekeeper, sometimes made her heartsick with innocent revelations.

"From the day his mother died, Mrs. Coppered, my dear, when poor little Master Duncan wasn't but three weeks old, I don't believe he and his father were separated an hour when they could be together! Mr. Coppered would take that little owl-faced baby downstairs with him when he came in before dinner, and 'way into the night they'd be in the library together, the baby laughing and crowing, or asleep on a pillow on the sofa. Why, the boy wasn't four when he let the nurse go, and carried the child off for a month's fishing in Canada! And when we first knew that the hip was bad, Mr. Coppered gave up his business and for five years in Europe he never let Master Duncan out of his sight. The games and the books--I should say the child had a million lead soldiers! The first thing in the morning it'd be, 'Is Dad awake, Paul?' and he running into the room; and at noon, coming back from his ride, 'Is Dad home?' Wonderful to him his father's always been."

"That's why I'm afraid he'll never like me," Margaret was quite simple enough to say wistfully, in response. "He never laughs out or chatters, as Mr. Coppered says he used to do."

And after such a conversation she would be especially considerate of Duncan--find some excuse for going upstairs when she heard the click of his crutch in the hall, so that he might find his father alone in the library, or excuse herself from a theatre trip so that they might be together.

"Oh, I'm so glad the Poindexters want us!" she said one night, over her letters.

"Why?" said Carey, amused by her ardor. "We can't go."

"I know it. But they're such nice people, Carey. Duncan will be so pleased to have them want me!"

Her husband laughed out suddenly, but a frown followed the laugh.

"You're very patient with the boy, Margaret. I--well, I've not been very patient lately, I'm afraid. He manages to exasperate me so, with these grandiose airs, that he doesn't seem the same boy at all!"

Mrs. Coppered came over to take the arm of his chair and put her white fingers on the little furrow between his eyes.

"It breaks my heart when you hurt him, Carey! He broods over it so. And, after all, he's only doing what they all--all the people he knows would do!"

"I thought better things of him," said his father.

"If you go to Yucatan in February, Carey," Margaret said, "he and I'll be here alone, and then we'll get on much smoother, you'll see."

"I don't know," he said. "I hate to go this year; I hate to leave you."

But he went, nevertheless, for the annual visit to his rubber plantation; and Margaret and Duncan were left alone in the big house for six weeks. Duncan took especial pains to be considerate of his stepmother in his father's absence, and showed her that he felt her comfort to be his first care. He came and went like a polite, un-responsive shadow, spending silent evenings with her in the library, or acting as an irreproachable and unapproachable escort when escort was needed. Margaret, watching him, began to despair of ever gaining his friendship.

Late one wintry afternoon the boy came in from a concert, and was passing the open door of his step-mother's room when she called him. He found her standing by one of the big windows, a very girlish figure in her trim walking-suit and long furs. The face she turned to him, under her wide hat, was rosy from contact with the nipping spring air.

"Duncan," she said, "I've had such a nice invitation from Mrs. Gregory."

Duncan's face brightened.

"Mrs. Jim?" said he.

"No, indeed!" exulted Margaret, gayly. "Mrs. Clement."

"Oh, I say!" said Duncan, smiling too. For if young Mrs. Jim Gregory's friend-ship was good, old Mrs. Clement's was much better. For the first time, he sat down informally in Margaret's room and laid aside his crutch.

"She's going to take General and Mrs. Wetherbee up to Snowhill for three or four days," pursued Margaret, "and the Jim Gregorys and Mr. Fred Gregory and me. Won't your father be pleased? Now, Duncan, what clothes do I need?"

"Oh, the best you've got," said Duncan, instantly interested; and, until it was time to dress for dinner, the two were deep in absorbed consultation.

Duncan was whistling as he went upstairs to dress, and his stepmother was apparently in high spirits. But twenty minutes later, when he found her in the library, there was a complete change. Her eyes were worried, her whole manner distressed, and her voice sharp. She looked up from a telegram as he came in.

"I've just had a wire from an old friend in New York," said she, "and I want you to telephone the answer for me, will you, Duncan? I've not a moment to spare. I shall have to leave for New York at the earliest possible minute. After you've telephoned the wire, will you find out about the trains from South Station? And get my ticket and reservation, will you? Or send Paul for them--whatever's quickest."

Duncan hardly recognized her. Her hesitation was gone, her diffidence gone. She did not even look at him as she spoke; his scowl passed entirely unnoticed. He stood coldly disapproving.

"I don't really see how you can go," he began. "Mrs. Gregory--"

"Yes, I know!" she agreed hastily. "I telephoned. She hadn't come in yet, so I had to make it a message--simply that Mrs. Coppered couldn't manage it tomorrow. She'll be very angry, of course. Duncan, would it save any time to have Paul take this right to the telegraph station--"

"Surely," Duncan interrupted in turn, "you're not going to rush off--"

"Oh, surely--surely--surely--I am!" she answered, fretted by his tone. "Don't tease me, dear boy! I've quite enough to worry over! I- -I"--she pushed her hair childishly off her face--"I wish devoutly that your father was here. He always knows in a second what's to be done! But--but fly with this telegram, won't you?" she broke off suddenly.

Duncan went. The performance of his errand was not reassuring. The telegram was directed to Philip Penrose, at the Colonial Theatre, and read:

Will be with you this evening. Depend on me. Heartsick at news. MARGARET.

When he went upstairs again, he rapped at his stepmother's door. Hatted, and with a fur coat over her arm, she opened it.

"Are you taking Fanny?" said Duncan, icily. Fanny, the maid, middle- aged, loyal, could be trusted with the honor of the Coppereds.

"Heavens, no!" said Mrs. Coppered, vigorously.

"Then I hope you will not object to my escort," said the boy, flushing.

If he meant it for reproach, it missed its mark. Mrs. Coppered's surprised look became doubtful, finally changed to relief.

"Why, that's very sweet of you, Duncan," she said graciously, "especially as I can't tell you what I'm going for, my dear, for it may not occur. But I think, of all people in the world, you're the one to go with me!"

Duncan eyed her severely.

"At the same time," he said, "I can't for one moment pretend--"

"Exactly; so that it's all the nicer of you to volunteer to come along!" she said briskly. "You'll have to hurry, Duncan. And ask Paul to come up for my trunk, will you? We leave the house in half an hour!"

Mrs. Coppered advised her stepson to supply himself with magazines on the train.

"For I shall have to read," she said, "and perhaps you won't be able to sleep."

And read she did, with hardly a look or a word for him. She turned and re-turned the pages of a little paper-covered book, moving her lips and knitting her brows over it as she read.

Duncan, miserably apprehensive that they would meet some acquaintance and have to give an explanation of their mad journey, satisfied himself that there was no such immediate danger, and, assuming a forbidding expression, sat erect in his seat. But he finally fell into an uneasy sleep, not rousing himself until the train drew into the Forty-second Street station late in the evening. His stepmother had made a rough pillow of his overcoat and put it between his shoulder and the window-frame; but he did not comment upon it as he slipped it on and followed her through the roaring, chilly station to a taxicab.

"The Colonial Theatre, as fast as you can!" said she, as they jumped in. She was obviously nervous, biting her lips and humming under her breath as she watched the brilliantly lighted streets they threaded so slowly. Almost before it stopped she was out of the cab, at the entrance of a Broadway theatre. Duncan, alert and suspicious, read the name "Colonial" in flaming letters, and learned from a larger sign that Miss Eleanor Forsythe and an all-star cast were appearing therein in a revival of Reade's "Masks and Faces."

In the foyer Mrs. Coppered asked authoritatively for the manager. It was after ten o'clock, the curtain had risen on the last act, and a general opinion prevailed that Mr. Wyatt had gone home. But Mrs. Coppered's distinguished air, her magnificent furs, her beauty, all had their effect, and presently Duncan followed her into the hot, untidy little office where the manager was to be found.

He was a pleasant, weary-looking man, who wheeled about from his desk as they came in, and signed the page to place chairs.

"Mr. Wyatt," said Mrs. Coppered, with her pleasantest smile, "can you give us five minutes?"

"I can give you as many as you like, madam," said the manager, patiently, but with a most unpromising air.

"Only five!" she reassured him, as they sat down. Then, with an absolutely businesslike air, she continued: "Mr. Wyatt, you have Mr. and Mrs. Penrose in your company, I think, both very old friends of mine. She's playing Mabel Vane,--Mary Archer is the name she uses,-- and he's Triplet. Isn't that so?"

The manager nodded, eying her curiously.

"Mr. Wyatt, you've heard of their trouble, of course? The accident this morning to their little boy?"

"Ah, yes--yes," said Wyatt. "Of course. Hurt by a fall, poor little fellow. Very serious. Yes, poor things! Did you want to see--"

"You know that one of your big surgeons here--I've forgotten the name!--is to operate on little Phil tomorrow?" asked Mrs. Coppered.

"So Penrose said," assented the manager, slowly, watching her as if a little surprised at her insistence.

"Mr. Wyatt." said Mrs. Coppered,--and Duncan noticed that she had turned a little pale,--"Mrs. Penrose wired me news of all this only a few hours ago. She is half frantic at the idea that she must go on tomorrow afternoon and evening; yet the understudy is ill, and she felt it was too short notice to ask you to make a change now. But it occurred to me to come to see you about it. I want to ask you a favor. I want you to let me play Mrs. Penrose's part tomorrow afternoon and tomorrow night. I've played Mabel Vane a hundred times; it's a part I know very well," she went on quickly. "I--I am not in the least afraid that I can't take it. And then she can be with the little boy through the operation and afterward--he's only five, you know, at the unreasonable age when all children want their mothers! Can't that be arranged, Mr. Wyatt?"

Duncan, holding a horrified breath, fixed his eyes, as he did, on the manager's face. He was relieved at the inflexible smile he saw there.

"My dear lady," said Wyatt, kindly, "that is--absolutely--OUT of the question! Anything in reason I will be delighted to do for Penrose and Miss Archer--but you must surely realize that I can't do that!"

"But wait!" said Mrs. Coppered, eagerly, not at all discouraged. "Don't say no yet! I AM an actress, Mr. Wyatt, or was one. I know the part thoroughly. And the circumstances--the circumstances are unusual, aren't they?"

While she was speaking the manager was steadily shaking his head.

"I have no doubt you could play the part," said he, "but I can't upset my whole company by substituting now. Tomorrow is going to be a big night. The house is completely sold out to the Masons--their convention week, you know. As it happens, there couldn't be a more inconvenient time. No, I can't consider it!"

Mrs. Coppered smiled at him. She had a very winning smile.

"It would mean a rehearsal; I suppose THAT would be inconvenient, to begin with," she said.

"Exactly," said Wyatt. "Friday night. I can't ask my people to rehearse to-morrow."

"But suppose you put it to them and they were all willing?" pursued the lady.

"My dear lady, I tell you it's absolutely--" He made a goaded gesture. Then, making fierce little dashes and dots on his blotter with his pencil, and eying each one ferociously as he made it, he added irritably, but in a quieter tone: "You're an actress, eh? Where'd you get your experience?"

"With various stock companies on the Pacific Coast," she answered readily. "My name was Margaret Charteris. I don't suppose you ever heard it?"

"As it happens, I HAVE," he returned, surprised into interest. "You knew Joe Pitcher, of course. He spoke of you. I remember the name very well."

"Professor Pitcher!" she exclaimed radiantly. "Of course I knew him- -dear old man! Where is he--still there?"

"Still there," he assented absently. "You married, I think?"

"I am Mrs. Coppered now--Mrs. Carey Coppered," she said. The man gave her a suddenly awakened glance.

"Surely," he said thoughtfully. They looked steadily at each other, and Duncan saw the color come into Margaret's face. There was a little silence.

Then the manager flung down his pencil, wheeled about in his chair, and rubbed his hands briskly together.

"Well!" he said. "And you think you can take Miss Archer's place, Mrs. Coppered?"

"If you will let me."

"Why," he said,--and Duncan would not have believed that the somewhat heavy face could wear a look so pleasant,--"you are doing so much, Mrs. Coppered, in stepping into the gap this way, that I'll do my share if I can! Perhaps I can't arrange it, but we can try. I'll call a rehearsal and speak to Miss Forsythe to-night. If you know the part, it's just possible that by going over it now we can get out of a rehearsal tomorrow. She wants to be with the little boy, eh?" he added musingly. "Yes, I suppose it might make a big difference, his not being terrified by strangers." And then, turning toward Margaret, he said warmly and a little awkwardly: "This is a remarkably kind thing for you to do, Mrs. Coppered."

"Oh, I would do more than that for Mary Penrose," said she, with a little difficulty. "She knows it. She wired me as a mad last hope today, and we came as fast as we could, Mr. Coppered and I." And she introduced Duncan very simply: "My stepson, Mr. Wyatt."

Duncan, fuming, could be silent no longer.

"I hope my--Mrs. Coppered is not serious in offering to do this," said he, very white, and in a slightly shaking voice. "I assure you that my father--that every one!--would think it a most extraordinary thing to do!"

Mrs. Coppered laid her hand lightly on his arm.

"Yes, I know, Duncan!" said she, quickly, soothingly. "I know how you feel! But--"

Duncan slightly repudiated the touch.

"I can't think how you can consider it!" he said passionately, but in a low voice. "A thing like this always gets out! You know--you know how your having been on the stage is regarded by our friends! It is simply insane--"

He had said a little more than he meant, in his high feeling, and Margaret's face had grown white.

"I asked you only for your escort, Duncan," she said gently, but with blazing eyes. There was open hostility in the look they exchanged.

"I can't see what good my escort does," said the boy, childishly, "when you won't listen to what you know is true!"

"Nevertheless, I still want it," she answered evenly. And after a moment Duncan, true to his training, and already a little ashamed of his ineffectual outburst,--for to waste a display of emotion was, in his code, a lamentable breach of etiquette,--shrugged his shoulders.

"Still want to stay with it?" said Mr. Wyatt, giving her a shrewd, friendly look.

"Certainly," she said promptly; but she was breathing fast.

"Then we might go and talk things over," he said; and a moment later they were crossing the theatre to the stage door. The final curtain had fallen only a moment before, but the lights were up, the orchestra halfway through a swift waltz, and the audience, buttoning coats and struggling with gloves, was pouring up the aisles. Duncan, through all his anger and apprehension, felt a little thrill of superiority over these departing playgoers as he and his stepmother were admitted behind the scenes. He was young, and the imagined romance of green-rooms and footlights appealed to him.

The company, suddenly summoned, appeared in various stages of street and stage attire. Peg, a handsome young woman with brilliant color and golden hair, still wore her brocaded gown and patches, and wore, in addition, a slightly affronted look at this unprecedented proceeding. The other members of the cast, yawning, slightly curious, were grouped about in the great draughty space between the wings that it cost Duncan some little effort to realize was the stage.

From this group, as Margaret followed the stage manager into the circle of light, a little woman suddenly detached herself, and, running across the stage and breaking into sobs as she ran, she was in Margaret's arms in a second.

"Oh, Meg, Meg, Meg!" she cried, laughing and crying at the same time. "I knew you'd come! I knew you'd manage it somehow! I've been praying so--I've been watching the clock! Oh, Meg," she went on pitifully, fumbling blindly for a handkerchief, "he's been suffering so, and I had to leave him! They thought he was asleep, but when I tried to loosen his little hand he woke up!"

"Mary--Mary!" said Mrs. Coppered, soothingly, patting the bowed shoulder.

No one else moved; a breathless attention held the group. "Of course I came," she went on, with a little triumphant laugh, "and I think everything's ALL right!"

"Yes, I know," said Mrs. Penrose, with a convulsive effort at self- control. She caught Margaret's soft big muff, and drew it across her eyes. "I'm ru-ru-ruining your fur, Margaret!" she said, laughing through tears, "but--but seeing you this way, and realizing that I could go--go--go to him now--"

"Mary, you must NOT cry this way," said Mrs. Coppered, seriously. "You don't want little Phil to see you with red eyes, do you? Mr. Wyatt and I have been talking it over," she went on, "but it remains to be seen, dear, if all the members of the company are willing to go to the trouble." Her apologetic look went around the listening circle. "It inconveniences every one, you know, and it would mean a rehearsal tonight--this minute, in fact, when every one's tired and cold." Her voice was soothing, very low. But the gentle tones carried their message to every one there. The mortal cleverness of such an appeal struck Duncan sharply, as an onlooker.

The warm-hearted star, Eleanor Forsythe, whose photographs Duncan had seen hundreds of times, was the first to respond with a half- indignant protest that SHE wasn't too tired and cold to do that much for the dear kiddy, and other volunteers rapidly followed suit. Ten minutes later the still tearful little mother was actually in a cab whirling through the dark streets toward the hospital where the child lay, and a rehearsal was in full swing upon the stage of the Colonial. Only the few actors actually necessary to the scenes in which Mabel figures need have remained; but a general spirit of sympathetic generosity kept almost the entire cast. Mr. Penrose, as Triplet, had the brunt of the dialogue to carry; and he and Margaret, who had quite unaffectedly laid aside her furs and entered seriously into the work of the evening, remained after all the others had lingered away, one by one.

Duncan watched from one of the stage boxes, his vague, romantic ideas of life behind the footlights rather dashed before the three hours of hard work were over. This was not very thrilling; this had no especial romantic charm. The draughts, the dust, the wide, icy space of the stage, the droning voices, the crisp interruptions, the stupid "business," endlessly repeated, all seemed equally disenchanting. The stagehands had set the stage for the next day's opening curtain, and had long ago departed. Duncan was cold, tired, headachy. He began to realize the edge of a sharp appetite, too; he and Margaret had barely touched their dinner, back at home those ages ago.

He could have forgiven her, he told himself, bitterly, if this plunge into her old life had had some little glory in it. If, for instance, Mrs. Gregory had asked her to play Lady Macbeth or Lady Teazle in amateur theatricals at home, why one could excuse her for yielding to the old lure. But this, this secondary part, these commonplace, friendly actors, this tiring night experience, this eager deference on her part to every one, this pitiful anxiety to please, where she should, as Mrs. Carey Coppered, have been proudly commanding and dictatorial--it was all exasperating and disappointing to the last degree; it was, he told himself, savagely, only what one might have expected!

Presently, when Duncan was numb in every limb, Margaret began to button herself into her outer wraps, and, escorted by Penrose, they went to supper. Duncan hesitated at the door of the cafe.

"This is an awful place, isn't it?" he objected. "You can't be going in here!"

"One must eat, Duncan!" Mrs. Coppered said blithely, leading the way. "And all the nice places are closed at this hour!" Duncan sullenly followed; but, in the flood of reminiscences upon which she and Penrose instantly embarked, his voice was not missed. Mollified in spite of himself by delicious food and strong coffee, he watched them, the man's face bright through its fatigue, his stepmother glowing and brilliant.

"I'll see this through for Dad's sake," said Duncan, grimly, to himself; "but, when he finds out about it, she'll have to admit I kicked the whole time!"

At four o'clock they reached the Penroses' hotel, where rooms were secured for Duncan and Margaret. The boy, dropping with sleep, heard her cheerfully ask at the desk to be called at seven o'clock.

"I've a cloak to buy," she explained, in answer to his glance of protest, "and a hairdresser to see, and a hat to find--they may be difficult to get, too! And I must run out and have just a glimpse of little Phil, and get to the theatre by noon; there's just a little more going over that second act to do! But don't you get up."

"I would prefer to," said Duncan, with dignity, taking his key.

But he did not wake until afternoon, when the thin winter sunlight was falling in a dazzling oblong on the floor of his room; and even then he felt a little tired and stiff. He reached for his watch-- almost one o'clock! Duncan's heart stood still. Had SHE overslept?

He sat up a little dazed, and, doing so, saw a note on the little table by his bed. It was from Margaret, and ran:

DEAR DUNCAN:

If you don't wake by one they're to call you, for I want you to see Mabel's entrance. I've managed my hat and cloak, and seen the child- -he's quiet and not in pain, thank God. Have your breakfast, and then come to the box-office; I'll leave a seat for you there. Or come behind and see me, if you will, for I am terribly nervous and would like it. So glad you're getting your sleep. MARGAEET.

P.S. Don't worry about the nerves; I ALWAYS am nervous.

Duncan looked at the note for three silent minutes, sitting on the edge of his bed.

"I'm sorry. She--she wanted me. I wish I'd waked!" he said slowly, aloud.

And ten minutes later, during a hurried dressing, he read the note again, and said, aloud again:

"'Have breakfast'! I wonder if she had HERS?"

He entered the theatre so late, for all his hurry, that the first act was over and the second well begun, and was barely in his seat before the now familiar opening words of Mabel Vane's part fell clearly on the silence of the darkened house.

For a moment Duncan thought, with a great pang of relief, that some one else was filling his stepmother's place; but he recognized her in another minute, in spite of rouge and powder and the piquant dress she wore. His heart stirred with something like pride. She was beautiful in her flowered hat and the caped coat that showed a foam of lacy frills at the throat; and she was sure of herself, he realized in a moment, and of her audience. She made a fresh and appealing figure of the plucky little country bride, and the old lines fell with delicious naturalness from her lips.

Duncan's heart hardly beat until the fall of the curtain; tears came to his eyes; and when Margaret shared the applause of the house with the gracious Peg, he found himself shaking with a violent nervous reaction.

He was still deeply stirred when he went behind the scenes after the play. His stepmother presently came up from her dressing-room, dressed in street clothes and anxious to hurry to the hospital and have news of the little boy.

Duncan called a taxicab, for which she thanked him absently and with worried eyes; and presently, with her and with the child's father, he found himself speeding toward the hospital. It was a silent trip. Margaret kept her ungloved fingers upon Penrose's hand, and said only a cheerful word of encouragement now and then.

Duncan waited in the cab, when they went into the big building. She was gone almost half an hour. Darkness came, and a sharp rain began to fall.

He was half drowsy when she suddenly ran down the long steps and jumped in beside him. Her face was radiant, in spite of the signs of tears about her eyes.

"He took the ether like a little soldier!" she said, as the motor- car slowly wheeled up the wet street. "Mary held his hand all the while. Everything went splendidly, and he came out of it at about four. Mary sang him off to sleep, sitting beside him, and she's still there--he hasn't stirred! Dr. Thorpe is more than well satisfied; he said the little fellow had nerves of iron! And the other doctor isn't even going to come in again! And Thorpe says it is LARGELY because he could have his mother!"

But the exhilaration did not last. Presently she leaned her head back against the seat, and Duncan saw how marked was the pallor of her face, now that the rouge was gone. There was fatigue in the droop of her mouth, and in the deep lines etched under her eyes.

"It's after six, Duncan," she said, without opening her eyes, "so I can't sleep, as I hoped! We'll have to dine, and then go straight to the theatre!"

"You're tired," said the boy, abruptly. She opened her eyes at the tone, and forced a smile.

"No--or, yes, I am, a little. My head's been aching. I wish to-night was over." Suddenly she sighed. "It's been a strain, hasn't it?" she said. "I knew it would be, but I didn't realize how hard! I just wanted to do something for them, you know, and this was all I could think of. And I've been wishing your father had been here; I don't know what he will say. I don't stop to think--when it's the people I love--" she said artlessly. "I dread--" she began again, but left the sentence unfinished, after all, and looked out of the window. "I suspect you're tired, too!" she went on brightly, after a moment. "I shan't forget what a comfort it's been to have you with me through this queer experience, Duncan. I know what it has cost you, my dear."

"Comfort!" echoed Duncan. He tried to laugh, but the laugh broke itself off gruffly. He found himself catching her hand, putting his free arm boyishly about her shoulders. "I'm not fit to speak to you, Margaret!" he said huskily. "You're-- you're the best woman I ever knew! I want you to know I'm sorry--sorry for it all--everything! And as for Dad, why, he'll think what I think--that you're the only person in the world who'd do all this for another woman's kid!"

Mrs. Coppered had tried to laugh, too, as she faced him. But the tears came too quickly. She put her wet face against his rough overcoat and for a moment gave herself up to the luxury of tears.

"Carey," said his wife, on a certain brilliant Sunday morning a month later, when he had been at home nearly a month. She put her head in at the library door. "Carey, will you do me a favor?"

He looked up to smile at her, in her gray gown and flowered hat, and she came in to take the seat opposite him at the broad table.

"I will. Where are you going?"

"Duncan and I are going to church, and you're to meet us at the Gregorys' for lunch," she reminded him.

"Yes'm. And what do you two kids want? What's the favor?"

"Oh!" She became serious. "You remember what I told you of our New York trip a month ago, Carey? The Penroses, you know?"

"I do."

"Well, Carey, I've discovered that it has been worrying Duncan ever since you got home, because he thinks I'm keeping it from you."

"Thinks you haven't told me, eh?"

"Yes. Don't laugh that way, Carey! Yes. And he asked me in the sweetest little way, a day or two ago, if I wouldn't tell you all about it."

"What did you do--box his young ears?"

"No." Margaret's eyes laughed, but she shook her head reprovingly. "I thought it was so DEAR of him to feel that way, yet never give you even a hint, that I--"

"Well?" smiled her husband, as she paused.

"Well," hesitated Mrs. Coppered. And then in a little burst she added: "I said, 'Duncan, if you ask me to I WILL tell him!'"

"And what do you think you gain by THAT, Sapphira?" said Carey, much amused.

"Why, don't you see? Don't you see it means EVERYTHING to him to have stood by me in this, and now to clear it all up between us! Don't you see that it makes him one of us, in a way? He's done his adored father a real service--"

"And his adored mother, too?"

His tone brought the happy tears to her eyes.

"And the favor?" he said presently.

"Oh! Well, you see, I'm supposed to be 'fessing up the whole horrible business, Carey, and in a day or two I want you to thank him, just in some general way,--you'll know how!--for looking out for me so well while you were away. Will you?"

"I will," he promised slowly.

"He's coming downstairs--so good-by!" said she. She came around the table to kiss him, and, suddenly smitten with a sense of youth and well-being and the glory of the spring morning, she added a little wistfully:

"I wonder what I've done to be so happy, Carey--I wonder what I've ever done to be so loved?"

"I wonder!" said Carey, smiling.

MISS MIX, KIDNAPPER

I

W ell, he has done it now, confound his nerve!" said Anthony Fox, Sr., in a tone of almost triumphant fury. He spread the loosely written sheets of a long letter on the breakfast table. "Here I am, just out of a sick-bed!" he pursued fretfully; "just home from a month's idling abroad, and now I'll have to go away out to California to lick some sense into that young fool!"

"For Heaven's sake, Tony, don't get yourself all worked up!" said handsome, stately Mrs. Fox, much more concerned for father than for son. She sighed resignedly as she folded a flattering request from her club for an address entitled, "Do We Forget Our Maids?" and gave him her full attention. "Read me the letter, dear," said she, placidly.

"Of course I always knew some woman would get hold of him," said Anthony, Sr., fumbling blindly for his mouth with a bit of toast, his eyes still on the letter; "but, by George, this sounds like Charlie Ross!"

"Woman!" repeated Mrs. Fox, with a relieved laugh. "Buddy's in love, is he? Don't worry, Tony, it won't last! Of all boys in the world he's the least likely to be foolish that way!"

"Of all boys in the world he's the kind that is easiest taken in!" said his father, dryly, securing the toast at last with a savage snap. "H-m--she's his landlady! Keeps fancy fowls and takes boarders--ha! Says they rather hope to be married in June. This has quite a settled tone to it, for Buddy. I don't like the look of it!"

"Nonsense!" said Mrs. Fox, with dawning uneasiness. "You don't mean to say he considers himself seriously engaged? At twenty! And to his landlady, too--I never heard such nonsense! Buddy's in no position to marry. Who IS the girl, anyway?"

"GIRL is good!" said the reader, bitterly. "She's thirty-two!"

Mrs. Fox, her hand hovering over a finger-bowl, grew rigid.

"Thirty-two!" she echoed blankly. Then sharply: "Anthony, do you think you can stop it?"

"I'll do what I can, believe me!" he assured her grimly. "Yes, sir, she's thirty-two! By the way, Fanny, this letter's already a month old. Why haven't I had it before?"

"You told them to hold only the office mail while you were travelling, you know," Mrs. Fox reminded him. "That one evidently has been following you. Anthony, can Tony marry without your consent?"

"No-o, but of course he's of age in five months, and if she's got her hooks deep enough into him, she--oh, confound such a complication, anyway!"

"It looks to me as if she wanted his money," said Mrs. Fox.

"H-m!" said his father, again deep in the letter. "That's just occurred to you, has it? Poor old Buddy--poor old Bud!"

"Oh, he'll surely get over it," said Mrs. Fox, uncertainly.

"He may, but you can bet SHE won't! Not before they're married, anyway. No, Bud's the sort that gets it hard, when he does get it!" his father said. "There's a final tone about the whole thing that I don't like. Listen to this!" He quoted from the letter with a rueful shake of the head. "'I don't know what the darling girl sees in me, dad, but she has turned down enough other fellows to know her own mind. At last I realize what Mrs. Browning's wonderful sonnets--'"

"He DOESN'T say that?" ejaculated the listener, incredulously.

"'She doesn't know I am writing you,'" Mr. Fox read on grimly, "'because I don't want her to worry about your objecting. But you won't object when you know her. She doesn't care anything about money, and says she will stick by me if we have to begin on an eighty-dollar-a-month job. You don't know how I love her, dad; it has changed my whole life. It's not just because she's beautiful, and all that. You will say that I am pretty young, but I know I can count on you for some sort of job to begin with, and things will work out all right.'"

"H-m!" said Mrs. Fox. "Yes, you're right, Tony. This is serious!"

"All worked out, you see," said the man, gloomily, as he drummed absently on the letter.

"Oh, Anthony, I can't help thinking of the Page boy, and that awful woman! Anthony, shall I go? Could I do any good if I went?"

"No," he said thoughtfully. "No, I'll go myself. Don't worry, Fanny, there's still time. Isn't it a curious thing that it's a quiet little fellow like Bud that--well, we'll see what can be done. I'll talk to this woman. She may think he has money of his own, you know. I'll buy her off if I can. Perhaps I can get him to go off somewhere with me for a trip. I'll see. Barker can look me up a train, and things here will have to wait. You'll see about my things, will you, Fanny--have 'em packed? Oh, and here's the letter--pretty sick reading you'll find it!"

"Be gentle with him!" said Mrs. Fox, deep in the boy's letter. "Thirty-two! Why, she might be his mother--in some countries she might, anyway. Anthony!"--her voice stopped him at the door--"IS her name Sally Mix?"

"Apparently," he said. "Can you beat it? It sounds like a drink!"

"Well," said Mrs. Fox, firmly, as if the name clenched the matter, "it must be STOPPED, that's all! Sally Mix! I hope she's WHITE!"

II

Just a week later, in Palo Alto, California, Anthony Fox slammed the gate of Miss Mix's garden loudly behind him, and eyed the Mix homestead with disapproval. The house was square and white, with doors and windows open to spring sunlight and air, and was surrounded by a garden space of flowers and trees and trim brick walks. The click of the gate brought a maid to the doorway.

"Mr. Fox won't be here until noon," said the maid, in answer to his question.

"Does Miss--could I see Miss Mix?" substituted Anthony, after a moment's thought.

He took a porch chair while she departed to find out.

"If you please," said the maid, suddenly reappearing, "Miss Mix is setting a Plymouth, and will you step right down?"

"Setting a--" scowled Anthony.

"Plymouth," supplied the maid, mildly.

Anthony eyed her suspiciously, but there was evidently nothing concealed behind her innocence of manner. Finally he followed the path she indicated as leading to Miss Mix. He followed it past the house, past clothes drying on lines, past scattered apple trees with whitewashed trunks, and down a board walk to the chicken yard.

No one was in sight. Anthony rattled the gate tentatively. A slim, neat, black Minorca fowl made an insulting remark about him to another hen. Both chuckled.

"Come in--come in and shut it!" called a clear voice from the interior of the chicken house.

Anthony's jaw stiffened.

"May I speak to you?" he called, with as much dignity as a person shouting at an utter stranger across an unfamiliar chicken yard may command.

"Certainly! Come right in!" called the voice, briskly.

Seeing nothing else to do, Anthony unwillingly crossed the yard, and stepped into the pleasant, whitewashed gloom of the chicken house. Loose chaff was scattered on the floor, and whitewashed boxes lined the walls. An adjoining shed held the roosts, which a few murmuring fowls were looping with heavy flights.

As he entered, a young woman in blue linen shut a gray hen into a box, and turned a pleasantly inquiring glance upon him.

"Good morning!" she said, smiling. "I knew you would want to see the thing sooner or later, so I asked Statia to show you right down here. Now, there's the trap"--she indicated a mass of loose chains and metal teeth on the floor--"and here's the key; but it simply WON'T work!"

Anthony was not following. He was staring at her. She was extremely pretty; that he had expected. But he had not expected that she--she- -well, he was not prepared for this sort of a woman at all! He must go slow here. He--she--Bud--

"I beg your pardon," he interrupted himself to stammer apologetically, "I didn't catch--you were saying--"

"The trap!" she said, smiling.

"Ah, the trap!" repeated Anthony, inanely.

"Certainly!" she said, with a hint of impatience. Then, as he still stared, she added quickly: "You're the man from Peterson's? From San Mateo? You came to fix it, didn't you?"

"Not at all," said Anthony, smiling. "I came from New York."

Light dawned in the girl's eyes. She gave a horrified laugh.

"Well, how stupid of me!" she ejaculated. "Of course, I thought you were. I'm expecting a man to fix the trap, any day, and you sent no name. I bought this affair a week ago; there's a coon, or a fox, or something, that's been coming down from the hills after my pullets; but it won't work."

"I don't know anything about traps," said Anthony.

He was wondering how he had best introduce himself. The vague campaign that he had outlined on those restless nights in the train would be useless here, he had decided. As he spoke, he absently touched the tangled chains and bolts with his foot.

"Don't do that!" screamed Miss Mix.

At the same second there was a victorious convulsion of metal teeth, and Anthony found himself frantically jerking at his foot, which was fast in the trap.

"Oh, you're caught! You are caught!" cried the girl, distressedly. "Oh, please don't hurt yourself tugging that way--you can't do it!"

Her eyes, full of concern and sympathy, met his for a second; then, suddenly, she broke into laughter.

"Why, confound the thing!" said Anthony, in pained surprise, as he struggled and twisted. "How does it open?"

"It DOESN'T!" choked Miss Mix, her mirth quite beyond control, as she gave various futile little tugs and twitches at the trap. "That's the trouble! The key never has had the slightest effect. Oh, I will NOT laugh this way!" she upbraided herself sternly. "Bu--bu-- but you did look so--" She abruptly turned her back upon him for a moment, facing him again with perfect calm, although with lashes still wet, and suspicious little dimples about her mouth. "Now, I'll get you out of it immediately, "she assured him gravely; "and meanwhile I can't tell you how sorry I am that--just sit on this box, you'll be more comfortable. I'll run and telephone a plumber, or some one." She paused in the doorway. "But I don't know your name?"

"Appropriately enough, it's Fox," said he, briefly; "Anthony Fox."

Miss Mix gasped, opened her mouth, shut it without speaking, and gasped again. Then she sat down heavily on a box.

"Of New York--I see!" said she, but more as if speaking to herself than to him. "Tony's father; he's written to you, and you've come all the way from New York to break it off. I see!" Desperation seemed to seize her. "Oh, my heavenly day!" she ejaculated. "Why didn't I think of this? This serves me right, you know," she said seriously, bringing her attention to bear fully upon Anthony; "but let me tell you, Mr. Fox, that this is about the worst thing you could have done!"

"The worst!" said Anthony, dully.

He felt utterly stupefied.

"Absolutely," said she, calmly. "You know you only hasten a thing like this by making an out-and-out fight of it. That's no way to stop it!"

"Are you Miss Mix?" said Anthony, feebly.

"I am." She nodded impatiently. "Sarah Mix."

"Then you and my son--" Anthony pursued patiently. "Didn't he write? Aren't you--"

"Engaged? Certainly we are," admitted the lady, with dignity. "And it would no more than serve you right if we got married, after all!" she added, with a sudden smile.

Anthony liked the smile. He smiled broadly in return.

"IF you got married! Do you mean you don't intend to?"

"I see I'll have to tell you," said Miss Mix, suddenly casting hesitation to the winds. "Then we can talk. Yes, we're engaged, Mr. Fox. What else could I do? Anthony's twenty; one can't treat him quite as if he were six. He's absolutely unable to take care of himself; and I've always liked him--always! How COULD I see a girl like Mollie Temple--but of course you don't know her. She's with the 'Giddy Middy' company, playing in San Francisco now."

"No, I don't know her," said Mr. Fox, stiffly.

"Well," continued Miss Mix, "her mother lives here in Palo Alto, and Mollie came home for September. Tony was just what she was looking for. A secret marriage, a sensational divorce, and alimony--Mollie asks nothing more of Fate! She made him her slave."

"Lord!" said Anthony.

"Every one was talking about it," continued Miss Mix; "but I never dreamed of interfering until Thanksgiving, when the Temples planned a week's house-party in Santa Cruz, and asked Tony to go. That would have settled it; so I managed to see Tony, and from that day on I may say I never let go of him. I took him about, I accompanied him when he sang--just big-sistered him generally! I'm thirty-two, you know, and I never dreamed he would--but he DID. New Year's night, Mr. Fox. Well, then I either had to say no, and let him go again, or say yes, and hold him. So I said yes. I couldn't stop him from planning, and I never dreamed he'd write you! Now, do you begin to see?"

"I see," said Anthony, huskily.

He cleared his throat.

"Meanwhile," pursued Miss Mix, glowing delightedly in the sympathy of her listener, "I introduced him to the Rogerses and the Peppers, and lots of jolly people, who are doing him a world of good. He goes about--he's developing. And now, just as I began to hope that the time had come when we could quietly break off our engagement, here YOU are, to make him feel in honor bound to stick to it!"

"Well, I am--" Anthony left it unfinished. "What can I do?" he asked meekly.

"We'll find a plan somehow," said Miss Mix, approvingly. "But you must be got out first!"

"And meanwhile," said Anthony, awkwardly, "I don't really know how to thank you--"

"Oh, nonsense!" she said lightly. "You forget how fond I am of him! Now, I'll go up to the house, and--" Her confident voice faltered, and Anthony was astonished to see a look of dismay cross her face. "Oh, my goodness gracious heavenly day!" she ejaculated softly. "Whatever shall we do now? Now we never can get you out!"

"Then I'll stay in," laughed Anthony, philosophically.

Miss Mix echoed his laugh nervously. She glanced across the yard.

"It's that disgusting newspaper contest!" she said.

"That WHAT?"

"Please don't shout!" she begged, sitting down on her box again, "I'll explain. You see, the San Francisco CALL, one of the big city dailies, has offered the job of being its local press representative to the college man who brings in the best newspaper story between now and the first of May--that's less than ten days. Of course, all the boys have gone crazy over it. It's a job that a boy could easily hold down with his regular class work, and it might lead to a permanent position on the paper's staff after graduation. About ten boys are working furiously for it, and all their friends are working for them. Tony's helping Jerry Billings, and Jerry has already taken in a couple of good stories, and has a good chance. This, of course, would land it!"

"What would?"

"Why, THIS!" She was laughing again. "Can't you see? Think of the head-lines! Even your New York papers would play it up. Think of the chance to get funny! 'Old Fox in a Trap!' 'Goes to Bed with the Chickens!' 'Iron King Plays Chanticleer!'"

"Thunder!" said Anthony, uncomfortably.

"There'd be no end of it, for you or me," said Miss Mix. "I know this town."

"Yes, you're right!" agreed Anthony. "The idea is for me to sit here until after the first of May, eh?" he continued uncertainly.

Her eyes danced.

"Oh, we MAY think of some other way!"

"Tony's not to be trusted, you think?"

"No-o! I wouldn't dare. He's simply mad to have Jerry win. He'd let it out involuntarily."

"The maid can go for a plumber?"

"Statia? She's working for Joe Bates. And both the boys in the plumber's shop are in college, anyway."

"You might telephone for a plumber from San Francisco?" suggested Anthony, afterthought.

"Yes, I could do that." Miss Mix brightened. "No, I can't, either," she lamented. "Elsie White, the long-distance operator, is working for Joe Bates, too." She meditated again for a space, then raised her head, listening. "They're calling me!" she whispered.

With a gesture for silence, she sprang to the door. Outside, some one shouted: "O Sally!"

"Hello, Tony!" she called hardily, in answer. "Lunch, is it? No, don't come down! I'm just coming up!"

With a warning glance over her shoulder for Anthony, she closed the door and was gone.

III

A long hour followed, the silence broken only by occasional low comments from the chickens, and by voices and footsteps coming and going on the side of the chicken house where the street lay. Anthony, his back against the rough wall, his hands in his pockets, had fallen into a smiling revery when Miss Mix suddenly returned. She carried a plate of luncheon, and two files.

"We are safe!" she reassured him. "The boys think I am playing bridge, and I've locked the gate on the inside. Now, files on parade!"

She tucked the filmy skirts of her white frock about her, sat down on a box, and began to grate away his bonds without an instant's delay. Her warm, smooth hands he found very charming to watch. Loose strands of hair fell across her flushed, smooth cheek. Anthony attacked his lunch with sudden gayety.

"How much we have to talk about!" he said, observing contentedly that five minutes' filing made almost no impression upon his chains. She colored suddenly, but met his eyes with charming gravity.

"Haven't we?" she assented simply.

"Why, no, it won't break his heart, Mr. Fox. I think he'll even be a little relieved to be able to go on serenely with the Peppers and the Rogerses. He's having lovely times there!"

"Oh, if his mother had lived, of course I should have written to her; but I knew you were a very busy man, Mr. Fox. Tony hardly ever speaks of his Aunt Fanny. She's a great club woman, I know. So I had to do the best I could."

"Why, I didn't think much about it, I suppose. But I certainly should have said that Tony's father was more than forty-five!"

"Ye-es, I suppose it might. But--but what a very funny subject for us to get on! I suppose--look at that white hen coming in, Mr. Fox! She's my prize winner. Isn't she a beauty?"

"Yes, indeed, he's all of that, dear old Tony! And then, as I say, he reminded me of--of that other, you know, years ago. I was only nineteen, hardly more than a child, but the memory is very sweet, and it made me want to be a good friend to

Tony!"

"There's the six o'clock bell, and you're all but free! Now, I'll let you out by this door, on the street side, and you can find your hotel? Then, when you call this evening, we needn't say anything of this. It hasn't been such a long afternoon, has it?"

Just after dinner, as Miss Mix and her youthful fiance were sitting on the porch in the spring twilight, a visitor entered the garden from the street. At sight of him, the boy sprang to his feet with a cry of "Dad!"

Miss Mix was introduced, and to young Tony's delight, she and his father chatted as comfortably as old friends. Presently, when Jerry Billings appeared with an invitation for the lady to accompany him to the post office for possible mail, father and son were left alone together.

Young Anthony beamed at his father's praise of his choice, but his comments seemed to come more easily on other matters. He told his father of the Rogers boys, of the Pepper girls, and of tennis and theatricals, and spoke hopefully of a possible camping trip with these friends.

"When did you think of announcing your engagement, Bud?"

The boy shifted in his chair, and laughed uneasily.

"Sally doesn't want to," he temporized, adding shyly, after a minute's silence, "and I didn't think you'd be in any hurry, dad!"

"But look here, son, you wrote that you planned being married in June!"

There was a pause. Then the boy said:

"I did think so; but now I don't see how we can. Sally sees that, too. I can't get married until I have a good job, and I've got another year here. We don't want to tell every one and then have to wait two or three years, do we, sir?"

"H-m!" said his father. "And yet you don't want to ask me to support you and your wife for indefinite years, Bud?"

Bud squeezed his father's hand.

"I'll never ask you to do that!" he promised promptly.

IV

A week drifted pleasantly over the college town, and still no definite step had been taken in the matter that had carried Anthony Fox over so many weary miles of country. If business matters in the Eastern city gave him any concern, he gave no sign of it to young Anthony or Sally, seeming entirely content with the passing moment.

The three were constantly together, except when the boy was in the class-room. During these intervals Miss Mix piloted her friend's father over lovely Palo Alto; they visited museum and library together, took drives and walks. One long evening was spent at the Peppers', where young Anthony was the centre of a buzz-ing and hilarious group, and where Sally, with her black evening gown and her violin, presented an entirely new phase.

On the evening of a certain glorious day, to young Anthony, sitting in silence on the porch steps, came Sally, who seated herself beside him.

"Tony," said she, firmly, "what have we decided about our engagement?"

Young Anthony eyed her expectantly, almost nervously, but he did not speak.

"We must either announce it or NOT announce it, Tony!"

"Why, you see, Sally," said Anthony, after a pause, "I wanted to, a while back, but--" "I know you did," she said heartily, to his great relief.

"But now, he pursued slowly," it would look pretty funny to the Rogerses, and the Peppers, and all, you know. JUST now, I mean. I've been up there all the time, right in things, and I've never said a word--"

"Well, well!" said a voice behind them; and to the unspeakable confusion of both, Jerry Billings rose from a porch chair and came down to them.

"I couldn't help hearing," explained that gentleman, joyously. "I was there first. I wish you joy, children. Miss Sally, here's my best wishes! I never dreamed you two--and yet I knew SOMETHING had brought father all the way from New York. But I never dreamed of this! This ought to land me the Call job, all right! Hasn't that occurred to either of you? Why, nobody has turned in anything to touch it!" He looked at his watch. "I had better be getting down there, too," he said excitedly.

"Tomorrow's the first of May, by George! and I've got to get any stuff in by ten. And there I've been sitting, cursing my luck for an hour! Here goes!"

"Look here, Jerry," began Sally and Anthony together, "look here--"

"You mean you don't want it announced?" said Mr. Billings, blankly. A pained look clouded the radiance of his face. "Isn't it TRUE?"

"We don't wish it announced yet," said Sally, feebly, as Anthony was silent.

"I call that pretty mean!" ejaculated Mr. Billings, after a pause. "It's TRUE," he went on aggrievedly. "I landed it--every old woman in town will be on to it in a few weeks--it's a corking job for me-- every one's wondering what Mr. Fox is doing here--and now you two hang back, just because you've not had time to tell your friends! Aw, be sports," he said ingratiatingly. "PLEASE, Miss Sally! I'd do as much for you two. You know I may not be able to make it at all, next year, if I haven't a job! I can have it, can't I? I get it, don't I, Tony? What do you two care--you've got what YOU want--"

"Oh, take your scoop!" half groaned young Anthony Fox.

Sally began to laugh, but it was curiously shaken laughter. Mr. Billings wisely seized this moment for a rapid departure. Mr. Fox, coming to the door a moment later, found the others silent on the steps.

"Now we are in for it!" said Sally, ruefully, as they made room for him between them. "What shall we do? Jerry's got it for the Call--we couldn't LIE about it! And, oh, we CAN'T have it in print to-morrow! Can you--can't you stop it?"

"Too late now!" said young Anthony, with a bad attempt at unconcern.

"Tell me what happened," said his father.

The recent developments were rapidly reviewed, and then Sally, removing herself and her wide-spreading ruffles to young Anthony's side of the steps, so that she might from time to time give his hand an affectionate and enlightening squeeze, confessed the deception of her engagement to him, and, with her blue eyes very close to his, asked him meekly to forgive her.

Young Anthony's forgiveness was a compound of boyish hurt and undisguised relief. It is probable that at no moment of their friendship had she seemed more dear to him.

"But--there's Jerry!" said Sally, suddenly, smitten with unpleasant recollection in the midst of this harmonious readjustment. "He--he heard, you know. And we can't deny THAT, and it means so much to him! He'll have telephoned up to town by this time, and the Call will run it anyway--newspaper editors are such beasts about those things!"

And again she and young Anthony drooped, and clung to each other's hands.

"I have been thinking," said the other Anthony, slowly, "that I see a way out of this. I HOPE I see one! I'd like--I'd like to discuss it with Miss Sally. If you'll just step down to the--the chicken yard, Bud, for five minutes, say. We'll call you. And it's just possible that we can--can arrange matters."

Half an hour later, Jerry Billings succeeded a second time in getting the city editor of the Call on the long-distance wire.

"Hello, Mr. Watts! Say, about that engagement of young Fox, Mr. Watts," he began.

"Well, what's the matter with it?" came back the editor's voice, sharply.

"Nothing's the matter with it," said Jerry, "only it's better than I thought! It's--it's old Fox that Miss Mix is going to marry! Old A.F. himself!"

"Who said so?" snapped the other.

"Fox did."

"FOX?"

"Yes, sir. He just telephoned to me. Gave me the whole thing. Said he wanted it to be published straight."

There was a pregnant silence for a few moments, then:

"This is no jolly, Billings? It's big stuff if it's true, you know."

"Oh, it's true enough," said Jerry, trying to control his voice.

"Well, we've got his picture--I'm sure!" said Mr. Watts, calmly. Then in obedience to Mr. Watts' curt "Hold the wire!" Jerry, with the receiver pressed to his ear, heard the city editor's voice on another telephone on his desk talking presumably to the make-up man on the next floor.

"Hello, Frank!" said Watts. "Tell Mike Williams to run that suffragette stuff on the third page. I've got a big story. I want room for a double cut and a column on the front!"

Then: "Hello, Billings! You telephone me six hundred words on this thing inside of an hour. No frills you understand. Just give me the straight facts. We'll fix the yarn up here."

SHANDON WATERS

For mercy's sakes, here comes Shandon Waters!" said Jane Dinwoodie, of the post-office, leaving her pigeonholes to peer through the one small window of that unpretentious building. "Mother, here's Shandon Waters driving into town with the baby!" breathed pretty Mary Dickey, putting an awed face into the sitting-room. "I declare that looks terrible like Shandon!" ejaculated Johnnie Larabee, straightening up at her wash-tubs and shading her eyes with her hand. "Well, what on earth brought her up to town!" said all Deaneville, crowding to the windows and doorways and halting the march of the busy Monday morning to watch a mud-spattered cart come bumping up and down over the holes in the little main street.

The woman--or girl, rather, for she was but twenty--who sat in the cart was in no way remarkable to the eye. She had a serious, even sullen face, and a magnificent figure, buttoned just now into a tan ulster that looked curiously out of keeping with her close, heavy widow's bonnet and hanging veil. Sprawled luxuriously in her lap, with one fat, idle little hand playing above her own gauntleted one on the reins, was a splendid child something less than a year old, snugly coated and capped against the cool air of a California February. She watched him closely as she drove, not moving her eyes from his little face even for a glance at the village street.

Poor Dan Waters had been six months in his grave, now, and this was the first glimpse Deaneville had had of his widow. For an unbroken half year she had not once left the solitude of the big ranch down by the marsh, or spoken to any one except her old Indian woman servant and the various "hands" in her employ.

She had been, in the words of Deaneville, "sorta nutty" since her husband's death. Indeed, poor Shandon had been "sorta nutty" all her life. Motherless at six, and allowed by her big, half civilized father to grow up as wild as the pink mallow that fringed the home marshes, she was regarded with mingled horror and pity by the well-ordered Deaneville matrons. Jane Dinwoodie and Mary Dickey could well remember the day she was brought into the district school, her mutinous black eyes gleaming under a shock of rough hair, her clumsy little apron tripping her with its unaccustomed strings. The lonely child had been frantic for companionship, and her direct, even forceful attempts at friendship had repelled and then amused the Deaneville children. As unfortunate chance would have it, it was shy, spoiled, adored little Mary Dickey that Shandon instantly selected for especial worship, and Mary, already bored by admiration, did not like it. But the little people would have adjusted matters in their own simple fashion presently had they been allowed to do so. It was the well-meant interference of the teacher that went amiss. Miss Larks explained to the trembling little newcomer that she mustn't smile at Mary, that she mustn't leave her seat to sit with Mary: it was making poor Mary cry.

Shandon listened to her with rising emotion, a youthful titter or two from different parts of the room pointing the moral. When the teacher had finished, she rose with a sudden scream of rage, flung her new slate violently in one direction, her books in another, and departed, kicking the stove over with a well-directed foot as she left. Thus she became a byword to virtuous infancy, and as the years went by, and her wild beauty and her father's wealth grew apace, Deaneville grew less and less charitable in its judgment of her. Shandon lived in a houseful of men, her father's adored companion and greatly admired by the rough cattle men who came yearly to buy his famous stock.

When her father died, a little wave of pity swept over Deaneville, and more than one kind-hearted woman took the five-mile drive down to the Bell Ranch ready to console and sympathize. But no one saw her. The girl, eighteen now, clung more to her solitude than ever, spending whole days and nights in lonely roaming over the marsh and the low meadows, like some frantic sick animal.

Only Johnnie Larabee, the warm-hearted little wife of the village hotel keeper, persevered and was rewarded by Shandon's bitter confidence, given while they rode up to the ridge to look up some roaming steer, perhaps, or down by the peach-cutting sheds, while Shandon supervised a hundred "hands." Shandon laughed now when she recounted the events of those old unhappy childish days, but Johnnie did not like the laughter. The girl always asked particularly for Mary Dickey, her admirers, her clothes, her good times.

"No wonder she acts as if there wasn't anybody else on earth but her!" would be Shandon's dry comment.

It was Johnnie who "talked straight" to Shandon when big Dan Waters began to haunt the Bell Ranch, and who was the only witness of their little wedding, and the only woman to kiss the unbride-like bride.

After that even, Johnnie lost sight of her for the twelve happy months that Big Dan was spared to her. Little Dan came, welcomed by no more skillful hands than the gentle big ones of his wondering father and the practised ones of the old Indian. And Shandon bought hats that were laughed at by all Deaneville, and was tremulously happy in a clumsy, unused fashion.

And then came the accident that cost Big Dan his life. It was all a hideous blur to Shandon--a blur that enclosed the terrible, swift trip to Sacramento, with the blinking little baby in the hollow of her arm, and the long wait at the strange hospital. It was young Doctor Lowell, of Deaneville, who decided that only an operation could save Dan, and Doctor Lowell who performed it. And it was through him that Shandon learned, in the chill dawn, that the gallant fight was lost. She did not speak again, but, moving like a sleepwalker, reached blindly for the baby, pushed aside the hands that would have detained her, and went stumbling out into the street. And since that day no one in Deaneville had been able to get close enough to speak to her. She did not go to Dan's funeral, and such sympathizers as tried to find her were rewarded by only desolate glimpses of the tall figure flitting along the edge of the marshes like a hunted bird. A month old, little Danny accompanied his mother on these restless wanderings, and many a time his little mottled hand was strong enough to bring her safely home when no other would have availed.

Her old Chinese "boy" came into the village once a week, and paid certain bills punctiliously from a little canvas bag that was stuffed full of gold pieces; but Fong was not a communicative person, and Deaneville languished for direct news. Johnnie, discouraged by fruitless attempts to have a talk with the forlorn young creature, had to content herself with sending occasional delicacies from her own kitchen and garden to Shandon, and only a week before this bright February morning had ventured a note, pinned to the napkin that wrapped a bowl of cream cheese. The note read:

Don't shorten Danny too early, Shandy. Awful easy for babies to ketch cold this weather.

Of all the loitering curious men and women at doors and windows and in the street, Johnnie was the only one who dared speak to her to- day. Mrs. Larabee was dressed in the overalls and jersey that simplified both the dressing and the labor of busy Monday mornings; her sleek black hair arranged fashionably in a "turban swirl." She ran out to the cart with a little cry of welcome, a smile on her thin, brown face that well concealed the trepidation this unheard-of circumstance caused her. "Lord, make me say the right thing!" prayed Johnnie, fervently. Mrs. Waters saw her coming, stopped the big horse, and sat waiting. Her eyes were wild with a sort of savage terror, and she was trembling violently.

"Well, how do, Shandon?" said Mrs. Larabee, cheerfully. Then her eyes fell on the child, and she gave a dramatic start. "Never you tell me this is Danny!" said she, sure of her ground now. "Well, you--old--buster--you! He's IMMENSE, ain't he, Shandon?"

"Isn't he?" stammered Shandon, nervously.

"He's about the biggest feller for nine months I ever saw," said Mrs. Larabee, generously. "He could eat Thelma for breakfast!"

"Johnnie--and he ain't quite seven yet!" protested Shandon, eagerly.

Mrs. Larabee gave her an astonished look, puckered up her forehead, nodded profoundly.

"That's right," she said. Then she dragged the wriggling small body from Shandon's lap and held the wondering, soft little face against her own.

"You come to Aunt Johnnie a minute," said she, "you fat old muggins! Look at him, Shandon. He knows I'm strange. Yes, 'course you do! He wants to go back to you, Shandy. Well, what do you know about that? Say, dearie," continued Mrs. Larabee, in a lower tone, "you've got a terrible handsome boy, and what's more, he's Dan's image."

Mrs. Waters gathered the child close to her heart. "He's awful like Dan when he smiles," said she, simply. And for the first time their eyes met. "Say, thank you, for the redishes and the custard pie and that cheese, Johnnie," said Shandon, awkwardly, but her eyes thanked this one friend for much more.

"Aw, shucks!" said Johnnie, gently, as she dislodged a drying clod of mud from the buggy robe. There was a moment's constrained silence, then Shandon said suddenly:

"Johnnie, what d'you mean by 'shortening' him?"

"Puttin' him in short clothes, dearie. Thelma's been short since Gran'ma Larabee come down at Christmas," explained the other, briskly.

"I never knew about that," said Mrs. Waters, humbly. "Danny's the first little kid I ever touched. Lizzie Tom tells me what the Indians do, and for the rest I just watch him. I toast his feet good at the fire every night, becuz Dan said his mother useter toast his; and whenever the sun comes out, I take his clothes off and leave him sprawl in it, but I guess I miss a good deal." She finished with a wistful, half-questioning inflection, and Mrs. Larabee did not fail her.

"Don't ask me, when he's as big and husky as any two of mine!" said she, reassuringly. "I guess you do jest about right. But, Shandy, you've got to shorten him."

"Well, what'll I get?" asked Shandon.

Mrs. Larabee, in her element, considered.

"You'll want about eight good, strong calico rompers," she began authoritatively. Then suddenly she interrupted herself. "Say, why don't you come over to the hotel with me now," she suggested enthusiastically. "I'm just finishing my wash, and while I wrench out the last few things you can feed the baby; than I'll show you Thelma's things, and we can have lunch. Then him and Thel can take their naps, and you 'n' me'll go over to Miss Bates's and see what we can git. You'll want shoes for him, an' a good, strong hat--"

"Oh, honest, Johnnie--" Shandon began to protest hurriedly, in her hunted manner, and with a miserable glance toward the home road. "Maybe I'll come up next week, now I know what you meant--"

"Shucks! Next week nobody can talk anything but wedding," said Johnnie, off guard.

"Whose wedding?" Shandon asked, and Johnnie, who would have preferred to bite her tongue out, had to answer, "Mary Dickey's."

"Who to?" said Shandon, her face darkening. Johnnie's voice was very low.

"To the doc', Shandy; to Arnold Lowell."

"Oh!" said Shandon, quietly. "Big wedding, I suppose, and white dresses, and all the rest?"

"Sure," said Johnnie, relieved at her pleasant interest, and warming to the subject. "There'll be five generations there. Parker's making the cake in Sacramento. Five of the girls'll be bridesmaids--Mary Bell and Carrie and Jane and the two Powell girls. Poor Mrs. Dickey, she feels real bad. She--"

"She don't want to give Mary up?" said Shandon, in a hard voice. She began to twist the whip about in its socket. "Well, some people have everything, it seems. They're pretty, and their folks are crazy about 'em, and they can stand up and make a fuss over marrying a man who as good as killed some other woman's husband,--a woman who didn't have any one else either."

"Shandy," said Johnnie, sharply, "ain't you got Danny?"

Something like shame softened the girl's stern eyes. She dropped her face until her lips rested upon the little fluffy fringe that marked the dividing line between Danny's cap and Danny's forehead.

"Sure I have," she said huskily. "But I've--I've always sort of had it in for Mary Dickey, Johnnie, I suppose becuz she IS so perfect, and so cool, and treats me like I was dirt--jest barely sees me, that's all!"

Johnnie answered at random, for she was suddenly horrified to see Dr. Lowell and Mary Dickey themselves come out of the post-office. Before she could send them a frantic signal of warning, the doctor came toward the cart.

"How do you do, Mrs. Waters?" said he, holding out his hand.

Shandon brought her startled eyes from little Danny's face. The child, with little eager grunts and frowning concentration, was busy with the clasp of her pocketbook, and her big, gentle hand had been guarding it from his little, wild ones. The sight of the doctor's face brought back her bitterest memories with a sick rush, at a moment when her endurance was strained to the utmost. HE had decreed that Dan should be operated on, HE had decided that she should not be with him, HE had come to tell her that the big, protecting arm and heart were gone forever--and now he had an early buttercup in his buttonhole, and on his lips the last of the laughter that he had just been sharing with Mary Dickey! And Mary, the picture of complacent daintiness, was sauntering on, waiting for him.

Shandon was not a reasonable creature. With a sound between a snarl and a sob she caught the light driving whip from its socket and brought the lash fairly across the doctor's smiling face. As he started back, stung with intolerable pain, she lashed in turn the nervous horse, and in another moment the cart and its occupants were racketing down the home road again.

"And now we never WILL git no closer to Shandon Waters!" said Johnnie Larabee, regretfully, for the hundredth time. It was ten days later, and Mrs. Larabee and Mrs. Cass Dinwoodie were high up on the wet hills, gathering cream-colored wild iris for the Dickey wedding that night.

"And serve her right, too!" said Mrs. Dinwoodie, severely. "A great girl like that lettin' fly like a child."

"She's--she's jest the kind to go crazy, brooding as she does," Mrs. Larabee submitted, almost timidly. She had been subtly pleading Shandon's cause for the past week, but it was no use. The last outrage had apparently sealed her fate so far as Deaneville was concerned. Now, straightening her cramped back and looking off toward the valleys below them, Mrs. Larabee said suddenly:

"That looks like Shandon down there now."

Mrs. Dinwoodie's eyes followed the pointing finger. She could distinguish a woman's moving figure, a mere speck on the road far below.

"Sure it is," said she. "Carryin' Dan, too."

"My goo'ness," said Johnnie, uneasily, "I wish she wouldn't take them crazy walks. I don't suppose she's walking up to town?"

"I don't know why she should," said Mrs. Dinwoodie, dryly, "with the horses she's got. I don't suppose even Shandon would attempt to carry that great child that far, cracked as she seems to be!"

"I don't suppose we could drive home down by the marsh road?" Johnnie asked. Mrs. Dinwoodie looked horrified.

"Johnnie, are you crazy yourself?" she demanded. "Why, child, Mary's going to be married at half-past seven, and there's the five-o'clock train now."

The older matron made all haste to "hitch up," sending not even another look into the already shadowy valley. But Johnnie's thoughts were there all through the drive home, and even when she started with her beaming husband and her four young children to the wedding she was still thinking of Shandon Waters.

The Dickey home was all warmth, merriment, and joyous confusion. Three or four young matrons, their best silk gowns stretched to bursting over their swelling bosoms, went busily in and out of the dining-room. In the double parlors guests were gathering with the laughter and kissing that marked any coming together of these hard- working folk. Starched and awed little children sat on the laps of mothers and aunts, blinking at the lamps; the very small babies were upstairs, some drowsily enjoying a late supper in their mothers' arms, others already deep in sleep in Mrs. Dickey's bed. The downstairs rooms and the stairway were decorated with wilting smilax and early fruit-blossoms.

To Deaneville it seemed quite natural that Dr. Lowell, across whose face the scar of Shandon Waters' whip still showed a dull crimson, should wait for his bride at the foot of the hall stairway, and that Mary's attendants should keep up a continual coming and going between the room where she was dressing and the top of the stairs, and should have a great many remarks to make to the young men below. Presently a little stir announced the clergyman, and a moment later every one could hear Mary Dickey's thrilling young voice from the upper hallway:

"Arnold, mother says was that Dr. Lacey?"

And every one could hear Dr. Lowell's honest, "Yes, dear, it was," and Mary's fluttered, diminishing, "All right!"

Rain began to beat noisily on the roof and the porches. Johnnie Larabee came downstairs with Grandpa and Grandma Arnold, and Rosamund Dinwoodie at the piano said audibly, "Now, Johnnie?"

There was expectant silence in the parlors. The whole house was so silent in that waiting moment that the sound of sudden feet on the porch and the rough opening of the hall door were a startlingly loud interruption.

It was Shandon Waters, who came in with a bitter rush of storm and wet air. She had little Dan in her arms. Drops of rain glittered on her hanging braids and on the shawl with which the child was wrapped, and beyond her the wind snarled and screamed like a disappointed animal. She went straight through the frightened, parting group to Mrs. Larabee, and held out the child.

"Johnnie," she said in a voice of agony, utterly oblivious of her surroundings, "Johnnie, you've always been my friend! Danny's sick!"

"Shandon,--for pity's sake!" ejaculated little Mrs. Larabee, reaching out her arms for Danny, her face shocked and protesting and pitying all at once, "Why, Shandy, you should have waited for me over at the hotel," she said, in a lower tone, with a glance at the incongruous scene. Then pity for the anguished face gained mastery, and she added tenderly, "Well, you poor child, you, was this where you was walking this afternoon? My stars, if I'd only known! Why on earth didn't you drive?"

"I couldn't wait!" said Shandon, hoarsely. "We were out in the woods, and Lizzie she gave Danny some mushrooms. And when I looked he--his little mouth--" she choked. "And then he began to have sorta cramps, and kinda doubled up, Johnnie, and he cried so queer, and I jest started up here on a run. He--JOHNNIE!" terror shook her voice when she saw the other's face, "Johnnie, is he going to die?" she said.

"Mushrooms!" echoed Mrs. Larabee, gravely, shaking her head. And a score of other women looking over her shoulder at the child, who lay breathing heavily with his eyes shut, shook their heads, too.

"You'd better take him right home with me, dearie," Mrs. Larabee said gently, with a significant glance at the watching circle. "We oughtn't to lose any time."

Dr. Lowell stepped out beside her and gently took Danny in his arms.

"I hope you'll let me carry him over there for you, Mrs. Waters," said he. "There's no question that he's pretty sick. We've got a hard fight ahead."

There was a little sensation in the room, but Shandon only looked at him uncomprehendingly. In her eyes there was the dumb thankfulness of the dog who knows himself safe with friends. She wet her lips and tried to speak. But before she could do so, the doctor's mother touched his arm half timidly and said:

"Arnold, you can't very well--surely, it's hardly fair to Mary--"

"Mary--?" he answered her quickly. He raised his eyes to where his wife-to-be, in a startled group of white-clad attendants, was standing halfway down the stairway.

She looked straight at Shandon, and perhaps at no moment in their lives did the two women show a more marked contrast; Shandon muddy, exhausted, haggard, her sombre eyes sick with dread, Mary's always fragile beauty more ethereal than ever under the veil her mother had just caught back with orange blossoms. Shandon involuntarily flung out her hand toward her in desperate appeal.

"Couldn't you--could you jest wait till he sees Danny?" she faltered.

Mary ran down the remaining steps and laid her white hand on Shandon's.

"If it was ten weddings, we'd wait, Shandon!" said she, her voice thrilling with the fellowship of wifehood and motherhood to come. "Don't worry, Shandon. Arnold will fix him. Poor little Danny!" said Mary, bending over him. "He's not awful sick, is he, Arnold? Mother," she said, turning, royally flushed, to her stupefied mother, "every one'll have to wait. Johnnie and Arnold are going to fix up Shandon's baby."

"I don't see the slightest need of traipsing over to the hotel," said Mrs. Dickey, almost offended, as at a slight upon her hospitality. "Take him right up to the spare room, Arnold. There ain't no noise there, it's in the wing. And one of you chil'ren run and tell Aggie we want hot water, and--what else? Well, go ahead and tell her that, anyway."

"Leave me carry him up," said one big, gentle father, who had tucked his own baby up only an hour ago. "I've got a kimmoner in my bag," old Mrs. Lowell said to Shandon. "It's a-plenty big enough for you. You git dry and comfortable before you hold him." "Shucks! Lloydy ate a green cherry when he wasn't but four months old," said one consoling voice to Shandon. "He's got a lot of fight in him," said another. "My Olive got an inch screw in her throat," contributed a third. Mrs. Larabee said in a low tone, with her hand tight upon Shandon's shaking one, "He'll be jest about fagged out when the doctor's done with him, dearie, and as hungry as a hunter. Don't YOU git excited, or he'll be sick all over again."

Crowding solicitously about her, the women got her upstairs and into dry clothing. This was barely accomplished when Mary Dickey came into the room, in a little blue cotton gown, to take her to Danny.

"Arnold says he's got him crying, and that's a good sign, Shandon," said Mary. "And he says that rough walk pro'bly saved him."

Shandon tried to speak again, but failed again, and the two girls went out together. Mary presently came back alone, and the lessened but not uncheerful group downstairs settled down to a vigil. Various reports drifted from the sick-room, but it was almost midnight before Mrs. Larabee came down with definite news.

"How is he?" echoed Johnnie, sinking into a chair. "Give me a cup of that coffee, Mary. That's a good girl. Well, say, it looks like you can't kill no Deaneville child with mushrooms. He's asleep now. But say, he was a pretty sick kid! Doc' looks like something the cat brought home, and I'm about dead, but Danny seems to feel real chipper. And EAT! And of course that poor girl looks like she'd inherited the earth, as the Scriptures say. The ice is what you might call broken between the whole crowd of us and Shandon Waters. She's sitting there holding Danny and smiling softly at any one who peeks in!" And, her voice thickening suddenly with tears on the last words, Mrs. Larabee burst out crying and fumbled in her unaccustomed grandeur for a handkerchief.

Mary Dickey and Arnold Lowell were married just twenty-four hours later than they had planned, the guests laughing joyously at the wilted decorations and stale sandwiches. After the ceremony the bride and bridegroom went softly up stairs, and the doctor had a last approving look at the convalescent Danny.

Mary, almost oppressed by the sense of her own blessedness on this day of good wishes and affectionate demonstration, would have gently detached her husband's arm from her waist as they went to the door, that Shandon might not be reminded of her own loss and aloneness.

But the doctor, glancing back, knew that in Shandon's thoughts to- day there was no room for sorrow. Her whole body was curved about the child as he lay in her lap, and her adoring look was intent upon him. Danny was smiling up at his mother in a blissful interval, his soft little hand lying upon her contented heart.

GAYLEY THE TROUBADOUR

Through the tremulous beauty of the California woods, in the silent April afternoon, came Sammy Peneyre, riding Clown. The horse chose his own way on the corduroy road, for the rider was lost in dreams. Clown was a lean old dapple gray so far advanced in years and ailments that when Doctor Peneyre had bought him, the year before, the dealer had felt constrained to remark:

"He's better'n he looks, Doc'. You'll get your seven dollars' worth out of him yet!"

To which the doctor had amiably responded:

"Your saying so makes me wonder if I WILL, Joe. However, I'll have my boy groom him and feed him, and we'll see!"

But, as Clown had stubbornly refused to respond to grooming and feeding, he was, like other despised and discarded articles, voted by the Peneyre family quite good enough for Sammy, and Sammy accepted him gratefully.

The spirit of spring was affecting them both to-day--a brilliant day after long weeks of rain. Sammy whistled softly. Clown coquetted with the bit, danced under the touch of the whip, and finally took the steep mountain road with such convulsive springs as jolted his rider violently from dreams.

"Why, you fool, are you trying to run away?" said Sammy, suddenly alive to the situation. The road here was a mere shelf on the slope of the mountain, constantly used by descending lumber teams, and dangerous at all times. A runaway might easily be fatal. Sammy pulled at the bit; but, at the first hard tug, the old bridle gave way, and Clown, maddened by a stinging blow from the loose flying end of the strap, bolted blindly ahead.

Terrified now, Sammy clung to the pommel and shouted. The trees flew by;

great clods of mud were flung up by the horse's feet. From far up the road could be heard the creaking of a lumber team and the crack of the lumberman's long whip.

"My Lord!" said Sammy, aloud, in a curious calm, "we'll never pass THAT!"

And then, like a flash, it was all over. Clown, suddenly freed from his rider, galloped violently for a moment, stopped, snorted suspiciously, galloped another twenty feet, and stood still, his broken bridle dangling rakishly over one eye. Sammy, dragged from the saddle at the crucial instant to the safety of Anthony Gayley's arms, as he brought his own horse up beside her, wriggled to the ground.

"That was surely going some!" said Anthony, breathing hard. "Hurt?"

"No-o!" said Sammy. But she leaned against the tall, big fellow, as he stood beside her, and was glad of his arm about her shoulders.

They had known each other by sight for years, but this was the first speech between them. Anthony suddenly realized that the doctor's youngest daughter, with her shy, dark eyes and loosened silky braids, had grown from an awkward child into a very pretty girl. Sammy, glancing up, thought--what every other woman in Wheatfield thought--that Anthony Gayley was the handsomest man she had ever seen, in his big, loose corduroys, with a sombrero on the back of his tawny head.

"I was awfully afraid I'd grate against your leg," said the boy, with his sunny smile; "but I couldn't stop to figure it out. I just had to hustle!"

"There's a lumber wagon ahead there," Sammy said. "I'm--I'm very much obliged to you!"

They both laughed. Presently Anthony made the girl mount his own beautiful mare.

"Ride Duchess home. I'll take your horse," said he.

"Oh, no, indeed; PLEASE don't bother!" protested Sammy, eagerly.

But Anthony only laughed and gave her a hand up. Sammy settled herself on the Spanish saddle with a sigh of satisfaction.

"I've always wanted to ride your horse!" said she, delightedly, as the big muscles moved smoothly under her.

Anthony smiled. "She's the handsomest mare here-abouts," said he. "I wouldn't take a thousand dollars for her!"

Sammy watched him deftly repair the broken bridle of the now docile and crestfallen Clown, and spring to the saddle.

"I'm taking you out of your way!" she pleaded, and he answered gravely:

"Oh, no; I'll be much happier seeing you safe home."

When they reached her gate, the two changed horses, and Sammy rode slowly up the dark driveway alone. Even on this brilliant afternoon the old Peneyre place looked dull and gloomy. Dusty dark pines and eucalyptus trees grew close about the house. There was no garden, but here and there an unkempt geranium or rank great bush of marguerites sprawled in the uncut grass, and rose bushes, long grown wild, stood in spraying clusters that were higher than a man's head. Pampas trees, dirty and overgrown, outlined the drive at regular intervals, their shabby plumes uncut from year to year.

The house was heavy, bay-windowed, three-storied. Ugly, immense, unfriendly, it struck an inharmonious note in the riotous free growth of the surrounding woods. The dark entrance-hall was flanked by a library full of obsolete, unread books, and by double drawing- rooms, rarely opened now. All the windows on the ground floor were darkened by the shrubbery outside and by heavy red draperies within.

Sammy, entering a side door, seemed to leave the day's brightness behind her. The air indoors was chill, flat. A half-hearted little coal fire flickered in the grate, and Koga was cleaning silver at the table. Sammy took David Copperfield from the mantel and settled herself in a great chair.

"Koga, you go fix Clown now," she suggested.

Koga beamed assent. Departing, he wrestled with a remark: "Oh! Nise day. I sink so."

Sammy agreed. "You don't have weather like this in Japan in April!"

"Oh, yis," said Koga, and, drunk with the joy of speech, he added: "I sink so. Awe time nise in Jap-pon! I sink so."

"All the time nice in Japan?" echoed Sammy, lazily. "Oh, what a story!"

But Koga was convulsed with innocent mirth. However excruciating the effort, he had produced a remark in English. He retired, repeating between spasms of enjoyment: "Oh, I sink so. Awe time nise in Jap- pon!"

The day dragged on, to all outward seeming like all of Sammy's days. Twilight made her close her book and straighten her bent shoulders. Pong came in to set the table. The slamming of the hall door announced her father.

Presently Mrs. Moore, the housekeeper, came downstairs. Lamps were lighted; dinner loitered its leisurely way. After it the doctor set up one of his endless chess problems on the end of the table, and Sammy returned to David Copperfield.

"Father, you know Anthony Gayley--that young carpenter in Torney's shop?"

"I do, my dear."

"Well, Clown ran away to-day, and he really saved me from a bad smash."

A long pause.

"Ha!" said the doctor, presently. "Set this down, will you, Sammy? Rook to queen's fourth. Check. Now, knight--any move. No--hold on. Yes. Knight any move. Now, rook--wait a minute!"

His voice fell, his eyes were fixed. Sammy sighed.

At eight she fell to mending the fire with such vigor that her colorless little face burned. Then her spine felt chilly. Sammy turned about, trying to toast evenly; but it couldn't be done. She thought suddenly of her warm bed, put her finger in her book, kissed her father's bald spot between two yawns, and went upstairs.

The dreams went, too. There was nothing in this neglected, lonely day, typical of all her days, to check them. It was delicious, snuggling down in the chilly sheets, to go on dreaming.

Again she was riding alone in the woods. Again Clown was running away. Again, big gentle Anthony Gayley was galloping behind her. Again for that breathless moment she was in his arms. Sammy shut her eyes....

Her father, coming upstairs, wakened her. She lay smiling in the dark. What had she been thinking of? Oh, yes! And out came the dream horses and their riders again....

The next day she rode over the same bit of road again, and the day after, and the day after that. The rides were absolutely uneventful, but sweet with dreams.

A week later Sammy teased Mrs. Moore into taking her to the Elks' concert and dance at the Wheatfield Hall over the post-office. When Mrs. Moore protested at this unheard-of proceeding, the girl used her one unfailing threat: "Then I'll tell father I want another governess!"

Mrs. Moore hated governesses. There had been no governess at the doctor's for two years. She looked uneasy. "You've nothing to wear," said she.

"I'll wear my embroidered linen," said Sammy, "and Mary's spangled scarf."

"You oughtn't borrow your sister's things without permission," said Mrs. Moore, half-heartedly.

"Mary's in New York," said Sammy, recklessly. "She's not been home for two years, and she may not be back for two more! She won't care. I'm eighteen, and I've never been to a dance, and I'm GOING--that's all there is about it!"

And she burst into tears, and presently laughed herself out of them, and went to her sister's orderly empty room to see what other treasures besides the spangled scarf Mary had left behind her.

Three months later, on a burning July afternoon, the Wheatfield "Terrors" played a team from the neighboring town of Copadoro. Wheatfield's population was reputedly nine hundred, and certainly almost that number of onlookers had gathered to watch the game. The free seats were packed with perspiring women in limp summer gowns, and restless, crimson-faced children; and a shouting, vociferous line of men fringed the field. But in the "grand stand," where chairs rented for twenty-five cents, there was still some room.

Three late-comers found seats there when the game was almost over-- Sammy's sister Mary, an extremely handsome young woman in a linen gown and wide hat, her brother Tom, a correct young man whose ordinary expression indicated boredom, and their aunt, a magnificent personage in gray silk, with a gray silk parasol. Their arrival caused some little stir.

"Well, for pit--!" exclaimed a stout matron seated immediately in front of them. "If it ain't Mary Peneyre--an' Thomas too! An' Mrs. Bond--for goodness' sake! Well, say, you folks ARE strangers. When 'jew all get here? Sammy never told me you was coming!"

"How d'you do, Mrs. Pidgeon?" said Sammy's aunt, cordially. "No, Samantha didn't know it. We came--ah--rather suddenly. Yes, I've not been in Wheatfield for ten years. We got here on the two o'clock train."

"Going to stay long, Mary?" said Mrs. Pidgeon, sociably.

"Only a few days," said Miss Peneyre, distantly. ("That's the worst of growing up in a place," she said to herself. "Every one calls you 'Mary'!") "We are going to take Samantha back to New York with us," she added.

"Look out you don't find you're a little late," said Mrs. Pidgeon, with great archness. "I'm surprised you ain't asked me if there's any news from Sammy. Whole village talking about it."

The three smiles that met her gaze were not so unconcerned as their wearers fondly hoped. Mrs. Bond ended a tense moment when she exclaimed, "There's Sammy now!" and indicated to the others the last row of seats, where a girl in blue, with a blue parasol, was sitting alone. Mrs. Pidgeon delivered a parting shot. "Sammy might do lots worse than Anthony Gayley," said she, confidentially. "Carpenter or no carpenter, he's an elegant fellow. I thought Lizzie Philliber was ace high, an' then folks talked some of Bootsy White. I guess Bootsy'd like to do some hair-pulling."

"I dare say it's just a boy-and-girl friendship," said Mrs. Bond, lightly, but trembling a little and pressing Mary's foot with her own. When they were climbing over the wooden seats a moment later, on their way to join Sammy, she added:

"Oh, really, it's insufferable! I'd like to spank that girl!"

"Apparently the whole village is on," contributed Tom, bitterly.

A moment later Sammy saw them; and if her welcome was a little constrained, it was merely because of shyness. She settled down radiantly between her sister and aunt, with a hand for each.

"Well, this is FUN!" said Sammy. "Did you get my letter? Were you surprised? Are you all going to stay until September?"

Her happy fusillade of questions distressed them all. Mary said the unwise thing, trying to laugh, as she had always laughed, at Sammy:

"DON'T talk as if you were going to be married, Sammy! It's too awful--you don't know how aunty and I feel about it! Why, darling, we want you to go back with us to New York! Sammy--"

The firm pressure of her aunt's foot against her own stopped her.

"I knew you would feel that way about it, Mary," said Sammy, very quietly, but with blazing cheeks; "but I am of age, and father says that Anthony has as much right to ask for the girl he loves as any other man, and that's all there is to it!"

"You have it all thought out," said Mary, very white; "but, I must say, I am surprised that a sister of mine, and a granddaughter of Judge Peters--a girl who could have EVERYTHING!--is content to marry an ordinary country carpenter! You won't have grandmother's money until you're twenty-one; there's three years that you will have to cook and sweep and get your hands rough, and probably bring up--"

"Mary! MARY!" said Mrs. Bond.

"Well, I don't care!" said Mary, unreproved. "And when she DOES get grandma's money," she grumbled, "what good will it do her?"

"We won't discuss it, if you please, Mary," said little Sammy, with dignity.

There was a silence. Tom lighted a cigarette. They watched the game, Mary fighting tears, Sammy defiant and breathing hard, Mrs. Bond with absent eyes.

"Stunning fellow who made that run!" said the elder woman presently. "Who is he, dear?"

"That's Anthony!" said Sammy, shortly, not to be won.

"Anthony!" Mrs. Bond's tone was all affectionate interest. She put up her lorgnette. "Well, bless his heart! Isn't he good to look at!" she said.

"He's all hot and dirty now," Sammy said, relenting a little.

"He's MAGNIFICENT," said Mrs. Bond, firmly. She cut Mary off from their conversation with a broad shoulder, and pressed Sammy's hand. "We'll all love him, I'm sure," said she, warmly.

Sammy's lip trembled.

"You WILL, Aunt Anne," said she, a little huskily. Pent up confidence came with a rush. "I know perfectly well how Mary feels!" said Sammy, eagerly. "Why, didn't you yourself feel a little sorry he's a carpenter?"

"Just for a moment," said Aunt Anne.

"I wish MYSELF he wasn't," Sammy pursued; "but he likes it, and he's making money, and he's liked by EVERY one. He's on the team, you know, and sings in all the concerts. Wild horses couldn't drag him away from Wheatfield. And why should he go away and study some profession he hates," she rushed on resentfully, "when I'm PERFECTLY satisfied with him as he is? Father asked him if he wouldn't like to study a profession--I don't see why he SHOULD!"

"Surely," said Mrs. Bond, sympathetically, but quite at a loss. After a thoughtful moment she added seriously: "But, darling, what about your trousseau? Why not make it November, say, and take a flying trip to New York with your old aunty? I want the first bride to have all sorts of pretty things, you know. No delays,--everything ready-made, not a moment lost--?"

Sammy hesitated. "You do like him, don't you, Aunt Anne?" she burst out.

"My dear, I HOPE I'm going to love him!"

"Do--do you mind my talking it over with him before I say I'll go?" Sammy's eyes shone.

"My darling, no! Take a week to think it over!" Mrs. Bond had never tried fishing, but she had some of the instincts of the complete angler.

A mad burst of applause interrupted her, and ended the game. Strolling from the field in the level, pitiless sunshine, the Peneyres were joined by young Gayley. He was quite the hero of the hour, stalwart in his base-ball suit, nodding and shouting greetings in every direction. He transferred a bat to his left hand to give Mrs. Bond a cheerfully assured greeting, and, with the freedom of long-gone days when he had played in the back lot with the Peneyre children, he addressed the young people as "Mary" and "Tom." If three of the party thought him decidedly "fresh," Sammy had no such criticism. She evidently adored her lover.

It was at her suggestion, civilly indorsed by the others, that he came to the house a few hours later for dinner. It was a painful meal. Mr. Gayley did not hesitate to monopolize the conversation. He was accustomed to admiration--too completely accustomed, in fact, to perceive that on this occasion it was wanting.

After dinner he sang--having quite frankly offered to sing. Mary played his accompaniments, and Sammy leaned on the closed cover of her mother's wonderful old grand piano--sadly out of tune in these days!--and watched him. Tom, frankly rude, went to bed. Mary, determined that the engaged pair should not be encouraged any further than was unavoidable, stuck gallantly to her post.

Mrs. Bond sat watching, useless regrets filling her heart. How sweet the child was! How full of possibilities! How true the gray eyes were! How stubborn the mouth might be! Sammy's power to do what she willed to do, in the face of all obstacles, had been notable since her babyhood. Her aunt looked from the ardent, virginal little head to the florid, handsome face of the singer, and her heart was sick within her. Anthony Gayley came to the train to see them off, two weeks later, and Sammy kissed him good-by before the eyes of all Wheatfield. She had made her own conditions in consenting to make the Eastern visit. She was going merely to buy her trousseau; the subject of her engagement was never to be discussed; and every one--EVERY one--she met was to know at once that she was going back to Wheatfield immediately to be married in December.

Anthony had agreed to wait until then.

"It isn't as if every one knew it, Kid," he said sensibly to his fiancee; "it gives me a chance to save a little, and it's not so hard on mother. Besides, I'm looking out for a partner, and I'll have to work him in."

"I wonder you don't think of entering some other business, Anthony," Mrs. Bond said, to this remark. "You're young enough to try anything. It's such a--it's such hard work, you know."

"I've often thought I'd like to be an actor," said Mr. Gayley, carelessly; "but there's not much chance to break into that."

"You could take a course of lessons in New York," suggested Mary, and Sammy indorsed the idea with an eager look. But Anthony laughed.

"Not for mine! No, sir. I'll stick to Wheatfield. I was a year in San Francisco a while back, and it was one lonesome year, believe me. No place like home and friends for your Uncle Dudley!"

"Don't you meet a bunch of swell Eastern fellows and forget me," he said to Sammy, as they stood awaiting the train. "I'll be getting a little home ready for you; I'll--I'll trust you, Kid."

"You may," said Sammy. She looked at the burning, dry little main street, the white cottages that faced the station from behind their blazing gardens; she looked at the locust trees that almost hid the church spire, at the straggling line of eucalyptus trees that followed the country road to the graveyard a mile away. It was home. It was all she had known of the world--and she was going away into a terrifying new life. Her eyes brimmed.

"I swear to you that I'll be faithful, Anthony," she said solemnly. "On my sacred oath, I will!"

And ten minutes later they were on their way. The porter had pinned her new hat up in a pillow-case and taken it away, and Sammy was laughing because another porter quite seriously shouted: "Last call for luncheon in the dining-car!"

"I always knew they did it, but I never supposed they really DID!" said Sammy, following her aunt through the shaded brightness of the Pullman to an enchanted table, from which one could see the glorious landscape flashing by.

It was all like a dream--the cities they fled through, the luxury of the big house at Sippican, the capped and aproned maids that were so eager to make one comfortable. The people she met were like dream people; the busy, useless days seemed too pleasant to be real.

August flashed by, September was gone. With the same magic lack of effort, they were all in the New York house. Sammy wore her first dinner gown, wore her first furs, made her youthful conquests right and left.

From the first, she told every one of her engagement. The thought of it, always in her mind, helped to give her confidence and poise.

"You must have heard of me, you know," said her first dinner partner, "for your sister's told me a lot about YOU. Piet van Soop."

"Piet van SOOP!" ejaculated Sammy, seriously.

"Certainly. Don't you think that's a pretty name?"

"But--but that can't be your name," argued Sammy, smilingly.

"Why can't it?"

"Why, because no one with a name like van Soop to begin with would name a little darling baby PIET," submitted Sammy.

"Oh, come," said Mr. van Soop. "Your own name, now! Sammy, as Mary always calls you--that's nothing to boast of, you know, and I'll bet you were a very darling little baby yourself!"

Sammy laughed joyously, and a dozen fellow guests glanced sympathetically in the direction of the fresh, childish sound.

"Well, if that's really your name, of course you can't help it," she conceded, adding, with the naivete that Mr. van Soop already found delightful: "Wouldn't the COMBINATION be awful, though! Sammy van Soop!"

"If you'll consider it, I'll endeavor to make it the only sorrow you have to endure," said Mr. van Soop; and the ensuing laughter brought them the attention of the whole table.

"No danger!" said Sammy, gayly. "I'm going home in December, you know, to be married!"

Every one heard it. Mary winced. Mrs. Bond flushed. Tom said a word that gave his pretty partner a right to an explanation. But Sammy was apparently cheerful.

Only apparently, however. For that night, when she found herself in her luxurious room again, she took Anthony's picture from the bureau and studied it gravely under the lights.

"I said that right out," she said aloud, "and I'll KEEP ON saying it. Then, when the time comes to go, I simply CAN'T back out!"

She put the picture back, and sat down at her dressing-table and stared at her own reflection. Her hair was filleted with silver and tiny roses; her gown was of exquisite transparent embroidery, and more tiny roses rumpled the deep lace collar. But even less familiar than this finery were the cheeks that blazed with so many remembered compliments, the scarlet lips that had learned to smile so readily, the eyes brilliant with new dreams.

"I feel as if sorrow--SORROW," said little Sammy, shivering, "were just about two feet behind me, and as if--if it ever catches up-- I'll be the most unhappy girl in the world!"

And she gave herself a little shake and put a firm little finger-tip on Gabrielle's bell.

"Sammy," said Mr. van Soop, one dull gray afternoon some weeks later, "I've brought you out for a special purpose to-day."

"Tea?" said Sammy, contentedly.

"Tea, gluttonous one," he admitted, turning his big car into the park. "But, seriously, I want to ask you about your going away."

"I don't know that there's anything to say about it," said Sammy, carelessly. "I've had a wonderful time, and every one's been charming. And now I've got to go back."

"Sammy, I've no right to ask you a favor, but I've a REASON," Piet began. He halted. Both were crimson.

"Yes, yes; I know, Piet," said Sammy, fluttered.

The car slackened, stopped. Their faces were not two feet apart.

"Well! Will you let me BEG you--for your aunt, and sister, and for-- well, for me, and for your own sake, Sammy--will you let me BEG you just to wait? Here, or there, or anywhere else--will you just WAIT a while?"

Sammy was silent a moment. Then--

"For what reason?" she said.

"Because you may save yourself lifelong unhappiness."

Sammy pondered, her lashes dropped, her hands clasped in her muff.

"Piet," she said gravely, "it's not as bad as that. No--I'll not be unhappy. I love Wheatfield, and horses, and the old house, and--" she hesitated, adding more brightly: "and you can MAKE happiness, you know! Just because it's spring, or it's Thanksgiving, or you've got a good book! Please go on," she urged suddenly. "We're very conspicuous here."

They moved slowly along under the bare trees. A sullen sunset colored the western sky. The drive was filled with motor-cars, and groups of riders galloped on the muddy bridle-path. It was just dusk. Suddenly, as the lamplighters went their rounds, all the park bloomed with milky disks of light.

"You see," Sammy went on presently, "I've thought this all out. Anthony's a good man, and he loves me, and I--well, I've promised. What RIGHT have I to say calmly that I've changed my mind, and to hurt him and make him ridiculous before all the people he loves? He knows I'll have money some day--no, Piet, you needn't look so! That has nothing to do with it! But, of course, he KNOWS it; and I said we would have a motor,--he's wild for one!--and entertain, don't you know, and that's what he's waiting for and counting on. He doesn't DESERVE to be shamed and humiliated. And, besides, it would break his mother's heart. She's been awfully sweet to me. And it must be a BITTER thing to be told that you're not good enough for the woman you love. Anthony saved my life, you know, and I can't break my word. I said: 'On my oath, I'll come back.' And just because there IS a difference between him--and us," she hesitated, "he's all the prouder and more sensitive. And it's only a difference in surface things!" finished Sammy, loyally. Piet was silent.

"Why, Tom keeps telling me that mother was a Cabot, and grandfather a judge, and talking Winthrop Colony and Copleys and Gilbert Stuarts to me!" the girl burst out presently. "As if that wasn't the very REASON for my being honorable! That's what blood's for!"

Still Piet was silent, his kind, ugly face set and dark.

"And then, you know," said Sammy, with sudden brightness, "when I get back, and see the dear old place again, and get a good big breath of AIR,--which we don't have here!--why, it'll all straighten out and seem right again. My hope is," she added, turning her honest eyes to the gloomy ones so near her, "my hope is that Anthony will be willing to wait a while--"

"What makes you think he is likely to?" said Piet, dryly.

There was a silence. Then he added:

"When do you go?"

"The--the twenty-sixth, I believe. I've got aunty's consent--I go with the Archibalds to San Francisco."

"And this is--?"

"The twentieth."

For some time after that they wove their way along the sweeping Parkroads without speaking, and when they did begin to talk to one another again, the subject was a different one and Mr. van Soop was more cheerful. The tea hour was a fairly merry one. But when he left Sammy, an hour later, at her aunt's door, he took off his big glove, and grew a little white, and held out his hand to her and said:

"I won't see you again, Sammy. I've been thinking it over. You're right; it's all my own fault. I was very wrong to attempt to persuade you. But I won't see you again. Good-by."

"Why--!" began Sammy, in astonishment; then she looked down and stammered, "Oh--," and finally she put her little hand in his and said simply:

"Good-by."

Therefore it was a surprise to Mr. van Soop to find himself entering Mrs. Bond's library just twenty-four hours later, and grasping the hands of the slender young woman who rose from a chair by the fire.

"Sammy! You sent for me?"

Sammy looked very young in a little velvet gown with a skirt short enough to show the big bows on her slippers. Her eyes had a childishly bewildered expression.

"I wanted you," she said simply. "I--I've had a letter from Anthony. It came only an hour ago. I don't know whether to be sorry or glad. Read it! Read it!"

She sat on a little, low stool by the fire, and Piet flattened the many loose pages of the letter on his knee and read.

Anthony had written on the glazed, ruled single sheets of the "Metropolitan Star Hotel"--had covered some twenty of them with his loose, dashing hand-writing.

MY DEAR SAMMY [wrote Anthony, with admirable directness]: The boys wanted me to sit in a little game to-night, but the truth is I have been wanting for a long time to speak to you of a certain matter, and to-night seems a good chance to get it off my chest. A man feels pretty rotten writing a letter like this, but I've thought it over for more than a month now, and I feel that no matter how badly you and I both feel, the thing to do is not to let things go too far before we think the thing pretty thoroughly over and make sure that things--

"What the deuce is he getting at?" said Piet, breaking off suddenly.

"Go on!" said Sammy, bright color in her cheeks.--make sure that things are best for the happiness of all parties [resumed Piet]. You see, Sammy [the letter ran on], as far as I am concerned, I never would have said a word, but I have been talking things over with a party whose name I will tell you in a minute, and they feel as if it would be better to write before you come on. I mean Miss Alma Fay. You don't know her. She is Lucy Barbee's cousin. Lucy and I had a great case years ago, and she and Tom asked me up to their house a few weeks ago, and Alma was staying with Lucy. Well, I took her to the Hallowe'en dance, and it was a keen dance, the swellest we ever had at the hall. Some of us rowed the girls on the river between the dances; we had a keen time. Well, after that I took her riding once or twice. She rides the best of any girl I ever saw; her father has the finest horses in East Wood--I guess he counts for quite a lot up there, he has the biggest department store and runs his own motor. Well, Sammy, I never would of written one word of this to you, but when Alma came to go away we both realized how it was. You know I have often had cases, as the boys call them, and a girl I was engaged to in Petrie told me once she hoped some day I'd get MINE. Well, she would be pleased if she knew that I HAVE. I have not slept since--

"Sammy!" said Piet, suddenly stopping.

"Go on!" said she, again.

But Piet couldn't go on. He glanced at the next page, read, "Now, Sammy, it is up to you to decide," skipped another page or two and read, "Neither Alma nor I would ever be happy if--" glanced at a third; then the leaves fluttered in wild confusion to the floor, and, with something between a sob and a shout, he caught Sammy in his arms.

"My darling," said Piet, an hour later, "if I release your right hand for ten minutes, do you think you could write a line to Mr. Anthony Gayley? I would like to mail it when I go home to dress."

"I was thinking I might wire--" said Sammy, dreamily.

DR. BATES AND MISS SALLY

Sometimes Ferdie's jokes were successful; sometimes they were not. This was one of the jokes that didn't succeed; but as it led to a chain of circumstances that proved eminently satisfactory, Ferdie's wife praised him as highly for his share in it as if he really had done something rather meritorious.

At the time it occurred, however, nobody praised anybody, and feeling even ran pretty high for a time between Ferdie and Elsie, his wife, and her sister Sally, and Dr. Bates.

Dr. Samuel Bates was a rising young surgeon, plain, quiet, and kindly. He was spending a few busy months in California, and writing dutifully home to friends and patients in Boston that he really could not free his hands to return just yet. But Sally knew what that meant; she had known business to keep people in her neighborhood before. So she was studiously unkind to the doctor, excusing herself to Elsie on the ground that nothing on earth would ever make her consider a man with fuzzy red hair and low collars.

Sally was a "daughter" and a "dame"; the doctor was the son of "Bates's Blue-Ribbon Hair Renewer"--awful facts against which the additional fact that he was rich and she was not, counted nothing. Sally talked all the time; the doctor was the most silent of men. Sally was twenty-two, the doctor thirty-five. Sally loved to flirt; the doctor never paid any attention to women. Altogether, it was the most impossible thing ever heard of, and Elsie might just as well stop thinking about it!

"It's a wonderful proof of what he feels," said Elsie, "to have him so gentle when you are rude to him, and so eager to be friends when you get over it!"

"It's a wonderful example of hair-tonic spirit!" Sally responded.

"There's a good deal behind that quiet manner," argued Elsie.

"But NOT the three generations that make a gentleman!" finished Sally.

Sally was out calling one hot Saturday afternoon when Ferdie, as was his habit, brought Dr. Bates home with him to the Ferdies' little awninged and shingled summer home in Sausalito. Elsie, with an armful of delightfully pink and white baby, led them to the cool side porch, and ordered cool things to drink. Sally, she said, as they sank into the deep chairs, would be home directly and join them.

Presently, surely enough, some one ran up the front steps and came into the wide hall, and Sally's voice called a blithe "Hello!" There was a little rattle to show that her parasol was flung down, and then the voice again, this time unmistakably impeded by hat-pins.

"Where's this fam-i-ly? Did the gentlemen come?"

This gave an opening for the sort of thing Ferdie thought he did very well. He grinned at his guest, and raised a warning finger.

"Hello, Sally!" he called back. "Elsie and I are out here! Bates couldn't come--operation last minute!"

"What--didn't come?" Sally called back after an instant's pause. "Well, what has happened to HIM? But, thank goodness, now I can go to the Bevis dinner to-morrow! Operation? I must say it's mannerly to send a message the last minute like that!" She hummed a second, and then added spitefully: "What can you expect of hair-tonic, anyway?" The frozen group on the porch heard her start slowly upstairs. "Well, I might be willing to marry him," added Sally, cheerfully, as she mounted, "but it's a real relief to snatch this glorious afternoon from the burning! Down in a second--keep me some tea!"

Nobody moved on the porch. The doctor's face was crimson, Elsie's kind eyes wide with horror. Sally called a final reflection from the first landing:

"Too bad not to have him see me looking so beautiful!" she sang frivolously. "Operation--h'm! An important operation--I don't believe it!"

She proceeded calmly to her room, and was buttoning herself into a trim linen gown when Elsie burst in, flushed and furious, cast the baby dramatically upon the bed, and hysterically recounted the effects of her recent remarks. Sally, at first making a transparent effort to seem amused, and following it with an equally vain attempt at being dignified, finally became very angry herself.

"When Ferdie does things like this," said Sally, heatedly, "I declare I wonder--I was going to say I wonder he has a friend left in the world! As you say, it's done now, but it makes me so FURIOUS! And I don't think it shows very much savior faire on your part, Elsie. However, we won't discuss it! Ferdie will try one joke too many, one of these days, and then--Now, look here, Elsie," Sally interrupted her tirade to state with deadly deliberation, "unless that man goes home before dinner, as a man of any spirit would do, I'm going over to Mary Bevis's, and you can make whatever apologies you like!"

"Of course he won't go," said Elsie, with spirit. "The only thing to do is to ignore it entirely. And of course you'll come down."

Sally had resumed her ruffled calling costume, and was now pinning on an effective hat. Her mouth was set.

"Please!" pleaded her sister, inserting a gold bracelet tenderly between George's little jaws, without moving her eyes from Sally.

"I will not!" said Sally. "I never want to see him again--superior, big, calm codfish--too lofty to care what any one says about him! I don't like a man you can walk on, anyway!" She began to pack things in a suit-case--beribboned night-wear, slippers, powder, and small jars. Presently, hasping these things firmly in, she went to the door, and opened it a cautious crack.

"Where are they?" she asked.

"I don't know," said Mrs. Ferdie, dispiritedly. "I think you're very mean!"

The bedrooms of the Ferdies' house opened in charming Southern fashion upon open balconies, over whose slender rails one could look straight into the hall below. Sally listened intently.

"What a horrible plan this house is built upon!" she said heartily. "Nothing in the world is more humiliating than to have to sneak about one's own house like a thief, afraid of being seen! Where's the motor--at the side door? Good. I'll run it over to the Bevises' myself, and Billy can come back with it. That is, I will if I can manage to get to the side door. Those idiots of men are apparently looking at Ferd's rods and tackle, right down there in the hall! I can distinctly hear their voices! I wish Ferd had thought of situations like this when he planned this silly balcony business! The minute I open this door they'll look up; and I'll stay up here a week rather than meet them!"

"They'll go out soon," said Elsie, soothingly, as she removed a shoe-horn from contact with George's mouth.

"I knew Ferd would regret this balcony!" pursued Sally, eyes to the crack.

"Ferdie's not regretting it!" tittered her sister.

Sally cast her a withering glance. Elsie devoted herself suddenly to George.

"Go down and lure them into the garden," pleaded Sally, presently.

Elsie obligingly picked up her son and departed, but Sally, watching her go, was infuriated to notice that a mild request from George's nurse, who met them in the hall, apparently drove all thoughts of Sally's predicament from the little mother's mind, for Elsie went briskly toward the nursery, and an absolute silence ensued.

Sally went listlessly to the window, where her eye was immediately caught by a long pruning ladder, leaning against the house a dozen feet away. Alma, the little waitress, quietly mixing a mayonnaise on the kitchen porch, was pressed into service, and five minutes later Sally's suit-case was cautiously lowered, on the end of a Mexican lariat, and Sally was steadying the top of the ladder against her window-sill. Alma was convulsed with innocent mirth, but her big, hard hands were effective in steadying the lower end of the ladder.

Sally, who was desperately afraid of ladders, packed her thin skirts tightly about her, gave a fearful glance below, and began a nervous descent. At every alternate rung she paused, unwound her skirts, shut her eyes, and breathed hard.

"PLEASE don't shake it so!" she said.

"Aye dadden't!" said Alma, merrily.

The ladder slipped an inch, settling a little lower. Sally uttered a smothered scream. She dared not move her eyes from the rung immediately in front of them. Her face was flushed, her hair had slipped back from her damp temples. It seemed to her as if she must already have climbed down several times the length of the ladder. At every step she had to kick her skirts free.

"Permit me!" said a kind voice in the world of reeling brick walks and dwarfed gooseberry bushes below her.

Sally, with a thump at her heart, looked down to see Dr. Bates lay a firm hand upon the rocking ladder.

Speechless, she finished the descent, reeling a little unsteadily against the doctor's shoulder as she faced about on the walk. Her face was crimson. To climb down a ladder, with him looking pleasantly up from below, and then to fall into his very arms! Sally shook out her skirts like a furious hen, and walked, with one chilly inclination of the head for acknowledgment of his courtesy, toward the waiting motor.

"Ferdie has promised Bill Bevis that you will spin me over in the motor," said the doctor, a little timidly, when they reached it.

Sally eyed him stonily.

"Ferd--"

"Why, I had promised Bevis that I would look in to-day," pursued the doctor, uncomfortably; "and when they telephoned about it, a few minutes ago, one of the maids said that she believed that you were going right over, and would bring me."

"I have changed my mind," said Sally. "Perhaps you will drive yourself over?"

"I don't know anything about motors," apologized the doctor, gravely.

"Ferd told one of the maids to say I would?" Sally said pleasantly. "Very well. Will you get in?"

They got in, Sally driving. They swept in silence past the lawns, and into the wide, white highway. A watering-cart had just passed, and the air was fresh and wet. The afternoon was one of exquisite beauty. The steamer from San Francisco was just in, and the road was filled with other motor-cars and smart traps. Sally and the doctor nodded and waved to a score of friends.

"I am as sorry as you are," said the doctor, awkwardly, after the silence had grown very long.

"Don't mention it," said Sally, her face flaming again. "That's my brother's idea of humor. I--I shall stay at the Bevises' overnight."

"I--why, I said I would do that!" said Dr. Bates, hastily. "I just called in to the maid, when she telephoned Bevis, and said, 'Ask him if he can put me up over-night.' You see, I've got my things."

"Well, then, I won't," said Sally. Her tone was cold, but a side glance at his serious face melted her a little. "This is ALL Ferdie!" she burst out angrily.

"Too bad to make it so important," said the doctor, regretfully.

"I don't see why you should stay at the Bevises'," said the girl, fretfully. "It looks very odd--when you had come to us. I--I am going to Glen Ellen early to-morrow, anyway. I would hate to have the Bevises suspect--"

"Then I will go back with you," agreed the doctor, pleasantly.

Sally frowned. She opened her lips, but shut them without speaking. She had turned the car into a wide gateway, and a moment later they stopped at a piazza full of young people. The noisy, joyous Bevis girls and boys swarmed rapturously about them.

After an hour of laughter and shouting, Sally and the doctor rose to go, accompanied to the motor by all the young people.

"Ah, you just got in, doctor?" said gentle Mrs. Bevis, with a glance at the suit-cases.

Sally flushed, but the doctor serenely let the misunderstanding go. There was no good reason to give for the presence of two cases in the car.

"You look quite like an elopement!" said Page Bevis with a joyous shout.

"Put one of the cases in front, Bates, and rest your feet on it," suggested the older boy, Kenneth.

As he spoke, he caught up Sally's case, and gave it a mighty swing from the tonneau to the front seat. In mid-flight, the suit-case opened. Jars and powders, slippers and beribboned apparel scattered in every direction. Small silver articles, undeniably feminine in nature, lay on the grass; a spangled scarf which they had all admired on Sally's slender shoulders had to be tenderly extricated from the brake.

With shrieks of laughter, the Bevis family righted the case and repacked it. Sally was frozen with anger.

"Mother SAID she knew you two would run off and get married quietly some day!" said pretty, audacious Mary Bevis.

"Dearie!" protested her mother. "I only said--I only thought--I said I thought--Mary, that's very naughty of you! Sally, you know how innocently one surmises an engagement, or guesses at things!"

"Oh, mother, you're getting in deeper and deeper!" said her older son. "Never you mind, Sally! You can elope if you want to!"

"San Rafael's the place to go, Sally," said Mary. "All the elopers get married there. The court-house, you know. No delays about licenses!"

"They're very naughty," said their mother, beginning to see how unwelcome this joking was to the visitors. "Are you going straight home, dear?"

"Straight home!" said the doctor.

"Well, speaking of San Rafael," pursued the matron, kindly--"can't you two and Elsie and Ferd go with us all to-night, say about an hour from now, up to Pastori's and have dinner?"

"Oh, thanks!" said Sally, trying to smile naturally. "I'm afraid not to-night. I've got a headache, and I'm going home to turn in."

Amid cheerful good-bys, she wheeled the car, and drove it along rapidly, pursuing thoughts of the Bevis boys hardly short of murderous. The doctor was silent; but Sally, glancing at him, saw his quiet smile change to an apologetic look, and hated both the smile and the apology.

They went more slowly on the steep road from the water front to the hillside. The level light of the sinking sun shone brilliantly on daisies and nasturtiums at the roadside. Boats, riding at anchor, dipped in the wash of another incoming steamer. Dr. Bates hummed; but Sally frowned, and he was immediately hushed.

"Boy looking for you?" he said presently, as a small and dusty boy rose from a boulder at one side of the road and shouted something unintelligible.

"Why, I guess he is for me!" said Sally, in the first natural tone she had used that afternoon.

But the boy, upon being interrogated, said that the telegram was for "the doc that was visiting up to Miss Sally's house."

Dr. Bates read the little message several times, and absently dismissed the messenger with a coin, which Sally thought outrageously large, and a muttered worried word or two.

"Bad news?" she asked.

"In a way," he said quickly. "When's the next train for San Rafael, Miss Sally? I've got to be there to-night--right away! Do we have to stand here? Thank you. There's a case Field and I have been watching; he says that there's got to be an operation at eight--" His voice trailed off into troubled silence, and he drew out his watch. "Eight!" he muttered. "It's on seven now!"

"Oh, and you have to operate--horrible for you!" said Sally, taking the car skilfully toward the railroad station as she spoke. "But I don't see how you CAN! You've missed the six-thirty train, and there's not another until after nine. But you can wire Dr. Field that you will be there the first thing in the morning."

The doctor paid no attention.

"The livery stable is closed, I suppose?" he asked.

"Oh, long ago!"

He ruminated frowningly. Suddenly his face cleared.

"Funny how one thinks of the right solution last!" he said in relief. "How long would it take you to run me up there? Forty minutes?"

"I don't see how I could," said Sally, flushing. "I can take the car home, though, and ask Ferd to do it. But that woman's at the hotel, isn't she? I couldn't go up there and sit outside, with every one I knew coming out and wondering why I brought you instead of Ferd! Elsie wouldn't like it. You must see--"

"It would take us fifteen minutes at least to go up and get Ferd," objected the doctor, seriously; "and he's not much better than I am at running it, anyway!"

"Well, I'm sorry," said Sally, shortly, "but I simply couldn't do it. Dr. Field should have given you more notice. It would look simply absurd for me to go tearing over these country roads at night--Elsie would go mad wondering where I was--"

They were in the village now. Troubled and stubborn, Sally stopped the car, and looked mutinously at her companion. The doctor's rosy face was flushed under his flaming hair, and in his very blue eyes was a look that struck her with an almost panicky sensation of surprise. Sally had never seen any man regard her with an expression of distaste before, but the doctor's look was actually inimical.

"I feared that you would be the sort of woman to fail one utterly, like this," he said quietly. "I've often wondered--I've often said to myself, 'COULD she ever, under any circumstances, throw off that pretty baby way of hers, and forget that this world was made just for flirting and dressing and being admired?' By George, I see you can't! I see you can't! Well! Now, whom can I get to take me up there within the hour?" He appeared to ponder. Sally sat as if stupefied.

"Don't resent what I say when I'm upset," said the doctor, absently. "You can't help your limitations, I can't help mine. I see a young woman--she's just lost a little boy, and she's all her husband has left--I see her dying because we're too late. You see a few empty- headed women saying that Sally Reade actually went driving alone, without her dinner, for three hours, with a man she hardly knew. I am not blaming you. You have never pretended to be anything but what you are. I blame myself for hoping--thinking--but, by George, you'd be an utter dead weight on a man if it was ever up to you to face an epidemic, or run a risk, or do one-twentieth of the things that those very ancestors of yours, that you're so proud of, used to do!"

Sally set her teeth. She leaned from the car to summon a small girl loitering on the road.

"You're one of the White children, aren't you?" said she to the child. "I want you to go up to Mrs. Ferdie Potter's house, and tell Mrs. Potter that her sister won't be home for several hours, and that I'll explain later. Now," said Sally, turning superbly to the doctor, "pull your hat down tight. We're going FAST!"

They were three miles farther on their way before he saw that her little chin was quivering, and great tears were running down her small face. Time was precious, but for a few memorable moments they stopped the car again.

Miss Sally and Dr. Bates returned to the sleepy and excited Ferdies' at one o'clock that night. The light that never was on land or sea glittered in Sally's wonderful eyes; the doctor was white, shaken, and radiant. Sally flew to her sister's arms.

"We waited to see--and she came out of it--and she has a fair fighting chance!" said Sally, joyously; and the look she gave her doctor made Elsie's heart rise with a bound.

"Runaways," said Elsie, "come in and eat! I never knew a serious operation to have such a cheering effect on any one before!"

"It all went so well," said Sally, contentedly, over chicken and ginger ale. "But, Elsie! Such fun!" she burst out, her dimples suddenly again in view. "I am disgraced forever! After we had done everything to make the Bevis crowd think we were eloping, what did we do but run into the whole crowd at San Anselmo! I wish you could have seen their faces! We had said we couldn't possibly go; and we were going too fast to stop and explain!"

"We'll explain to-morrow," said the doctor, so significantly that Ferdie rose instantly to grasp his hand, and Elsie fell again upon Sally as if she had never kissed her before.

"Not--not really!" gasped Elsie, turning radiantly from one to the other.

"Oh, really!" said Sally, with her prettiest color. "He despises me, but he will take the case, anyway! And he has done nothing but mortify and enrage me all day, but I feel that I should miss it if it stopped! So we are going to sacrifice our lives to each other-- isn't it edifying and beautiful of us? We'll tell you all about it to-morrow. Jam--Sam?"

THE GAY DECEIVER

After the meat course, Mrs. Tolley and Min rather languidly removed the main platters and, by reaching backward, piled the dinner plates on the shining new oak sideboard. Thus room was made for the salad, which was always mantled in tepid mayonnaise, whether it was sliced tomatoes, or potatoes, or asparagus. After the salad there was another partial clearance, and then every available inch of the table was needed for peach pies and apple sauce and hot gingerbread and raspberries, or various similar delicacies, and the coffee and yellow cheese and soda-crackers with which the meal concluded.

By the time these appeared, on a hot summer evening, the wheezing clock in the kitchen would have struck six,--dinner was early at Kirkwood,--and the level rays of the sun would be pouring boldly in at the uncurtained western windows. The dining, room was bare, and not entirely free from flies, despite an abundance of new green screening at the windows. Relays of new stiff oak chairs stood against its walls, ready for the sudden need of occasional visitors. On the walls hung framed enlarged photographs of machinery, and factories, and scaffoldings, and the like. There was one of laborers and bosses grouped about great generators and water-wheels in transit, and another of a monster switchboard, with a smiling young operator, in his apron and overalls, standing beside it.

Mrs. Tolley sat at the head of the table--a big, joyous, vigorous widow, who had managed the Company House at Kirkwood ever since its erection two years before, and who had been an employee of the Light and Power Company, in one capacity or another, for some five years before that--or ever since, as she put it, "the juice got pore George." Mrs. Tolley loved every inch of Kirkwood; for her it was the captured dream.

Min Tolley, sitting next to her mother, loved Kirkwood, too, because she was going to marry Harry Garvey, who was one of the shift bosses at the plant. Harry sat next to Min. Then came her brother Roosy, ten years old; and then the Hopps--Mrs. Lou, and little Lou, spattering rice and potato all over himself and his chair, and big Lou, silently, deeply admiring them both. Then there were two empty chairs, for the Chisholms, the resident manager and superintendent and his sister, at the end of the table; and then Joe Vorse, the switchboard operator, and his little wife; and then Monk White, another shift boss; and lastly, at Mrs. Tolley's left, Paul Forster, newly come from New York to be Mr. Chisholm's stenographer and assistant.

Paul was the first to leave the table that night. He drank his coffee in three savage gulps, pushed back his crumpled napkin, and rose. "If you'll excuse me--" he began.

"You're cert'n'y excusable!" said Mrs. Tolley, elegantly--adding, when the door had closed behind him: "And leave me tell you right now that somebody was real fond of children to raise YOU!"

"An' I'm not planning to spend the heyday of my girlhood ironing napkins for you, Pauly Pet!" said Min, reaching for his discarded napkin and folding it severely into a wooden ring.

Paul did not hear these remarks, but he heard the laughter that greeted them, and he scowled as he selected a rocker on the front porch. He put his feet up on the rail, felt in one pocket for tobacco, in another for papers, and in a third for his match-case, and set himself to the congenial task of composing a letter in which he should resign from the employ of the Light and Power Company. It was a question of a broken contract, so it must be diplomatically worded. Paul had spent the five evenings since his arrival at Kirkwood in puzzling over the phrasing of that letter.

Below the porch, the hillside, covered with scrub-oak and chaparral and madrono trees, and the stumps where redwoods had been, dropped sharply to the little river, which came tumbling down from the wooded mountains to plunge roaring into one end of the big power- house, and which foamed out at the other side to continue its mad rush down the valley. The power-house, looming up an immense crude outline in the twilight, rested on the banks of the stream and stood in a rough clearing. A great gash in the woods above it showed whence lumber for buildings and fires came; another ugly gash marked the course of the "pole line" over the mountain. Near the big building stood lesser ones, two or three rough little unpainted cottages perched on the hill above it. There was a "cook-house," and a "bunk-house," and storage sheds, and Mrs. Tolley's locked provision shed, and the rough shack the builders lived in while construction was going on, and where the Hopps lived now, rent free.

Nasturtiums languished here and there, where some of the women had made an effort to fight the unresponsive red clay. Otherwise, even after two years, the power-house and its environs looked unfinished, crude, ugly. On all sides the mountains rose dark and steep, the pointed tops of the redwoods mounting evenly, tier on tier. Except for the lumber slide and the pole line, there was no break anywhere, not even a glimpse of the road that wound somehow out of the canyon- -up, up, up, twelve long miles, to the top of the ridge.

And even at the top, Paul reflected bitterly, there was only an unpainted farmhouse, where the stage stopped three times a week with mail. From there it was a fifty-mile drive to town--a California country town, asleep in the curve of two sluggish little rivers. And from "town" to San Francisco it was almost a day's trip, and from San Francisco to the Grand Central Station at Forty-second Street it was nearly five days more.

Paul shoved his hands in his pockets and began again: "Light and Power Co.--GENTLEMEN."

Night came swiftly to Kirkwood. For a few wonderful moments the last of the sunlight lingered, hot and gold, on the upper branches of the highest trees along the ridge; then suddenly the valley was plunged in soft twilight, and violet shadows began to tangle themselves about the great shafts of the redwoods. The heat of the day dropped from the air like a falling veil. A fine mist spun itself above the river; bats began to wheel on the edge of the clearing.

With the coming of darkness every window in the place was suddenly alight. The Company House blazed with it; the great power-house doorway sent a broad stream of yellow into the deepening shadows of the night; the "cook-house," where Willy Chow Tong cooked for a score of "hands" and oilers, showed a thousand golden cracks in its rough walls. The little cottages on the hill were hidden by the glare from their dangling porch lights. Light was so plentiful, at this factory of light, that even the Hopps' barnlike home blazed with a dozen "thirty-twos."

"Nothing like having a little light on the subject, Mr. Fo'ster," said Mrs. Tolley, coming out to the porch. The Vorses had small children that they could not leave very long alone; so, when Min and her mother had reduced the kitchen to orderly, warm, soap-scented darkness every night, and wound the clock, and hung up their aprons, they went up to the Vorses' to play "five hundred."

"Seems's if I never could get enough light, myself," the matron continued agreeably, descending the porch steps. "Before I come here I never had nothing in my kitchen but an oil lamp and a reflector. Jest as sure as I'd be dishing up dinner, hot nights, that lamp would begin to flicker and suck--well, shucks! I'd look up at it and I'd say, 'Well, why don't you go out? Go ahead!'" Mrs. Tolley laughed joyously. "Well, one night--George--" she was continuing with relish, when Min pulled at her sleeve and, with a sort of affectionate impatience, said, "Oh, f've'vens' sakes ma!"

"Yes, I'm coming," said Mrs. Tolley, recalled. "Wish't you played 'five hundred,' Mr. Fo'ster," she added politely.

"I don't play either that or old maid," said Paul, distinctly. This remark was taken in good part by the Tolleys.

"Old maid's a real comical game," Min conceded mildly.

"Well, you won't be s'lunsum next week when the Chisholms get back," said Mrs. Tolley, unaffectedly, gathering up the skirt of her starched gown to avoid contact with the sudden heavy dews. "He's an awful nice feller, and she--she's twenty-six, but she's as jolly as a girl. I declare, I just love Patricia Chisholm."

"Twenty-six, is she?" said Paul, disgustedly, to himself, when the Tolleys had gone. "Only one woman--of any class, that is--in this forsaken hole, and she twenty-six!" And he had been thinking of this Patricia with a good deal of interest, he admitted resentfully. Paul was twenty-four, and liked slender little girls well under twenty.

"Lord, what a place!" he said, for the hundredth time.

He sat brooding in the darkness, discouraged and homesick. So he had sat for all his nights at Kirkwood.

The men at the cook-house were playing cards, silently, intently. The cook, serene and cool, was smoking in the doorway of his cabin. Above the dull roar of the river Paul could hear Min Tolley's cackle of laughter from the cottages a hundred yards away, and Mrs. Hopps crooning over her baby.

Presently the night shift went down to the powerhouse, the men taking great boyish leaps on the steep trail. Some of the lighted windows were blotted out-- the Hopps', the cook-house light. The singing pole line above Paul's head ceased abruptly, and with a little rising whine the opposite pole line took up the buzzing currant. That meant that the copper line had been cut in, and the aluminum one would be "cold" for the night.

Minutes went by, eventless. Half an hour, an hour--still Paul sat staring into the velvet dark and wrestling with bitter discouragement and homesickness.

"Lord, what a PLACE!" he said once or twice under his breath.

Finally, feeling cramped and chilly, he went stiffly indoors, through the hot, bright halls, that smelled of varnish and matting, to his room.

The next day was exactly like the five preceding days--hot, restless, aimless; and the next night Paul sat on the porch again, and listened to the rush of the river, and Min Tolley's laugh at the "five hundred" table, and the Hopps' baby's lullaby. And again he composed his resignation, and calculated that it would take three days for it to reach San Francisco, and another three for him to receive their acceptance of it--another week at least of Kirkwood!

On the seventh day the Chisholms rode down the trail that followed the pole line, and arrived in a hospitable uproar. Alan Chisholm, some five years older than Paul, was a fine-looking, serious, dark youth, a fellow of not many words, being given rather to silent appreciation of his sister's chatter than to speech of his own. Miss Chisholm was very tall, very easy in manner, and powdered just now to her eyelashes with fine yellow dust. Paul thought her too tall and too large for beauty, but he liked her voice, and the fashion she had of crinkling up her eyes when she smiled. He sat on the porch while the Chisholms went upstairs to brush and change, and thought that the wholesome noise of their splashing and calling, opening draw- ers, and banging doors was a pleasant change from the usual quiet of the house.

Miss Chisholm was the first to reappear. She was followed by Min and Mrs. Tolley, and was asking questions at a rate that kept both answering at once. Had her kodak films come? Was Minnie going to have some little sense and be married in a dress she could get some use out of? How were the guinea-pigs, the ducks, the vegetables, the caged fox, the "boys" generally, Roosy's ear, Consuelo Vorse's lame foot? Did Mrs. Tolley know that she had made a deep impression on the old fellow who drove the stage? "Oh, look at her blush, Min! Well, really!"

She came, delightfully refreshed by toilet waters and crisp linen, to take a deep rocker opposite Paul, and leaned luxuriously back, showing very trim feet shod in white.

"Admit that you've fallen in love with Kirkwood, Mr. Forster," said she.

"I can't admit anything of the sort," said Paul, firmly, but smiling because she was so very good to look at. He had to admit that he had never seen handsomer dark eyes, nor a more tender, more expressive and characterful mouth than the one that smiled so readily and showed so even a line of big teeth.

"Oh, you will!" she assured him easily. "There's no place like Kirkwood, is there, Alan?" she said to her brother, as he came out. He smiled.

"We don't think there is, Forster. My sister's been crazy about the place since we got here--that's eighteen months ago; and I'm crazy about it myself now!"

"Wait until you've slept out on the porch for a while," said Miss Chisholm, "and wait until you've got used to a plunge in the pool before breakfast every morning. Alan, you must take him down to the pool to-morrow, and I'll listen for his shrieks. Where are you going now--the power-house? No, thank you, I won't go. I'm going out to find something special to cook you for your suppers."

The something special was extremely delicious; Paul had a vague impression that there was fried chicken in it, and mushrooms, and cream, and sherry. Miss Chisholm served it from a handsome little copper blazer, and also brewed them her own particular tea, in a Canton tea-pot. Paul found it much pleasanter at this end of the table. To his surprise, no one resented this marked favoritism--Mrs. Tolley observing contentedly that her days of messing for men were over, and Mrs. Vorse remarking that she'd "orghter reely git out her chafing-dish and do some cooking" herself.

Paul found that Miss Chisholm possessed a leisurely gift of fun; she was droll, whether she quite meant to be or not. Everybody laughed. Mrs. Tolley became tearful with mirth.

"Now, this is the nicest part of the day," said Patricia, when they three had carried their coffee out to the porch and were seated. "Did you ever watch the twilight come, sitting here, Mr. Forster?"

"It seems to me I have never done anything else," said Paul. She gave him a keen glance over her lifted teaspoon; then she drank her coffee, set the cup down, and said:

"Well! How is that combination of vaudeville and railway station and zotrope that is known as New York?"

"Oh, the little old berg is all there," said Paul, lightly. But his heart gave a sick throb. He hoped she would go on talking about it. But it was some time before any one spoke, and then it was Alan Chisholm, who took his pipe out of his mouth to say:

"Patricia hates New York."

"I can't imagine any one doing that," Paul said emphatically.

"Well, there was a time when I thought I couldn't live anywhere else," said Alan, good-naturedly; "but there's a lot of the pioneer in any fellow, if he gives it a chance."

"Oh, I had a nice enough time in New York," said Patricia, lazily, "but it just WEARS YOU OUT to live there; and what do you get out of it? Now, HERE--well, one's equal to the situation here!"

"And then some," Paul said; and the brother and sister laughed at his tone.

"But, honestly," said Miss Chisholm, "you take a little place like Kirkwood, and you don't need a Socialist party. We all eat the same; we all dress about the same; and certainly, if any one works hard here, it's Alan, and not the mere hands. Why, last Christmas there wasn't a person here who didn't have a present--even Willy Chow Tong! Every one had all the turkey he could eat; every one a fire, and a warm bed, and a lighted house. Mrs. Tolley gets only fifty dollars a month, and Monk White gets fifty--doesn't he, Alan? But money doesn't make much difference here. You know how the boys adore Monk for his voice; and as for Mrs. Tolley, she's queen of the place! Now, how much of that's true of New York!"

"Oh, well, put it that way--" Paul said, in the tone of an offended child.

"Apropos of Mrs. Tolley's being queen of the place," said Alan to his sister, "it seems she's rubbing it into poor little Mollie Peavy. Len brought Mollie and the baby down from the ranch a week ago, and nobody's been near 'em."

"Who said so?" flashed Miss Chisholm, reddening.

"Why, I saw Len to-night, sort of lurking round the power-house, and he told me he had 'em in that little cottage, across the creek, where the lumbermen used to live. Said Mollie was in agony because nobody came near her."

"Oh, that makes me furious!" said Patricia, passionately. "I'll see about it to-morrow. Nobody went near her? The poor little thing!"

"Who are they?" said Paul.

"Why, she's a little blonde, sickly-looking thing of sixteen," explained Miss Chisholm, "and Len's a lumberman. They have a little blue-nosed, sickly baby; it was born about six weeks ago, at her father's ranch, above here. She was--she had no mother, the poor child--"

"And in fact, my sister escorted the benefit of clergy to them about two months ago," said Alan, "and the ladies of the Company House are very haughty about it."

"They won't be long," predicted Miss Chisholm, confidently. "The idea! I can forgive Mrs. Hopps, because she's only a kid herself; but Mrs. Tolley ought to have been big enough! However!"

"This place honestly can't spare you for ten minutes, Pat," her brother said.

"Well, honestly," she was beginning seriously, when she saw he was laughing at her, and broke off, with a shamefaced, laughing look for Paul. Then she announced that she was going down to the power-house, and, packing her thin white skirts about her, she started off, and they followed.

Paul was not accustomed to seeing a lady in the power-house, and thought that her enthusiasm was rather nice to watch. She flitted about the great barnlike structure like a contented child, insisted upon displaying the trim stock-room to Paul, demanded a demonstration of the switchboard, spread her pretty hands over the whirling water that showed under the glass of the water-wheels, and hung, fascinated, over the governors.

"I never get used to it," said Patricia, above the steady roaring of the river. "Do you realize that you are in one of the greatest force factories of the world? Look at it!" She swept with a gesture the monster machinery that shone and glittered all about them. "Do you realize that people miles and miles away are reading by lights and taking street-cars that are moved by this? Don't talk to me about the subway and the Pennsylvania Terminal!"

"Oh, come, now!" said Paul.

"Well!" she flared. "Do you suppose that anything bigger was ever done in this world than getting these things--these generators and water-wheels and the corrugated iron for the roof, and the door- knobs and tiles and standards and switch-board, and everything else, up to the top of the ridge from Emville and down this side of the ridge? I see that never occurred to you! Why, you don't KNOW what it was. Struggle, struggle, struggle, day after day--ropes breaking, and tackle breaking, and roads giving way, and rain coming! Suppose one of these had slipped off the trail--well, it would have stayed where it fell. But wait--wait!" she said, interrupting herself with her delightful smile. "You'll love it as we do one of these days!"

"Not," said Paul to himself, as they started back to the house.

After that he saw Miss Chisholm every day, and many times a day; and she was always busy and always cheerful. She wanted her brother and Paul to ride with her up to the dam for a swim; she wanted to go to the woods for ferns for Min's wedding; she was going to make candy and they could come in. She packed delicious suppers, to be eaten in cool places by the creek, and to be followed by their smoking and her careless snatches of songs; she played poker quite as well as they; she played old opera scores and sang to them; she had jig-saw puzzles for slow evenings. She could not begin a game of what Mrs. Tolley called "halmy," with that good lady, without somehow attracting the boys to the table, where they hung, championing and criticising. Paul was more amused than surprised to find Mrs. Peavy having tea with the other ladies on the porch less than a week later. The little mother looked scared and shamed; but Mrs. Tolley had the baby, and was bidding him "love his Auntie Gussie," while she kissed his rounding little cheek. One night, some four weeks after his arrival, Patricia decided that Paul's room must be made habitable; and she and Alan and Paul spent an entire busy evening there, discussing photographs and books, and deciding where to cross the oars, and where to hang the Navajo blanket, and where to put the college colors. Miss Chisholm, who had the quality of grace and could double herself up comfortably on the floor like a child, became thoughtful over the class annual.

"The Dicky, and the Hasty Pudding!" she commented. "Weren't you the Smarty?"

Paul, who was standing with a well-worn pillow in his hand, turned and said hungrily:

"Oh, you know Harvard?"

"Why, I'm Radcliffe!" she said simply.

Paul was stupefied.

"Why, but you never SAID so! I thought yours was some Western college like your brother's!"

"Oh, no; I went to Radcliffe for four years," said she, casually. Then, tapping a picture thoughtfully, she went on: "There's a boy whose face looks familiar."

"Well, but--well, but--didn't you love it?" stammered Paul.

"I liked it awfully well," said Patricia. "Alan, you've got that one a little crooked," she added calmly. Paul decided disgustedly that he gave her up. His own heart was aching so for old times and old voices that it was far more pain than pleasure to handle all these reminders: the photographs, the yacht pennant, the golf-clubs, the rumpled and torn dominoes, the tumbler with "Cafe Henri" blown in the glass, the shabby camera, the old Hawaiian banjo. Oh, what fun it had all been, and what good fellows they were!

"It was lovely, of course," said Patricia, in a businesslike tone; "but this is real life! Cheer up, Paul," she went on (they had reached Christian names some weeks before). "I am going to have two darling girls here for two weeks at Thanksgiving, just from Japan. And think of the concert next month, with Harry Garvey and Laurette Hopps in a play, and Mrs. Tolley singing 'What Are the Wild Waves Saying?' Then, if Alan sends you to Sacramento, you can go to the theatre every night you're there, and pretend"--her eyes danced mischievously--"that you're going to step out on Broadway when the curtain goes down, and can look up the street at electric signs of cocoa and ginger beer and silk petticoats--"

"Oh, don't!" said Paul; and, as if she were a little ashamed of herself, she began to busy herself with the book-case, and was particularly sweet for the rest of the evening. But she wouldn't talk Radcliffe, and Paul wondered if her college days hadn't been happy; she seemed rather uneasy when he repeatedly brought up the subject.

But a day or two later, when he and she were taking a long ride and resting their horses by a little stream high up in the hills, she began to talk of the East; and they let an hour, and then another, go by, while they compared notes. Paul did most of the talking, and Miss Chisholm listened, with downcast eyes, flinging little stones from the crumbling bank into the pool the while.

A lazy leaf or two drifted upon the surface of the water, and where gold sunlight fell through the thick leafage overhead and touched the water, brown water-bugs flitted and jerked. Once a great dragon- fly came through on some mysterious journey, and paused for a palpitating bright second on a sunny rock. The woods all about were silent in the tense hush of the summer afternoon; even the horses were motionless, except for an occasional idle lipping of the underbrush. Now and then a breath of pine, incredibly sweet, crept from the forest.

Paul watched his companion as he talked. She was, as always, quite unself-conscious. She sat most becomingly framed by the lofty rise of oak and redwood and maple trees about her. Her sombrero had slipped back on her braids, and the honest, untouched beauty of her thoughtful face struck Paul forcibly. He wondered if she had ever been in love--what her manner would be to the man she loved.

"What did you come for, Paul?" She was ending some long sentence with the question.

"Come here?" Paul said. "Oh, Lord, there seemed to be reasons enough, though I can't remember now why I ever thought I'd stay."

"You came straight from college?"

"No," he said, a little uneasily; "no. I finished three years ago. You see, my mother married an awfully rich old guy named Steele, the last year I was at col-lege; and he gave me a desk in his office. He has two sons, but they're not my kind. Nice fellows, you know, but they work twenty hours a day, and don't belong to any clubs,-- they'll both die rich, I guess,--and whenever I was late, or forgot some-thing, or beat it early to catch a boat, they'd go to the old man. And he'd ask mother to speak to me."

"I see," said Patricia.

"After a while he got me a job with a friend of his in a Philadelphia iron-works," said the boy; "but that was a ROTTEN job. So I came back to New York; and I'd written a sketch for an amateur theatrical thing, and a manager there wanted me to work it up--said he'd produce it. I tinkered away at that for a while, but there was no money in it, and Steele sent me out to see how I'd like working in one of the Humboldt lumber camps. I thought that sounded good. But I got my leg broken the first week, and had to wire him from the hospital for money. So, when I got well again, he sent me a night wire about this job, and I went to see Kahn the next day, and came up here."

"I see," she said again. "And you don't think you'll stay?"

"Honestly, I can't, Patricia. Honest--you don't know what it is! I could stand Borneo, or Alaska, or any place where the climate and customs and natives stirred things up once in a while. But this is like being dead! Why, it just makes me sick to see the word 'New York' on the covers of magazines--I'm going crazy here."

She nodded seriously.

"Yes, I know. But you've got to do SOMETHING. And since your course was electrical engineering--! And the next job mayn't be half so easy, you know--!"

"Well, it'll be a little nearer Broadway, believe me. No, I'm sorry. I never knew two dandier people than you and your brother, and I like the work, but--!"

He drew a long breath on the last word, and Miss Chisholm sighed, too.

"I'm sorry," she said, staring at the big seal ring on her finger. "I tell you frankly that I think you're making a mistake. I don't argue for Alan's sake or mine, though we both like you thoroughly, and your being here would make a big difference this winter. But I think you've made a good start with the company, and it's a good company, and I think, from what you've said to-day, and other hints you're given me, that you'd make your mother very happy by writing her that you think you've struck your groove. However!"

She got up, brushed the leaves from her skirt, and went to her horse. They rode home through the columned aisles of the forest almost silently. The rough, straight trunks of the redwoods rose all about them, catching gold and red on their thick, fibrous bark from the setting sun. The horses' feet made no sound on the corduroy roadway.

For several days nothing more was said of Paul's going or staying. Miss Chisholm went her usual busy round. Paul wrote his letter of resignation and carried it to the dinner-table one night, hoping to read it later to her, and win her approval of its finely rounded sentences.

But a heavy mail came down the trail that evening, brought by the obliging doctor from Emville, who had been summoned to dress the wounds of one of the line-men who had got too close to the murderous "sixty thousand" and had been badly burned by "the juice." And after the letters were read, and the good doctor had made his patient comfortable, he proved an excellent fourth hand at the game of bridge for which they were always hungering.

So at one o'clock Paul went upstairs with his letter still unapproved. He hesitated in the dim upper hallway, wondering if Patricia, who had left the men to beer and crackers half an hour earlier, had retired, or was, by happy chance, still gossiping with Mrs. Tolley or Min. While he loitered in the hall, the door of her room swung slowly open.

Paul had often been in this room, which was merely a kind of adjunct to the sleeping-porch beyond. He went to the doorway and said, "Patricia!"

The room, wide and charmingly furnished, was quite empty. On the deep couch letters were scattered in a wide circle, and in their midst was an indentation as if some one had been kneeling on the floor with her elbows there. Paul noticed this with a curious feeling of unease, and then called softly again, "Patricia!"

No answer. He walked hesitatingly to his own room and to the window. Why he should have looked down at the dark path with the expectation of seeing her, he did not know; but it was almost without surprise that he recognized the familiar white ruffles and dark head moving away in the gloom. Paul unhesitatingly followed.

He followed her down the trail as far as he had seen her go, and was standing, a little undecidedly, wondering just which way she had turned, when his heart was suddenly brought into his throat by the sound of her bitter sobbing.

A moment later he saw her. She was sitting on a smooth fallen trunk, and had buried her face in her hands. Paul had never heard such sobs; they seemed to shake her from head to foot. Hardly would they lessen, bringing him the hope that her grief, whatever it was, was wearing itself out, when a fresh paroxysm would shake her, and she would abandon herself to it. This lasted for what seemed a long, long time.

After a while Paul cleared his throat, but she did not hear him. And again he stood motionless, waiting and waiting. Finally, when she straightened up and began to mop her eyes, he said, trembling a little:

"Patricia!"

Instantly she stopped crying.

"Who is that?" she said, with an astonishing control of her voice. "Is that you, Alan? I'm all right, dear. Did I frighten you? Is that you, Alan?"

"It's Paul," the boy said, coming nearer.

"Oh--Paul!" she said, relieved. "Does Alan know I'm here?"

"No," he reassured her; then, affectionately: "What is it, Pat?"

"Just--just that I happen to be a fool!" she said huskily, but with an effort at lightness. Paul sat down, beginning to see in the darkness. "I'm all right now," went on Patricia, hardily. "I just--I suppose I just had the blues." She put out a smooth hand in the darkness, and patted Paul's appreciatively. "I'm ashamed of myself!" said she, catching a little sob, as she spoke, like a child.

"Bad news--in your letters?" he hazarded.

"No, GOOD; that's the trouble!" she said, with her whimsical smile, but with trembling lips. "You see, all my friends are in the East, and some of them happened to be at the same house-party at Newport, and they--they were saying how they missed me," her voice shook a little, "and--and it seems they toasted me, all standing, and--and-- " And suddenly she gave up the fight for control, and began to cry bitterly again. "Oh, I'm so HOMESICK!" she sobbed, "and I'm so LONESOME! And I'm so sick, sick, sick of this place! Oh, I think I'll go crazy if I can't go home! I bear it and I BEAR it," said Patricia, in a sort of desperate self-defence, "and then the time comes when I simply CAN'T bear it!" And again she wept luxuriously, and Paul, in an agony of sympathy, patted her hand.

"My heart is just breaking!" she burst out again, her tears and words tumbling over each other. "It--it isn't RIGHT! I want my friends, and I want my youth--I'll never be twenty-six again! I want to put my things into a suit-case and go off with the other girls for country visits--and I want to dance!" She put her head down again, and after a moment Paul ventured a timid, "Patricia, dear, DON'T."

He thought she had not heard him, but after a moment, he was relieved to see her resolutely straighten up again, and dry her eyes, and push up her tumbled hair. "Well, I really will STOP," she said determinedly. "This will not do! If Alan even suspected! But, you see, I'm naturally a sociable person, and I had--well, I don't suppose any girl ever had such a good time in New York! My aunt did for me just what she did for her own daughters--a dance at Sherry's, and dinners--! Paul, I'd give a year of my life just to drive down the Avenue again on a spring afternoon, and bow to every one, and have tea somewhere, and smell the park--oh, did you ever smell Central Park in the spring?"

Both were silent. After a long pause Paul said:

"Why DO you stay? You've not got to ask a stepfather for a job."

"Alan," she answered simply. "No, don't say that," she interrupted him quickly; "I'm nothing of the sort! But my mother--my mother, in a way, left Alan and me to each other, and I have never done anything for Alan. I went to the Eastern aunt, and he stayed here; and after a while he drifted East--and he had too much money, of course! And I wasn't half affectionate enough; he had his friends and I had mine! Well then he got ill, and first it was just a cold and then it was, suddenly--don't you know?--a question of consultations, and a dry climate, and no dinners or wine or late hours. And Alan refused--refused flat to go anywhere, until I said I'd LOVE to come! I'll never forget the night it came over me that I ought to. I am--I was--engaged, you know?" She paused.

Paul cleared his throat. "No, I didn't know," he said.

"It wasn't announced," said Miss Chisholm. "He's a good deal older than I. A doctor." There was a long silence. "He said he would wait, and he will," she said softly, ending it. "It's not FOREVER, you know. Another year or two, and he'll come for me! Alan's quite a different person now. Another two years!" She jumped up, with a complete change of manner. "Well, I'm over my nonsense for another while!" said she. "And it's getting cold. I can't tell you how I've enjoyed letting off steam this way, Paul!"

"Whenever we feel this way," he said, giving her a steadying hand in the dark, "we'll come out for a jaw. But cheer up; we'll have lots of fun this winter!"

"Oh, lots!" she said contentedly. They entered the dark, open doorway together.

Patricia went ahead of him up the stairs, and at the top she turned, and Paul felt her hand for a second on his shoulder, and felt something brush his forehead that was all fragrance and softness and warmth.

Then she was gone.

Paul went into his room, and stood at the window, staring out into the dark. Only the door of the power-house glowed smoulderingly, and a broad band of light fell from Miss Chisholm's window.

He stood there until this last light suddenly vanished. Then he took a letter from his pocket, and began to tear it methodically to pieces. While he did so Paul began to compose another letter, this time to his mother.

THE RAINBOW'S END

Well, I am discovered--and lost." Julie, lazily making the announcement after a long silence, shut her magazine with a sigh of sleepy content; and braced herself more comfortably against the old rowboat that was half buried in sand at her back. She turned as she spoke to smile at the woman near her, a frail, keen-faced little woman luxuriously settled in an invalid's wheeled chair.

"Ann--you know you're not interested in that book. Did you hear what I said? I'm discovered."

"Well, it was sure to happen, sooner or later, I suppose." Mrs. Arbuthnot, suddenly summoned from the pages of a novel brought her gaze promptly to the younger woman's face, with the pitifully alert interest of the invalid. "You were bound to be recognized by some one, Ju!"

"Don't worry, a cannon wouldn't wake him!" said Julia, in reference to Mrs. Arbuthnot's lowered voice, and the solicitous look the wife had given a great opened beach umbrella three feet away, under which Dr. Arbuthnot slumbered on the warm sands. "He's forty fathoms deep. No," continued the actress, returning aggrievedly to her own affairs, "I suppose there's no such thing as escaping recognition-- even as late in the season as this, and at such an out-of-the-way place. Of course, I knew," she continued crossly, "that various people here had placed me, but I did rather hope to escape actual introductions!"

"Who is it--some one you know?" Mrs. Arbuthnot adjusted the pillow at her back, and settled herself enjoyably for a talk.

"Indirectly; it's that little butterfly of a summer girl--the one Jim calls 'The Dancing Girl'--of all people in the world!" said Julie, locking her arms comfortably behind her head. "You know how she's been haunting me, Ann? She's been simply

DETERMINED upon an introduction ever since she placed me as her adored Miss Ives of matinee fame. I imagine she's rather a nice child--every evidence of money--the ambitious type that longs to do something big--and is given to desperate hero worship. She's been under my feet for a week, with a Faithful Tray expression that drives me crazy. I've taken great pains not to see her."

"And now--?" prompted the other, as the actress fell silent, and sat staring dreamily at the brilliant sweep of beach and sea before them.

"Oh--now," Miss Ives took up her narrative briskly. "Well, a new young man arrived on the afternoon boat and, of course, the Dancing Girl instantly captivated him. She has one simple yet direct method with them all," she interrupted herself to digress a little. "She gets one of her earlier victims to introduce him; they all go down for a swim, she fascinates him with her daring and her bobbing red cap, she returns to white linen and leads him down to play tennis-- they have tea at the 'Casino,' and she promises him the second two- step and the first extra that evening. He is then hers to command," concluded Julie, bringing her amused eyes back to Mrs. Arbuthnot's face, "for the remainder of his stay!"

"That's exactly what she DOES do," said Mrs. Arbuthnot, laughing, "but I don't see yet--"

"Oh, I forgot to say," Miss Ives amended hastily, "that to-day's young man happens to be an acquaintance of mine; at least his uncle introduced him to me at a tea last winter. She led him by to the tennis courts an hour ago, and, to my disgust, I recognized him. That's all Miss Dancing Girl wants. Now--you'll see! They'll come up to our table in the dining-room to-night, and to-morrow she'll bring up a group of dear friends and he'll bring up another--to be introduced; and--there we'll be!"

"Oh, not so bad as that, Julie!"

"Oh, yes, indeed, Ann!" pursued Miss Ives with morose enjoyment. "You don't know how helpless one is. I'll be annoyed to death for the rest of the month, just so that the Dancing Girl can go back to the city this winter and say, 'Oh, girls, Julia Ives was staying where mamma and I were this summer, and she's just a DEAR! She doesn't make up one bit off the stage, and she dresses just as PLAIN! I saw her every day and got some dandy snapshots. She's just a darling when you know her.'"

"Well! What an unspoiled modest little soul you are, Julie!" interrupted the doctor's admiring voice. He wheeled away the umbrella and, lying luxuriously on his elbows in the sun, beamed at them both through his glasses.

"Jim," said the actress, severely, "it's positively indecent--the habit you're getting of evesdropping on Ann and me!"

"It gives me sidelights on your characters," said the doctor, quite brazenly.

"Ann--don't you call that disgraceful?"

"I certainly do, Ju," his wife agreed warmly. "But Jim has no sense of honor." Ann Arbuthnot, in the fifteen years of her married life, had never been able to keep a thrill of adoration out of her voice when she spoke, however jestingly, of her husband. It trembled there now.

"Well, what's wrong, Julie? Some old admirer turn up?" asked the doctor, sleepily content to follow any conversational lead, in the idle pleasantness of the hour.

"No--no!" she corrected him, "just some silly social complications ahead--which I hate!"

"Be rude," suggested the doctor, pleasantly.

"Now, you know, I'd love that!" said Mrs. Arbuthnot, youthfully. "I'd simply love to be followed and envied and adored!"

"No, you wouldn't, Ann!" Miss Ives assured her promptly. "You'd like it, as I did, for a little while. And then the utter USELESSNESS of it would strike you. Especially from such little complacent, fluffy whirlings as that Dancing Girl!"

"Yes, and that's the kind of a girl I like," persisted the other, smiling.

"That's the kind of a girl you WERE, Ann, I've no doubt," said the actress, vivaciously, "only sweeter. I know she wore white ruffles and a velvet band on her hair, didn't she, Jim? And roses in her belt?"

"She did," said the doctor, reminiscently. "I believe she flirted in her kindergarten days. She was always engaged to ride or dance or row on the river with the other men--and always splitting her dances, and forgetting her promises, and wearing the rings and pins of her adorers."

"And the fun was, Ju," said Mrs. Arbuthnot, girlishly, with bright color in her cheeks, "that when Jim came there to give two lectures, you know, all the older girls were crazy about him--and he was ten years older than I, you know, and I never DREAMED--"

"Oh, you go to, Ann! You never DREAMED!" said Miss Ives, lazily.

"Honestly, I didn't!" Mrs. Arbuthnot protested. "I remember my brother Billy saying, 'Babs, you don't think Dr. Arbuthnot is coming here to see ME, do you?' and then it all came over me! Why, I was only eighteen."

"And engaged to Billy's chum," said the doctor.

"Well," said the wife, naively, "he knew all along it wasn't serious."

"You must have been a rose," said Miss Ives, "and I would have hated you! Now, when I went to dances," she pursued half seriously, "I sat in one place and smiled fixedly, and watched the other girls dance. Or I talked with great animation to the chaperons. Ann, I've felt sometimes that I would gladly die, to have the boys crowd around me just once, and grab my card and scribble their names all over it. I didn't dress very well, or dance very well--and I never could talk to boys." She began to trace a little watercourse in the sand with an exquisite finger tip. "I was the most unhappy girl on earth, I think! I felt every birthday was a separate insult--twenty, and twenty-two, and twenty-four! We were poor, and life was--oh, not dramatic or big!--but just petty and sordid. I used to rage because the dining-room was the only place for the sewing-machine, and rage because my bedroom was really a back parlor. Well!--I joined a theatrical company--came away. And many a night, tired out and discouraged, I've cried myself to sleep because I'd never have any girlhood again!"

She stopped with a half-apologetic laugh. The doctor was watching her with absorbed, bright eyes. Mrs. Arbuthnot, unable to imagine youth without joy and beauty, protested:

"Julie--I don't believe you--you're exaggerating! Do you mean you didn't go on the stage until you were twenty-four!"

"I was twenty-six. I was leading lady my second season, and starred my third," said the actress, without enthusiasm. "I was starred in 'The Jack of Clubs.' It ran a season in New York and gave me my start. Lud, how tired we all got of it!"

"And then I hope you went back home, Ju, and were lionized," said the other woman, vigorously.

"Oh, not then! No, I'd been meaning to go--and meaning to go--all those three years. The little sisters used to write me--such forlorn little letters!--and mother, too--but I couldn't manage it. And then--the very night 'Jack' played the three hundredth time, as it happened--I had this long wire from Sally and Beth. Mother was very ill, wanted me--they'd meet a certain train, they were counting the hours--"

Miss Ives demolished her watercourse with a single sweep of her palm. There was a short silence.

"Well!" she said, breaking it. "Mother got well, as it happened, and I went home two months later. I had the guest room, I remember. Sally was everything to mother then, and I tried to feel glad. Beth was engaged. Every one was very flattering and very kind in the intervals left by engagements and weddings and new babies and family gatherings. Then I came back to 'Jack,' and we went on the road. And then I broke down and a strange doctor in a strange hospital put me together again," she went on with a flashing smile and a sudden change of tone, "and his wholly adorable wife sent me double white violets! And they--the Arbuthnots, not the violets--were the nicest thing that ever happened to me!"

"So that was the way of it?" said the doctor.

"That was the way of it."

"And as the Duchess would say, the moral of THAT is--?"

"The moral is for me. Or else it's for little dancing girls, I don't know which." Miss Ives wiped her eyes openly and, restoring her handkerchief to its place, announced that she perceived she had been talking too much.

Presently the Dancing Girl came down from the tennis-court, with her devoted new captive in tow. The captive, a fat, amiable-looking youth, was warm and wilted, but the girl was fresh and buoyant as ever. They heard her allude to the "second two-step" and something was said of the "supper dance," but her laughing voice stopped as she and her escort came nearer the actress, and she gave Julie her usual look of mute adoration. The boy, flushing youthfully, lifted his hat, and Julie bowed briefly.

They were lingering over their coffee two hours later, when the newly arrived young man made the expected move. He threaded the tables between his own and the doctor's carefully, the eager Dancing Girl in his wake.

"I don't know whether you remember me, Miss Ives--?" he began, when he could extend a hand.

Julie turned her splendid, unsmiling eyes toward him.

"Mr. Polk. How do you do? Yes, indeed, I remember you," she said, unenthusiastically. "How is Mr. Gilbert?"

"Uncle John? Oh, he's fine!" said young Polk, rapturously. "I wonder why he didn't tell me you were spending the summer here I"

"I don't tell any one," said Julie, simply. "My winters are so crowded that I try to get away from people in the summer."

"Oh!" said the boy, a little blankly. There was an instant's pause before he added rather uncomfortably:

"Miss Ives--Miss Carter has been so anxious to meet you--"

"How do you do, Miss Carter?" said Julie, promptly, politely. She gave her young adorer a ready hand. The usually poised Dancing Girl could not recall at the moment one of the things she had planned to say when this great moment came. But she thought of them all as she lay in bed that night, and the conviction that she had bungled the long-wished-for interview made her burn from her heels to the lobes of her ears. What HAD she said? Something about having longed for this opportunity, which the actress hadn't answered, and something about her desperate admiration for Miss Ives, at which Miss Ives had merely smiled. Other things were said, or half said--the girl reviewed them mercilessly in the dark--and then the interview had terminated, rather flatly. Marian Carter writhed at the recollection.

But the morning brought courage. She passed Julie, who was fresh from a plunge in the ocean, and briskly attacking a late breakfast, on her way from the dining-room.

"Good morning, Miss Ives! Isn't it a lovely morning?"

"Oh, good morning, Miss Carter. I beg pardon--?"

"I said, 'Isn't it a lovely morning?'"

"Oh--? Yes, quite delightful."

"Miss Ives--but I'm interrupting you?"

Julie gave her book a glance and raised her eyes expectantly to Miss Carter's face, but did not speak.

"Miss Ives," said Miss Carter, a little confusedly, "mamma was wondering if you've taken the trip to Fletcher's Forest? We've our motor-car here, you know, and they serve a very good lunch at the Inn."

"Oh, thank you, no!" said Julie, positively. "VERY good of you--but I'm with the Arbuthnots, you know. Thank you, no."

"I hoped you would," said Miss Carter, disappointed. "I know you use a motor in town," she answered daringly. "You see I know all about you!"

Miss Ives paid to this confession only the small tribute of raised eyebrows and an absent smile. She was quite at her ease, but in the little silence that followed Miss Carter had time to feel baffled-- in the way. "Here is Mrs. Arbuthnot," she said in relief, as Ann came slowly in on the doctor's arm. Before they reached the table the girl had slipped away.

That afternoon she asked Miss Ives, pausing beside the basking group on the sands to do so, if she would have tea informally with mamma and a few friends. Oh--thank you, Miss Ives couldn't, to-day. Thank you. The next day Miss Carter wondered if Miss Ives would like to spin out to the Point to see the sunset? No, thank you so much. Miss Ives was just going in. Another day brought a request for Miss Ives's company at dinner, with just mamma and Mr. Polk and the Dancing Girl herself. Declined. A fourth day found Miss Carter, camera in hand, smilingly confronting the actress as she came out on the porch.

"Will you be very cross if I ask you to stand still just a moment, Miss Ives?" asked the Dancing Girl.

"Oh, I'm afraid I will," said Julie, annoyed. "I DON'T like to be photographed!" But she was rather disarmed at the speed with which Miss Carter shut up her little camera.

"I know I bother you," said the girl, with a wistful sincerity that was most becoming and with a heightened color, "but--but I just can't seem to help it!" She walked down the steps beside Julie, laughing almost with vexation at her own weakness. "I've always admired so--the people who DO things! I've always wanted to do something myself," said Miss Carter, awkwardly. "You don't know how unhappy it makes me. You don't know how I'd love to do something for you!"

"You can, you can let me off being photographed, like a sweet child!" said Julie, lightly. But twenty minutes later when, very trim and dainty in her blue bathing suit and scarlet cap, she came out of the bath-house to join Ann and the doctor on the beach, she reproached herself. She might have met the stammered little confidence with something warmer than a jesting word, she thought with a little shame.

"You're not going in again!" protested Ann. "Oh, CHIL-dren!"

"I am," said Miss Ives, buoyantly. "I don't know about Jim. At Jim's age every step counts, I suppose. These fashionable doctors habitually overeat and oversleep,

I understand, and it makes them lazy."

"I AM going in, Ann," said the doctor, with dignity, rising from the sand and pointedly addressing his wife. A few moments later he and Julie joyously breasted the sleepy roll of the low breakers, and pushed their way steadily through the smoother water beyond.

"Oh, that was glorious, Jim!" gasped the actress, as they gained the raft that was always their goal and pulling herself up to sit siren- wise upon it. She was breathless, radiant, bubbling with the joy of sun and air and green water. She took off her cap and let the sunlight beat on her loosened braids.

"How you love the water, Julie!"

"Yes--best of all. I'm never so satisfied as when I'm in it!"

"You never look so happy as when you are," he said.

"Oh, these are happy days!" said Julie. "I wish they could last forever. Just resting and playing--wouldn't you like a year of it, Jim?"

The doctor eyed her quietly.

"I don't know that I would," he said seriously, impersonally.

There was a little silence. Then the girl began to pin up her braids with fingers that trembled a little.

"Ann's waving!" she said presently, and the doctor caught up her scarlet cap to signal back to the far blur on the beach that was Ann. He watched the tiny distant groups a moment.

"Here comes your admirer!" said he.

"Where?" Julie was ready at once to slip into the water.

"Oh--finish your hair--take your time! She's just in the breakers. We'll be off long before she gets here."

"That reminds me, Jim," Miss Ives was quite herself again, "that when I was in the bath-house a few moments ago your Dancing Girl and that pretty little girl who is visiting her came into the next room. You know how flimsy the walls are? I could hear every word they said."

"If you'd been a character in a story, Ju, you'd have felt it your duty to cough!"

"Well, I didn't," grinned Miss Ives; "not that I wanted to hear what they were saying. I didn't even know who they were until I heard little Miss Carter say solemnly, 'Ethel, I used to want mamma to get that Forty-eighth Street house, and I used to want to do Europe, but I think if I had ONE wish now, it would be to do something that would MAKE everybody know me--and everybody talk about me. I'd LOVE to be pointed out wherever I went. I'd love to have people stare at me. I'd like to be just as popular and just as famous as Julia Ives!'"

"She HAS got it badly, Ju!" the doctor observed.

"She has. And it will be fuel on the flames to have me start to swim back to shore while she is swimming as hard as she can to the raft!" said the lady, tucking the last escaping lock under her cap and springing up for the plunge that started the home trip.

It was only a little after midnight that night when Julie, lying wakeful in the sultry summer darkness, was startled by a person in her room.

"It's Emma, Miss Ives," said Mrs. Arbuthnot's maid, stumbling about, "Mrs. Arbuthnot wants you."

"She's ill!" Julie felt rather than said the words, instantly alert and alarmed, and reaching for her wrapper and slippers.

"No, ma'am. But the doctor feels like he ought to go down to the fire, and she's nervous--"

"The fire?"

"Yes'm," said Emma, simply, "the windmill is afire!"

"And I sleeping through it all!" Miss Ives was still bewildered, fastening the sash of her cobwebby black Mandarin robe as she followed Emma through the passage that joined her suite to the Arbuthnots'.

"Ann, dear--Emma tells me the laundry's on fire?" said she, entering the big room. "I had no idea of it!"

"Nor had we," the doctor's wife rejoined eagerly. "The first we knew was from Emma. Jim says there's no danger. Do you think there is?"

"Certainly not, Ann!" Julie laughed. "I'll tell you what we can do," she added briskly. "We'll wheel you down the hall here to the window; you can get a splendid view of the whole thing."

The doctor approving, the ladies took up their station at a wide hall window that commanded the whole scene.

Outside the velvet blackness and silence of the night were shattered. The great mill, ugly tongues of flame bursting from the door and windows at its base, was the centre of a talking, shouting, shrill-voiced crowd that was momentarily, in the mysterious fashion of crowds, gathering size.

"Wonderful sight, isn't it, Ann?"

"Wonderful. Does this cut off our water supply, Emma?"

"No, Mrs. Arbuthnot. They're using the little mill for the engines now."

"What did they use the big mill for, Emma?"

"The laundry, Miss Ives. And there's a sort of flat on the second floor where the laundry woman and her husband--he's the man that drives the 'bus--live."

"Good heavens!" said Ann. "I hope they got out!"

"Oh, sure," said the maid, comfortably. "It was all of an hour ago the fire started. They had lots of time."

The three watched for a while in silence. Ann's eyes began to droop from the bright monotony of the flames.

"I believe I'll wait until the tank falls, Ju? and then go back to my comfortable bed--Julie, what is it--!"

Her voice rose, keen with terror. The actress, her hand on her heart, shook her head without turning her eyes from the mill.

For suddenly above the other clamor there had risen one horrible scream, and now, following it, there was almost a silence.

"Why--what on earth--" panted Miss Ives, looking to Mrs. Arbuthnot for explanation after an endless interval in which neither stirred. But again they were interrupted, this time by such an outbreak of shouting and cries from the watching crowd about the mill as made the night fairly ring.

A moment later the entire top of the mill collapsed, sending a gush of sparks far up into the night. Then at last the faithfully played hoses began to gain control.

"Do run down and find out what the shouting was, Emma," said Julie. Emma gladly obeyed.

"She'd come back, if anything had happened," said Julie, some ten minutes later.

"Who--Emma?" Mrs. Arbuthnot was not alarmed. "Oh, surely!" she yawned, and drew her wraps about her.

"It's all over now. But I suppose it will burn for hours. I think I'll turn in again," she said.

"I've had enough, too!" Julie said, not quite easy herself, but glad to find the other so. "Let's decamp."

She wheeled the invalid carefully back to her room, where both women were still talking when a bell-boy knocked, bringing a message from the doctor. A woman had been hurt; he would be busy with her for an hour.

"Who was it?" Julie asked him, but the boy, obviously frantic to return to the fascinations of the fire, didn't know.

It was more than an hour later that the doctor came in. Julie had been reading to Ann. She shut the book.

"Jim! What on earth has kept you so long?"

"Frighten you, dear?" The doctor was very pale; he looked, between the dirt and disorder of his clothes, and the anxiety of his face, like an old man.

"Some one was hurt?" flashed Julie, solicitous at once.

"Has no one told you about it?" he wondered. "Lord! I should think it would be all over the place by this time!"

He dropped into an easy chair, and sank his head wearily into his hands.

"Lord--Lord--Lord!" he muttered. Then he looked up at his wife with the smile that never failed her.

"Jim--no one was killed?"

"Oh, no, dear! No, I'll tell you." He came over and sat beside her on the bed, patting her hand. The two women watched him with tense, absorbed faces.

"When I got there," said the doctor, slowly, "there was quite a crowd--the lower story of the mill was all aflame--and the firemen were keeping the people back. They'd a ladder up at the second story and firemen were pitching things out of the windows as fast as they could--chairs, rugs, pillows, and so on. Finally the last man came out, smoke coming after him--it was quick work! Now, remember, dear, no one was killed--"he stopped to pat his wife's hand reassuringly. "Well, just then, at the third-story windows--it seems the laundress has children--"

"Children!" gasped Miss Ives. "Oh, NO!"

"Yes, four of 'em--the oldest a little fellow of ten, had the baby in his arms--." The doctor stopped.

"Go ON, Jim!"

"Well, they put the ladder back again, but the sill was aflame then. No use! Just then the mother and father--poor souls--arrived. They'd been at a dance in the village. The woman screamed--"

"We heard."

"Ah? The man had to be held, poor fellow! It was--it was--" Again the doctor stopped, unable to go on. But after a few seconds he began more briskly: "Well! The mill was connected with this house, you know, by a little bridge, from the tank floor of the mill to the roof. No one had thought of it, because every one supposed that there was no one in the mill. Before the crowd had fairly seen that there WERE children caged up there, they left the window, and not a minute later we saw them come up the trap-door by the tank. Lord, how every one yelled."

"They'd thought of it, the darlings!" half sobbed Mrs. Arbuthnot.

"No, they'd never have thought of it--too terrified, poor little things. No. We all saw that there was some one--a woman--with them hurrying them along. I was helping hold the mother or I might have thought it was the mother. They scampered across that bridge like little squirrels, the woman with the baby last. By that time the mill was roaring like a furnace behind them, and the bridge itself burst into flames at the mill end. She--the woman--must have felt it tottering, for she flung herself the last few feet--but she couldn't make it. She threw the baby, by some lucky accident, for she couldn't have known what she was doing, safe to the others, and caught at the rail, but the whole thing gave way and came down.... I got there about the first--she'd only fallen some dozen feet, you know, on the flat roof of the kitchen, but she was all smashed up, poor little girl. We carried her into the housekeeper's room--and then I saw that it was little Miss Carter--your Dancing Girl, Ju!"

"Jim! Dead?"

"Oh, no! I don't think she'll die. She's badly burned, of course-- face and hands especially--but it's the spine I'm afraid for. We can tell better to-morrow. We made her as comfortable as we could. I gave her something that'll make her sleep. Her mother's with her. But I'm afraid her dancing days are over."

"Think of it--little Miss Carter!" Julie's voice sounded dazed.

"But, Jim," Ann said, "what was she doing in the mill?"

"Why, that's the point," he said. "She wasn't there when the fire started. She was simply one of the crowd. But when she heard that the children were there, she ran to the back of the mill, where there was a straight up-and-down ladder built against the wall outside, so that the tank could be reached that way. She went up it like a flash--says she never thought of asking any one else to go. She broke a window and climbed in--she says the floor was hot to her feet then--and she and the kids ran up the inside flight to the trap-door. They obeyed her like little soldiers! But the bridge side of the mill was the side the fire was on, and the wood was rotten, you know--almost explosive. Half a minute later and they couldn't have made it at all."

"How do you ACCOUNT for such courage in a girl like that?" marvelled Julie.

"I don't know," he said. "Take it all in all, it was the most extraordinary thing I ever saw. Apparently she never for one second thought of herself. She simply ran straight into that hideous danger--while the rest of us could do nothing but put our hands over our eyes and pray."

"But she'll live, Jim?" the actress asked, and as he nodded a thoughtful affirmative, she added: "That's something to be thankful for, at least!"

"Don't be too sure it is," said Ann.

Ten days later Miss Ives came cheerfully into the sunny, big room where Marian Carter lay. Bandaged, and strapped, and bound, it was a sorry little Dancing Girl who turned her serious eyes to the actress's face. But Julie could be irresistible when she chose, and she chose to be her most fascinating self to-day. Almost reluctantly at first, later with something of her old gayety, the Dancing Girl's laugh rang out. It stirred Julie's heart curiously to hear it, and made the little patient's mother, listening in the next room, break silently into tears.

"But this is what I really came to bring you," said the actress, presently, laying a score or more of newspaper clippings on the bed. "You see you are famous! I had my press-agent watch for these, and they're coming in at a great rate every mail. You see, here's a nattering likeness of you in a New York daily, and here you are again, in a Chicago paper!"

"Those aren't of ME," said Marian, smiling.

"It SAYS they are," Julie said. "One says you are petite and dark, and the other that you are a blond Gibson type. You wouldn't have believed that your wish could come true so quickly, would you, just the other day?"

"My wish?" stammered the girl.

"Yes. Don't you remember saying that you wished you could do something big?" pursued Julie. "You've done a thing that makes the rest of us feel pretty small, you know. Why, while there was any question of your getting better, there wasn't a dance given at any of the hotels between here and Surf Point, and all sorts of people came here with inquiries every day. This place was absolutely hushed. The maids used to fight for the privilege of carrying your trays up. None of us thought of anything but 'How is Miss Carter?' And you'll be 'The young lady who saved those children from the fire' for the rest of your life wherever you go!"

Miss Carter was watching her gravely.

"You say I got my wish," she said now, her blue eyes brimming with slow tears, and her lips trembling. "But--but--you see how I AM, Miss Ives! Dr. Arbuthnot says I MAY be able to walk in a month or two, but no swimming or riding or dancing for years--perhaps never. And my face--it'll always be scarred."

Julie laid a gentle hand on the little helpless fingers.

"But that's part of the process, you know, little girl," said the actress after a little silence. "I pay one way, perhaps, and you pay another, but we both pay. Don't you suppose," a smile broke through the seriousness of her face, "don't you suppose I have my scars, too?"

Marian dried her eyes. "Scars?"

"When you are pointed out--as you WILL be, wherever you go--" said Julie, "you'll think to yourself, 'Ah, yes, this is very lovely and very flattering, but I'll never dance again--I'll never rush into the waves again, I'll never spend a whole morning on the tennis court,' won't you?"

The Dancing Girl nodded, her eyes filling again, her lips trembling.

"And when people stare after me and follow me," said Julie, "I think to my-self--'Oh, this is very flattering, very delightful--but the young years are gone--the mother who missed me and longed for me is gone--the little sisters are married, and deep in happy family cares--they don't need me any more.' I have what I wanted, but I've paid the price! In a life like mine there's no room for the normal, wonderful ties of a home and children. Never--" she put her head back against her chair and shut her eyes--"never that happiness for me!" She finished, her voice lowered and carefully controlled.

They were both silent awhile. Then Marian stirred her helpless fingers just enough to deepen their light pressure on Julie's own.

"Thank you," she said shyly. "I see now. I think I begin to understand."

ROSEMARY'S STEPMOTHER

In the sunny morning-room there prevailed an atmosphere of business. Rosemary, at the desk, was rapidly writing notes and addressing envelopes. Theodore, a deep wrinkle crossing his forehead, was struggling to reduce to order a confused heap of crumpled and illegible papers. Before him lay little heaps of silver and small gold, which he moved and counted untiringly, referring now and then to various entries in a large, flat ledger. Mrs. Bancroft, stepmother of these two, was in a deep chair, with her lap full of letters. Now and then she quoted aloud from these as she opened and glanced over them. Lastly, Ann Weatherbee, a neighbor, seated on the floor with her back against Mrs. Bancroft's knee, was sorting a large hamperful of silver spoons and crumpled napkins into various heaps.

"There!" said Ann, presently. "I've finished the napkins--or nearly! Tell me, whose are these, Aunt Nell?"

Mrs. Bancroft reached a smooth hand for them and mused over the monograms.

"B--B--B--?" she reflected. "Both are B's, aren't they? And different, too. This is Mrs. Bayne's, anyway--I was with her when she bought these. But these--? Oh, I know now, Ann! That little cousin of the Potters',--what was her name, Rosemary?"

"Sutter, madam! Guess again."

"No; but her unmarried name, I mean?"

"Oh, Beatty, of course!" supplied Ann. "Aren't you clever to remember that! I'll tie them up. Oh, and should there only be eleven of the Whiteley Greek-borders?" she asked presently.

"One was sent home with a cake, dear,--we had too much cake."

"We always do, somehow," commented Rosemary, absently, and there was a silence. The last speaker broke it presently, with a long sigh.

"At your next concert, mamma, I shall insist upon having 'please omit flowers' on the tickets," said Rosemary, severely. "I think I have thanked forty people for 'your exquisite roses'!"

"Poor, overworked little Rosemary!" laughed her stepmother.

"You can look for a new treasurer, too," said Theodore. "This sort of thing needs an expert accountant. No ordinary brain...! What with some of these women rubbing every item out three or four times, and others using pale green water for ink, nobody could get a balance."

Mrs. Bancroft, smiling serenely, leaned back in her chair,

"Aren't they unkind to me, Ann?" she complained. "They would expect a poor, forlorn old woman--Now, Rosemary!"

For Rosemary had interrupted her. Seating herself upon the arm of her stepmother's chair, she laid a firm hand over the speaker's mouth.

"Now she will fish, Ann," said Rosemary, calmly.

"Fish!" said Ann, indignantly. "After last night she doesn't have to FISH!"

"You bet she doesn't," said Theodore, affectionately. "Not she! She got enough compliments last night to last her a long while."

"I was ashamed of myself," confessed Rosemary, with her slow smile; "for, after all, WE'RE only her family! But father, Ted, and I went about the whole evening with broad, complacent grins--as if WE'D been doing something."

"Oh, I was boasting aloud most of the time that I knew her intimately," Ann added, laughing. "Just being a neighbor and old friend shed a sort of glory even on me!"

"Oh, well, it was the dearest concert ever," summarized Rosemary, contentedly. "The papers this morning say that the flowers were like an opera first night--though I never saw any opera singer get so many here--and that hundreds were turned away!"

"'Hundreds'!" repeated Mrs. Bancroft, chuckling at the absurdity of it.

"Well, mamma, the hall WAS packed," Ted reminded her promptly. He grinned over some amusing memory. "...Old lady Barnes weeping over 'Nora Creina,'" he added.

"Ann, I didn't tell you that Dad and I met Herr Muller at the gate this morning," said Rosemary, "shedding tears over the thought of some of the Franz songs, and blowing his nose on his blue handkerchief!"

"And you certainly did look stunning, mamma," contributed Ted.

"Children... children!" protested Mrs. Bancroft. But the pleased color flooded her cheeks.

Another busy silence was broken by a triumphant exclamation from Theodore, who turned about from his table to announce:

"Three hundred and seven dollars, ladies, and thirty-five cents, with old lady Baker still to hear from, and eight dollars to pay for the lights."

"WHAT!" said the three women together. Theodore repeated the sum.

"Nonsense!" cried Rosemary. "It CAN'T be so much."

Mrs. Bancroft stared dazedly.

"TWO hundred, Ted...?" she suggested.

"Three hundred!" the boy repeated firmly, beaming sympathetically as both the young women threw themselves upon Mrs. Bancroft, and smothered her in ecstatic embraces.

"Oh, Aunt Nell," said Ann, almost tearfully, "I don't know what the girls will SAY. Why, Rose, it'll all but clear the ward. It's three times what we thought!"

"Your father will be pleased," said Mrs. Bancroft, winking a little suspiciously. "He's worried so about you girlies assuming that debt. I must go tell him." She began to gather her letters together. "Do you know where he is, Ted? Has he come in from his first round?" she asked.

"She's the dearest...!" said Ann, when the door closed behind her. "There's nobody quite like your mother."

"Honestly there isn't," assented Rosemary, thoughtfully. "When you think how unspoiled she is--with that heavenly voice of hers, you know, and every one so devoted to her. She doesn't do a THING, whether it's arranging flowers, or apron patterns, or managing the maids, that people don't admire and copy."

"She can't wait now to tell father the news," commented Theodore, smiling.

"He'll be perfectly enchanted," said Rosemary. "He sent her violets last night, and this morning, when we were taking all her flowers out of the bathtub, and looking at the cards, she gave me such a funny little grin and said, 'I'll thank the gentleman for these myself, Rose!' Ted and I roared at her."

"But that was dear," said Ann, romantically.

"She simply does what she likes with Dad," said Ted, ruminatively. Rosemary, facing the others over the back of her chair, nodded. Ann had her arms about her knees. They were all idle.

"She got Dad to give me my horse," the boy went on, "and she'll get him to let us go off to the Greers' next month--you'll see! I can't think how she does it."

"I can remember the first day she came here," said Rosemary. She rested her chin in her hands; her eyes were dreamy.

"George! We were the scared, miserable little rats!" supplemented Theodore. Rosemary smiled pitifully, as if the mother asleep in her could feel for the children of that long-passed day.

"I was only six," she said, "and when we heard the wheels we ran--"

"That's right! We ran upstairs," agreed her brother.

"Yes. And she followed us. I can remember the rustling of her dress.... And she had roses on--she pinned one on Bess's little black frock. And she carried me down to dinner in her arms, and I sat in her lap."

"And that year you had a party," said Ann. "I remember that, for I came. And the playhouse was built for Bess's birthday."

"So it was," said Rosemary, struck afresh. "That was all her doing, too. She just has to want a thing, and it gets done! I'll never forget Bess's wedding."

"Nor I," said Ann. "It was the most perfect little wedding I ever saw. Not a hitch anywhere. And wasn't the house a bower? I never had so much fun at any wedding in my life. Bess was so fresh and gay, and she and George helped us until the very last minute--do you remember?--gathering the roses and wrapping the cake. It was all ideal!"

"Bess told me the other day," said Rosemary, soberly, and in a lowered tone, "that on her wedding-day, when she was dressed, you know, mamma put on her veil, and pinned on the orange blossoms, and kissed her. And Bess saw the tears in her eyes. And mamma laughed, and put her arm about her and said: 'It is silly and wrong of me, dearest, but I was thinking who might have been doing this for you to-day--of how proud she would have been!' Then they came down, and Bess was married."

"Wasn't that like her?" said Ann. They were all silent a moment. Then the visitor jumped up.

"Well, I must trot home to my deserted parent, my children," she exclaimed briskly. "He rages if he comes in and doesn't find me. But, if you ask me, I'll be over later to help you, Rose. Every one in the world will be here for tea. And, meantime, make her rest, Ted. She looks tired to death."

"I'll see thee home, Mistress," said Ted, gallantly, and Rosemary was left alone. Her brother, coming in again nearly an hour afterward, found her still in the same thoughtful attitude, her big eyes fixed upon space. He knelt, and put his arm about her, and she drooped her soft, cool little cheek against his, tightening her own arm about his neck. There was a little silence.

"What is it?" said the boy, presently.

"Nothing, Teddy. But you're SUCH a comfort!"

"Well, but it's SOMETHING, old lady. Out with it!"

Rosemary tumbled his hair with her free hand.

"I was thinking of--mother," she confessed, very low.

His eyes were fast on hers for another short silence.

"Well,"--he spoke as if to a small child--"what were you thinking, dear?"

"Oh, I was just thinking, Ted, that it's not fair. It isn't fair," said Rosemary, with a little difficulty. "Not only Dad and Bess and the maids, but you and I, too, we can't help idolizing mamma. And sometimes we never think of mother--our own mother!--except as tired and sick and struggling--that's all I remember, anyway. And mamma is all strength and sweetness and health."

"I--I know it, old lady."

"Oh, and Ted!--to-day, and sometimes before, it's hurt me so! I can't feel--I don't want to!--anything but what I do to mamma, but sometimes--"

She struggled for composure. Her brother cleared his throat.

"She was so wistful for pretty things and good times, even I can remember that," said Rosemary, with pitiful recollection. "And she never had them! SHE would have loved to stand there last night, in lace and pearls, bowing and smiling to every one. She would have loved the applause and the flowers. And it stings me to think of us, you and I, proud to be mamma's stepchildren!"

"Dad worshipped mother," submitted the boy, hesitatingly.

"Yes, of course! But he was working day and night, and they were poor, and then she was ill. I don't think she managed very well. Those frightful, sloppy servants we used to have, and smoky fires, and sticky summer dinners--and three bad little kids crying and leaving screen doors open, and spilling the syrup! I remember her at the stove, flushed and hot. You think I don't, but I do!"

"Yes, I do, too," he assented uncomfortably, frowningly.

"And do you remember the Easter eggs, Ted?"

Theodore nodded, wincing.

"She forgot to buy them, you know, and then walked two miles in the hot spring weather, just to surprise and please us!"

"And then the eggs smashed, didn't they?"

"On the way home, yes. And we cried with fury, little beasts that we were!" said Rosemary, as if unable to stop the sad little train of memories. "I can remember that awful Belle that we had, making her drink some port. I wouldn't kiss her. And she said that she would see if she couldn't get me another egg the next day. And then Dad came in, and scolded us all so, and carried her upstairs!"

She suddenly burst out crying, and clung to her brother. And he let her cry for a while, patting her shoulder and talking to her until control and even cheerfulness came back, and she could be trusted to go upstairs and bathe her eyes for lunch.

When the lunch bell rang, Rosemary went downstairs, to find her stepmother at the wide hall doorway with a yellow telegram in her hand.

"News from Bess," said Mrs. Bancroft, quickly. "Good news, thank God! George wires that she and the little son are doing well. The baby came at eleven this morning. Dad's just come in, and he's telephoning that you and I will come over right after lunch. Think of it! Think of it!"

"Bess!" said Rosemary, unsteadily. She read the telegram, and clung a little limply to the firm hand that held it. "Bess's baby!" she said dazedly.

"Bess's darling baby--think of holding it, Aunt Rose!"

Rosemary's sober eyes flashed joyously.

"Oh, I am--so I am! An aunt! DOESN'T it seem queer?"

"It seems very queer to me," said Mrs. Bancroft, as they sat down on a wide window-seat to revel in the news, "for I went to see your mother, on just such a morning, when Bess herself was just a day old--it seems only a year ago! Bless us, how old we get! Your mother was younger than I, you know, and I remember that

SHE seemed to me mighty young to have a baby! And now here's her baby's baby! Your mother was like an exquisite child, Rosey-posy, showing off little Bess. They lived in a little playhouse of a cottage, with blue curtains, and blue china, and a snubnosed little maid in blue! I passed it on my way to school,--I had been teaching for seven years or so, then,--and your mother would call out from the garden and make me come in, and dance about me like a little witch. She wanted me to taste jam, or to hold Teddy, or to see her roses--I used to feel sometimes as if all the sunshine in the world was for Rose! Your father had boarded with my mother for three years before they were married, you know, and I was fighting the bitterest sort of heartache over the fact that I liked him and missed him--not that he ever dreamed it! Perhaps she did, for she was always generous with you babies--loaned you to me, and was as sweet to me as she could be." Mrs. Bancroft crumpled the telegram, smiled, and sighed. "Well, it all comes back with another baby--all those times when we were young, and gay, and unhappy, and working together. Bess will look back at these days sometime, with the same feeling. There is nothing in life like youth and work, and hard times and good times, when people love each other, Rose."

Rosemary suddenly leaned over to kiss her. Her eyes were curiously satisfied.

"I see where the fairness comes in--I see it now," she said dreamily. But even her stepmother did not catch the whisper or its meaning.

AUSTIN'S GIRL

In the blazing heat of a July afternoon, Mrs. Cyrus Austin Phelps, of Boston, arrived unexpectedly at the Yerba Buena rancho in California. She was the only passenger to leave the train at the little sun-burned platform that served as a station, and found not even a freight agent there, of whom to ask the way to Miss Manzanita Boone's residence. There were a few glittering lizards whisking about on the dusty boards, and a few buzzards hanging motionless against the cloudless pale blue of the sky overhead. Otherwise nothing living was in sight.

The train roared on down the valley, and disappeared. Its last echo died away. All about was the utter silence of the foot-hills. The even spires of motionless redwood trees rose, dense and steep, to meet the sky-line with a shimmer of heat. The sun beat down mercilessly, there was no shadow anywhere.

Mrs. Phelps, trim, middle-aged, richly and simply dressed, typical of her native city, was not a woman to be easily disconcerted, but she felt quite at a loss now. She was already sorry that she had come at all to Yerba Buena, sorry that, in coming, she had not written Austin to meet her. She already disliked this wide, silent, half-savage valley, and already felt out of place here. How could she possibly imagine that there would not be shops, stables, hotels at the station? What did other people do when they arrived here? Mrs. Phelps crisply asked these questions of the unanswering woods and hills.

After a while she sat down on her trunk, though with her small back erect, and her expression uncompromisingly stern. She was sitting there when Joe Bettancourt, a Portuguese milkman, happened to come by with his shabby milk wagon, and his lean, shaggy horses, and-- more because Joe, not understanding English, took it calmly for granted that she wished to drive with him, than because she liked the arrangement--Mrs. Phelps got him to take her trunk and herself upon their way. They drove steadily upward, through apple orchards that stretched in hot zig-zag lines, like the spokes of a great wheel, about them, and through strips of forest, where the corduroy road was springy beneath the wagon wheels, and past ugly low cow sheds, where the red-brown cattle were already gathering for the milking.

"You are taking me to Mr. Boone's residence?" Mrs. Phelps would ask, at two-minute intervals. And Joe, hunched lazily over the reins, would respond huskily:

"Sure. Thaz th' ole man."

And presently they did turn a corner, and find, in a great gash of clearing, a low, rambling structure only a little better than the cow sheds, with wide, un-painted porches all about it, and a straggling line of out-houses near by. A Chinese cook came out of a swinging door to stare at the arrival, two or three Portuguese girls, evidently house-servants, entered into a cheerful, nasal conversation with Joe Bettancourt, from their seats by the kitchen door, and a very handsome young woman, whom Mrs. Phelps at first thought merely another servant came running down to the wagon. This young creature had a well-rounded figure, clad in faded, crisp blue linen, slim ankles that showed above her heavy buckled slippers, and a loosely-braided heavy rope of bright hair. Her eyes were a burning blue, the lashes curled like a doll's lashes, and the brows as even and dark as a doll's, too. She was extraordinarily pretty, even Mrs. Phelps could find no fault with the bright perfection of her face.

"Don't say you're Mother Phelps!" cried this young person, delightedly, lifting the older woman almost bodily from the wagon. "But I know you are!" she continued joyously. "Do you know who I am? I'm Manzanita Boone!"

Mrs. Phelps felt her heart grow sick within her. She had thought herself steeled for any shock,--but not this! Stricken dumb for a moment, she was led indoors, and found herself listening to a stream of gay chatter, and relieved of hat and gloves, and answering questions briefly and coldly, while all the time an agonized undercurrent of protest filled her heart: "He cannot--he SHALL NOT marry her!"

Austin was up at the mine, of course, but Miss Boone despatched a messenger for him in all haste. The messenger was instructed to say merely that Manzanita had something she wanted to show him, but the simple little ruse failed. Austin guessed what the something was, and before he had fairly dismounted from his wheeling buckskin, his mother heard his eager voice: "Mater! Where are you! Where's my mother?"

He came rushing into the ranch-house, and caught her in his arms, laughing and eager, half wild with the joy of seeing his mother and his girl in each other's company, and too radiant to suspect that his mother's happiness was not as great as his own.

"You got my letter about our engagement, mater? Of course,--and you came right on to meet my girl yourself, didn't you? Good little mater, that was perfectly great of you! This is just about the best thing that ever--and isn't she sweet--do you blame me?" He had his arm about Manzanita, their eyes were together, his tender and proud, the girl's laughing and shy,--they did not see Mrs. Phelps's expression. "And what did you think?" Austin rushed on, "Were you surprised? Did you tell Cornelia? That's good. Did you tell every one--have the home papers had it? You know, mother," Austin dropped his voice confidentially, "I wasn't sure you'd be awfully glad,-- just at first, you know. I knew you would be the minute you saw Manz'ita; but I was afraid--But now, it's all right,--and it's just great!"

"But I thought Yerba Buena was quite a little village, dear," said Mrs. Phelps, accusingly.

"What's the difference?" said Austin, cheerfully, much concerned because Manzanita was silently implying that he should remove his arm from her waist.

"Why, I thought I could stay at a hotel, or at least a boarding- house--" began his mother. Miss Boone laughed out. She was a noisy young creature.

"We'll 'phone the Waldorf-Astoria," said she.

"Seriously, Austin--" said Mrs. Phelps, looking annoyed.

"Seriously, mater," he met her distress comfortably, "you'll stay here at the ranch-house. I live here, you know. Manz'ita'll love to have you, and you'll get the best meals you ever had since you were born! This was certainly a corking thing for you to do, mother!" he broke off joyfully. "And you're looking awfully well!"

"I find you changed, Austin," his mother said, with a delicate inflection that made the words significant. "You're brown, dear, and bigger, and--heavier, aren't you?"

"Why don't you say fat?" said Manzanita, with a little push for her affianced husband. "He was an awfully pasty-looking thing when he came here," she confided to his mother. "But I fed him up, didn't I, Aus?" And she rubbed her cheek against his head like a little friendly pony.

"And he's going to marry her!" Mrs. Phelps said to herself, heartsick. She felt suddenly old and discouraged and helpless; out of their zone of youth and love. But on the heels of despair, her courage rose up again. She would save Austin while there was yet time, if human power could do it.

The three were sitting in the parlor, a small, square room, through whose western windows the sinking sun streamed boldly. Mrs. Phelps had never seen a room like this before. There was no note of quaintness here; no high-boy, no heavy old mahogany drop-leaf table, no braided rugs or small-paned windows. There was not even comfort. The chairs were as new and shining as chairs could be; there was a "mission style" rocker, a golden-oak rocker, a cherry rocker, heavily upholstered. There was a walnut drop-head sewing-machine on which a pink saucer of some black liquid fly-poison stood. There was a "body Brussels" rug on the floor. Lastly, there was an oak sideboard, dusty, pretentious, with its mirror cut into small sections by little, empty shelves.

It all seemed like a nightmare to poor little Mrs. Phelps, as she sat listening to the delighted reminiscences of the young people, who presently reviewed their entire acquaintanceship for her benefit. It seemed impossible that this was her Austin, this big- voiced, brown, muscular young man! Austin had always been slender, and rather silent. Austin had always been so close to her, so quick to catch her point of view. He had been nearer her even than Cornelia--

Cornelia! Her heart reached Cornelia's name with a homesick throb. Cornelia would be home from her club or concert or afternoon at cards now,--Mrs. Phelps did not worry herself with latitude or longitude,--she would be having tea in the little drawing-room, under the approving canvases of Copley and Gilbert Stuart. Her mother could see Cornelia's well-groomed hands busy with the Spode cups and the heavy old silver spoons; Cornelia's fine, intelligent face and smooth dark head well set off by a background of rich hangings and soft lights, polished surfaces, and the dull tones of priceless rugs.

"I beg your pardon?" she said, rousing herself.

"I asked you if you didn't have a cat-fit when you realized that Aus was going to marry a girl you never saw?" Manzanita repeated with friendly enjoyment. Mrs. Phelps gave her only a few seconds' steady consideration for answer, and then pointedly addressed her son.

"It sounds very strange to your mother, to have you called anything but Austin, my son," she said.

"Manz'ita can't spare the time," he explained, adoring eyes on the girl, whose beauty, in the level light, was quite startling enough to hold any man's eyes.

"And you young people are very sure of yourselves, I suppose?" the mother said, lightly, after a little pause. Austin only laughed comfortably, but Manzanita's eyes came suddenly to meet those of the older woman, and both knew that the first gun had been fired. A color that was not of the sunset burned suddenly in the girl's round cheeks. "She's not glad we're engaged!" thought Manzanita, with a pang of utter surprise. "She knows why I came!" Mrs. Phelps said triumphantly to herself.

For Mrs. Phelps was a determined woman, and in some ways a merciless one. She had been born with Bostonian prejudices strong within her. She had made her children familiar, in their very nursery days, with the great names of their ancestors. Cornelia, when a plain, distinguished-looking child of six, was aware that her nose was "all Slocumb," and her forehead just like "great-aunt Hannah Maria Rand Babcock's." Austin learned that he was a Phelps in disposition, but "the image of the Bonds and the Baldwins." The children often went to distinguished gatherings composed entirely of their near and distant kinspeople, ate their porridge from silver bowls a hundred years old, and even at dancing-school were able to discriminate against the beruffled and white-clad infants whose parents "mother didn't know." In due time Austin went to a college in whose archives the names of his kinsmen bore an honorable part; and Cornelia, having skated and studied German cheerfully for several years, with spectacles on her near-sighted eyes, her hair in a club, and a metal band across her big white teeth, suddenly blossomed into a handsome and dignified woman, who calmly selected one Taylor Putnam Underwood as the most eligible of several possible husbands, and proceeded to set up an irreproachable establishment of her own.

All this was as it should be. Mrs. Phelps, a bustling little figure in her handsome rich silks, with her crisp black hair severely arranged, and her crisp voice growing more and more pleasantly positive as years went by, fitted herself with dignity into the role of mother-in-law and grandmother. Cornelia had been married several years. When Austin came home from college, and while taking him proudly with her on a round of dinners and calls, his mother naturally cast her eye about her for the pearl of women, who should become his wife.

Austin, it was understood, was to go into Uncle Hubbard Frothingham's office. All the young sons and nephews and cousins in the family started there. When Austin, agreeing in the main to the proposal, suggested that he be put in the San Francisco branch of the business, Mrs. Phelps was only mildly disturbed. He had everything to lose and nothing to gain by going West, she explained, but if he wanted to, let him try California.

So Austin went, and quite distinguished himself in his new work for about a year. Then suddenly out of a clear sky came the astounding news that he had left the firm,--actually resigned from Frothingham, Curtis, and Frothingham!--and had gone up into the mountains, to manage a mine for some unknown person named Boone! Mrs. Phelps shut her lips into a severe line when she heard this news, and for several weeks she did not write to Austin. But as months went by, and he seemed always well and busy, and full of plans for a visit home, she forgave him, and wrote him twice weekly again,--charming, motherly letters, in which newspaper clippings and concert programmes likely to interest him were enclosed, and amateur photographs,--snapshots of Cornelia in her furs, laughing against a background of snowy Common, snapshots of Cornelia's children with old Kelly in the motor-car, and of dear Taylor and Cornelia with Sally Middleton on the yacht. Did Austin remember dear Sally? She had grown so pretty and had so many admirers.

It was Cornelia who suggested, when the staggering news of Austin's engagement came to Boston, that her mother should go to California, stay at some "pretty, quiet farm-house near by," meet this Miss Manzanita Boone, whoever she was, and quietly effect, as mothers and sisters have hoped to effect since time began, a change of heart in Austin.

And so she had arrived here, to find that there was no such thing in the entire valley as the colonial farmhouse of her dreams, to find that, far from estranging Austin from the Boone family, she must actually be their guest while she stayed at Yerba Buena, to find that her coming was interpreted by this infatuated pair to be a sign of her entire sympathy with their plans. And added to all this, Austin was different, noisier, bigger, younger than she remembered him: Manzanita was worse than her worst fears, and the rancho, bounded only by the far-distant mountain ridges, with its canyons, its river, its wooded valleys and trackless ranges, struck actual terror to her homesick soul.

"Well, what do you think of her? Isn't she a darling?" demanded Austin, when he and his mother were alone on the porch, just before dinner.

"She's very PRETTY, dear. She's not a college girl, of course?"

"College? Lord, no! Why, she wouldn't even go away to boarding- school." Austin was evidently proud of her independent spirit. "She and her brothers went to this little school over here at Eucalyptus, and I guess Manz'ita ran things pretty much her own way. You'll like the kids. They have no mother, you know, and old Boone just adores Manzanita. He's a nice old boy, too."

"Austin, DEAR!" Mrs. Phelps's protest died into a sigh.

"Well, but he is, a fine old fellow," amended Austin.

"And you think she's the sort of woman to make you happy, dear. Is she musical? Is she fond of books?"

Austin, for the first time, looked troubled.

"Don't you LIKE her, mother?" he asked, astounded.

"Why, I've just met her, dear. I want you to tell me about her."

"Every one here is crazy about her," Austin said half sulkily. "She's been engaged four times, and she's only twenty-two!"

"And she TOLD you that, dear? Herself?"

The boy flushed quickly.

"Why shouldn't she?" he said uncomfortably. "Every one knows it."

His mother fanned for a moment in silence.

"Can you imagine Cornelia--or Sally--engaged four times, and talking about it?" she asked gently.

"Things are different here," Austin presently submitted, to which Mrs. Phelps emphatically assented, "Entirely different!"

There was a pause. From the kitchen region came much slamming of light wire door, and the sound of hissing and steaming, high-keyed remarks from the Chinese and the Portuguese girls, and now and then the ripple of Manzanita's laughter. A farm-hand crossed the yard, with pails of milk, and presently a dozen or more men came down the steep trail that led to the mine.

These were ranch-hands, cow-boys, and road-keepers, strong, good- natured young fellows, who had their own house and their own cook near the main ranch-house, and who now began a great washing and splashing, at a bench under some willow trees, where there were basins and towels. An old Spanish shepherd, with his dogs, came down from the sheep range; other dogs lounged out from barns and stables; there was a cheerful stir of reunion and relaxation as the hot day dropped to its close.

A great hawk flapped across the canyon below the ranch-house, bats began to wheel in the clear dusk, owls called in the woods. Just before Manzanita appeared in the kitchen doorway to ring a clamorous bell for some sixty ear-splitting seconds, her father, an immense old man on a restless claybank mare, rode into the yard, and the four brothers, Jose, Marty, Allen, and the little crippled youngest, eight-year-old Rafael, appeared mysteriously from the shadows, and announced that they were ready for dinner. Martin Boone, Senior, gave Mrs. Phelps a vigorous welcome.

"Well, sir! I never thought I'd be glad to see the mother of the fellow who carried off my girl," said Martin Boone, wringing Mrs. Phelps's aching fingers, "but you and I married in our day, ma'am, and it's the youngsters' turn. But he'll have to be a pretty fine fellow to satisfy Manzanita!" And before the lady could even begin the spirited retort that rose to her lips, he had led the way to the long, overloaded dinner-table.

"I am too terribly heartsick to go into details," wrote the poor little lady, when Manzanita had left her for the night in her bare, big bedroom and she had opened her writing-case upon a pine table over which hung, incongruously enough, a large electric light. "Austin is apparently blind to everything but her beauty, which is really noticeable, not that it matters. What is mere beauty beside such refinement as Sally's, for instance, how far will it go with OUR FRIENDS when they discover that Austin's wife is an untrained, common little country girl? Even when I tell you that she uses such words as 'swell,' and 'perfect lady,' and that she asked me who Phillips Brooks was, and had never heard of William Morris or Maeterlinck you can really form no idea of her ignorance! And the dinner,--one shudders at the thought of beginning to teach her of correct service; hors d'oeuvres, finger-bowls, butter-spreaders, soup-spoons and salad-forks will all be mysteries to her! And her clothes! A rowdyish-looking little tight-fitting cotton a servant would not wear, and open-work hose, and silver bangles! It is terrible, TERRIBLE. I don't know what we can do. She is very clever. I think she suspects already that I do not approve, although she began at once to call me 'Mother Phelps'--with a familiarity that is quite typical of her. My one hope is to persuade Austin to come home with me for a visit, and to keep him there until his wretched infatuation has died a natural death. What possible charm this part of the world can have for him is a mystery to me. To compare this barn of a house to your lovely home is enough to make me long to be there with all my heart. Instead of my beautiful rooms, and Mary's constant attendance, imagine your mother writing in a room whose windows have no shades, so that one has the uncomfortable sensation that any one outside may be looking in. Of course the valley descends very steeply from the ranch-house, and there are thousands of acres of silent woods and hills, but I don't like it, nevertheless, and shall undress in the dark. ...I shall certainly speak seriously to Austin as soon as possible."

But the right moment for approaching Austin on the subject of his return to Boston did not immediately present itself, and for several days Manzanita, delighted at having a woman guest, took Mrs. Phelps with her all over the countryside.

"I like lady friends," said Manzanita once, a little shyly. "You see it's 'most always men who visit the rancho, and they're no fun!"

She used to come, uninvited but serene, into her prospective mother- in-law's room at night, and artlessly confide in her, while she braided the masses of her glorious hair. She showed Mrs. Phelps the "swell" pillow she was embroidering to represent an Indian's head, and which she intended to finish with real beads and real feathers. She was as eagerly curious as a child about the older woman's dainty toilet accessories, experimenting with manicure sets and creams and powders with artless pleasure. "I'm going to have that and do it that way!" she would announce, when impressed by some particular little nice touch about Cornelia's letters, or some allusion that gave her a new idea.

"If you ever come to Boston, you will be expected to know all these things," Mrs. Phelps said to her once, a little curiously.

"Oh, but I'll never go there!" she responded confidently.

"You will have to," said the other, sharply. "Austin can hardly spend his whole life here! His friends are there, his family. All his traditions are there. Those may not mean much to him now, but in time to come they will mean more."

"We'll make more money than we can spend, right here," Manzanita said, in a troubled voice.

"Money is not everything, my dear."

"No--" Manzanita's brown fingers went slowly down to the last fine strands of the braid she was finishing. Then she said, brightening:

"But I AM everything to Aus! I don't care what I don't know, or can't do, HE thinks I'm fine!"

And she went off to bed in high spirits. She was too entirely normal a young woman to let anything worry her very long,--too busy to brood. The visitor soon learned why the ranch-house parlor presented so dismal an aspect of unuse. It was because Manzanita was never inside it. The girl's days were packed to the last instant with duties and pleasures. She needed no parlor. Even her bedroom was as bare and impersonal as her father's. She was never idle. Mrs. Phelps more than once saw the new-born child of a rancher's or miner's wife held in those capable young arms, she saw the children at the mine gathering about Manzanita, the women leaving their doorways for eager talk with her. And once, during the Eastern woman's visit, death came to the Yerba Buena, and Manzanita and young Jose spent the night in one of the ranch-houses, and walked home, white, tired, and a little sobered, in the early morning, for breakfast.

Manzanita rode and drove horses of which even her brothers were afraid; she handled a gun well, she chattered enough Spanish, Portuguese, Indian, and Italian to make herself understood by the ranch hands and dairy-men. And when there was a housewarming, or a new barn to gather in, she danced all night with a passionate enjoyment. It might be with Austin, or the post-office clerk, or a young, sleek-haired rancher, or a miner shining from soap and water; it mattered not to Manzanita, if he could but dance. And when she and Mrs. Phelps drove, as they often did, to spend the day with the gentle, keen, capable women on other ranches thereabout, it was quite the usual thing to have them bring out bolts of silk or gingham for Manzanita's inspection, and seriously consult her as to fitting and cutting.

Mrs. Phelps immensely enjoyed these day-long visits, though she would have denied it; hardly recognized the fact herself. One could grow well acquainted in a day with the clean, big, bare ranch- houses, the very old people in the shining kitchens, the three or four capable companionable women who managed the family; one with a child at her breast, perhaps another getting ready for her wedding, a third newly widowed, but all dwelling harmoniously together and sharing alike the care of menfolk and children. They would all make the Eastern woman warmly welcome, eager for her talk of the world beyond their mountains, and when she and Manzanita drove away, it was with jars of specially chosen preserves and delicious cheeses in their hands, pumpkins and grapes, late apples and perhaps a jug of cider in the little wagon body, and a loaf of fresh-baked cake or bread still warm in a white napkin. Hospitable children, dancing about the phaeton, would shout generous offers of "bunnies" or "kitties," Manzanita would hang at a dangerous angle over the wheel to accept good-by kisses, and perhaps some old, old woman, limping out to stand blinking in the sunlight, would lay a fine, transparent, work-worn hand on Mrs. Phelps and ask her to come again. It was an "impossible" life, of course, and yet, at the moment, absorbing enough to the new-comer. And it was at least surprising to find the best of magazines and books everywhere,--"the advertisements alone seem to keep them in touch with everything new," wrote Mrs. Phelps.

Her whole attitude toward Manzanita might have softened sometimes, if long years of custom had not made the little things of life vitally important to her. A misused or mispronounced word was like a blow to her; inner forces over which she had no control forced her to discuss it and correct it. She had a quick, horrified pity for Manzanita's ignorance on matters which should be part of a lady's instinctive knowledge. She winced at the girl's cheerful acknowledgement of that ignorance. No woman in Mrs. Phelps's own circle at home ever for one instant admitted ignorance of any important point of any sort; what she did not know she could superbly imply was not worth knowing. Even though she might be secretly enjoying the universal, warm hospitality of the rancho, Mrs. Phelps never lost sight of the fact that Manzanita was not the wife for Austin, and that the marriage would be the ruin of his life. She told herself that her opposition was for Manzanita's happiness as well as for his, and plotted without ceasing against their plans.

"I've had a really remarkable letter from Uncle William, dear!" she said, one afternoon, when by some rare chance she was alone with her son.

"Good for you!" said Austin, absently, clicking the cock of the gun he was cleaning. "Give the old boy my love when you write."

"He sends you a message, dear. He wants to know--but you're not listening," Mrs. Phelps paused. Austin looked up.

"Oh, I'm listening. I hear every word."

"You seem so far from me these days, Austin," said his mother, plaintively. But--" she brightened, "I hope dear Uncle William's plan will change all that. He wants you to come home, dear. He offers you the junior partnership, Austin." She brought it out very quietly.

"Offers me the--WHAT?"

"The junior partnership,--yes, dear. Think of it, at your age, Austin! What would your dear father have said! How proud he would have been! Yes. Stafford has gone into law, you know, and Keith Curtis will live abroad when Isabel inherits. So you see!"

"Mighty kind of Uncle William," mused Austin, "but of course there's nothing in it for me!" He avoided her gaze, and went on cleaning his gun. "I'm fixed here, you know. This suits me."

"I hope you are not serious, my son." Austin knew that voice. He braced himself for unpleasantness.

"Manzanita," he said simply. There was a throbbing silence.

"You disappoint one of my lifelong hopes for my only son, Austin," his mother said very quietly.

"I know it, mother. I'm sorry."

"For the first time, Austin, I wish I had another son. I am going to beg you--to beg you to believe that I can see your happiness clearer than you can just now!" Mrs. Phelps's voice was calm, but she was trembling with feeling.

"Don't put it that way, mater. Anyway, I never liked office work much, you know."

"Austin, don't think your old mammy is trying to manage you," Mrs. Phelps was suddenly mild and affectionate. "But THINK, dear. Taylor says the salary is not less than fifteen thousand. You could have a lovely home, near me. Think of the opera, of having a really formal dinner again, of going to Cousin Robert Stokes's for Christmas, and yachting with Taylor and Gerry."

Austin was still now, evidently he WAS thinking.

"My idea," his mother went on reasonably, "would be to have you come on with me now, at once. See Uncle William,--we mustn't keep his kindness waiting, must we?--get used to the new work, make sure of yourself. Then come back for

Manzanita, or have her come on--" She paused, her eyes a question.

"I'd hate to leave Yerba Buena--" Austin visibly hesitated.

"But, Austin, you must sooner or later." Mrs. Phelps was framing a triumphant letter to Cornelia in her mind.

But just then Manzanita came running around the corner of the house, and seeing them, took the porch steps in two bounds, and came to lean on Austin's shoulder.

"Austin!" she burst out excitedly. "I want you to ride straight down to the stock pens,--they've got a thousand steers on the flats there going through from Portland, and the men say they aren't to leave the cars to-night! I told them they would HAVE to turn them out and water them, and they just laughed! Will you go down?" She was breathing hard like an impatient child, her cheeks two poppies, her eyes blazing. "Will you? Will you?"

"Sure I will, if you'll do something for me." Austin pulled her toward him.

"Well, there!" She gave him a child's impersonal kiss. "You'll make them water them, won't you, Austin?"

"Oh, yes. I'll 'tend to them." Austin got up, his arm about her. "Look here," said he. "How'd you like to come and live in Boston?"

Her eyes went quickly from him to his mother.

"I wouldn't!" she said, breathing quickly and defiantly.

"Never?"

"Never, never, never! Unless it was just to visit. Why, Austin--" her reproachful eyes accused him, "you said we needn't, ever! You KNOW I couldn't live in a street!"

Austin laughed again. "Well, that settles Uncle William!" he announced comfortably. "I'll write him to-morrow, mother. Come on, now, we'll settle this other trouble!"

And he and Manzanita disappeared in the direction of the stable.

Mrs. Phelps sat thinking, deep red spots burning in her cheeks. Things could not go on this way. Yet she would not give up. She suddenly determined to try an idea of Cornelia's.

So the word went all over the ranch-house next day that Mrs. Phelps was ill. The nature of the illness was not specified, but she could not leave her bed. Austin was all filial sympathy, Manzanita an untiring nurse. Hong Fat sent up all sorts of kitchen delicacies, the boys brought trout, and rare ferns, and wild blackberries in from their daily excursions, for her especial benefit, and before two days were over, every hour found some distant neighbor at the rancho with offers of sympathy and assistance. An old doctor came up from Emville at once, and Jose and Marty accompanied him all the twenty miles back into town for medicines.

But days went by, and the invalid was no better. She lay, quiet and uncomplaining, in the airy bedroom, while October walked over the mountain ranges, and the grapes were gathered, and the apples brought in. She took the doctor's medicine, and his advice, and agreed pleasantly with him that she would soon be well enough to go home, and would be better off there. But she would not try to get up.

One afternoon, while she was lying with closed eyes, she heard the rattle of the doctor's old buggy outside, and heard Manzanita greet him from where she was labelling jelly glasses on the porch. Mrs. Phelps could trace the old man's panting approach to a porch chair, and heard Manzanita go into the house with a promise of lemonade and crullers. In a few minutes she was back again, and the clink of ice against glass sounded pleasantly in the hot afternoon.

"Well, how is she?" said the doctor, presently, with a long, wet gasp of satisfaction.

"She's asleep," answered Manzanita. "I just peeked in.--There's more of that," she added, in apparent reference to the iced drink. And then, with a change of tone, she added, "What's the matter with her, anyway, Doc' Jim?"

To which the old doctor with great simplicity responded:

"You've got me, Manz'ita. I can diagnose as good as any one," he went on after a pause, "when folks have GOT something. If you mashed your hand in a food cutter, or c't something poisonous, or come down with scarlet fever, I'd know what to do for ye. But, these rich women--"

"Well, you know, I could prescribe for her, and cure her, too," said Manzanita. "All I'd do is tell her she'd got to go home right off. I'd say that this climate was too bracing for her, or something."

"Shucks! I did say that," interrupted the doctor.

"Yes, but you didn't say you thought she'd ought to take her son along in case of need," the girl added significantly. There was a long pause.

"She don't want ye to marry him, hey?" said the doctor, ending it.

Manzanita evidently indicated an assent, for he presently resumed indignantly: "Who does she want for him--Adelina Patti?" He marvelled over a third glass. "Well, what do you know about that!" he murmured. Then, "Well, I'll be a long time prescribing that."

"No, I want you to send her off, and send him with her," said Manzanita, decidedly, "that's why I'm telling you this. I've thought it all over. I don't want to be mean about it. She thinks that if he saw his sister, and his old friends, and his old life, he'd get to hate the Yerba Buena. At first I laughed at her, and so did Aus. But, I don't know, Doc' Jim, she may be right!"

"Shucks!" said the doctor, incredulously.

"No, of course she isn't!" the girl said, after a pause. "I know Aus. But let her take him, and try. Then, if he comes back, she can't blame me. And--" She laughed. "This is a funny thing," she said, "for she doesn't like me. But I like her. I have no mother and no aunts, you know, and I like having an old lady 'round. I always wanted some one to stay with me, and perhaps, if Aus comes back some day, she'll get to liking me, too. She'll remember," her tone grew a little wistful, "that I couldn't help his loving me! And besides-- "and the tone was suddenly confident again--"I AM good--as good as his sister! And I'm learning things. I learn something new from her every day! And I'd LIKE to feel that he went away from me--and had to come back!"

"Don't you be a fool," cautioned the doctor. "A feller gets among his friends for a year or two, and where are ye? Minnie Ferguson's feller never come back to her and she was a real pretty, good girl, too."

"Oh, I think he'll come back," the girl said softly, as if to herself.

"I only hope, if he don't show up on the minute, you'll marry somebody else so quick it'll make her head spin!" said the doctor, fervently. Manzanita laughed out, and the sound of it made Mrs. Phelps wince, and shut her eyes.

"Maybe I will!" the girl said hardily. "You'll suggest his taking her home, anyway, won't you, Doc' Jim?" she asked.

"Well, durn it, I'd jest as soon," agreed the doctor. "I don't know as you're so crazy about him!"

"And you'll stay to dinner?" Manzanita instantly changed the subject. "There's ducks. Of course the season's over, but a string of them came up to Jose and Marty, and pushed themselves against their guns--you know how it is."

"Sure, I'll stay," said the doctor. "Go see if she's awake, Manz'ita, that's a good girl. If she ain't--I'll walk up to the mine for a spell."

So Manzanita tiptoed to the door of Mrs. Phelps's room and noiselessly opened it, and smiled when she saw the invalid's open eyes.

"Well, have a nice nap?" she asked, coming to put a daughterly little hand over the older woman's hand. "Want more light? Your books have come."

"I'm much better, dear," said Mrs. Phelps. The Boston woman's tone would always be incisive, her words clear. But she kept Manzanita's hand. "I think I will get up for dinner. I've been lying here thinking that I've wasted quite enough time, if we are to have a wedding here before I go home--"

Manzanita stared at her. Then she knelt down beside the bed and began to cry.

On a certain Thursday afternoon more than a year later, Mrs. Phelps happened to be alone in her daughter's Boston home. Cornelia was attending the regular meeting of a small informal club whose reason for being was the study of American composers. Mrs. Phelps might have attended this, too, or she might have gone to several other club meetings, or she might have been playing cards, or making calls, but she had been a little bit out of humor with all these things of late, and hence was alone in the great, silent house. The rain was falling heavily outside, and in the library there was a great coal fire. Now and then a noiseless maid came in and replenished it.

Cornelia was always out in the afternoons. She belonged to a great many clubs, social, literary, musical and civic clubs, and card clubs. Cornelia was an exceptionally capable young woman. She had two nice children, in the selection of whose governesses and companions she exercised very keen judgment, and she had a fine husband, a Harvard man of course, a silent, sweet-tempered man some years her senior, whose one passion in life was his yacht, and whose great desire was that his wife and children should have everything in life of the very best. Altogether, Cornelia's life was quite perfect, well-ordered, harmonious, and beautiful. She attended the funeral of a relative or friend with the same decorous serenity with which she welcomed her nearest and dearest to a big family dinner at Christmas or Thanksgiving. She knew what life expected of her, and she gave it with calm readiness.

The library in her beautiful home, where her mother was sitting now, was like all the other drawing-rooms Cornelia entered. Its mahogany reading-table bore a priceless lamp, and was crossed by a strip of wonderful Chinese embroidery. There were heavy antique brass candlesticks on the mantel, flanking a great mirror whose carved frame showed against its gold rare touches of Florentine blue. The rugs on the floor were a silken blend of Oriental tones, the books in the cases were bound in full leather. An oil portrait of Taylor hung where his wife's dutiful eyes would often find it, lovely pictures of the children filled silver frames on a low book-case.

Eleanor, the ten-year-old, presently came into the room, with Fraulein Hinz following her. Eleanor was a nice child, and the only young life in the house since Taylor Junior had been sent off to boarding-school.

"Here you are, grandmother," said she, with a kiss. "Uncle Edward brought us home. It's horrid out. Several of the girls didn't come at all to-day."

"And what have you to do now, dear?" Mrs. Phelps knew she had something to do.

"German for to-morrow. But it's easy. And then Dorothy's coming over, for mamma is going out. We'll do our history together, and have dinner upstairs. She's not to go home until eight!"

"That's nice," said Mrs. Phelps, claiming another kiss before the child went away. She had grown quite used to seeing Eleanor only for a moment now and then.

When she was alone again, she sat staring dreamily into the fire, a smile coming and going in her eyes. She had left Manzanita's letter upstairs, but after all, she knew the ten closely covered pages by heart. It had come a week ago, and had been read several times a day since. It was a wonderful letter.

They wanted her--in California. In fact, they had always wanted her, from the day she came away. She had stayed to see the new house built, and had stayed for the wedding, and then had come back to Boston, thinking her duty to Austin done, and herself free to take up the old life with a clear conscience. But almost the first letters from the rancho demanded her! Little Rafael had painfully written to know where he could find this poem and that to which she had introduced him. Marty had sent her a bird's nest, running over with ants when it was opened in Cornelia's breakfast-room, but he never knew that. Jose had written for advice as to seeds for Manzanita's garden. And Austin had written he missed her, it was "rotten" not to find mater waiting for them, when they came back from their honeymoon.

But best of all, Manzanita had written, and, ah, it was sweet to be wanted as Manzanita wanted her! News of all the neighbors, of the women at the mine, pressed wildflowers, scraps of new gowns, and questions of every sort; Manzanita's letters brimmed with them. She could have her own rooms, her own bath, she could have everything she liked, but she must come back!

"I am the only woman here at the house," wrote Manzanita, "and it's no fun. I'd go about ever so much more, if you were here to go with me. I want to start a club for the women at the mine, but I never belonged to a club, and I don't know how. Rose Harrison wants you to come on in time for her wedding, and Alice has a new baby. And old Mrs. Larabee says to tell you--"

And so on and on. They didn't forget her, on the Yerba Buena, as the months went by. Mrs. Phelps grew to look eagerly for the letters. And now came this one, and the greatest news in the world--! And now, it was as it should be, Manzanita wanted her more than ever!

Cornelia came in upon her happy musing, to kiss her mother, send her hat and furs upstairs, ring for tea, and turn on the lights, all in the space of some sixty seconds.

"It was so interesting to-day, mater," reported Cornelia. "Cousin Emily asked for you, and Edith and the Butlers sent love. Helen is giving a bridge lunch for Mrs. Marye; she's come up for Frances' wedding on the tenth. And Anna's mother is better; the nurse says you can see her on Wednesday. Don't forget the Shaw lecture Wednesday, though. And there is to be a meeting of this auxiliary of the political study club,--I don't know what it's all about, but one feels one must go. I declare," Cornelia poured a second cup, "next winter I'm going to try to do less. There isn't a single morning or afternoon that I'm not attending some meeting or going to some affair. Between pure milk and politics and charities and luncheons,- -it's just too much! Belle says that women do all the work of the world, in these days--"

"And yet we don't GET AT anything," said Mrs. Phelps, in her brisk, impatient little way. "I attend meetings, I listen to reports, I sit on boards--But what comes of it all! Trained nurses and paid workers do all the actual work--"

"But mother, dear, a great deal will come of it all," Cornelia was mildly reproachful. "You couldn't inspect babies and do nursing yourself, dear! Investigating and tabulating and reporting are very difficult things to do!"

"Sometimes I think, Cornelia, that the world was much pleasanter for women when things were more primitive. When they just had households and babies to look out for, when every one was personally NEEDED."

"Mother, DEAR!" Cornelia protested indulgently. "Then we haven't progressed at all since MAYFLOWER days?"

"Oh, perhaps we have!" Mrs. Phelps shrugged doubtfully. "But I am sometimes sorry," she went on, half to herself, "that birth and wealth and position have kept me all my life from REAL things! I can't help my friends in sickness or trouble, Cornelia, I don't know what's coming on my own table for dinner, or what the woman next door looks like! I can only keep on the surface of things, dressing a certain way, eating certain things, writing notes, sending flowers, making calls!"

"All of which our class--the rich and cultivated people of the world--have been struggling to achieve for generations!" Cornelia reminded her. "Do you mean you would like to be a laborer's mother, mater, with all sorts of annoying economies to practice, and all sorts of inconveniences to contend with?"

"Yes, perhaps I would!" her mother laughed defiantly.

"I can see you've had another letter from California," said Cornelia, pleasantly, after a puzzled moment. "You are still a pioneer in spite of the ten generations, mater. Austin's wife is NOT a lady, Austin is absolutely different from what he was, the people out there are actually COMMON, and yet, just because they like to have you, and think you are intelligent and instructive, you want to go. Go if you want to, but I will think you are mad if you do! A girl who confused 'La Boheme' with 'The Bohemian Girl,' and wants an enlarged crayon portrait of Austin in her drawing-room! Really, it's--well, it's remarkable to me. I don't know what you see in it!"

"Crayon portraits used to be considered quite attractive, and may be again," said Mrs. Phelps, mildly. "And some day your children will think Puccini and Strauss as old-fashioned as you think 'Faust' and Offenbach. But there are other things, like the things that a woman loves to do, for instance, when her children are grown, and her husband is dead, that never change!"

Cornelia was silent, frankly puzzled.

"Wouldn't you rather do nothing than take up the stupid routine work of a woman who has no money, no position, and no education?" she asked presently.

"I don't believe I would," her mother answered, smiling. "Perhaps I've changed. Or perhaps I never sat down and seriously thought things out before. I took it for granted that our way of doing things was the only way. Of course I don't expect every one to see it as I do. But it seems to me now that I belong there. When she first called me 'Mother Phelps,' it made me angry, but what sweeter thing could she have said, after all? She has no mother. And she needs one, now. I don't think you have ever needed me in your life, Cornelia--actually NEEDED me, my hands and my eyes and my brain."

"Oh, you are incorrigible!" said Cornelia, still with an air of lenience. "Now," she stopped for a kiss, "we're going out to-night, so I brought you The Patricians to read; it's charming. And you read it, and be a good mater, and don't think any more about going out to stay on that awful, uncivilized ranch. Visit there in a year or two, if you like, but don't strike roots. I'll come in and see you when I'm dressed."

And she was gone. But Mrs. Phelps felt satisfied that enough had been said to make her begin to realize that she was serious, and she contentedly resumed her dreaming over the fire.

The years, many or few, stretched pleasantly before her. She smiled into the coals. She was still young enough to enjoy the thought of service, of healthy fatigue, of busy days and quiet evenings, and long nights of deep sleep, with slumbering Yerba Buena lying beneath the moon outside her open window. There would be Austin close beside her and other friends almost as near, to whom she would be sometimes necessary, and always welcome.

And there would be Manzanita, and the child,--and after a while, other children. There would be little bibs to tie, little prayers to hear, deep consultations over teeth and measles, over morals and manners. And who but Grandmother could fill Grandmother's place?

Mrs. Phelps leaned back in her chair, and shut her eyes. She saw visions. After a while a tear slipped from between her lashes.

RISING WATER

I f only my poor child had a sensible mother," said Mrs. Tressady, calmly, "I suppose we would get Big Hong's 'carshen' for him, and that would do perfectly! But I will not have a Chinese man for Timothy's nurse! It seems all wrong, somehow."

"Big Hong hasn't got a female cousin, I suppose?" said Timothy's father; "a Chinese woman wouldn't be so bad." "Oh, I think it would be as bad--nearly," Mrs. Tressady returned with vivacity. "Anyway, this particular carshen is a man--'My carshen lun floot store'-- that's who it is!"

"Will you kindly explain what 'My carshen lun floot store' means?" asked a young man who was lying in a hammock that he lazily moved now and then by means of a white-shod foot. This was Peter Porter, who, with his wife, completed the little group on the Tressadys' roomy, shady side porch.

"It means my cousin who runs a fruit store," supplied Mrs. Porter--a big-boned, superb blonde who was in a deep chair sewing buttons on Timothy Tressady's new rompers. "Even I can see that--if I'm not a native of California."

"Yes, that's it," Mrs. Tressady said absently. "Go back and read those Situations Wanted over again, Jerry," she commanded with a decisive snip of the elastic she was cunningly inserting into more new rompers for Timothy.

Jerry Tressady obediently sat up in his steamer chair and flattened a copy of the Emville Mail upon his knee.

The problem under discussion this morning was that of getting a nurse for Timothy Tressady, aged two years. Elma, the silent, undemonstrative Swedish woman who had been with the family since Timothy's birth, had started back to Stockholm two months ago, and since then at least a dozen unsatisfactory applicants for her position had taken their turn at the Rising Water Ranch.

Mrs. Tressady, born and brought up in New York, sometimes sighed as she thought of her mother's capped and aproned maids; of Aunt Anna's maids; of her sister Lydia's maids. Sometimes in the hot summer, when the sun hung directly over the California bungalow for seven hours every day, and the grass on the low, rolling hills all about was dry and slippery, when Joe Parlona forgot to drive out from Emville with ice and mail, and Elma complained that Timmy could not eat his luncheon on the porch because of buzzing "jellow yackets," Molly Tressady found herself thinking other treasonable thoughts-- thoughts of packing, of final telegrams, of the Pullman sleeper, of Chicago in a blowing mist of rain, of the Grand Central at twilight, with the lights of taxicabs beginning to move one by one into the current of Forty-second Street--and her heart grew sick with longings. And sometimes in winter, when rain splashed all day from the bungalow eaves, and Beaver Creek rose and flooded its banks and crept inch by inch toward the garden gate, and when from the late dawn to the early darkness not a soul came near the ranch--she would have sudden homesick memories of Fifth Avenue, three thousand miles away, with its motor-cars and its furred women and its brilliant tea-rooms. She would suddenly remember the opera-house and the long line of carriages in the snow, and the boys calling the opera scores.

However, for such moods the quickest cure was a look at Jerry-- strong, brown, vigorous Jerry--tramping the hills, writing his stories, dreaming over his piano, and sleeping deep and restfully under the great arch of the stars. Jerry had had a cold four years ago--"just a mean cold," had been the doctor's cheerful phrase; but what terror it struck to the hearts that loved Jerry! Molly's eyes, flashing to his mother's eyes, had said: "Like his father--like his aunt--like the little sister who died!" And for the first time Jerry's wife had found herself glad that little Jerry Junior--he who could barely walk, who had as yet no words--had gone away from them fearlessly into the great darkness a year before. He might have grown up to this, too.

So they came to California, and big Jerry's cold did not last very long in the dry heat of Beaver Creek Valley. He and Molly grew so strong and brown and happy that they never minded restrictions and inconveniences, loneliness and strangeness--and when a strong and brown and happy little Timothy joined the group, Molly renounced forever all serious thoughts of going home. California became home. Such friends as chance brought their way must be their only friends; such comfort as the dry little valley and the brown hills could hold must suffice them now. Molly exulted in sending her mother snapshots of Timmy picking roses in December, and in heading July letters: "By our open fire--for it's really cool to-day."

Indeed it was not all uncomfortable and unlovely. All the summer nights were fresh and cool and fragrant; there were spring days when all the valley seemed a ravishing compound of rain-cooled air and roses, of buttercups in the high, sun-flecked grass under the apple- trees, crossed and recrossed by the flashing blue and brown of mating jays and larks. It was not a long drive to the deep woods; and it was but six miles to Emville, where there was always the pleasant stir and bustle of a small country town; trains puffing in to disgorge a dozen travelling agents and their bags; the wire door at the post-office banging and banging; the maid at the Old Original Imperial Commercial Hotel coming out on the long porch to ring a wildly clamorous dinner-bell. Molly grew to love Emville.

Then, two or three times a year, such old friends as the Porters, homeward bound after the Oriental trip, came their way, and there was delicious talk at the ranch of old days, of the new theatres, and the new hotels, and the new fashions. The Tressadys stopped playing double Canfield and polished up their bridge game; and Big Hong, beaming in his snowy white, served meals that were a joy to his heart. Hong was a marvellous cook; Hong cared beautifully for all his domain; and Little Hong took care of the horses, puttered in the garden, swept, and washed windows. But they needed more help, for there were times when Molly was busy or headachy or proof- reading for Jerry or riding with him. Some one must be responsible every second of the day and night for Timmy. And where to get that some one?

"Aren't they terrors!" said Mrs. Porter in reference to the nurse- maids that would not come to the ranch on any terms. "What do they expect anyway?"

"Oh, they get lonesome," Molly said in discouragement, "and of course it is lonely! But I should think some middle-aged woman or some widow with a child even--"

"Molly always returns to that possible widow!" said her husband. "I think we might try two!"

"I would never think of that!" said the mistress of the ranch firmly. "Four ser-vants always underfoot!"

"Did you ever think of trying a regular trained nurse, Molly?" Peter Porter asked.

"But then you have them at the table, Peter--and always in the drawing-room evenings. And no matter how nice they are--"

"That's the worst of that!" agreed Peter.

Jerry Tressady threw the Mail on the floor and sat up.

"Who's this coming up now, Molly?" he asked.

He had lowered his voice, because the white-clad young woman who was coming composedly up the path between the sunflowers and the overloaded rose-bushes was already within hearing distance. She was a heavy, well-developed young person upon closer view, with light- lashed eyes of a guileless, childlike blue, rosy cheeks, and a mass of bright, shining hair, protected now only by a parasol. Through the embroidery insertion of her fresh, stiff dress she showed glimpses of a snowy bosom, and under her crisp skirt a ruffle of white petticoat and white-shod feet were visible. She was panting from her walk and wiped her glowing face with her handkerchief before she spoke.

"Howdy-do, folks?" said the new-comer, easily, dropping upon the steps and fanning herself with the limp handkerchief. "I don't wonder you keep a motor-car; it's something fierce walking down here! I could of waited," she went on thoughtfully, "and had my brother brought me down in the machine, but I hadn't no idea it was so far. I saw your ad in the paper," she went on, addressing Mrs. Tressady directly, with a sort of trusting simplicity that was rather pretty, "and I thought you might like me for your girl."

"Well,--" began Molly, entirely at a loss, for until this second no suspicion of the young woman's errand had occurred to her. She dared not look at husband or guests; she fixed her eyes seriously upon the would-be nurse.

"Of course I wouldn't work for everybody," said the new-comer hastily and proudly. "I never worked before and mamma thinks I'm crazy to work now, but I don't think that taking care of a child is anything to be ashamed of!" The blue eyes flashed dramatically--she evidently enjoyed this speech. "And what's more, I don't expect any one of my friends to shun me or treat me any different because I'm a servant--that is, so long as I act like a lady," she finished in a lower tone. A sound from the hammock warned Mrs. Tressady; and suggesting in a somewhat unsteady voice that they talk the matter over indoors, she led the new maid out of sight.

For some twenty minutes the trio on the porch heard the steady rise and fall of voices indoors; then Molly appeared and asked her husband in a rather dissatisfied voice what he thought.

"Why, it's what you think, dear. How's she seem?"

"She's competent enough--seems to know all about children, and I think she'd be strong and willing. She's clean as a pink, too. And she'd come for thirty and would be perfectly contented, because she lives right near here--that house just before you come to Emville which says Chickens and Carpentering Done Here--don't you know? She has a widowed sister who would come and stay with her at night when we're away." Mrs. Tressady summed it up slowly.

"Why not try her then, dear? By the way, what's her name?"

"Darling--Belle Darling."

"Tell her I'm English," said Mr. Porter, rapturously, "and that over there we call servants--"

"No, but Jerry,"--Mrs. Tressady was serious,--"would you? She's so utterly untrained. That's the one thing against her. She hasn't the faintest idea of the way a servant should act. She told me she just loved the way I wore my hair, and she said she wanted me to meet her friend. Then she asked me, 'Who'd you name him Timothy for?'"

"Oh, you'd tame her fast enough. Just begin by snubbing her every chance you get--"

"I see it!" laughed Mrs. Porter, for Mrs. Tressady was a woman full of theories about the sisterhood of woman, about equality, about a fair chance for every one--and had never been known to hurt any one's feelings in the entire course of her life.

Just here Belle stepped through one of the drawing-room French windows, with dewy, delicious Timothy, in faded pale-blue sleeping- wear, in her arms.

"This darling little feller was crying," said Belle, "and I guess he wants some din-din--don't you, lover? Shall I step out and tell one of those Chinese boys to get it? Listen! From now on I'll have mamma save all the banty eggs for you, Timmy, and some day I'll take you down there and show you the rabbits, darling. Would you like that?"

Molly glanced helplessly at her husband.

"How soon could you come, Belle?" asked Jerry, and that settled it. He had interpreted his wife's look and assumed the responsibility. Molly found herself glad.

Belle came two days later, with every evidence of content. It soon became evident that she had adopted the family and considered herself adopted in turn. Her buoyant voice seemed to leap out of every opened door. She rose above her duties and floated along on a constant stream of joyous talk.

"We're going to have fried chicken and strawberries--my favorite dinner!" said Belle when Molly was showing her just how she liked the table set. After dinner, cheerfully polishing glasses, she suddenly burst into song as she stood at the open pantry window, some ten feet from the side porch. The words floated out:

"And the band was bravely playing
The song of the cross and crown--
Nearer, my god, to thee--
As the ship--"

Mrs. Tressady sat up, a stirring shadow among the shadows of the porch.

"I must ask her not to do that," she announced quietly, and disappeared.

"And I spoke to her about joining in the conversation at dinner," she said, returning. "She took it very nicely."

Belle's youthful spirits were too high to succumb to one check, however. Five minutes later she burst forth again:

"Ring, ting-a-ling, ting-a-ling, on your telephone--
And ring me up tonight--"

"Soft pedal, Belle!" Jerry called.

Belle laughed.

"Sure!" she called back. "I forgot."

Presently the bright blot of light that fell from the pantry window on the little willow trees vanished silently, and they could hear Belle's voice in the kitchen.

"Good-natured," said Molly.

"Strong," Mrs. Porter said.

"And pretty as a peach!" said Peter Porter.

"Oh, she'll do!" Jerry Tressady said contentedly.

She was good-natured, strong, and pretty indeed, and she did a great deal. Timmy's little garments fluttered on the clothes-line before breakfast; Timmy's room was always in order: Timmy was always dainty and clean. Belle adored him and the baby returned her affection. They murmured together for hours down on the river bank or on the shady porch. Belle always seemed cheerful.

Nor could it be said that Belle did not know her place. She revelled in her title. "This is Mrs. Tressady's maid," Belle would say mincingly at the telephone, "and she does not allow her servants to make engagements for her." "My friends want me to enter my name for a prize for the most popular girl in the Emville bazaar, Mrs. Tressady; but I thought I would ask your permission first."

But there was a sort of breezy familiarity about her very difficult to check. On her second day at the ranch she suddenly came behind Jerry Tressady seated on the piano bench and slipped a sheet of music before him.

"Won't you just run over that last chorus for me, Mr. Tress'dy?" asked Belle. "I have to sing that at a party Thursday night and I can't seem to get it."

No maid between Washington Square and the Bronx Zoo would have asked this favor. Yes, but Rising Water Ranch was not within those limits, nor within several thousand miles of them; so Jerry played the last chorus firmly, swiftly, without comment, and Belle gratefully withdrew. The Porters, unseen witnesses of this scene, on the porch, thought this very amusing; but only a day later Mrs. Porter herself was discovered in the act of buttoning the long line of buttons that went down the back of one of Belle's immaculate white gowns.

"Well, what could I do? She suddenly backed up before me," Mrs. Porter said in self-defence. "Could I tell her to let Hong button her?"

After dinner on the same day Peter Porter cleared a space before him on the table and proceeded to a demonstration involving a fork, a wedding ring, and a piece of string. While the quartet, laughing, were absorbed in the mysterious swinging of the suspended ring, Belle, putting away her clean silver, suddenly joined the group.

"I know a better one than that," said she, putting a glass of water before Mrs. Tressady. "Here--take your ring again. Now wait--I'll pull out one of your hairs for you. Now swing it over the water inside the glass. It'll tell your age."

Entirely absorbed in the experiment, her fresh young face close to theirs, her arms crossed as she knelt by the table, she had eyes only for the ring.

"We won't keep you from your dishes, Belle," said Molly.

"Oh, I'm all through," said Belle, cheerfully. "There!" For the ring was beginning to strike the glass with delicate, even strokes-- thirty.

"Now do it again," cried Belle, delightedly, "and it'll tell your married life!"

Again the ring struck the glass--eight.

"Well, that's very marvellous," said Molly, in genuine surprise; but when Belle had gone back to her pantry, Mrs. Tressady rose, with a little sigh, and followed her.

"Call her down?" asked Jerry, an hour later.

"Well, no," the lady admitted, smiling. "No! She was putting away Timmy's bibs, and she told me that he had seemed a little upset to- night, she thought; so she gave him just barley gruel and the white of an egg for supper, and some rhubarb water before he went to bed. And what could I say? But I will, though!"

During the following week Mrs. Tressady told Belle she must not rush into a room shouting news--she must enter quietly and wait for an opportunity to speak; Mrs. Tressady asked her to leave the house by the side porch and quietly when going out in the evening to drive with her young man; Mrs. Tressady asked her not to deliver the mail with the announcement: "Three from New York, an ad from Emville, and one with a five-cent stamp on it;" she asked her not to shout out from the drive, "White skirt show?" She said Belle must not ask, "What's he doing?" when discovering Mr. Tressady deep in a chess problem; Belle must not drop into a chair when bringing Timmy out to the porch after his afternoon outing; she must not be heard exclaiming, "Yankee Doodle!" and "What do you know about that!" when her broom dislodged a spider or her hair caught on the rose-bushes.

To all of these requests Belle answered, "Sure!" with great penitence and amiability.

"Sure, Mis' Tress'dy--Say, listen! I can match that insertion I spilled ink on--in Emville. Isn't that the limit? I can fix it so it'll never show in the world!"

"I wouldn't stand that girl for--one--minute," said Mrs. Porter to her husband; but this was some weeks later when the Porters were in a comfortable Pullman, rushing toward New York.

"I think Molly's afraid of flying in the face of Providence and discharging her," said Peter Porter--"but praying every day that she'll go."

This was almost the truth. Belle's loyalty, affection, good nature, and willingness were beyond price, but Belle's noisiness, her slang, and her utter lack of training were a sore trial. When November came, with rains that kept the little household at Rising Water prisoners indoors, Mrs. Tressady began to think she could not stand Belle much longer.

"My goodness!" Belle would say loudly when sent for to bring a filled lamp. "Is that other lamp burned out already? Say, listen! I'll give you the hall lamp while I fill it." "You oughtn't to touch pie just after one of your headaches!" she would remind her employer in a respectful aside at dinner. And sometimes when Molly and her husband were busy in the study a constant stream of conversation would reach them from the nursery where Belle was dressing Timothy:

"Now where's the boy that's going to let Belle wash his face? Oh, my, what a good boy! Now, just a minny--minny--minny--that's all. Now give Belle a sweet, clean kiss--yes, but give Belle a sweet, clean kiss--give Belle a kiss--oh, Timmy, do you want Belle to cry? Well, then, give her a kiss--give Belle a sweet kiss--"

When Molly was bathing the boy Belle would come and take a comfortable chair near by, ready to spring for powder or pins, but otherwise studying her fingernails or watching the bath with genial interest. Molly found herself actually lacking in the strength of mind to exact that Belle stand silently near on these occasions, and so listened to a great many of Belle's confidences. Belle at home; Belle in the high school; Belle trying a position in Robbins's candy store and not liking it because she was not used to freshness--all these Belles became familiar to Molly. Grewsome sicknesses, famous local crimes, gossip, weddings--Belle touched upon them all; and Molly was ashamed to find it all interesting, it spite of herself. One day Belle told Molly of Joe Rogers, and Joe figured daily in the narratives thereafter--Joe, who drove a carriage, a motor, or a hay wagon, as the occasion required, for his uncle who owned a livery stable, but whose ambition was to buy out old Scanlon, the local undertaker, and to marry Belle.

"Joe knows more about embalming than even Owens of Napa does," confided Belle. "He's got every plat in the cemetery memorized--and, his uncle having carriages and horses, it would work real well; but Scanlon wants three thousand for the business and goodwill."

"I wish he had it and you this minute!" Molly would think. But when she opened Timmy's bureau drawers, to find little suits and coats and socks in snowy, exquisite order; when Timmy, trim, sweet, and freshly clad, appeared for breakfast every morning, his fat hand in Belle's, and "Dea' Booey"--as he called her--figuring prominently in his limited vocabulary, Molly weakened again.

"Is he mad this morning?" Belle would ask in a whisper before Jerry appeared. "Say, listen! You just let him think I broke the decanter!" she suggested one day in loyal protection of Molly. "Why, I think the world and all of Mr. Tressady!" she assured Molly, when reproved for speaking of him in this way. "Wasn't it the luckiest thing in the world--my coming up that day?" she would demand joyously over and over. Her adoption of and by the family of Tressady was--to her, at least--complete.

In January Uncle George Tressady's estate was finally distributed, and this meant great financial ease at Rising Water. Belle, Molly said, was really getting worse and worse as she became more and more at home; and the time had come to get a nice trained nurse--some one who could keep a professional eye on Timmy, be a companion to Molly, and who would be quiet and refined, and gentle in her speech.

"And not a hint to Belle, Jerry," Molly warned him, "until we see how it is going to work. She'll see presently that we don't need both."

When Miss Marshall, cool, silent, drab of hair and eye, arrived at the ranch, Belle was instantly suspicious.

"What's she here for? Who's sick?" demanded Belle, coming into Mrs. Tressady's room and closing the door behind her, her eyes bright and hard.

Molly explained diplomatically. Belle must be very polite to the new-comer; it was just an experiment--"This would be a good chance to hint that I'm not going to keep both," thought Molly, as Belle listened.

Belle disarmed her completely, however, by coming over to her with a suddenly bright face and asking in an awed voice:

"Is it another baby? Oh, you don't know how glad I'd be! The darling, darling little thing!"

Molly felt the tears come into her eyes--a certain warmth creep about her heart.

"No," she said smiling; "but I'm glad you will love it if it ever comes!" This was, of course, exactly what she did not mean to say.

"If we got Miss Marshall because of Uncle George's money," said Belle, huffily, departing, "I wish he hadn't died! There isn't a thing in this world for her to do."

Miss Marshall took kindly to idleness--talking a good deal of previous cases, playing solitaire, and talking freely to Molly of various internes and patients who admired her. She marked herself at once as unused to children by calling Timothy "little man," and, except for a vague, friendly scrutiny of his tray three times a day, did nothing at all--even leaving the care of her room to Belle.

After a week or two, Miss Marshall went away, to Belle's great satisfaction, and Miss Clapp came. Miss Clapp was forty, and strong and serious; she did not embroider or confide in Molly; she sat silent at meals, chewing firmly, her eyes on her plate. "What would you like me to do now?" she would ask Molly, gravely, at intervals.

Molly, with Timothy asleep and Belle sweeping, could only murmur:

"Why, just now,--let me see,--perhaps you'd like to write letters-- or just read--"

"And are you going to take little Timothy with you when he wakes up?"

Molly would evade the uncompromising eyes.

"Why, I think so. The sun's out now. You must come, too."

Miss Clapp, coming, too, cast a damper on the drive; and she persisted in talking about the places where she was really needed.

"Imagine a ward with forty little suffering children in it, Mrs. Tressady! That's real work--that's a real privilege!"

And after a week or two Miss Clapp went joyously back to her real work with a generous check for her children's ward in her pocket. She kissed Timothy good-by with the first tenderness she had shown.

"Didn't she make you feel like an ant in an anthill?" asked Belle, cheerfully watching the departing carriage. "She really didn't take no interest in Timothy because there wasn't a hundred of him!"

There was a peaceful interval after this, while Molly diligently advertised for

"A competent nurse. One child only. Good salary. Small family in country."

No nurse, competent or incompetent, replied. Then came the January morning when Belle casually remarked: "Stupid! You never wound it!" to the master of the house, who was attempting to start a stopped clock. This was too much! Mrs. Tressady immediately wrote the letter that engaged Miss Carter, a highly qualified and high-priced nursery governess who had been recommended by a friend.

Miss Carter, a rosy, strong, pleasant girl, appeared two days later in a driving rain and immediately "took hold." She was talkative, assured in manner, neat in appearance, entirely competent. She drove poor Belle to frenzy with her supervision of Timothy's trays, baths and clothes, amusements and sleeping arrangements. Timmy liked her, which was point one in her favor. Point two was that she liked to have her meals alone, liked to disappear with a book, could amuse herself for hours in her own room.

The Tressadys, in the privacy of their own room, began to say to each other: "I like her--she'll do!"

"She's very complacent," Molly would say with a sigh.

"But it's nothing to the way Belle effervesces all over the place!"

"Oh, I suppose she is simply trying to make a good impression-- that's all." And Mrs. Tressady began to cast about in her mind for just the words in which to tell Belle that--really--four servants were not needed at the ranch. Belle was so sulky in these days and so rude to the new-comer that Molly knew she would have no trouble in finding good reason for the dismissal.

"Are we going to keep her?" Belle asked scornfully one morning--to which her mistress answered sharply:

"Belle, kindly do not shout so when you come into my room. Do you see that I am writing?"

"Gee whiz!" said Belle, sorrowfully, as she went out, and she visibly drooped all day.

It was decided that as soon as the Tressadys' San Francisco visit was over, Belle should go. They were going down to the city for a week in early March--for some gowns for Molly, some dinners, some opera, and one of the talks with Jerry's doctor that were becoming so delightfully unnecessary.

They left the ranch in a steady, gloomy downpour. Molly did her packing between discouraged trips to the window, and deluged Belle and Miss Carter with apprehensive advice that was not at all like her usual trusting outlook.

"Don't fail to telephone me instantly at the hotel if anything--but, of course, nothing will," said Molly. "Anyway you know the doctor's number, Belle, and about a hot-water bag for him if his feet are cold, and oil the instant he shows the least sign of fever--"

"Cert'n'y!" said Belle, reassuringly.

"This is Monday," said Molly. "We'll be back Sunday night. Have Little Hong meet us at the Junction. And if it's clear, bring Timmy."

"Cert'n'y!" said Belle.

"I hate to go in all this rain!" Molly said an hour or two later from the depths of the motor-car.

Miss Carter was holding Timmy firmly on the sheltered porch railing. Belle stood on an upper step in the rain. Big Hong beamed from the shadowy doorway. At the last instant Belle suddenly caught Timmy in her arms and ran down the wet path.

"Give muddy a reel good kiss for good-by!" commanded Belle, and Molly hungrily claimed not one, but a score.

"Good-by, my heart's heart!" she said. "Thank you, Belle." As the carriage whirled away she sighed. "Was there ever such a good- hearted, impossible creature!"

Back into the house went Belle and Timmy, Miss Carter and Big Hong. Back came Little Hong with the car. Silence held the ranch; the waning winter light fell on Timmy, busy with blocks; on Belle darning; on Miss Carter reading a light novel. The fire blazed, sank to quivering blue, leaped with a sucking noise about a fresh log, and sank again. At four the lamps were lighted, the two women fussed amicably together over Timothy's supper. Later, when he was asleep, Miss Carter, who had no particular fancy for the shadows that lurked in the corners of the big room and the howling wind on the roof, said sociably: "Shall we have our dinner on two little tables right here before the fire, Belle?" And still later, after an evening of desultory reading and talking, she suggested that they leave their bedroom doors open. Belle agreed. If Miss Carter was young, Belle was younger still.

The days went by. Hong served them delicious meals. Timmy was angelic.

They unearthed halma, puzzles, fortune-telling cards. The rain fell steadily; the eaves dripped; the paths were sheets of water.

"It certainly gets on your nerves--doesn't it?" said Miss Carter, when the darkness came on Thursday night. Belle, from the hall, came and stood beside her at the fireplace.

"Our 'phone is cut off," said she, uneasily. "The water must of cut down a pole somewheres. Let's look at the river."

Suddenly horror seemed to seize upon them both. They could not cross the floor fast enough and plunge fast enough into the night. It was dark out on the porch, and for a moment or two they could see nothing but the swimming blackness, and hear nothing but the gurgle and drip of the rain-water from eaves and roof. The rain had stopped, or almost stopped. A shining fog seemed to lie flat--high and level over the river-bed.

Suddenly, as they stared, this fog seemed to solidify before their eyes, seemed curiously to step into the foreground and show itself for what it was. They saw it was no longer fog, but water--a level spread of dark, silent water. The Beaver Creek had flooded its banks and was noiselessly, pitilessly creeping over the world.

"It's the river!" Belle whispered. "Gee whiz, isn't she high!"

"What is it?" gasped Miss Carter, from whose face every vestige of color had fled.

"Why, it's the river!" Belle answered, slowly, uneasily. She held out her hand. "Thank God, the rain's stopped!" she said under her breath. Then, so suddenly that Miss Carter jumped nervously, she shouted: "Hong!"

Big Hong came out, and Little Hong. All four stood staring at the motionless water, which was like some great, menacing presence in the dark--some devil-fish of a thousand arms, content to bide his time.

The bungalow stood on a little rise of ground in a curve of the river. On three sides of it, at all seasons, were the sluggish currents of Beaver Creek, and now the waters met on the fourth side. The garden path that led to the Emville road ran steeply now into this pool, and the road, sloping upward almost imperceptibly, emerged from the water perhaps two hundred feet beyond.

"Him how deep?" asked Hong.

"Well, those hollyhocks at the gate are taller than I am," Belle said, "and you can't see them at all. I'll bet it's ten feet deep most of the way."

She had grown very white, and seemed to speak with difficulty. Miss Carter went into the house, with the dazed look of a woman in a dream, and knelt at the piano bench.

"Oh, my God--my God--my God!" she said in a low, hoarse tone, her fingers pressed tightly over her eyes.

"Don't be so scared!" said Belle, hardily, though the sight of the other woman's terror had made her feel cold and sick at her stomach. "There's lots of things we can do--"

"There's an attic--"

"Ye-es," Belle hesitated. "But I wouldn't go up there," she said. "It's just an un-floored place under the roof--no way out!"

"No--no--no--not there, then!" Miss Carter said heavily, paler than before. "But what can we do?"

"Why, this water is backing up," Belle said slowly, "It's not coming downstream, so any minute whatever's holding it back may burst and the whole thing go at once--or if it stops raining, it won't go any higher."

"Well, we must get away as fast as we can while there is time," said Miss Carter, trembling, but more composed. "We could swim that distance--I swim a little. Then, if we can't walk into Emville, we'll have to spend the night on the hills. We could reach the hills, I should think." Her voice broke. "Oh--this is terrible!" she broke out frantically--and she began to walk the floor.

"Hong, could we get the baby acrost?" asked Belle.

"Oh, the child--of course!" said Miss Carter, under her breath. Hong shook his head.

"Man come bimeby boat," he suggested. "Me no swim--Little Hong no swim."

"You can't swim" cried Miss Carter, despairingly, and covered her face with her hands.

Little Hong now came in to make some earnest suggestion in Chinese. His uncle, approving it, announced that they two, unable to swim, would, nevertheless, essay to cross the water with the aid of a floating kitchen bench, and that they would fly for help. They immediately carried the bench out into the night.

The two women followed; a hideous need of haste seemed to possess them all.

The rain was falling heavily again.

"It's higher," said Miss Carter, in a dead tone. Belle eyed the water nervously.

"You couldn't push Timmy acrost on that bench?" she ventured.

It became immediately evident, however, that the men would be extremely fortunate in getting themselves across. The two dark, sleek heads made slow progress on the gloomy water. The bench tipped, turned slowly, righted itself, and tipped again. Soon they worked their slow way out of sight.

Then came silence--silence!

"She's rising!" said Belle.

Miss Carter went blindly into the house. She was ashen and seemed to be choking. She sat down.

"They'll be back in no time," said she, in a sick voice.

"Sure!" said Belle, moistening her lips.

There was a long silence. Rain drummed on the roof.

"Do you swim, Belle?" Miss Carter asked after a restless march about the room.

"Some--I couldn't swim with the baby--"

Miss Carter was not listening. She leaned her head against the mantelpiece. Suddenly she began to walk again, her eyes wild, her breath uneven.

"Well, there must be something we can do, Belle!"

"I've been trying to think," said Belle, slowly. "A bread board wouldn't float, you know, even if the baby would sit on it. We've not got a barrel--and a box--"

"There must be boxes!" cried the other woman.

"Yes; but the least bit of a tip would half fill a box with water. No--" Belle shook her head. "I'm not a good enough swimmer."

Another short silence.

"Belle, does this river rise every winter?"

"Why, yes, I suppose it does. I know one year Emville was flooded and the shops moved upstairs. There was a family named Wescott living up near here then--" Belle did not pursue the history of the Westcott family, and Miss Carter knew why.

"Oh, I think it is criminal for people to build in a place like this!" Miss Carter burst out passionately. "They're safe enough--oh, certainly!" she went on with bitter emphasis. "But they leave us--"

"It shows how little you know us, thinking we'd run any risk with Timmy--" Belle said stiffly; but she interrupted herself to say sharply: "Here's the water!"

She went to the door and opened it. The still waters of Beaver Creek were lapping the porch steps.

Miss Carter made an inarticulate exclamation and went into her room. Belle, following her to her door, saw her tear off her shoes and stockings, and change her gown for some brief, dark garment.

"It's every one for himself now!" said Miss Carter, feverishly. "This is no time for sentiment. If they don't care enough for their child to--This is my gym suit-- I'm thankful I brought it. Don't be utterly mad, Belle! If the water isn't coming, Timmy'll be all right. If it is, I don't see why we should be so utterly crazy as not to try to save ourselves. We can easily swim it, and then we can get help--You've got a bathing suit--go put it on. My God, Belle, it's not as if we could do anything by staying. If we could, I'd--"

Belle turned away. When Miss Carter followed her, she found her in Mrs. Tressady's bedroom, looking down at the sleeping Timmy. Timmy had taken to bed with him a box of talcum powder wrapped in a towel, as a "doddy." One fat, firm little hand still held the meaningless toy. He was breathing heavily, evenly--his little forehead moist, his hair clinging in tendrils about his face.

"No--of course we can't leave him!" said Miss Carter, heavily, as the women went back to the living-room. She went frantically from window to window. "It's stopped raining!" she announced.

"We'll laugh at this to-morrow," said Belle. They went to the door. A shallow sheet of water, entering, crept in a great circle about their very feet.

"Oh, no--it's not to be expected; it's too much!" Miss Carter cried. Without an instant's hesitation she crossed the porch and splashed down the invisible steps.

"I take as great a chance in going as you do in staying," she said, with chattering teeth. "If--if it comes any higher, you'll swim for it--won't you, Belle?"

"Oh, I'd try it with him as a last chance," Belle answered sturdily. She held a lamp so that its light fell across the water. "That's right. Keep headed that way!" she said.

"I'm all right!" Miss Carter's small head was bravely cleaving the smooth dark water. "I'll run all the way and bring back help in no time," she called back.

When the lamp no longer illumined her, Belle went into the house. The door would not shut, but the water was not visibly higher. She went in to Timmy's crib, knelt down beside him, and put her arms about his warm little body.

Meanwhile Timmy's father and mother, at the hotel, were far from happy. They stopped for a paper on their way to the opera on Thursday night; and on their return, finding no later edition procurable, telephoned one of the newspapers to ask whether there was anything in the reports that the rivers were rising up round Emville. On Friday morning Jerry, awakening, perceived his wife half-hidden in the great, rose-colored window draperies, barefoot, still in her nightgown, and reading a paper.

"Jerry," said she, very quietly, "can we go home today? I'm worried. Some of the Napa track has been washed away and they say the water's being pushed back. Can we get the nine o'clock train?"

"But, darling, it must be eight now."

"I know it."

"Why not telephone to Belle, dear, and have them all come into Emville if you like."

"Oh, Jerry--of course! I never thought of it." She flew to the telephone on the wall. "The operator says she can't get them-- they're so stupid!" she presently announced.

Jerry took the instrument away from her and the little lady contentedly began her dressing. When she came out of the dressing- room a few moments later, her husband was flinging things into his suitcase.

"Get Belle, Jerry?"

"Nope." He spoke cheerfully, but did not meet her eyes. "Nope. They can't get 'em. Lines seem to be down. I guess we'll take the nine."

"Jerry,"--Molly Tressady came over to him quietly,--"what did they tell you?"

"Now, nothing at all--" Jerry began. At his tone terror sprang to Molly's heart and sank its cruel claws there. There was no special news from Rising Water he explained soothingly; but, seeing that she was nervous, and the nine was a through train, and so on--and on--

"Timmy--Timmy--Timmy!" screamed Molly's heart. She could not see; she could not think or hear, or taste her breakfast. Her little boy- -her little, helpless, sturdy, confident baby, who had never been frightened, never alone--never anything but warm and safe and doubly, trebly guarded--

They were crossing a sickening confusion that was the hotel lobby. They were moving in a taxicab through bright, hideous streets. The next thing she knew, Jerry was seating her in a parlor car.

"Yes, I know, dear--Of course--Surely!" she said pleasantly and mechanically when he seemed to expect an answer.--She thought of how he would have come to meet her; of how the little voice always rang out: "Dere's my muddy!"

"Raining again!" said Jerry. "It stopped this morning at two. Oh, yes, really it did. We're almost there now. Hello! Here's the boy with the morning papers. See, dear, here's the head-line: Rain Stops at One-fifty--"

But Molly had seen another headline--a big headline that read: "Loss of Life at Rising Water! Governess of Jerome Tressady's Family Swims One Mile to Safety!"--and she had fainted away.

She was very brave, very reasonable, when consciousness came back, but there could be no more pretence. She sat in the demoralized little parlor of the Emville Hotel--waiting for news--very white, very composed, a terrible look in her eyes. Jerry came and went constantly; other people constantly came and went. The flood was falling fast now and barges were being towed down the treacherous waters of Beaver Creek; refugees--and women and children whom the mere sight of safety and dry land made hysterical again--were being gathered up. Emville matrons, just over their own hours of terror, were murmuring about gowns, about beds, about food: "Lots of room-- well, thank God for that--you're all safe, anyway!" "Yes, indeed; that's the only thing that counts!" "Well, bless his heart, we'll tell him some day that when he was a baby--" Molly caught scraps of their talk, their shaken laughter, their tears; but there was no news of Belle--of Timmy--

"Belle is a splendid, strong country girl, you know, dear," Jerry said. "Belle would be equal to any emergency!"

"Of course," Molly heard herself say.

Jerry presently came in from one of his trips to draw a chair close to his wife's and tell her that he had seen Miss Carter.

"Or, at least, I've seen her mother," said Jerry, laying a restraining hand upon Molly, who sat bolt upright, her breast heaving painfully--"for she herself is feverish and hysterical, dear. It seems that she left--Now, my darling, you must be quiet."

"I'm all right, Jerry. Go on! Go on!"

"She says that Hong and Little Hong managed to get away early in the evening for help. She didn't leave until about midnight, and Belle and the boy were all right then--"

"Oh, my God!" cried poor Molly.

"Molly, dear, you make it harder."

"Yes, I know." Her penitent hot hand touched his own. "I know, dear- -I'm sorry."

"That's all, dear. The water wasn't very high then. Belle wouldn't leave Timmy-" Jerry Tressady jumped suddenly to his feet and went to stare out the window with unseeing eyes. "Miss Carter didn't get into town here until after daylight," he resumed, "and the mother, poor soul, is wild with fright over her; but she's all right. Now, Molly, there's a barge going up as far as Rising Water at four. They say the bungalow is still cut off, probably, but they'll take us as near as they can. I'm going, and this Rogers--Belle's friend--will go, too."

"What do you think, Jerry?" she besought him, agonized.

"My darling, I don't know what to think."

"Were--were many lives lost, Jerry?"

"A few, dear."

"Jerry,"--Molly's burning eyes searched his,--"I'm sane now. I'm not going to faint again; but--but--after little Jerry--I couldn't bear it and live!"

"God sent us strength for that, Molly."

"Yes, I know!" she said, and burst into bitter tears.

It had been arranged that Molly should wait at the hotel for the return of the barge; but Jerry was not very much surprised, upon going on board, to find her sitting, a shadowy ghost of herself, in the shelter of the boxed supplies that might be needed. He did not protest, but sat beside her; and Belle's friend, a serious, muscular young man, took his place at her other side.

The puffing little George Dickey started on her merciful journey only after some agonizing delays; but Molly did not comment upon them once, nor did any one of the trio speak throughout the terrible journey. The storm was gone now, and pale, uncertain sunlight was falling over the altered landscape--over the yellow, sullen current of the river; over the drowned hills and partly submerged farms. A broom drifted by; a child's perambulator; a porch chair. Now and then there was frantic signalling from some little, sober group of refugees, huddled together on a water-stained porch or travelling slowly down the heavy roads in a spattered surrey.

"This is as near as we can go," Jerry said presently. The three were rowed across shallow water and found themselves slowly following on foot the partly obliterated road they knew so well. A turn of the road brought the bungalow into view.

There the little house stood, again high above the flood, though the garden was a drenched waste, and a shallow sheet of water still lay across the pathway. The sinking sun struck dazzling lights from all the windows; no living thing was in sight. A terrible stillness held the place!

To the gate they went and across the pool. Then Jerry laid a restraining hand on his wife's arm.

"Yes'm. You'd 'a' better wait here," said young Rogers, speaking for the first time. "Belle wouldn't 'a' stayed, you may be sure. We'll just take a look."

They were not ten feet from the house, now--hesitating, sick with dread. Suddenly on the still air there was borne a sound that stopped them where they stood. It was a voice--Belle's voice--tired and somewhat low, but unmistakably Belle's:

"Then i'll go home, my crown to wear;
for there's a crown for me--"

"Belle!" screamed Molly. Somehow she had mounted the steps, crossed the porch, and was at the kitchen door.

Belle and Timothy were in the kitchen--Timothy's little bib tied about his neck, Timothy's little person securely strapped in his high chair, and Timothy's blue bowl, full of some miraculously preserved cereal, before him. Belle was seated--her arms resting heavily and wearily upon his tray, her dress stained to the armpits, her face colorless and marked by dark lines. She turned and sprang up at the sound of voices and feet, and had only time for a weak smile before she fell quite senseless to the floor. Timmy waved a welcoming spoon, and shouted lustily: "Dere's my muddy!"

Presently Belle was resting her head upon Joe's big shoulder, and laughing and crying over the horrors of the night. Timothy was in his mother's arms, but Molly had a hand free for Belle's hand and did not let it go through all the hour that followed. Her arms might tighten about the delicious little form, her lips brush the tumbled little head--but her eyes were all for Belle.

"It wasn't so fierce," said Belle. "The water went highest at one; and we went to the porch and thought we'd have to swim for it-- didn't we, Timmy? But it stayed still a long time, and it wasn't raining, and I came in and set Timmy on the mantel--my arms were so tired. It's real lucky we have a mantel, isn't it?"

"You stood, and held Tim on the mantel: that was it?" asked Jerry.

"Sure--while we was waiting," said Belle. "I wouldn't have minded anything, but the waiting was fierce. Timmy was an angel! He set there and I held him--I don't know--a long time. Then I seen that the water was going down again; I could tell by the book-case, and I begun to cry. Timmy kept kissing me--didn't you, lover?" She laughed, with trembling lips and tearful eyes. "We'll have a fine time cleaning this house," she broke off, trying to steady her voice; "it's simply awful--everything's ruined!"

"We'll clean it up for your marriage, Belle," said Jerry, cheerfully, clearing his throat. "Mrs. Tressady and I are going to start Mr. Rogers here in business--"

"If you'd loan it to me at interest, sir-" Belle's young man began hoarsely. Belle laid her hand over Molly's, her voice tender and comforting--for Molly was weeping again.

"Don't cry, Mis' Tress'dy! It's all over now, and here we are safe and sound. We've nothing to cry over. Instead," said Belle, solemnly, "we'd ought to be thanking God that there was a member of the family here to look out for Timmy, instead of just that hired governess and the Chinee boys!"

www.bookjungle.com *email: sales@bookjungle.com fax: 630-214-0564 mail: Book Jungle PO Box 2226 Champaign, IL 61825*

The Codes Of Hammurabi And Moses
W. W. Davies

QTY

The discovery of the Hammurabi Code is one of the greatest achievements of archaeology, and is of paramount interest, not only to the student of the Bible, but also to all those interested in ancient history...

Religion   **ISBN:** *1-59462-338-4*

Pages:132
MSRP $12.95

The Theory of Moral Sentiments
Adam Smith

QTY

This work from 1749. contains original theories of conscience amd moral judgment and it is the foundation for systemof morals.

Philosophy ISBN: *1-59462-777-0*

Pages:536
MSRP $19.95

Jessica's First Prayer
Hesba Stretton

QTY

In a screened and secluded corner of one of the many railway-bridges which span the streets of London there could be seen a few years ago, from five o'clock every morning until half past eight, a tidily set-out coffee-stall, consisting of a trestle and board, upon which stood two large tin cans, with a small fire of charcoal burning under each so as to keep the coffee boiling during the early hours of the morning when the work-people were thronging into the city on their way to their daily toil...

Childrens   ISBN: *1-59462-373-2*

Pages:84
MSRP $9.95

My Life and Work
Henry Ford

QTY

Henry Ford revolutionized the world with his implementation of mass production for the Model T automobile. Gain valuable business insight into his life and work with his own auto-biography... "We have only started on our development of our country we have not as yet, with all our talk of wonderful progress, done more than scratch the surface. The progress has been wonderful enough but..."

Biographies/   **ISBN:** *1-59462-198-5*

Pages:300
MSRP $21.95

The Art of Cross-Examination
Francis Wellman

QTY

I presume it is the experience of every author, after his first book is published upon an important subject, to be almost overwhelmed with a wealth of ideas and illustrations which could readily have been included in his book, and which to his own mind, at least, seem to make a second edition inevitable. Such certainly was the case with me; and when the first edition had reached its sixth impression in five months, I rejoiced to learn that it seemed to my publishers that the book had met with a sufficiently favorable reception to justify a second and considerably enlarged edition. ..

Pages:412

Reference   **ISBN:** *1-59462-647-2*   *MSRP $19.95*

On the Duty of Civil Disobedience
Henry David Thoreau

QTY

Thoreau wrote his famous essay, On the Duty of Civil Disobedience, as a protest against an unjust but popular war and the immoral but popular institution of slave-owning. He did more than write—he declined to pay his taxes, and was hauled off to gaol in consequence. Who can say how much this refusal of his hastened the end of the war and of slavery ?

Law   **ISBN:** *1-59462-747-9*   **Pages:48**

MSRP $7.45

Dream Psychology Psychoanalysis for Beginners
Sigmund Freud

QTY

Sigmund Freud, born Sigismund Schlomo Freud (May 6, 1856 - September 23, 1939), was a Jewish-Austrian neurologist and psychiatrist who co-founded the psychoanalytic school of psychology. Freud is best known for his theories of the unconscious mind, especially involving the mechanism of repression; his redefinition of sexual desire as mobile and directed towards a wide variety of objects; and his therapeutic techniques, especially his understanding of transference in the therapeutic relationship and the presumed value of dreams as sources of insight into unconscious desires.

Dream Psychology
Psychoanalysis for Beginners

Sigmund Freud

Pages:196

Psychology   **ISBN:** *1-59462-905-6*   *MSRP $15.45*

The Miracle of Right Thought
Orison Swett Marden

QTY

Believe with all of your heart that you will do what you were made to do. When the mind has once formed the habit of holding cheerful, happy, prosperous pictures, it will not be easy to form the opposite habit. It does not matter how improbable or how far away this realization may see, or how dark the prospects may be, if we visualize them as best we can, as vividly as possible, hold tenaciously to them and vigorously struggle to attain them, they will gradually become actualized, realized in the life. But a desire, a longing without endeavor, a yearning abandoned or held indifferently will vanish without realization.

Pages:360

Self Help   **ISBN:** *1-59462-644-8*   *MSRP $25.45*

www.**bookjungle**.com *email: sales@bookjungle.com fax: 630-214-0564 mail: Book Jungle PO Box 2226 Champaign, IL 61825*

QTY

The Rosicrucian Cosmo-Conception Mystic Christianity by *Max Heindel* ISBN: *1-59462-188-8* **$38.95**
The Rosicrucian Cosmo-conception is not dogmatic, neither does it appeal to any other authority than the reason of the student. It is: not controversial, but is: sent forth in the, hope that it may help to clear... New Age/Religion Pages 646

Abandonment To Divine Providence by *Jean-Pierre de Caussade* ISBN: *1-59462-228-0* **$25.95**
"The Rev. Jean Pierre de Caussade was one of the most remarkable spiritual writers of the Society of Jesus in France in the 18th Century. His death took place at Toulouse in 1751. His works have gone through many editions and have been republished... Inspirational/Religion Pages 400

Mental Chemistry by *Charles Haanel* ISBN: *1-59462-192-6* **$23.95**
Mental Chemistry allows the change of material conditions by combining and appropriately utilizing the power of the mind. Much like applied chemistry creates something new and unique out of careful combinations of chemicals the mastery of mental chemistry... New Age Pages 354

The Letters of Robert Browning and Elizabeth Barret Barrett 1845-1846 vol II ISBN: *1-59462-193-4* **$35.95**
by *Robert Browning* and *Elizabeth Barrett* Biographies Pages 596

Gleanings In Genesis (volume I) by *Arthur W. Pink* ISBN: *1-59462-130-6* **$27.45**
Appropriately has Genesis been termed "the seed plot of the Bible" for in it we have, in germ form, almost all of the great doctrines which are afterwards fully developed in the books of Scripture which follow... Religion/Inspirational Pages 420

The Master Key by *L. W. de Laurence* ISBN: *1-59462-001-6* **$30.95**
In no branch of human knowledge has there been a more lively increase of the spirit of research during the past few years than in the study of Psychology, Concentration and Mental Discipline. The requests for authentic lessons in Thought Control, Mental Discipline and... New Age/Business Pages 422

The Lesser Key Of Solomon Goetia by *L. W. de Laurence* ISBN: *1-59462-092-X* **$9.95**
This translation of the first book of the "Lernegton" which is now for the first time made accessible to students of Talismanic Magic was done, after careful collation and edition, from numerous Ancient Manuscripts in Hebrew, Latin, and French... New Age/Occult Pages 92

Rubaiyat Of Omar Khayyam by *Edward Fitzgerald* ISBN:*1-59462-332-5* **$13.95**
Edward Fitzgerald, whom the world has already learned, in spite of his own efforts to remain within the shadow of anonymity, to look upon as one of the rarest poets of the century, was born at Bredfield, in Suffolk, on the 31st of March, 1809. He was the third son of John Purcell... Music Pages 172

Ancient Law by *Henry Maine* ISBN: *1-59462-128-4* **$29.95**
The chief object of the following pages is to indicate some of the earliest ideas of mankind, as they are reflected in Ancient Law, and to point out the relation of those ideas to modern thought. Religion/History Pages 452

Far-Away Stories by *William J. Locke* ISBN: *1-59462-129-2* **$19.45**
"Good wine needs no bush, but a collection of mixed vintages does. And this book is just such a collection. Some of the stories I do not want to remain buried for ever in the museum files of dead magazine-numbers an author's not unpardonable vanity..." Fiction Pages 272

Life of David Crockett by *David Crockett* ISBN: *1-59462-250-7* **$27.45**
"Colonel David Crockett was one of the most remarkable men of the times in which he lived. Born in humble life, but gifted with a strong will, an indomitable courage, and unremitting perseverance... Biographies/New Age Pages 424

Lip-Reading by *Edward Nitchie* ISBN: *1-59462-206-X* **$25.95**
Edward B. Nitchie, founder of the New York School for the Hard of Hearing, now the Nitchie School of Lip-Reading, Inc, wrote "LIP-READING Principles and Practice". The development and perfecting of this meritorious work on lip-reading was an undertaking... How-to Pages 400

A Handbook of Suggestive Therapeutics, Applied Hypnotism, Psychic Science ISBN: *1-59462-214-0* **$24.95**
by *Henry Munro* Health/New Age/Health/Self-help Pages 376

A Doll's House: and Two Other Plays by *Henrik Ibsen* ISBN: *1-59462-112-8* **$19.95**
Henrik Ibsen created this classic when in revolutionary 1848 Rome. Introducing some striking concepts for the realist genre, this play has been studied the world over. Fiction/Classics/Plays 308

The Light of Asia by *sir Edwin Arnold* ISBN: *1-59462-204-3* **$13.95**
In this poetic masterpiece, Edwin Arnold describes the life and teachings of Buddha. The man who was to become known as Buddha to the world was born as Prince Gautama of India but he rejected the worldly riches and abandoned the reigns of power when... Religion/History/Biographies Pages 170

The Complete Works of Guy de Maupassant by *Guy de Maupassant* ISBN: *1-59462-157-8* **$16.95**
"For days and days, nights and nights, I had dreamed of that first kiss which was to consecrate our engagement, and I knew not on what spot I should put my lips..." Fiction/Classics Pages 240

The Art of Cross-Examination by *Francis L. Wellman* ISBN: *1-59462-309-0* **$26.95**
Written by a renowned trial lawyer, Wellman imparts his experience and uses case studies to explain how to use psychology to extract desired information through questioning. How-to/Science/Reference Pages 408

Answered or Unanswered? by *Louisa Vaughan* ISBN: *1-59462-248-5* **$10.95**
Miracles of Faith in China Religion Pages 112

The Edinburgh Lectures on Mental Science (1909) by *Thomas* ISBN: *1-59462-008-3* **$11.95**
This book contains the substance of a course of lectures recently given by the writer in the Queen Street Hall, Edinburgh. Its purpose is to indicate the Natural Principles governing the relation between Mental Action and Material Conditions... New Age/Psychology Pages 148

Ayesha by *H. Rider Haggard* ISBN: *1-59462-301-5* **$24.95**
Verily and indeed it is the unexpected that happens! Probably if there was one person upon the earth from whom the Editor of this, and of a certain previous history, did not expect to hear again... Classics Pages 380

Ayala's Angel by *Anthony Trollope* ISBN: *1-59462-352-X* **$29.95**
The two girls were both pretty, but Lucy who was twenty-one who supposed to be simple and comparatively unattractive, whereas Ayala was credited, as her Bombwhat romantic name might show, with poetic charm and a taste for romance. Ayala when her father died was nineteen... Fiction Pages 484

The American Commonwealth by *James Bryce* ISBN: *1-59462-286-8* **$34.45**
An interpretation of American democratic political theory. It examines political mechanics and society from the perspective of Scotsman James Bryce Politics Pages 572

Stories of the Pilgrims by *Margaret P. Pumphrey* ISBN: *1-59462-116-0* **$17.95**
This book explores pilgrims religious oppression in England as well as their escape to Holland and eventual crossing to America on the Mayflower and their early days in New England... History Pages 268

QTY

The Fasting Cure *by Sinclair Upton*   ISBN: *1-59462-222-1*   **$13.95**
In the Cosmopolitan Magazine for May, 1910, and in the Contemporary Review (London) for April, 1910, I published an article dealing with my experi-
ences in fasting. I have written a great many magazine articles, but never one which attracted so much attention... New Age/Self Help/Health Pages 164

Hebrew Astrology *by Sepharial*   ISBN: *1-59462-308-2*   **$13.45**
In these days of advanced thinking it is a matter of common observation that we have left many of the old landmarks behind and that we are now pressing
forward to greater heights and to a wider horizon than that which represented the mind-content of our progenitors... Astrology Pages 144

Thought Vibration or The Law of Attraction in the Thought World   ISBN: *1-59462-127-6*   **$12.95**

by William Walker Atkinson   Psychology/Religion Pages 144

Optimism *by Helen Keller*   ISBN: *1-59462-108-X*   **$15.95**
Helen Keller was blind, deaf, and mute since 19 months old, yet famously learned how to overcome these handicaps, communicate with the world, and
spread her lectures promoting optimism. An inspiring read for everyone... Biographies/Inspirational Pages 84

Sara Crewe *by Frances Burnett*   ISBN: *1-59462-360-0*   **$9.45**
In the first place, Miss Minchin lived in London. Her home was a large, dull, tall one, in a large, dull square, where all the houses were alike, and all the
sparrows were alike, and where all the door-knockers made the same heavy sound... Childrens/Classic Pages 88

The Autobiography of Benjamin Franklin *by Benjamin Franklin*   ISBN: *1-59462-135-7*   **$24.95**
The Autobiography of Benjamin Franklin has probably been more extensively read than any other American historical work, and no other book of its kind
has had such ups and downs of fortune. Franklin lived for many years in England, where he was agent... Biographies/History Pages 332

Name	
Email	
Telephone	
Address	
City, State ZIP	

☐ **Credit Card**   ☐ **Check / Money Order**

Credit Card Number	
Expiration Date	
Signature	

Please Mail to: Book Jungle
PO Box 2226
Champaign, IL 61825
or Fax to: 630-214-0564

ORDERING INFORMATION

web*: www.bookjungle.com*
email*: sales@bookjungle.com*
fax*: 630-214-0564*
mail*: Book Jungle PO Box 2226 Champaign, IL 61825*
or PayPal *to sales@bookjungle.com*

Please contact us for bulk discounts

DIRECT-ORDER TERMS

20% Discount if You Order
Two or More Books
Free Domestic Shipping!
Accepted: Master Card, Visa,
Discover, American Express